ELIZABETH APPLETON

ELIZABETH APPLETON

A NOVEL *by*

John O'Hara

RANDOM HOUSE · NEW YORK

To Pat Outerbridge

ELIZABETH APPLETON

I

The house was at the corner of Harvard Road and Bucknell Street, set back on two sides from the unpaved sidewalks, and with a garage at the rear. It was built according to a standard design of the days before the first world war; substantial, comfortable, respectable. It was a brick house because locally brick was cheap and would go for years without painting. On the street floor there were the diningroom and kitchen on one side of the hall; on the other side, a livingroom that matched in size the diningroom, and a study that matched in size the kitchen. On the second story there were four bedrooms, two and connecting bath on each side of the hall. There was a cellar, there was an attic, and that was all. The garage had once undergone alterations to provide space for a second car. There were four elms in front of the plot on the Harvard Road side of the property; there were five horse-chestnut trees on the Bucknell Street side.

(3)

This was the home of John Appleton and his wife Elizabeth in the Year of Our Lord 1950, in the college town of Spring Valley, Stratford County, Pennsylvania.

Snow had begun to fall during the third quarter of the Spring Valley-Mount St. Joseph's game. It came down in large flakes that melted on the faces of the spectators. It was the first snow of the season and a decorative one, unlikely to last long enough to create the problems that arrived with every winter in the mountains. The only man in the stadium who could object to this light fall was Duffy, the St. Joe's safety man, whose judgment of a high punt was momentarily thrown off by a single snowflake in his right eye. Duffy fumbled, Spring Valley recovered, and Spring Valley was on its way to a fourth touchdown.

"Wouldn't this be a good time to leave?" said Elizabeth Appleton.

"Are you cold?" said her husband.

"No, but I'd like to be home when Jean arrives."

"Well, I guess this puts the game on ice," said John Appleton. "All right."

People made little jokes as the Appletons rose from their seats and climbed the steps to the exit. "What's the matter, Dean? Can't you take a little snow? . . . Hey, John, a hot buttered rum for me . . . Hey, Appie, don't forget 1935. Five touchdowns in the fourth quarter . . . John, you're the only one's got any sense." When John Appleton left a game early he had a good reason.

In the car Elizabeth Appleton said: "You don't mind leaving, do you? I do want to be there when Jean arrives."

"No, I don't mind. God, I've seen—I wonder how many games I *have* seen. I started going to football games when I was about five years old, with my father. Thirty-seven years. Played two years in high school and four years in college. I didn't see any games in '43 or '44, so that cuts down the average. Say I've seen an average of five games a year for thirty-seven years. A hundred and eighty-five games. Is that all? I guess it must be. Do you realize that a major league baseball team plays a hundred and fifty-four games in a season? In one season a ballplayer gets to see almost as much baseball as I've seen of football in my whole life. Not only that. Baseball takes longer than football. I'm not sure about this, but it's my impression that the average baseball game takes about two hours minimum."

"She was coming by bus from Pittsburgh," said Elizabeth Appleton.

"I thought she was coming all the way by bus."

"She is, and it was supposed to arrive in Pittsburgh around one o'clock this afternoon. I think she was hoping to get a bus that left Pittsburgh at two or two-thirty."

"All the way from Reno to Pittsburgh in one bus? She won't be able to hear anything for a couple of days."

"No, she had to change buses two or three times, but I didn't try to memorize her schedule."

"She'll be exhausted. She must be pretty damn short of cash, too. And when I think of Jean, in that black Continental. How did she get rid of all her money? Well, that's a foolish question. *That* is one of the most foolish questions I ever asked myself. But she must have got rid of over three hundred thousand in nine years. That's better than thirty thousand a year. She had the same amount you had, didn't she? From your father's estate, I mean."

"Yes, and another hundred thousand from Mother's. Oh, she got rid of it. And she had a lot of help."

"From Tommy. But I thought, I always thought Neal Roberts was a big advertising tycoon."

"He was, and is. And that makes me wonder."

"You've been wondering about something for over a month."

"Well, I'll tell you what it is I've been wondering about. I never liked Neal Roberts. He's cheap. Gaudy and cheap. But I think Jean must be very much in the wrong in this divorce. If she'd been in the right, she'd have got alimony and she wouldn't have to travel by bus. I have no idea whether I'm right or wrong, but I'll just bet you there's another man.

(5)

And Neal just said to her, 'All right, you're having an affair with someone else. Don't expect *me* to pay for your divorce.'"

"Plausible, but let's give her the benefit of the doubt, at least till we've heard her side of it. I always thought Neal Roberts was a prime horse's ass."

"And you've always had a little sneaker for Jean."

"Well, you've always said I had. If I did have, *she* never knew anything about it."

"But *you* did."

"Why call it a sneaker? I love Jean. I have a wholehearted love for her. I've seen her waste her life and throw away her money. But she has a sweetness that's very rare."

"She also happens to be a very pretty girl."

"Very pretty, and a magnificent shape. But I'll tell you something, Elizabeth. No matter how much I may admire her looks and her shape, I wouldn't want to be in any way responsible for hurting Jean. She's very dear to me. If you want to go deeper than that, I'm sure you'd find that sex was at the bottom of my feeling for her. But let's keep it the way it is, me with my illusions."

"I'm perfectly willing to keep it the way it is if you are."

"That's the kind of remark that makes me sore. Now I'll be self-conscious all the time Jean's here. And you did that deliberately."

"Yes. I did it deliberately," said Elizabeth Appleton.

"Why?"

"Because I have fewer illusions about my sister than you have. I adore Jean, but she's had two husbands already, and I don't imagine they represent all her activity in that line."

"Probably not. But she's not after me, and besides, I don't like the feeling that I'm under surveillance."

"I should think it would be very complimentary, especially after nineteen years."

"You wouldn't have thought it was complimentary."

"I don't think it ever occurred to you to put me under surveillance."

(6)

"It didn't, not even during the war."

"Well, I didn't really mean to make you self-conscious, John. I just hope the next two weeks aren't going to be any more difficult than they have to be. We're not used to having visitors stay that long, and I'm just hoping that Jean will stay long enough to tell me what she wants, and then be on her way. And she wants something. It isn't just sororal love. Is there such a word?"

"If there isn't there should be, although there doesn't seem to be much of it lost here."

"That isn't nice, just for the sake of a wisecrack."

"I think what I'll do is drop you at the house and leave you to cope with Jean."

"Cope with?"

"It's an expression I got from you. Deal with. Cope with. In other words, you be there to greet her and I'll give you two an hour by yourselves. I'll go up to the Beta house and have a drink with the brothers while you two sisters are sniffing at each other."

"What a horrid expression. But all right, that may be a good idea. You can just say that I'm waiting for my sister."

"I don't have to say anything. When will you get over the idea that I always have to explain, every time I go somewhere without you?"

"We've always done it. This is Spring Valley, not Old Westbury. And particularly now—"

"Oh, the hell with particularly now. If the trustees want me for president, it's not going to be on a basis of what we do now. If they don't know all about me by this time, they never will."

"Oh, very well. But I'll just bet you that at least six people at the Beta house ask where I am."

"Would you like to be president of Spring Valley, dear heart?"

"I want *you* to be president of Spring Valley, dear heart. And that isn't all."

"Isn't it too bad Griswold got that job at Yale? If they'd known *I* was available . . ."

(7)

"The president of Princeton didn't go to Princeton, and Yale once had a president that went to the University of Michigan."

"Now how do you know that?"

"Because I made a point of finding out, that's how. And because I believe in you."

He was silent for a moment.

"What, John?"

"President of Spring Valley used to be as high as a man could go. When I was a boy, and old Prexy Witherspoon came to our house for his annual Sunday dinner, he and Mrs. Witherspoon, it was more important than as if Woodrow Wilson were coming. I can remember old Prexy and his cane, walking along Harvard Road, kicking up the leaves, but never losing his dignity. If he saw me playing with the other boys he'd always speak to me. 'Good afternoon, Johnny.' And I'd always tell my mother that Prexy spoke to me. I remember after a St. Joe's game, a battle royal between their crowd and ours. The police didn't even try to stop it, but when it got really bad Prexy and the priest that was head of St. Joe's, those two old men went down on the field and by God they stopped it. I *saw* that." John Appleton paused. "I couldn't do it."

"I don't see why not."

"I know I couldn't. I wouldn't be afraid to go down on the field. It's what I'd do after I got there. Prexy took one of our fellows by the arm and the priest took one of the St. Joe's boys, and the two old men made the students shake hands, right then and there, right in the middle of the riot. Then Prexy took Father What's His Name by the arm and the two of them marched off together. One of the greatest sights I've ever seen. They just turned their backs on the whole thing and marched off. You had to have real presence to get away with that, and I haven't got it. Nobody of my generation has it. Anyway, that's the kind of man that was once president of Spring Valley, so I don't look on the job as a stepping-stone to something else."

"You almost took that job at Amherst three years ago."

(8)

"That was a job in my field. Amherst is a better college than Spring Valley, and a professorship at Amherst means more than a professorship here."

"Do you think I talked you out of taking the Amherst job?"

"I talked myself out of it because I had a chance to be president of Spring Valley. But I didn't know then that you had other plans for me. And remember this, Elizabeth. I've never said I'd quit the presidency of Spring Valley. I've never made you any promises on that score."

"I've never asked you for any."

He stopped the car in Harvard Road. "The phone will be busy at the Beta house, so I won't be able to call you and you won't be able to call me. Can I get you anything?"

"No, but please be home before six. That's when the others will be coming."

"I like that cape. Is that the stuff you got from Scotland?"

"Thank you. Yes, the suit and the cape and the hat, it's the material Evangeline brought back last summer."

"I'd like to have the nerve to wear a cape. See you later."

Elizabeth Appleton went directly to the kitchen. "Hello, Mrs. Klein. No sign of my sister?"

"Not so far. Say, I like your outfit. That's the material from Mrs. Ditson. It isn't every woman that could wear a hat like that and stay feminine."

"Thank you very much."

"I wish capes would come back. They're more handier than a coat for like going next door. But unless you have the figure, you look as if you were expecting."

"Fortunately, I'm not."

"Well, you never can tell."

"I always can. Have you started on the appetizers?"

"Well, I got the little sausages in the oven, and the bacon. I thought I'd wait the toast till they got here. You don't want anchovies hot, do you?"

"No, I guess not. I can't decide whether to have my bath now."

"There's plenty of hot water."

"I wasn't thinking of that so much as not being here when Mrs. Roberts arrives. I think I'll have a quick bath and change. If she does come while I'm in the tub . . ."

"Take your bath now, and that way there'll be plenty of hot water for when she gets here. All that way by bus. Not me. I went to Gettysburg with the Auxiliary last May, by bus. You'll never get me on another ride like that. To tell you the honest truth, I don't even like the bus from here to downtown. I wish they never got rid of the trolleys."

"It shouldn't take me more than fifteen minutes," said Elizabeth Appleton. "Twenty at the most."

"Oh, have a good soak. It relaxes you, and I notice it started snowing. Twenty-eight to nothing. Is that the last you heard? I had the radio on till a few minutes ago."

"Twenty-eight nothing. Excuse me."

Mrs. Klein snapped the toggle switch of the radio and presently the WSVC announcer was saying: ". . . about wraps it up, folks, here in Witherspoon Stadium. Once again, the final score, Spring Valley 35, Mount St. Joseph's, a big fat goose-egg. Thirty-five to nothing, the worst shellacking in this traditional series since 1935, when the score was exactly reversed. That was the year I believe St. Joe's made all five touchdowns in the fourth period. This broadcast came to you through the courtesy of Schumacher-Chevrolet in Spring Valley, who bring you all the Spring Valley home games. See Shooey now for your best buy in a brand-new 1950 Chevrolet. This is Frank De Marco returning you to our studio in the Ditson Building in downtown Spring Valley for five minutes of—" Mrs. Klein turned off the radio.

"Downtown Spring Valley. You'd think he was KDKA," said Mrs. Klein. Always, when alone, Mrs. Klein answered back to the radio. "Our studio in the Ditson Building. That old firetrap." Mrs. Klein had a sort of proprietary interest in the Ditson Building; Evangeline Ditson employed Mrs. Klein on the alternate days when she was not helping out with Elizabeth Appleton. Mrs. Klein would not work full time for anyone, and she had to be paid in cash at the end of each day's helping out. She did not regard herself as a servant and would not permit herself to be so regarded. She was very firm about the use of the term, helping out, and it was understood by Elizabeth Appleton and Evangeline Ditson that there was to be no report to the federal government concerning the arrangements. "Mr. Klein paid his money into the pension fund right up till he passed on," said Mrs. Klein, "and I pay income tax on his pension. That's enough. If I want to work, the government don't have to know about it. It's enough that a widow has to pay that income tax on the pension. If Mr. Klein didn't provide for me, the government would of had to." At $1.50 an hour, six days a week, six hours a day, Mrs. Klein collected $54 a week from Mrs. Ditson and Mrs. Appleton, tax free.

It was in the nature of a compliment to Evangeline Ditson and Elizabeth Appleton that Mrs. Klein consented to help them out. There were certain other women in Spring Valley who would have been glad to have her help them out, but she was not interested. Only Evangeline Ditson and Elizabeth Appleton measured up: they were not the kind of women who would go tattling to the government if things did not work out. In Mrs. Klein's world the worst sin was tattling; in one form or another it was responsible for most of the trouble people got into. In the form of gossip it was especially deplorable, and if Mrs. Klein had any preference between the two women she helped out with, it was Mrs. Appleton. Mrs. Ditson gave Mrs. Klein most of her old dresses, but Mrs. Appleton did not gossip. Mrs. Appleton's clothes would not fit Mrs. Klein, but Mrs. Ditson wanted to know everything that was going on. If it ever came to a choice between helping out with Mrs. Ditson and helping out with —the doorbell rang, and Mrs. Klein went to answer it.

A blonde, hatless young woman was standing on the brick walk, and a step or two behind her was a taxi driver holding two large suitcases. "Is this Mrs. Appleton's house?" said the young woman.

"I *know* it is," said the driver.

"Yes, are you Mrs. Roberts?" said Mrs. Klein.

"Oh, good," said Mrs. Roberts. "Just let me pay this nice man. How much do I owe you?"

"Oh, make it two and a quarter. Hello, Mildred. I thought you's with Mrs. Ditson."

"Hello, Jimmy. Bring the valises inside," said Mrs. Klein.

"Three dollars," said Mrs. Roberts. "You keep the change."

"Thanks a lot," said the driver, leaving.

"He had the 'off duty' sign in his taxi but he took pity on me," said Mrs. Roberts. "Is my sister at home?"

"Taking a bath, but there'll be plenty of hot water for you."

"How did you know I'm dying for a bath, and what's your name?"

"I'm Mrs. Klein, I help out with the housework. I been with Mrs. Appleton five years next May."

"Jean? Is that you?"

"Hello, Elizabeth, it's me."

"Leave your bags downstairs, John'll bring them up later."

"If you take the one I'll take the other," said Mrs. Klein.

"I'll take both. They're not very heavy, thanks," said Jean Roberts.

Elizabeth Appleton, holding her bathrobe so that it would not fall open, was standing on the second-floor landing. "You might as well take them into your room. Betty's room, actually." Elizabeth kissed her sister, whose hands were engaged with the suitcases. "Do you want a bath right away? There'll be some people dropping in in a little while, and if you'd like to have anything pressed, give it to me and I'll take it down to Mrs. Klein while you're in the tub."

"You look just the same."

"Well, it's only been two years, Jean."

"*Only* two years?"

"Unpack what you want to wear and we can talk while you're having your bath."

"All right."

"I'll run your tub. Very warm?"

"You bet. I haven't had a bath in almost a week. I'd like to take all these clothes off and just burn them. But I guess not, in my present circumstances."

"Was it a perfectly awful trip?"

"It was no luxury cruise, but a good scrub, and maybe you have some perfume. This snow you're getting, it followed me all the way across the country, and they never opened a window in the bus. Actually it was quite exciting going through I think it was Nebraska. In one town there were five or six buses, westward bound, and they wouldn't let them go through. Luckily we were eastward bound."

Jean now stood naked and lit a cigarette.

"Put something on, Jean. John may be home any minute," said Elizabeth.

"I'm sorry. I'll have to watch that, won't I?" Jean Roberts put on a wrinkled dressing-gown. "How is John? And I haven't asked you about the children."

"Well, you'll see John in a few minutes. Peter is hanging on at St. Paul's by the skin of his teeth, very poor in geometry and history. Fair in French and quite good in English. Betty is passing everything, but she really hates Farmington. Of course she was determined to hate boarding-school, no matter where she went. She's convinced that we're trying to get rid of her, and in one sense we are. You can't bring up a young girl on a college campus."

"Don't they have girls at Spring Valley?"

"They have. But they're more trouble than they're worth. Coeducation may be all right for the big places, but not in a small place like this. We have nearly sixty married couples here under the G. I. Bill, and we'll be glad when they're gone, too. Very disrupting. They aren't really good students, and there's no discipline. They drink too much, and they quarrel, and it's a known fact that several of them have been exchanging husbands and wives. You can imagine what that does for the morale, not to mention the morals. The unmarried students take their cue from the married ones. Is this the dress you'd like to have pressed?"

"Yes, if it isn't too much trouble."

"I can press some other things tomorrow, and Monday we can take the rest downtown. You have your bath now and I'll be back in a minute."

"Good."

"Lock the other bathroom door, the one leading to Peter's room. John sometimes wanders in there when I'm using the other bathroom."

"Imagine his surprise, coming in to take a leak and finding a nude woman in the tub."

"Surprise and pleasure, but let's deprive him of both."

"He's your man, Elizabeth. I have no designs on him."

"Nevertheless, you have quite a lot to offer."

"Not *too* much, I hope, and anyway, it's all spoken for."

"Oh? We must talk about that when we have more time."

"Try and stop me," said Jean. "I'm glad I'm here."

"I'm delighted you are," said her sister.

The only young man at the party got up to refill Jean's glass, and his chair was almost immediately occupied by a man who, if not the oldest caller, was made to seem so by his beard and his garb. The beard was carefully trimmed, a rounded Vandyke, streaked with black but for the most part grey. The man wore a black suit, with lapels on the waistcoat; a brightly shining Phi Beta Kappa key hung from a few links of golden chain that also anchored the principal chain to the waistcoat. He wore a standup collar and a black four-in-hand tie with a large knot, and high laced shoes of black vici kid, with a tab at the back. "I was studying you from across the room," he said. "You don't *mind* being studied, I hope?"

"That all depends," said Jean. "I didn't get your name, and I don't know what you do."

"I'm Old Hillenketter. Professor emeritus, psychology. Sometimes known as Old Prof Hillenketter."

"I've always steered clear of—"

"The head shrinkers, I believe you'd call them?"

She smiled. "I was on the verge of saying it."

"Well, that isn't my profession, although the teaching of

(14)

psychology of course involves some knowledge of psychiatry and psychoanalysis. However, that isn't what I was studying. I was fascinated by a discovery I made. Shall I tell you what it is?"

"Why, yes."

"I know, of course, that you're Elizabeth's sister, and I was first struck by the almost complete lack of resemblance between you two. But that isn't so. There is a very strong, very subtle resemblance. Not the usual family resemblance, so-called. But you in repose, do resemble Elizabeth. While Elizabeth in animation, resembles you. It isn't actually so much physical resemblance as evocation. In other words, Mrs. Roberts, a transference occurs, a personality transference. When you're not speaking, making the social effort, you almost become the Elizabeth that I've known for so many years. But when Elizabeth is making the social effort, as hostess today, she momentarily resembles you."

"I can explain that."

"You can? Please do."

"When we're pepped up, we're like my father. When we're calmed down, we're like my mother."

"You think it's so easily explained?"

"Yes, I do."

"Do I detect perhaps a note of hostility toward the head-shrinking profession?"

"You do. All I know about it is that the man I just got a divorce from used to use it like a massage. A Turkish bath. Twice a week for five years he was on the couch. I didn't mind, as long as he kept me out of it. I wouldn't go to a Turkish bath, either. But his analyst wanted to make it a family affair, and I told Neal, my husband, that I—well, never mind what I told him."

Hillenketter smiled. "I wish you'd tell me. The recollection amuses you."

"Well—I told him I'd get in bed with him any time, but not on a couch. Not very funny, but it amused me at the time. Under the circumstances."

"What were the circumstances?"

"The circumstances were that my husband was going to bed with a lot of other people."

"And you knew it?"

"The whole town knew it."

"And did that irritate you, or hurt you? I should think that a comely young woman such as you—"

"Comely. I haven't heard that word for a long time. If you mean did I do the same as he did? No. I was in love with him, or thought I was. But he thought I was dull, and told me so."

"Then I would say that he was dulled. D, u, double-l, e, d. There is no such thing as a dull woman. There are only dulled appetites, Mrs. Roberts. Does that fit in with what you know of your husband?"

"It certainly does. Very clever of you, though, considering how little I've told you."

"You've told me a great deal. Was your husband a practising homosexual?"

"Neal? God, no."

"What makes you so sure?"

She laughed. "He wouldn't have had time."

"That's a frivolous answer, Mrs. Roberts."

"Well, we're getting too serious anyway, aren't we? I didn't know your name ten minutes ago, and now you want to know if my husband, my ex-husband, was a fairy. Maybe he was, but you'll have to ask him that. And I'm sure he'd tell you."

"Perhaps I should explain that my interest is friendly, and clinical. Friendly, because I'm a friend of your sister's and John's. Clinical, because while I've retired from teaching, I haven't retired from thought. I'm much too old for—"

"Oh, no you're not, Professor."

"You don't know what I was going to say."

"Yes I do."

He shrugged his shoulders. "Hmm. Perhaps you do. You are a *very* interesting young woman."

"Well, anyway, I'm not dull. I have your word for that," said Jean Roberts. "That young man that went to get me a drink—is he afraid of you, Professor? He took one look at us talking, and he's been standing there sipping his own drink and holding mine in the other hand."

"The young man doesn't know enough about me to be afraid of me. And never will. He'll go through life holding people's drinks and not knowing how to interrupt a conversation. What you see isn't politeness. Good manners. It's the insecurity of the second-rater. He may be awed by my reputation, my professional standing, that is. But he takes it entirely for granted, never questioning it, not really curious about it. He is not, in other words, a scholar. His name, by the way, is Jake Rodeheaver. Not Jacob. Jake. He was christened Jake, and he comes from Texas. He is a young man of considerable means, and I've been told that he's attached himself to the teaching profession because his mother wants it so. I understand that he and his mother are looking around for a kindly university that will guarantee Jake a Ph.D. They could save a lot of time by buying one. A university, I mean. Not just a Ph.D."

"Tell me about some of the other people here."

"I thought my little vignette would amuse you. Well, I don't think I need waste much of our time on Brice Ditson. What you see is what there is. A rich man in his fifties, married to a rich woman. They are used to having their own way in this part of the world, and naturally they have no real interest in any place else. They go abroad every year, when there's no war on, but they always travel on the same steamships and stay at the same hotels. Consequently London and Paris and Rome are scarcely more than an extension of Spring Valley. Brice went to Princeton and graduated very inconspicuously and came home and married the daughter of J. W. Framingham, as he was expected to do. The Framinghams have been prominent in this part of the world since —oh—Braddock's Defeat. Timber. Coal. And electric power. The Ditsons have always owned a hardware store, but they also own the Spring Valley Supply Company, which sells explosives to the mining companies and such things as cable and transformers to the power company. Brice is chairman of the board of the Spring Valley Bank & Trust. Don't miss going to their house. It will be a revelation to you. They live very simply. But then if they like you they'll invite you to what they call their camp. That's in the mountains, about forty miles from here. Your sister's been there, and John. And so have I. But we're the only faculty people that have. They have I forget whether it's two or three thousand acres where they can go and live off the land in case there's a revolution. They have a lake, several streams. Enough canned goods to last a year. Firearms—and both of them are very proficient with firearms. Brice began planning it in 1932, when there was a great deal of uneasiness in this part of the world. Unemployment and so forth."

"You sort of contradict yourself. You said that what I can see is all there is."

"That's all there is. You could see that, given time. Isn't Brice Ditson obviously the kind of man that would have a camp, and isn't Evangeline the kind of woman that would run her house with two servants when she could afford six or seven? How many children do you suppose they have?"

"Oh—I'd say none."

"You passed the test. They have none."

"Who is the man in the blue suit?"

"Harry W. Jeffries, M.D. Local boy. Great athlete. Not a great surgeon, but a successful one. The woman with the fur neckpiece is his wife."

"Yes, I was introduced to them together."

"She was a trained nurse. She comes to your sister for advice on social problems. Matters of taste. How to decorate her house. It's the rather familiar story of the wife who can't keep up with her husband's success. It's not a good marriage, and Jeffries would have been wiser to have divorced her years ago. She'd have been better off, too. She's one of the unhappiest women I know. They have a child, but it's a mongoloid. In an institution, and must be at least eighteen years old, by this time. Harry and Frances Jeffries have spent eighteen years blaming each other for the child, but never coming right out and saying so."

"Now who are these, just arriving?"

"Roy and Mary Leslie."

"She's attractive."

"You warm to her right away, don't you?"

"Of course I do. *He's* a stick."

"He was quite a catch when she married him. He was head of student government, president of the interfraternity council, manager of football. All those things."

"And now look at him. Those glasses, and that big Adam's apple."

"I'll tell you one thing about him that will change your mind about him."

"What?"

"She's just as crazy about him today as she was when they were in college. Think that over."

She looked at the professor, and he nodded slowly.

"Sex?" she said.

"You watch. Every man in this room will pay some attention to Mary, because she's so pretty. And she'll flirt with them. But if she has enough to drink—well, you'll see. You're about to meet them."

Elizabeth Appleton brought the newcomers to Jean and the professor. "Hello, Professor," said Roy Leslie. "Go to the game?"

"Prof Hillenketter at a football game?" said Mary Leslie. "Hello, Jean. You don't mind if I call you Jean?"

"Wait to be introduced, honey," said Roy Leslie.

"Oh, I knew she was coming a week ago."

"Yes, but she doesn't know who we are."

"Well, this is Mr. and Mrs. Leslie," said Elizabeth. "Now you *have* met and what would you like to drink?"

"Don't you drink, Jean?" said Mary Leslie.

"Oh, indeed I do. I'm temporarily without."

"I'll get the drinks, Elizabeth," said Roy Leslie. "What were you drinking, Jean?"

"Bourbon on the rocks."

"That's what I was drinking," said Mary Leslie.

"No you weren't," said her husband. "You were drinking a long, mild bourbon and soda, and that's what you're going to get. Professor, can I get you anything?"

"No thanks. I'll have my two ounces when I get to the Faculty Club. You ought to know my habits by this time, Roy."

"Well, you could always change, you know," said Roy Leslie.

Mary Leslie whispered to Jean Roberts: "And *should* change *some* of his habits."

"What was that, Mary?" said Roy Leslie. "It's impolite to whisper."

"Not what *she* whispered," said Jean Roberts. She took Mary's arm and they left the room and went upstairs.

"Say, that was quick thinking, thanks," said Mary Leslie. "I was afraid the professor got it."

"Oh, what if he did? He's a sanctimonious old jack-rabbit."

"How do you know I'm not madly in love with him?"

"I'll bet you saw through him in two minutes."

"Five."

"Topic A, as soon as he gets alone with a pretty girl. Never in front of the men. Oh my, no. They all think he's a great scientist. Even your brother-in-law, John. He's pretty smart about people, but he's got a blind spot where old Bluebeard's concerned."

"Old Bluebeard never mentioned a wife. Did he have one?"

"I guess he did a long time ago, but I guess he cut her up and ate her, like a Charles Addams character. How long are you going to be here?"

"About two weeks, I think."

"Oh, that's good. Roy is so immersed in this new thing. Roy, my husband, he's just started this new company to manufacture plywood, and when we have anybody to the house it's always people like Brice Ditson and Charley Mossler, older men that are putting money in the company. He promised me faithfully that next year we'll see some people our own age, but meanwhile. You haven't met Charley Mossler and his wife. Elizabeth never has them—"

"Why not?"

"Why not? Well, I don't know."

"Yes you do. Why not the Mosslers?"

"Oh—I guess it's because they don't fit in."

"You're holding out on me, but I won't pursue it. If you mean that Elizabeth's inclined to be snobbish, that's no news."

"No, I don't mean that. If Elizabeth were snobbish there's no reason why she should have me here. I'm nobody. No, Bertha Mossler and Elizabeth had some kind of a falling-out several years ago, what about I don't know. They speak, but that's all. No, Elizabeth isn't so snobbish, really. She has Harry and Frances Jeffries here, and Harry is Bertha Mossler's brother."

"I'm going to have to get all this straightened out or I'm liable to make a faux pas. Harry Jeffries and Mrs. *Charles?* Mossler are brother and sister. Who else is related here today?"

"Well, Roy, my husband. He's a distant cousin of Evangeline's. Evangeline Ditson. But very distant. The Distant Ditsons, we call them. Not to their faces, though. But that isn't why Elizabeth has us."

"I'm sure."

"Oh, you'll find out soon enough. Roy is vice-president of the alumni association, and automatically next year he'll be elected president. And he's one of those that are rooting for John Appleton for next president of Spring Valley. Personally I think John Appleton is the *logical* choice, but Elizabeth wants to be sure. I have a reason for telling you this, Jean."

"Oh? What?"

"It's a sort of a warning, you might call it."

"Against what?"

"Not exactly against anything, but don't do anything or say anything that Elizabeth can construe to hurt John's chances. It's a phobia with Elizabeth."

"Is it as obvious as all that?"

"It is to some people. John is the only person that's been mentioned by name, he's so logical a choice. But that's what makes people notice what Elizabeth does. If there were several other teachers in the running it wouldn't be so noticeable. And *I* don't think Elizabeth ought to do a thing. Oh, it's just something to talk about in a small town, and Elizabeth wasn't always so polite to everybody. Am I bitchy to say all this? I don't mean to be, but you may take umbrage."

"I think it's very friendly of you. I knew there was something on Elizabeth's mind, but I haven't had much chance to talk to her."

"Then I'll tell you something else. The damn awful part of the whole thing is, I don't think John wants the job. He told me at our house after he got out of the Navy. He said he didn't really want to go back to teaching. He wanted to go away some place, Maine or some place like that, and write a book that he'd been thinking about all the time he was in the service. But I don't know what ever happened to that idea."

"Why, I guess Elizabeth decided he ought to be president. Don't you imagine that's what happened?"

Mary Leslie nodded. "But *I'd* never say it. Of course John is immersed in his own work the same way Roy is in his—not that there's any comparison. But I'm thankful that my Roy—I don't want to say this wrong. I'm glad that Roy's in business. Put it that way. I wouldn't want to be in Elizabeth's position. The less I have to do with Roy's business, the better he likes it. But the wife of a professor that's being talked about for president of a college, she's the cynosure of all eyes."

"You know, Mary, you're very bright."

"No, I'm not very bright. I guess you heard I was Phi Beta Kappa. I suppose Elizabeth told you. People always say, 'Mary Leslie was Phi Beta Kappa,' and then they sort of add, 'Believe it or not.' No, I'm not bright, but my parents made me study while I was in college. They were very strict and I lived at home. One night out a week was all I was allowed."

"Elizabeth didn't tell me anything about you. In fact she didn't mention you or Roy."

"Well, she'll have a few remarks to make, and I guess I deserve some of them. But I wouldn't be Elizabeth Appleton for anything I can think of."

"Neither would I, but why wouldn't you?"

"Because you see, if John *doesn't* get to be president— you see, *John* hasn't tried to get the job, but Elizabeth has. And she's not going to blame herself. She's going to blame John."

"But you're so sure he *is* going to get it."

"He's the logical one, that's what I said. But they don't always give it to the logical one."

"When will they know?"

Mary Leslie was silent, and Jean saw that her new friend was troubled by the question. "If you were in my sorority, I'd know how to swear you to secrecy," said Mary Leslie.

"Pretend I am," said Jean. "I'm not a blabbermouth."

"There's a secret meeting on Monday night. The trustees are all here for the game. Tomorrow they're all going up to Brice Ditson's camp and talk it over informally, and they're meeting again on Monday night. There are only four people in this house that know any of this. Five, with you. The Ditsons know it, and Roy and I. They're going to vote Monday night, but they're not going to announce it till the end of the year."

"Why do they wait so long?"

"Well, they always do. They have to tell the new man and give him a chance to make his plans. Have him ready for when the official announcement is made public."

"Are you sure Elizabeth doesn't know any of this?"

"I'm positive. The reason I'm so positive is that not even Roy knows where they're having the meeting Monday night. They'll be told that tomorrow, at Brice's camp."

"And Roy is a trustee, of course."

"You get to be a trustee when you're vice-president of the alumni association, because vice-president I told you automatically moves up to president. Roy's in on everything."

"I know I shouldn't ask this, but will he tell you who they decide on Monday night?"

"Oh, Jean. You know darn well I'll know that the first minute he gets home."

"If all the trustees' wives know it, it won't be a secret very long."

"Only five of the trustees live in town, and one of them's a bachelor and the other's a widower. That leaves Evangeline, who won't open her mouth, and Bertha Mossler, and me. Bertha, it's hard to tell about. She'd want to talk, but maybe Charley won't even tell her. Charley's a real old-fashioned Pennsylvania Dutchman, and he mostly grunts at her. I guess I might as well do what I came up here for." She went in the bathroom that had been assigned to Jean, and Jean went to the bathroom on the other side of the hall.

Mary was smoking a cigarette when Jean returned to her bedroom. "I wish you were staying longer," said Mary. "Do you have a lot of friends you see in New York?"

"I know a lot of people, having been born there, and always went to school there. But the husband that I just divorced had other friends. The trouble was, he didn't like my friends, and he didn't want me to meet his. That wasn't the *only* trouble, of course. But for the past five or six years —I haven't really known what's been going on. It would be hard to describe our life and expect anyone to believe it. We'd have theater tickets and I'd be all set to go, and at quarter of eight Neal would telephone and tell me to pack his bag, he had to fly to the coast, that night. Oh, things like that. One night we were having dinner, for instance, and he said, 'Oh, I ran into your friend Starkweather.' Well, Ed Starkweather lives in Chicago and I said, 'Where's he staying? I'd like to ask him in for a drink.' 'Oh, this was in Chicago. I was in Chicago today.' He'd flown out to Chicago and had lunch and transacted his business and flown back.

The point of that is that if Neal hadn't happened to mention seeing an old beau of mine, I never would have known
he'd been in Chicago. That isn't my idea of marriage. But
I guess we'd better go join the merrymakers."

"Yes, I guess we'd better."

"Although I'd much rather sit and talk to you. Come
over tomorrow afternoon, can you?"

"I will. Three o'clock, around there?"

"Any time. I don't think Elizabeth has anything
planned."

The young women returned to the party.

It was past noon when Jean Roberts went to the kitchen
and made some toast and reheated the coffee in the percola-
tor. There were some patches of snow on the hard ground
of the backyard; without going outside she knew it to be a
cold and windy day. An unseen car in a nearby garage was
having difficulty in starting, until finally the battery died
down with a sound from the starter like a deflating bag-
pipe. The coffee was hot and strong, and Jean's first cigarette of the day made her slightly, inexplicably dizzy, until
she realized that she had not smoked in thirteen hours.
The party had lasted until eight; Elizabeth had prepared
ham and eggs, and the three ate supper in the kitchen. They
sat in the kitchen until the eleven o'clock news, and then all
three retired.

Now the front door was being closed.

"Hello, Sleeping Beauty," said Elizabeth.

"I'll bet I don't look it, the beauty, I mean," said Jean.

"You were certainly knocking it off," said John.

"Good Lord, not snoring, was I?"

"No, but Elizabeth opened your door and you were
breathing like somebody that planned to make a winter of
it. Hibernating."

"We've been to church, and then we stopped on the
way home to get the New York papers. They don't get here
until too late to be delivered with the Pittsburgh paper. And

(25)

at one o'clock they're all gone. They won't save them for us, either."

"Any more of that battery acid left?" said John.

"I'll make some fresh," said Jean.

"This man became a coffee addict in the Navy. I don't think it's good for your nerves," said Elizabeth.

"What's the matter with my nerves?" John wiggled his hands in an exaggerated ague. "I I I I I I I'm all ruh-ruh-right."

"What does the thermometer say?" said Elizabeth.

"Thirty-two," said John.

"I knew it must be below freezing. Too cold to play golf. Oh, I didn't tell you, Jean. We be*long* to the *country* club. We joined last year. Evangeline's a golfer and she finally persuaded me to take it up again after all these years."

"How are you?" said Jean.

"Modesty forbids," said Elizabeth.

"She beat Evangeline in the women's handicap tournament."

"Oh, Evangeline was a good sport about it."

"Yes, but she won't be next year when you have the same handicap she has."

"She may win."

"Do you play, John?"

"I do, but Madam beats me."

"You could play a very good game if you wanted to. You need a few lessons, that's all. He hits the ball a mile, but his short game is erratic, and his putting is terrible. Your trouble is you can hardly wait to get to the next tee and drive. That isn't the way you score in golf. I almost never three-putt a green, and I'm very steady with my irons."

"The answer is, you're a good golfer, and I'm not."

"That's it, she is a good golfer and always was. And tennis, too."

"Well, I guess I know about the tennis. Tennis is how I met the charming Miss Elizabeth Webster."

"I didn't know tennis had anything to do with it," said Jean.

"Tennis had everything to do with it. If I hadn't creamed her she never would have paid the slightest attention to me."

"True," said Elizabeth.

"Was that when you were tutoring the Castle boy? Bobby Castle?"

"Yes. Tell her," said John. "I'm not a boasting type."

"Oh, I had a date to play singles with Frannie Castle and I forget now why he couldn't play. Sunburn. He'd been out deep-sea fishing and got sunburned. So he called up and said he was sorry he couldn't keep our date. But then he said there was this young man from the Harvard Graduate School—"

"Not from Spring Valley College. Harvard Graduate School," said John. "And I hadn't even started."

"Who was tutoring his younger brother, Bobby, and played nice tennis. So I said all right. I wanted to play men, because I was getting ready for East Hampton. So this young gentleman from the Harvard Graduate School arrived in the Castles' station wagon, wearing a white sweater with the letters S. V. in front. Not in back. In front. Nobody wore their letters in front, but of course I was too polite to say anything. In fact neither of us said anything all the way over to the Meadow Club, and to make matters worse, we had to wait for a court. The only thing he said to me was, 'How are you? Are you pretty good?'"

"And what did you say?" said Jean.

"I said, 'Well, I hope I'll be able to give you a game.' And *he* said, 'Baby, you're going to give me *six* games, the first set.' I never detested anyone so in my whole life. 'We'll see,' I said."

"And what happened? I never knew this part," said Jean.

"He beat me six-love."

"You did, John? You must have been pretty good."

"Well, I was all right. But that day I couldn't make a mistake. Everything was working for me. My serve—"

"I couldn't get a ball back to him. And on my serve, if I went to net, he'd pass me. If I stayed back, he'd go to net

(27)

and drop one over with a soft racquet, you know. I *hated* him. I was *such* a bad sport. And I spent the rest of the summer trying to beat him, and never did. And never have."

"I remember that summer so well," said Jean. "Not so much what happened. But I remember it was the first summer that I wanted to be older. I suppose it was because I noticed you two. You may have been trying to beat him in tennis, but you certainly were in love with him."

"Not till the very end of the summer," said Elizabeth. "Not till I realized that he was leaving for good, the day after Labor Day. And that I might never see him again."

"You knew better than that," said John.

"No, not really. It was very hard for me to believe that I was in love with a man that wanted to be a teacher. I'd never known a boy that not only wanted to be a teacher, but was actually studying to be one. A teacher? A teacher was Mr. Chips, or Mr. Bhaer in *Little Women*."

"Not Mr. Brooke?" said John.

"He wasn't my idea of a teacher. He was a tutor."

"Well, I was a tutor," said John.

"Well, I was smarter than both of you. I knew you were in love with each other," said Jean. Suddenly, and with suddenness, she said: "That's why I'm here now."

"It is? Why?" said Elizabeth.

"I don't want to make a big thing of it, but I thought if I came and visited you for a while I might overcome my feelings about marriage."

"How do you mean?" said Elizabeth.

"I'm for it. I'm for marriage. But I don't know that I'm for it for me. A two-time loser before I'm thirty, and now I have somebody I *want* to marry, to have a marriage with, but I have very serious doubts about me and marriage."

"Who is the man?" said Elizabeth. "Do I know him?"

"You don't know *him*. You used to know his sister a long time ago. Penelope Collins."

"Nip Collins, of course I knew her. And which brother

(28)

is it? Bill? It must be Bill, because I think Harry's dead."

"It's Bill."

"But he's in his forties."

"How old do you think Neal Roberts was? He's thirty-eight. He always subtracted a little from his age, but he's actually thirty-eight."

"And you're thinking of marrying Bill Collins?"

"I'm thinking of not marrying him."

"Does he still live in Philadelphia?"

"Yes, he lives in Philadelphia. His wife died about two years ago. He has two sons at the Hill School."

"Did you divorce Neal on account of Bill Collins?"

"Yes, I did, but not exactly the way you might think. If I hadn't fallen in love with Bill I'd have gone on in the same old rat race with Neal. But when I fell in love with Bill I couldn't stand another minute of it with Neal. It was a very expensive decision on my part."

"How so?"

"Well—I've known all along that Neal was sleeping with other women. *I* was *not* sleeping with other men, any other men. But when I told him *I* wanted a divorce he said he *didn't*. If I wanted to get a divorce I could expect nothing from him. No alimony, and not even the money he'd allegedly borrowed from me. The divorce was all my idea, not his, and if I went ahead with it he wouldn't contest it, but I'd never get a cent out of him. So I went ahead and got the divorce, on his terms. I even signed some kind of a financial agreement that my lawyer said I was a fool to sign, but I signed it anyway. By that time I couldn't even bear to look at Neal. He said quite frankly that he knew there must be another guy, but he wasn't even going to try to find out who it was unless I tried to hold him up for money. Hold him up? A lot of it was my money."

"And now you have nothing? No money at all?" said Elizabeth. "It's all gone?"

"I have three government bonds that will be worth fifteen thousand dollars, God knows when. And I have

Mother's diamond-and-ruby pin and Aunt Charlotte's diamond earrings. And some clothes."

"That's all that's left of over four hundred thousand dollars?" said Elizabeth. "Where did it go, Jean? How could you spend that much money?"

"That's one of the things I did to occupy my time in Reno, figure out where it went. Rent and servants, to start with. We had a duplex, and I paid the rent and the couple. Theoretically Neal paid the food and liquor bills, but that was only theoretically. Most of the time I paid them, after we were dunned. One big lump went to pay some of Neal's back income tax. And in fairness to Neal, I spent some of the money while I was married to Tommy. Tommy and I had the boat, and I bought that black Continental, and those trips to Sun Valley. But then in fairness to Tommy, he always paid half. Neal never came near paying half. And finally took what was left."

"When Tommy was killed didn't you get any insurance?"

"Insurance? Tommy? And even if I had, it would have gone with the rest. I don't think even Lloyd's of London would have insured Tommy, not after they checked his accident record. He couldn't get a driver's license in New York State. And when he slammed into that truck at Canoe Place the first thing the state policeman said was they'd all been alerted to pick him up if they saw him driving a car. Well, they picked him up, the poor thing. But in what? You know, I can hardly remember being married to Tommy."

"She couldn't have got insurance anyway," said John. "She was divorced from him, and wasn't he married again?"

"Yes, I suppose you're right," said Elizabeth. "He couldn't get a driver's license, but he had no trouble getting a marriage license."

"Oh, don't be hard on Tommy, Elizabeth," said Jean. "He didn't have a brain in his head but neither did I."

"I'm afraid that was all too true then," said Elizabeth. "I'm not being hard on Tommy. Maybe if you'd waited till he'd settled down a little—but I suppose that's a foolish thing to say at this late date."

"If Tommy had to wait for anything he lost interest in it. He'd have lost interest in me, and that was what I was afraid of. He had asked other girls to marry him. I knew that. But they'd all been sensible. I wasn't a bit sensible. I was crazy about him, and crazy is the right word. And he was crazy about me—for three or four months."

"Just think of all that's happened to the world since then," said Elizabeth.

"Is happening now, look at Korea," said John.

"Yes, Korea," said Elizabeth.

"I don't understand anything about Korea," said Jean.

"You'll have plenty of time to," said John. "You can start reading up on it now, here are the Sunday papers."

"Are we going to have another war?" said Jean.

"Going to?" said John. "It must seem like it on the Yalu River."

"The Yalu River, even that's only a name I heard on the radio in Reno. I don't know a thing about Korea. I just hope we don't have to use the atom bomb."

"I just hope it'll be settled before Peter's old enough to go. I'm not committing myself on the atom bomb till I see what happens. John and I aren't in agreement on that, of course."

"However, I hasten to point out that we approve of marriage," said John. "Even though we may disagree on big things and some little things."

"Oh, I knew that," said Jean. "I didn't expect you to be a *Ladies Home Journal* couple."

"Oddly enough, we come pretty close," said John. "However, we'd like you to stay. I'm not suggesting that you go back to New York and read back issues of the *Ladies Home Journal*. Stay and have a good look at us, but if you find out our secret, for God's sake don't tell us."

Elizabeth looked at him. "It isn't much of a secret, is it? I hope not."

(31)

"No, I'm being facetious. Facetious, by the way, is the only word I know of that contains all the vowels and in their proper order."

"All right," said Jean. "If you'd like to change the subject."

"It isn't that he wants to change the subject, Jean. He just wants to take the spotlight off *us*," said Elizabeth.

"No, Jean is right. I want to change the subject. You're right too. I'd rather not have the spotlight on us. But as I told you yesterday in another connection, I don't like to be made self-conscious. Now if you'll excuse me, I'm going to change my suit and do a few chores. What time is dinner?"

"Two o'clock."

"I'll be in my study. Call me when you're ready for a cocktail."

When he had gone Jean said: "I blurted that out, about why I wanted to visit you. I should have kept it to myself."

"No, I'm glad you told us."

"But then all that stuff about Neal and Tommy."

"Don't you think we'd already guessed quite a lot of it? I almost wish you hadn't taken a bus, Jean. That, uh, proclaims it a little too obviously. That your finances are at a low ebb. However, it's done."

"But no harm's done by proclaiming it, Elizabeth. If I have no money it's going to be found out soon enough."

"Having no money is no disgrace. Heaven knows, the wife of a college professor sees the meanest kind of poverty, and usually knows it first-hand. We often have people here just to give them a square meal. I mean that literally. I could name at least three couples that I'm sure never see a steak except when they're invited out. Everybody knows we have some outside money, because we live in this house. John is entitled to one of the college houses because he's head of a department and dean, but those houses are beginning to fall apart and I wouldn't live in one of them. So we have an arrangement with the college. John takes five hundred a year over and above his salary, in return for which one of the college houses is made available. Five hundred barely pays our taxes on this house, but it's something."

"Elizabeth, I don't want to talk about money. I don't want to pry into your financial affairs."

"I know you don't. But don't do things like taking buses. It tells everybody in the world that you got no alimony from Neal Roberts, so they naturally draw their own conclusions. That you were the guilty party in your divorce."

"Well, technically I suppose I was. I've certainly committed adultery with Bill, and I guess Neal could have proved it." She laughed. "I wouldn't have been a bit surprised if he'd had detectives on us, and then sent me the bill. Oh, that's a real son of a bitch. While I was in Reno I got a bill from Saks-Fifth Avenue, and I hadn't bought anything there. I wrote them about it, and of course it was for two new suits that my beloved had got there. The charge was still in my name. Five hundred and thirty dollars."

"I hope you didn't pay it," said Elizabeth indignantly.

"Well, you just bet I didn't. I just wrote on the bill, 'Nice try, but no cigar,' and sent it to my beloved."

"Jean, why did you *ever* marry him?"

Jean looked at her sister. "That's something I hope you'll never understand. And you won't. At least not from experience."

"Oh," said Elizabeth. "Well, why don't you take the Sunday papers in the front room and I'll get started on dinner?"

They had a good roast beef for dinner and the sisters stayed on safe topics as they washed and put away the dishes and table silver. Then it was three o'clock by the bell in College Hall, followed almost immediately by the doorbell. "Now who can that be?" said Elizabeth. "We don't encourage the drop-in trade, as John calls it."

"I think it may be Mary Leslie," said Jean.

"Oh, you asked her to come?" said Elizabeth.

"Yes. It's all right, isn't it?"

"Oh, of course. The only thing is—before you ask anyone else, it might be better if you found out—this is a very close-knit community. Not everybody gets invited here that would like to be, and they might wheedle an invitation out of you that they'd never get from me."

"But Mary was here yesterday," said Jean.

"Oh, I didn't say Mary was one of those."

"But she's almost one," said Jean, hurrying to the door.

"I was punctual," said Mary Leslie. "Was I too punctual?"

"Not a bit. We just finished the dishes," said Jean.

"How would you like to go for a ride? There isn't much to see, but we can get some fresh air."

"Fresh air. Yes," said Jean.

"Oh, hello, Mary," said Elizabeth.

"Hello, Elizabeth. I thought I'd take Jean for a ride. Show her what there is to see, and then maybe have some tea at the club."

"All right. She's yours till five-thirty."

"What's at five-thirty?" said Jean.

"Well, Professor Hillenketter said he might stop in. I knew when the doorbell rang it wasn't he. He wouldn't miss his Philharmonic."

"I'll see you at five-thirty, then," said Jean. "If not before."

Mary's car was a grey Studebaker coupe. "If I were going to get a car I'd get one of these," said Jean. "I like the lines."

"That's why I bought it. It's second-hand, but it was a good buy. It seems extravagant for us to have two cars, especially now, but Roy's car is gone all day, and the kids have no other way of getting to school."

"Your children?"

"Yes, I have two. Martin is seven and Wendy is five. They go to Model School. That's not what it sounds like. It's part of the Education course at Spring Valley. I'll show it to you. We can do the whole campus in fifteen minutes."

The older buildings showed their age—more than a century—and the slightly newer and much newer buildings indicated the growth of the college. Plainly there had once been one building of red brick, to which had been added wings and a white cupola. Three more buildings had followed, and the four now formed a quadrangle. Away from this quadrangle there was no uniformity to the architecture. One dormitory was collegiate Gothic, another was Dutch Colonial, the choices of the respective donors and no more heterogeneous than the styles of the houses of the older, wealthier fraternities. The library, built in 1920, owed something to the Parthenon; the Science Building, four years older, copied the simpler features of Italian Renaissance design, particularly in the tall windows. The gymnasium, which was halfway between the quadrangle and the football stadium, was a tan brick eyesore on which ivy refused to grow, and represented mutual connivance on the part of the architect and the builder.

"I had no idea this place was so rich," said Jean.

"It isn't. It was. But it isn't poor," said Mary Leslie. "All the rich people didn't go to Yale. I guess there were quite a few went here because they couldn't get into places like Yale. Roy was one. He wanted to go to Princeton, but he couldn't pass the college boards."

"I thought he was one of the brightest students."

"Oh, not in studies. He was a campus politician and things like that. But his marks were awful. Still, he's a credit to Spring Valley. Some day he'll give them a building. Made of plywood, probably. Most of these buildings were given one at a time, and usually by one person. Framingham Hall, the men's dorm, was given by Evangeline Ditson's father. Ditson Hall was given by Brice and his brother in memory of their mother. She was a student here. Nowadays when somebody wants to give a building the college tries to talk them out of it and give the money instead, unless they want to give a building and endow it. Of course some fatheads, all they care about is to have a big pile of bricks named after them. If John gets to be president one of the worst parts of his job is going to be raising money, and trying to find people that will give money without strings attached. I don't know how good he'll be at that."

"Is John going to get that job? I'm not trying to pump

you for inside information, and don't answer if it involves that."

"Without giving you any inside information, John stands a chance."

"Is that all?"

"Well, I could be wrong, but I know these people. I know them a lot better than Elizabeth does. I'm one of them."

"Isn't John one of them?"

"No. John is a teacher. I'm talking about the trustees and the influential people that aren't trustees. A lot of the people I mean never go up to the campus except for football games and class reunions. They influence each other, Jean. They're not influenced by the faculty. There's a man in Cleveland. Not a trustee, and not one of those that are at Brice Ditson's today. But they'll be on the phone to him today or tomorrow, before they vote on the next prexy. A man in Detroit. Same thing. If *you* have a half a million dollars that you may leave to Spring Valley, they'll listen to what you have to say."

"I don't know whether I want John to get it or not."

"Well, you know what I told you yesterday."

"That's why I sort of *do* want him to."

"She may get over it, if he doesn't get it."

"Mary, everything you say practically tells me he isn't going to get it."

"*He isn't*," said Mary Leslie. "That isn't anything I know, factually. But all my instincts tell me he isn't. I don't know what I base it on. Little looks here and there. People clamming up when the conversation goes a certain way. Intuition. But intuition that *is* based on facts. Unfortunately I can't put my finger on those facts, so I call it intuition."

"A girl with your looks shouldn't have so much intelligence. It isn't fair."

"It wouldn't be if that's all life was. But it's more than that, and I've had plenty of things go wrong. I've had my disappointments," said Mary Leslie. She spoke, and stopped speaking, in a manner that closed the subject. "Why look

(36)

who's out for a stroll and not listening to his Philharmonic. Do you see him? With the cane?"

"Professor Hickenbucker."

"Hillenketter. I think I'll turn left here so we don't have to give him a lift. I don't want to hear how he happens to be missing his Philharmonic. And I'm sure you don't want to have passes made at you. Not the kind he makes, anyway."

"You really have it in for him, haven't you?"

"Yes I have. I despise him."

"Why?"

"Because he's a louse," said Mary Leslie. For the second time in a single minute she abruptly ended a topic of conversation. "I'll show you my sorority house. I'm a Kappa, short for Kappa Kappa Gamma. I got in because I was pretty, and then they wished they hadn't taken me because I turned out to be a grind. Then they changed their minds all over again when Roy pinned me. Then they changed their minds *again* because another Kappa spread it around that I'd stolen Roy from her. Hectic, to say the least. I hardly ever go there except to use the loo, but if you'd like to see the inside we can stop."

"Not particularly."

"My parents spent all that money on my education, and then as soon as I graduated I got married."

"But aren't you glad you got an education? I wish I'd had more."

"It was different with you. My parents weren't poor, but they could have done other things with the money. My father's a photographer. He makes a good living. Class pictures. Fraternal organizations. Weddings."

"I'll bet you were his favorite subject," said Jean.

"Oh, no. He took pictures of me, but he never put one in the window. He said that if he took a picture of another girl and it didn't turn out well, they'd have said he was showing favoritism. A photographer, especially a small-town photographer like my father, has to be very diplomatic. To say the least. You'd think with all these candids people would grow accustomed to how they look. But they haven't.

People won't buy a wedding picture if the bride isn't made to look pretty. And why should they? That's supposed to be the big day in a girl's life, and I don't blame her if she doesn't want a picture sitting around the house, showing her bad complexion, her crooked teeth. Why have that to remind your husband of what he got? . . . The new hospital. Harry Jeffries, chief surgeon. You met him and his wife yesterday. I'm convinced she's crazy. She used to be a nurse and she was all right when they were first married, but they had a baby that had to be put in an institution, a defective. But that isn't the whole trouble. Harry came up in the world, and she stayed where she was. A man that gets to be successful, people will overlook his vulgarities and cheapness. But a woman like Frances Jeffries, she's what my mother calls common. 'My old mink.' 'My Cadillac,' only she calls it 'my Cad.' 'My Delmans.' 'My Harry.' And everybody knows he isn't her Harry. Speaking of Frances." Mary Leslie waved to a police sergeant, a tall stout man in uniform, arctics and ear-muffs, who was stamping his feet and beating his gauntleted hands. He saluted Mary. "Milton Stauffer. Frances Jeffries' brother. Milton went to Spring Valley and played on the football team with Harry Jeffries, but now the only time Frances sees him—well, *not* the *only* time, but one of the times is when there's a church wedding and when Frances comes out to get in her Cad, there's her big fat brother directing traffic. She *dies*." Mary giggled. "This is mean, but when Frances starts talking about her Cad and her last year's mink, I've been tempted to ask her if she could get Milton to fix a parking ticket for me. But I wouldn't dare. I'm afraid of that woman. If you weren't Elizabeth's sister you'd be on Frances's hate-list automatically. Even so, don't have any more to do with her than you have to. City Hall. The old Pennsy station, now a bus terminal."

"That's where I got off the bus."

"Ditson's hardware store. Spring Valley Hotel. Go there if you want to have your hair done, it's the only good beauty parlor in town. My father's studio, upstairs over the Cut-Rate Drug Company."

"B. F. Phillips Photo Studio?" said Jean.

"That's where the family fortune came from. Lazarus Furrier, where I got my silver fox. Dr. Moorhead, in case you have to have a filling, God forbid. *And* the Spring Valley Bank & Trust Company. Brice Ditson, president. Roy Leslie, director. One of them. That's it, that's the works. Now we go out to the club. I don't think there was enough snow for any skiing but we can have tea and watch them skating on the tennis courts. The porch is enclosed during the winter, so we won't have to freeze. I hope you're not expecting a drink. The bar is closed on Sundays, even during the summer. The men have bottles in their lockers, but officially the club doesn't serve any alcoholic drinks on Sunday. J. W. Framingham's influence. He gave the land for the original club, and that was one of the conditions. Bar closes midnight Saturday."

"There are a lot of people here this afternoon, judging by the number of cars," said Jean.

"I love this place on Sunday, in the winter. Everybody seems more relaxed. The dances are like all club dances, and during the summer it's just like any other club. But in the winter people come out and sit around and have tea, and read the Sunday papers and there's no fuss. It's something to do on Sunday afternoon, and it's a much nicer place." A waitress brought tea and cinnamon toast and set it on a wicker table on the glassed-in porch.

"Here comes a character," said Jean. A middle-aged man in an old raccoon coat, wearing a black beret and carrying skates, approached the porch from the flooded tennis courts.

"He *is* a character," said Mary Leslie. "Porter Ditson. Brice's younger brother. Never been known to do a tap of work, but the busiest man in town. I'm quoting my father." Porter Ditson reached the porch, shed his beret and fur coat, and was revealed to be wearing a jacket and knickerbockers of reddish Harris tweed, cable-stitch tennis sweater, and striped scarf.

"Now you *knew* I was going to make a bee-line for your

(39)

table," said Porter Ditson. "Why didn't you tell Mae to bring another cup?"

"Yes, I should have known. Jean, this is Porter Ditson. Porter, Mrs. Roberts."

"How do you do, Mrs. Roberts. Am I right in guessing that you must be Elizabeth Appleton's sister?"

"Yes, I am," said Jean Roberts.

"I know a friend of yours. Bill Collins," said Porter Ditson. "As a matter of fact, I saw you with him at the theater one night."

"But I didn't meet you."

"No. I was, uh, I was with a party."

"I'll bet you were," said Mary Leslie. "Have a seat, Porter."

"Thanks. Actually, old Bill is a bit of a stuffed shirt, if you don't mind my saying so. He saw me that night, but he gave me that nod that's almost the cut direct. Truth be told, he didn't want to be put in the position of being forced to introduce you to the lady I was with. Simple as that. *I* knew it. I've known Bill for going on twenty-five years. Twenty-five years ago he said to me, 'Porter, I'd *like* to have you as one of my ushers, but I just can't. I just can't.' The thing is, if he'd had me for an usher, I'd have laid off him. But I fixed him."

"How?" said Jean Roberts.

"Had him arrested," said Porter Ditson. "Called up the state police and gave them the license number of his car. Reported it stolen. He and his brand-new bride got pinched somewhere near Reading. On their way to Canada on their wedding trip. I wish I'd been there. What are you doing here, Mrs. Roberts? Visiting Elizabeth, obviously, but are you going to stay a while? Decorate the local scene? Not that our little Mary doesn't do that, but we can always use some new talent."

"I'll be here about two weeks."

"Any chance old Bill might be getting out this way? I'd love to see him again. He could stay with me. That would interest him, because old Bill never likes to part with a dollar unnecessarily."

"I won't have you say these things about Bill," said Jean Roberts. "He's neither a stuffed shirt nor a tightwad." She smiled as she spoke.

"If you know Bill, you know he's both, but I love him just the same," said Porter Ditson. "Mary, you're not up at the camp today. Is my brother having one of his fate-of-the-nation meetings?"

"I guess so. Roy's there," said Mary Leslie.

"I knew Roy was there. I saw him in Brice's car, but I didn't know whether the girls were going or not. My brother likes to get the local big shots up at his camp. When they're going up there to shoot, he has to have me, so they don't come away empty-handed. But when I'm not invited I always know they're going to bring out a new stock issue, or elect a congressman. This time I imagine they're going to put that fellow from Haverford in as the new president of Spring Valley. Mallard. Ballard. Some name like that. Ballard. It couldn't be Mallard. Thank the Lord *that's* all settled."

"Oh, it's all settled?" said Mary Leslie.

"Sure thing. Brice went over to Philadelphia and saw the fellow about two-three weeks ago. I suppose your brother-in-law John Appleton could have had it if he'd wanted it, but I don't know why he would. When is John leaving? I understand he's taking time off to write a book?"

"I don't really know. I just got here yesterday."

"Well, not too soon, I hope. Maybe I could persuade you to let me give a small dinner party for you while you're here. After all, I'm an old friend of a friend."

"That would be lovely."

"Well, then, done and done. I'll be in touch with Elizabeth and we'll fix up a date. You'll come, Mary, of course? I'll put Mrs. Roberts on my right and you on my left, and the others can all go to hell. Thanks for the tea, young ladies. Got to buzz off, take a hot bath, or I'll be stiff tomorrow."

He bowed to Jean Roberts, affectionately patted Mary Leslie on the shoulder, and was gone.

"I can hardly look at you," said Mary Leslie.

"I know."

"I hope you believe me, that I was only guessing."

"Of course I believe you, Mary."

"Roy doesn't know about this Ballard man. Oh, I guess he does now. But he didn't. He was for John."

"I don't know whether I'm glad I'm here or not. This may be a time when they'd want to be alone. On the other hand—"

"It may be a good thing you're here. Elizabeth doesn't confide in anybody, except possibly Prof Hillenketter, and I don't think she'll want to talk to him when she finds out."

"I wonder if I ought—"

"To tell her? Don't even hint at it. Let her tell you. If you so much as hint at knowing, she'll manage to blame you. That's not a nice thing to say, but it's true."

Jean smiled sadly. "Well, at least now I won't have to struggle against pumping you tomorrow."

"I'd have told you as soon as I knew."

"I know you would have, Mary. Now I think you'd better take me back to their house."

II

The man entered the room without seeing John Appleton and went to a desk on which rested several piles of mail. John Appleton deliberately scraped his chair noisily and rose and said, "Good morning, sir." The man's startled expression was disproportionate to the noise and the slight shock that normally would go with finding oneself not alone.

"Oh, good morning. Good morning, young man," said the man. "Are you calling for Elizabeth? Do they know you're here? I'm Elizabeth's father."

"My name is John Appleton. I'm supposed to play tennis with Miss Webster."

"Well, I'm Jarvis Webster. I don't think she'll be long. I see you've won your letters. Saint Something? What does S. V. stand for?"

"Spring Valley. It's a small college in Pennsylvania."

"Oh, yes. I've seen the name in the football scores. Spring Valley. You play, uh—Carnegie Tech? Washington & Jefferson?"

"Yes sir. Not every year. When we play those teams it's the first game of the season, and we always get beaten, but we get a good guarantee and we need the money."

"You always get beaten the first game of the season? I should think that would get you off to a bad start psychologically."

"No. We know we're going to get beaten. Just as long as they don't cripple us, physically, I mean. And if we can score on them once or twice it's a moral victory for us."

"How are you against teams your own size?"

"Well, last year we won four, lost one—to W. and J.—and tied one."

"That's a very good record. It seems to me you could almost consider yourselves undefeated."

"We did," said John Appleton.

Jarvis Webster smiled. "Good. What did you play?"

"I was an end."

"Yes, you're tall enough, and I imagine you're fairly quick on your feet. I never played in college, and where I went to school we didn't play outside teams, but I've always followed football. I go to at least one game every year. How's your tennis?"

"Well, I guess it's all right. I played second man on our team and first-team doubles. I got to the semi-finals in our district. Singles. I didn't play in the doubles. We had a chance there, but my partner got ptomaine poisoning, and we had to default."

"Hard luck, but I'm glad you're a good player. Elizabeth prides herself on playing like a man. She doesn't, but she can beat a lot of the boys down here. She wants to make a good showing at East Hampton. Not that she has a chance of winning. I suppose Helen Wills and that little Palfrey girl will be entered, and the English girl, Betty Nuthall. Fast company for Elizabeth."

"Well, it's like us playing Tech and W. and J."

"Exactly. Exactly," said Jarvis Webster. "The same idea. But don't you hold back because she's a girl. If you do, you may find yourself love-2. She likes to win the first two games. She tries harder in the first two games than later on."

"I'll turn on everything I've got."

"That's the idea. If you have a hard serve, and I'll bet you have, you give it all you've got. I'm on her side, mind you, but she's been having a too easy time of it this summer. Where are you staying?"

"I'm tutoring the Castle boy."

"Bobby? You must have your hands full. I wrote a letter for that kid. He's going to my school, and I perjured myself because his father and mother are friends of mine. What are you tutoring him in?"

"Latin and algebra."

"You must be pretty bright yourself to be able to do that. I know I couldn't, and I went as far as trigonometry and Horace. When do you graduate, or have you?"

"I just did. I'm going to Harvard next year. Graduate work, and then I'm going to teach."

"You're going to teach? What?"

"I want to teach history. American history."

"You could teach a lot of it in this house. My younger daughter especially. You should have heard me trying to explain the difference between the Constitution and the Declaration of Independence. On some things I must admit I'm pretty shaky myself. Here's Elizabeth. Hello, my dear. You look trim and efficient. This is Mr. Appleton."

"How do you do? Have you got a car?"

"I have the Castles' station wagon."

"Then I think we'd better go right away. We're going to have to wait for a court, I'm afraid."

John Appleton and Elizabeth Webster continued to play tennis together after she was put out of the East Hampton tournament in the second round, but until mid-August he never saw her in the evening, and he did not meet her mother, Amelia Webster, until a few days before the Labor Day weekend.

"I'm having a party a week from Friday," said Elizabeth, one day on the way home from the tennis courts.

"I know you are," said John Appleton.

"You do? How did you know?"

"I saw it in the paper."

"Well, will you come?"

"Sure, if it's all right with your mother."

"Why do you say that? What's my mother got to do with it?"

"I've talked to your father, I guess a dozen times, and your kid sister, but I've never even seen your mother. I get the feeling that she doesn't approve of me."

"Well, she doesn't," said Elizabeth.

"I knew she didn't. She went to such trouble to avoid seeing me. Your father's one of the friendliest men I ever knew. That is, after you get to know him a little."

"He can afford to be friendly."

"What do you mean by that? You sound as if you didn't like him."

"Well, maybe I don't. Not that it's any of your business."

"All right, then let's drop the whole matter."

"My father isn't nice to my mother."

"Oh, come on, Elizabeth."

"Come on yourself. You take my father's side, but if you knew what my mother went through. Didn't the Castles ever tell you anything about my father? No, probably not."

"Do you know what I am at the Castles'? I'm somewhere between a male nursemaid and a golf caddy. I eat my dinner with their daughter's governess and Mr. Castle's secretary, when he's here. Not that I give a damn. Good food and plenty of it, and very good pay. But no social stuff at all. They all call me Mr. Appleton, even that infant prodigy Bobby."

"Well, anyway, it's settled that you're coming to my party?"

"I just thought of something. I'll have to hire a Tuck."

"My father will lend you one."

"Has he got an extra one?"

"He has unless he gave his old one away. He's using my party as an excuse to get a new one. I'll ask him, if you don't mind."

"Why should I mind? I have a Tuck at home, but it might not get here in time. I wouldn't mind wearing all your father's clothes. He's what I call a well-dressed man."

"He's that, all right."

"And I like him. What's the matter? Has he got a girl friend?"

"Who told you that?"

"What else would your mother be sore about?"

"Yes, he's having an affair with a perfectly dreadful woman. Forty-eight years old, and chasing around after another woman."

"He's a damn good-looking man. Maybe she's chasing him. And forty-eight isn't old for a man. We've got a prof at Spring Valley, he must be around that age, and if half the stories are true, boy, he gets plenty."

"Why haven't they discharged him?"

"I don't know. I guess they couldn't prove it."

"Men are horrible."

"Believe you me, they're no worse than women."

"How do you know?"

"How do you think I know?"

"Because you've had experience, I suppose."

"Certainly I've had experience. I'm twenty-two years old."

"What experience?"

"The experience you're talking about."

"I don't believe you."

"Well, you can believe it or not, Ripley, but I have. And not just once or twice."

"What kind of girls were they? Not anybody you'd want to be seen in public with."

"Listen, Elizabeth, Southampton and Spring Valley aren't very different. Your father's girl friend may be society, but when they—"

"Stop it!"

"All right, but *you* stop, too. 'Girls you'd be seen in public with.' Answer me this, did you ever neck anybody?"

"No."

"Oh, come on. Did you ever kiss a boy?"

"Yes."

"But you never necked?"

"No."

"All right, what *is* necking?"

"Why ask *me*? *You* know so much about it."

"I want to see where you draw the line between kissing and necking. You're one of those girls that know exactly when to stop, huh?"

"Yes."

"I thought so. Then you must know what the next step is."

"Everybody knows."

"All right. What is it?"

"I don't want to discuss it."

"Putting your hand down the girl's dress. That's it, isn't it?"

"Stop saying such things."

"Answer my question. That's the next step, isn't it?"

"What if it is?"

"So that's where you stop, huh?"

"I certainly do."

"And always have, I suppose."

"How dare you ask me—"

"I wasn't asking you if I could. I was asking you if you always have."

"I won't even deign to answer."

"No. Because you know the next question."

"Stop the car. I'm going to walk home."

"All right, if that's the way you feel about it." He stopped the car and she got out and began to walk on the footpath.

"Hey, you forgot your tennis racquet," he said.

She kept on walking. He drove past her, stopped the

car, and placed the racquet on the path ahead of her. He then got in the station wagon and drove off.

They did not meet again the next day, but in the mail on the second day there was an invitation to her party. He observed that the postmark indicated the invitation had been mailed after their quarrel. On a calling card—the first time he had used one all summer—he wrote his acceptance and sent it with a dozen roses from a florist on Hill Street. In the afternoon she telephoned him.

"Your flowers are perfectly lovely," she said.

"Thank you. I hoped you'd like them."

"Oh, I do, very much. They're quite lovely. I was wondering if you were possibly free for dinner this evening. Not a party. Just family. Just a quiet dinner with Mother and Father and I."

"What time?"

"Say eight o'clock?"

Her matter-of-factness was maintained throughout dinner, and in other circumstances would have had John Appleton's complete, if somewhat mystified, admiration. On this occasion, however, Elizabeth's performance had only half his attention: he was equally interested in Mrs. Webster and in the Websters together. Oddly enough, Elizabeth, with her sang-froid, her determined effort to rise above a petty quarrel in ladylike fashion, seemed younger than she had all summer. The effect she created was of a fourteen-year-old girl who was wearing high heels for the first time. She had her own manner, a personal, rather severe aloofness that passed for dignity; but this evening's gracious coolness was a copied affectation and John Appleton recognized it for an affectation and was moreover in a position to study the original from whom the copy was made. Amelia Webster was a woman who always made her own first impression on strangers, and it was always the same impression on everyone meeting her for the first time. She was a woman of whom strangers always said that she had some sort of secret, and of the secret that it was not a happy one. Even without the special knowledge he had been given by Elizabeth in her criticism of her father, John Appleton would have been like all other strangers in his response to Amelia Webster's tense, strained beauty.

"Have you enjoyed your summer in Southampton, Mr. Appleton?" she said. It was apparently an insignificant small-talk remark, but from this woman at this time it was an admission that she had known all along of his presence in Southampton, frequently in this house, and that she had no intention of making amends for ignoring him up to now.

"Very much," said John Appleton.

"Where do you think you'll go next summer?" said Amelia Webster. This, too, was a question that had its own obvious inference, namely, that he would certainly not be back in Southampton again. Indeed, in the slight emphasis on the word *next* she almost seemed to imply that he was a footloose, irresponsible youth who went from one summer resort to another but never to the same one twice, for reasons that quite possibly had to do with his morals, the integrity of well-born young womanhood, the security of the silverware. He could not overcome the suspicion that everything she said was a calculated attempt to say two things at once.

"I'd like to get a job on a boat," he replied, immediately conscious of the interpretation she could put on that.

"On a boat? A steamship?" said Amelia Webster.

"Yes, one of those United Fruit boats. Or any kind. I'd like to go abroad somewhere."

"You must write to me next spring," said Jarvis Webster. "I have a friend that might be able to do something for you."

"You have? Who?" said Amelia Webster.

"Tom Laidley."

"I thought he was in the steel business," said Amelia.

"He is, but his company owns a fleet of boats."

"I didn't know that," said Amelia. Now Jarvis Webster was the object of her lofty disdain, and so, by extension, was Mr. Tom Laidley, who kept a fleet of boats without telling her about it.

"I'm going abroad next summer," said Elizabeth.

"It isn't certain," said Amelia Webster, lest John Appleton plan his voyages with a rendezvous in mind.

"Why yes it is, Mother."

"We haven't made final arrangements. I still have to talk to the other mothers," said Amelia Webster. "Elizabeth and three very nice friends of hers may go on a tour that an old schoolmate of mine takes every summer. It's really the only way for a young girl to travel abroad. Someone responsible and trustworthy in charge."

"I'll say that much for Betty Chrystie. She's responsible and trustworthy," said Jarvis Webster.

"Now, dear, you always manage to add a touch of sarcasm when you mention Betty Chrystie. But I've seen what can happen to young American girls traveling abroad without someone reliable. Especially in France and even more so in Italy. You don't see French girls and Italian girls wandering about in *our* cities. That's because French and Italian fathers and mothers are more protective."

"They'd be safe here as long as they stayed out of the subway during rush hour," said Jarvis Webster.

"Really, Jarvis, I'm trying to be serious."

"So am I. The fact remains that a girl is safer in a New York speakeasy than she is in broad daylight in that big square in Florence."

"You're arguing *my* point."

"I didn't finish. What I said goes for an Italian girl as well as an American girl. The Italians don't look to see if an American flag is pinned to the girl's bottom."

"Really, Jarvis."

"And any number of Betty Chrysties isn't going to prevent pinching."

"I'm afraid you're talking in circles," said Amelia Webster.

"If an Italian pinched my bottom I'd slap his face," said Elizabeth.

"Exactly," said Jarvis Webster. "And you'd develop a strong arm by the end of the summer. But that's the way to deal with it. What do you think, John?"

"I don't see why you have to make Mr. Appleton take sides," said Amelia Webster.

"Well, if I was with a girl and an Italian pinched her, I'd give him a punch in the nose."

"And then you'd be in trouble," said Jarvis Webster.

"Let's change the subject," said Amelia Webster, as the waitress came in to change the plates.

"How did we get on this one anyway?" said Elizabeth.

"It started when I said I wanted to work on a boat," said John Appleton.

"Yes," said Amelia, not quite implying that he had started a conversation to provoke a family quarrel. "Well, there was something I wanted to ask you. Oh, yes. I understand you're going to Harvard this fall. Will you have friends there?"

"Two fellows I know are there," said John Appleton.

"I see. I wondered why you'd picked Harvard."

"What's the matter with Harvard?" said Jarvis Webster.

"Nothing. I just wondered why Mr. Appleton picked it. I've known a great many men that went to Harvard, beginning with my own father, but most of them went there because their fathers did."

"That's partly the reason I'm going."

"Oh?" said Amelia Webster. She sounded as though something had stung her. "Your father went to Harvard?"

"Yes," said John Appleton.

"I didn't know that. Elizabeth, I don't remember your telling me that Mr. Appleton's father went to Harvard."

"I didn't know it myself till just this minute," said Elizabeth.

"Neither did I," said Jarvis Webster.

"There wasn't any particular reason for telling anyone that my father went to Harvard. *I* didn't go there."

"How did your father happen to go to Harvard?" said Amelia Webster.

"I guess because his father went there and one of his grandfathers. His other grandfather went to Dartmouth."

"You sound as though you had a strong New England background," said Jarvis Webster.

"Only on my father's side. My mother's people are all from Pennsylvania, and I am too. I was born in Spring Valley, P A."

"But not your father. *He* didn't come from Pennsylvania," said Amelia Webster.

"No, he came from a little town in New Hampshire."

"What town? I went to school in New Hampshire," said Jarvis Webster.

"A place called Penacook."

"Oh, I know where it is. Not far from where I went to school, in Concord."

"I think it's near Concord, yes," said John Appleton, who knew that it was less than ten miles from Concord and that Concord was the seat of St. Paul's School.

"How did your father happen to migrate from Penacook, New Hampshire, to Spring Valley, Pennsylvania?" said Jarvis Webster.

"Well, I guess it was through Harvard. My grandfather —is this boring you?—"

"Not at all," said Jarvis Webster.

"Well, it isn't very interesting," said John Appleton. "My grandfather happened to be a preacher. Most of the Appletons seemed to have been preachers or teachers. Some, both. My father was sent to Harvard, and then he was offered a job teaching at Spring Valley."

"Now *that's* interesting," said Jarvis Webster. "A college in Western Pennsylvania getting its teachers from Harvard."

"Well, Spring Valley was founded by two Harvard men in 1837. Two brothers named Everett. John and Robert Everett. They were Congregationalists, but they switched to Presbyterian, and Spring Valley's always been Presbyterian more than anything else. Anyway, there always have been one or two Harvard men on the faculty at Spring Valley."

"A tradition, you might say," said Jarvis Webster.

"Yes sir. A tradition. I couldn't tell you how many presidents of Spring Valley there've been, but I remember hearing that nearly all of them had some Harvard degree."

"What did your father teach?" said Jarvis Webster.

"Latin and Greek."

"Did your mother go to that school?" said Amelia Webster.

"Yes, that's how she met my father. She was one of his students."

"Did he pass her?" said Elizabeth.

"He had to. She graduated *summa cum laude*."

"A lot of brains in your family," said Jarvis Webster. "Did you find it hard to live up to?"

"Father, that isn't a very nice question."

"I want to know, and John doesn't mind telling me. I should think it would be very hard to follow in their footsteps."

"You're right, Mr. Webster, it was. And I didn't. I was fair in some subjects but not all. If I'd been better in high school I might have got a scholarship to Harvard, but my high school record was nothing to brag about. So I went to Spring Valley—for practically nothing."

"Football scholarship?"

"No. Although I guess I could have had one in junior and senior years. No, my father was on the faculty and I got tuition free, and I lived at home. I made a little money in college, marking papers and in the library, and I sold ads for this and that. Last summer I was a counsellor at a boys' camp, and the summer before that I had a job washing cars."

"You seem to have done extremely well. I think that's fine," said Jarvis Webster. "I congratulate you."

"Thank you. If I had to do over again I wouldn't play basketball. The trips were fun. We played colleges in Ohio and Indiana and West Virginia and Maryland, and we played Princeton and Yale, Fordham, Cornell, Buffalo, Canisius, Niagara, Western Reserve, and the colleges in our own section of the State. But basketball season came too soon after football, and the winter's the best time to crack the books."

"I've never seen a basketball game," said Amelia Webster. "I didn't know they played it at Yale."

"Oh, sure. Yale's in the League with Harvard, Princeton, Dartmouth, Penn, Cornell, Columbia, and Brown."

"I haven't seen much basketball, either," said Jarvis Webster. "But I think you're right. It does come too soon after football, if you've been playing football. Then in the spring did you play baseball?"

John Appleton smiled. "Tennis. We usually only played five or six matches. The whole tennis budget was three hundred dollars, so most of the time we supplied our own balls, and no long trips. We'd always have a day student for manager, a boy that could borrow his family's car. He'd get a minor sports letter, but if he wanted a sweater he had to buy it himself. This year we wouldn't have had any team at all, but a fellow named Porter Ditson came through with the money. He wasn't even an alumnus."

"I *know* he wasn't," said Jarvis Webster. "I know Porter Ditson. He went to Princeton. He was on the hockey team at my school, and he played on the Princeton team one year. A young fellow just a few years older than you?"

"Yes."

"He was a damn good hockey player. Hockey and football are the only games I like to watch. But isn't Ditson a pretty fair tennis player, too? I've seen him play squash at the club. Not that a good squash player is necessarily a good lawn tennis player, but I'll bet Ditson can give a good account of himself."

"He isn't a very good tennis player, Mr. Webster. I can beat him."

"Well, I like that," said Elizabeth.

"So he comes from Spring Valley, too."

"Yes sir. The club you mean, is that the Tennis and Racquet Club?"

"No, that's in Boston. This is the Racquet and Tennis. New York."

"That's the one I meant. Yes, he belongs to that," said John Appleton.

"You can be sure of that. Father doesn't make any mistakes about who belongs to the Racquet Club. He practically lives there."

"Well, as I often tell your mother, at least you always know where I am," said Jarvis Webster.

"I wish I cared more about sports, but I don't," said Amelia Webster. "Swimming is the only exercise I ever indulge in. I used to envy the girls my age that enjoyed tennis, but when I see how wrought up Elizabeth can become before a tournament, I'm glad I never took it up. By the way, Jarvis, that person I spoke to you about. He was in bathing again today without a top. Can't you write him a really sharp letter, the board of governors?"

"I'll make a note of it."

"Please do, because I think it's downright disgusting." Amelia Webster had resumed command of the conversation and did not relinquish it again until dinner was over.

"Cigar, John?" said Jarvis Webster.

"If you're going to smoke a cigar, Elizabeth and I will join you later," said Amelia Webster. "We'll be on the porch."

John Appleton and Jarvis Webster stayed in the dining-room with their cigars and Benedictine frappés. "Only a few more days and the summer'll be gone, to all intents and purposes. Week from Tuesday most of the people will be packed and gone. And actually the fall is the best time of year down here. It's quite beautiful right through Thanksgiving. We've often gone bathing as late as the middle of October, and then a little later there's duck-shooting for those who like it. I don't happen to, but I've kept the house open for friends who do. A few fellows. Colored man. Actually part Indian, part colored. He does the cooking and cleaning up. Just a few of us for weekends. It's the best time of the year down here. Although this year, I don't know. A lot of fellows are retrenching, and if things don't begin to show a decided improvement, I don't know where the hell

we'll be. I don't know where the hell we *are*. I used to think
it would be nice to retire at fifty, but here I am almost that
and suddenly all my plans have changed. No longer a question of making money. Now the problem is to try to hold on
to what you've got, and you don't dare to turn your back on
the ticker, for fear of what might happen while your back is
turned."

Jarvis Webster spoke between puffs on his cigar, and
was not so much speaking to John Appleton as thinking
aloud, airing his apprehensions, unconsciously sighing for
the companionship of weekends in autumns past.

"I suppose the sensible thing to do is close up when
everyone else does," said Jarvis Webster, and then, with a
smile: "And hope it'll all be here next summer. It might not,
you know. And you, John, you're just starting out."

"Just starting out. Not even that. Still at school."

"Well, we'll always need teachers, so I think you're very
fortunate to have your career more or less mapped out for
you. Will you teach at Spring Valley when you get through
at Harvard?"

"If they'll have me."

"Oh, they'll have you. Glad to, I imagine. You know, it
used to be that a young fellow whose father was a partner in
a Wall Street firm, he was usually considered to be set for
life. But a year, one year, has changed that. Now not even
the father is set for life. You, on the other hand, your father
was a teacher and you're going to be one, and you *are* set
for life."

"A lot of things can happen."

"They can, but barring some mishap, you are set for life.
I don't know whether a year or two ago you might have en-
vied a boy who could step into a ready-made partnership
and a lot of money, but now the tables have turned. If my
boy had lived, I'd much rather be able to help him with a
teaching career than start him out in Wall Street."

"Your boy?"

"Yes, Mrs. Webster and I had three children. A son between Elizabeth and Jean. His name was Hamilton, but he was nicknamed Dan. Daniel Webster. All we Websters get that, naturally."

"He died?"

"He was drowned, the second of August, 1926. Twelve years old. It doesn't surprise me that you haven't heard about it. It's made an enormous difference in this household."

"Yes, I imagine it would."

Jarvis Webster leaned forward and with one finger tapped John Appleton on the knee. "But it doesn't explain *everything*, John. Don't attribute everything to my son's death." Jarvis Webster rose, and John Appleton realized that this man, this pleasant, well-mannered, conventional gentleman, had been observing him for weeks, watching him as he gained information and formed impressions of the Webster family. At this moment Jarvis Webster was reading his thoughts, and the older man smiled. John Appleton smiled in return, slightly embarrassed but with an affection for the older man and for the understanding that was revealed in his observation. The two men were smiling as they left the diningroom.

"Is there a movie you'd like to see?" said Jarvis Webster to his daughter.

"They're showing a prison picture, and I hate them," said Elizabeth. "As soon as there's one prison picture the movies are full of nothing but prison pictures. And this has Wallace Beery, to make it worse. Or are you trying to get rid of us, Father?"

"I'm not trying to get rid of you, but your mother and I are playing bridge with Mr. and Mrs. Watley."

"At their house?"

"Yes."

"Then maybe I can get John to take me to Canoe Place."

"I don't like you going to Canoe Place, Elizabeth," said Amelia Webster.

"And I didn't bring any money with me," said John Appleton.

"We'll be all right here," said Elizabeth.

"Well, your father and I should be home by eleven-thirty."

"Or twelve," said Jarvis Webster.

Amelia Webster rose. "Goodnight, Mr. Appleton. Goodnight, dear. Get some sleep. You have a busy week ahead, getting ready for your party."

Mr. and Mrs. Webster drove off in a black Lincoln sedan-limousine, and John and Elizabeth did not speak until the tockle-tockle sound of the Lincoln exhaust began to fade.

"Have you met Mr. and Mrs. Watley?" said Elizabeth.

"Haven't met them and never even heard of them before."

"You've spent a whole summer in Southampton and you really might as well have been in Timbuktu."

"That's why I came here. I'm getting ready for Timbuktu. Next summer. Trying out my French here, first."

"I don't get it."

"Timbuktu is French. Owned by the French. It was a very feeble witticism. But who knows, I may get there next summer. Maybe I'll tutor some little black boy, and be adopted by a chieftain. What ever happened to John Appleton? Didn't you hear? He's living in Timbuktu, gone native, has fourteen wives."

"You're silly. You're talking nonsense."

"I know I am. I was under a strain. Your mother was trying so hard to put me in my place and keep me there."

"At first. But not later."

"Why should she be so impressed by Harvard? If I'd wanted to I could have told her that seven generations of my father's family went to Harvard. But when they started going to Harvard it wasn't as big as Spring Valley. Or as good."

"Then why are you going there?"

"Oh, it's better now. Harvard's three hundred years old and rich, and Spring Valley's only a hundred. Not quite that. Be a hundred in 1937. And Spring Valley isn't rich, not in

(59)

comparison with Harvard. But if I had a son I'd rather send him to Spring Valley, for his A.B. The Appletons of Harvard means nothing. But maybe the Appletons of Spring Valley will, in a couple of generations."

"My mother's father went to Harvard. That's why she was so impressed."

"But you can be damn sure her father didn't know any of my relations."

"Why do we have to quarrel about that? If you knew all about my mother you'd feel sorry for her and make allowances. Do you know who the Watleys are? No, you don't, but I'll tell you. Mrs. Watley is my father's girl friend, as you called her. Mother and Father go over there to play bridge, and my mother knows about Father and Mrs. Watley. Mr. Watley is such a sap it wouldn't make any difference whether he knew or not."

"Why does your mother go?"

"Because it would be worse to stay home. You pretend you don't know about those things."

"Do you? I wouldn't. Would you? If you were married and your husband was cheating on you, would you play bridge with his girl?"

"Of course I would. Especially in a place like Southampton. Mother doesn't have to see the Watleys in New York, but in the summer, in a small place like this, you see the same people every day, several times a day. You can't just drop people that are in your own circle. Everybody'd be uncomfortable. You'd have to be careful never to invite the Watleys when the Websters were coming or vice versa."

"I learned one thing this summer. I wouldn't live here if I inherited ten million dollars. Not that I ever expect to. But even if I did."

"You don't know what you'd do if you inherited ten million dollars. Or what you'd be like. I know what you think. You think we're all a bunch of snobs. But I'll just bet there's just as much snobbishness in Spring Valley as there is here. Only there it isn't money or who your family are. It's how many degrees you have, or how bright you are. But

I'll bet there's just as much snobbishness. And it would be the same in Timbuktu. I've gone to school with girls from families like yours, teachers' and ministers' daughters. They complain about snobbishness, but their families move heaven and earth to get them in the Mets and the Gets."

"What the hell are the Mets and the Gets?"

"Dances. The Metropolitans and the Get-Togethers."

"Did you go to the Mets and the Gets?"

"Of course I did, and I don't apologize. They're the people I was brought up with and was related to. The same way you were brought up with your highbrow friends and boys that washed cars. I never knew any boys that washed cars or sold ads, and I don't know why I should want to. What would we have to talk about? The kind of soap they use? I wouldn't know anybody they knew. I feel sorry for really poor people, but not for those girls that go to schools where they don't belong, and try to push their way into parties and dances where they won't know anybody. I don't like them, and I like their parents even less. There won't be any at my party, and I didn't have them when I came out, either."

"Then I guess I'd better not go to your party, either," said John Appleton. "Why did you invite me?"

"Because I wanted to."

"But I'm one of those people you were talking about."

"No you're not."

"Why not?" he said. "I washed cars, I sold ads."

"Well, if you don't want to come, don't. I sent you an invitation even after you were so rude the other day. But for heaven's sake, don't come if you don't want to, or if you're going to feel out of place."

"I know why you invited me. Because your father likes me."

"How wrong you are. If anything, that would have kept me from inviting you. I invited you because I enjoyed playing tennis with you this summer, and that'll probably be the last time I see you. Ever."

"Ever?"

"Won't it be?"

"Yes, I guess it probably will. A closed chapter in both our lives."

"Yes."

"Elizabeth?"

"What?"

"Do you want it to be a closed chapter?"

"No."

"I don't either. It *can't* be."

"But that's the way it is."

"You mean a lot to me."

"Do I? Why?"

"I was lonesome this summer. A couple of times I came close to quitting my job. If it hadn't been for you, I would have. I mean playing tennis with you, seeing you a couple of times a week. That was all that kept me from quitting that job. Last week I could hear the orchestra from the Meadow Club, the night of the dance. I could hear everybody having a good time, and I was alone in my room. I almost went downstairs and swiped a bottle of gin and got drunk. Instead of that I went for a walk. I stood there listening to the music and that close I could hear girls laughing. Then a policeman came along and asked me who I was and what I was doing. He thought I was getting ready to steal a car, I guess. He took me to the Castles' and woke up the butler to identify me. Otherwise I'd have spent the night in jail. I never felt so low in all my life. I was out of it, and homesick, and sore, and jealous. God, I felt awful. That's why I said I'd never live here if I had ten million dollars. I'll never come back here. But I don't want to stop seeing you, Elizabeth. If I come to New York will you go out with me? If I write you ahead of time?"

"Yes."

"Will you give me your address before I leave?"

"Yes."

"If I write to you will you answer it?"

"Yes. Why were you jealous? Because you weren't at the dance?"

"Worse than that. Because you *were,* and *with* somebody. Dancing with somebody, and I never got that close to you."

The moment had come and there was no more to say. He got up and sat beside her on the wicker sofa. He kissed her and they stretched out together. He put his knee between her legs and she caught her breath in the new excitement. Soon he had his unresisted hand wherever he wanted it to be, and she whispered to him, "I can't stop now. John, I can't stop. You have to do it, but be careful."

"We have to take a chance," he said.

"All right, all right we'll take a chance," she said. "Yes, let's take a chance. Oh, my darling. Is it over for you?"

"Yes," he said.

"I want to stay here, but I mustn't. I must go upstairs quickly and do something."

"Do you know what to do?"

"I think so. I'm pretty sure. Before I go—do you love me?"

He said the words, "I love you." And then he did.

The problem of entertaining for the groom's mother had disturbed Amelia Webster ever since the announcement of Elizabeth's engagement. More accurately, it had been a problem ever since Mrs. Appleton's visit to the Websters following the announcement in February. Ethel Stroud Appleton was forty-six, two years older than Amelia Webster, and her rather dumpy figure was not helped by the all too obviously ready-made clothes she brought with her to New York. She wore rimless pince-nez glasses that she was constantly taking off and putting on during conversations, now and then blowing on the lenses before polishing them. She stayed two nights at the Websters' apartment, and when the guests arrived for the small dinner party on the second night, Ethel Appleton was in Jean Webster's room, helping her with her homework. John Appleton had neglected to tell Amelia Webster that his mother was a substitute teacher in Spring Valley High School. She was a peppy little woman and *interested* in everyone equally.

She did not shake hands with the Webster servants (which Amelia had somehow expected her to do) or in any other way become over-familiar with them, but the friendliness of her smile was the same for Jean Webster, who was eleven years old, for the butler and the cook, and for the Fifth Avenue clergyman, the aged bibliophile, and the headmaster of a boys' day school who, with their wives—the bibliophile was a widower—had been invited to meet the mother of Elizabeth's fiancé. The dinner guests were all ten or more years older than Ethel Appleton, but as Amelia Webster told Jarvis Webster, it was the best she could do. But after he had met Ethel Appleton it was apparent to Jarvis Webster that she would actually have fitted in with a younger, or at least a more dashing group. She was certainly more animated than anyone else at the dinner party, and as the evening progressed she became much the youngest person in the room. The clergyman, who was notoriously a ladies' man, took her hand in both of his when he was saying goodnight. This was a small rite that he usually reserved for his wealthy parishioners and much younger women.

Aside from her unfamiliarity with the names that came up during the dinner party, Ethel Appleton could not be regarded as a social failure; she committed no gaffe. But Amelia Webster commented on her "ordinariness," and as far as possible wanted her kept out of the way over the wedding festivities. John Appleton had met so few people in Southampton that it had been difficult to explain to the Websters' friends how Elizabeth had come to know him. The Castles knew him, and so did a few young people who played tennis, but among the friends of Jarvis and Amelia Webster the engagement came like a bolt from the blue. Especially when their friends read the sparse information in the society columns: "Mr. Appleton, son of Mrs. Charles F. Appleton and the late Prof. Appleton, received the B.A. degree from Spring Valley College and is doing graduate work at Harvard. He is a member of Beta Theta Pi and Phi Beta Kappa." No clubs, no grandparents, no aid to identification or clue to the romance.

The Castles, to John Appleton's and Amelia Webster's astonishment, came through with an invitation to John and his mother to stay at their house over the wedding and to have free use of Mr. Castle's Lincoln convertible. "They hardly ever spoke a civil word to me all last summer," said John.

"Well, maybe they're nice people. And appreciate what you did for their little Bobby," said his mother. "You wouldn't have liked it if they'd gushed all over you, anyway."

"Mr. Castle even told Mr. Webster he'd be glad to second me for the University Club."

"Well, if you want to join I'll give it to you for a Christmas present."

John shook his head. "I'll do that when I'm a full professor."

"Well, I'll give it to you then. Your father used to stay there when he had meetings in New York."

"Not the Harvard Club? I thought he stayed at the Harvard Club."

"No. Dr. Witherspoon would always arrange to get him a room at the University Club. One advantage, it's cheaper than a hotel, and just as convenient."

"I wish Father could be here."

"To see you get married. The rest of it would bring on one of his attacks."

"As far as that goes, I wish it were over."

"This is the way they do things, John. A girl of Elizabeth's upbringing shouldn't be deprived of it. Going through it may give her nervous prostration, but they like to have it to remember. And they should. Once in her life a girl is entitled to be the center of the stage. Compliments and attentions. After that is another story. The husband must have the say, even when the wife may think he's wrong."

"Did you ever think Pop was wrong?"

"Yes, I did. But I gave in."

"When was he wrong?"

"Well, he took on the dean's job for the extra money,

and the five hundred dollars a year didn't make that much difference. I was subbing at High and we had enough, more than most. Oh, I know why he did it. He wanted to take out more insurance. But the extra work just wasn't worth it. He wasn't an administrator. He was a scholar. I argued, but there was no use arguing with that man. Once that Yankee mind was made up. I couldn't tell him that the extra work would hasten his death. He would have argued that that was all the more reason for increasing his insurance."

"Was that the only time he was wrong?"

"Oh, no. He wouldn't go to the doctor until the pain got so bad. And we had personal things."

"Like what?"

"You'll find out when you're married. Every married couple have personal things."

"Did you always give in on the personal things?"

"No, I didn't. Not always. But those things were personal. Husband and wife should never speak of personal things to a third party. Some they shouldn't even speak of to one another. Watch out for those little personal things, John, and don't always say what comes into your mind." She laughed. "Do you know what I used to do?"

"What?"

"When your father would make me angry, I'd wait till his back was turned, and then I'd stick my tongue out at him. Oh, that was a great relief."

"Did he ever catch you?"

"Dear me, no. But what a great relief. You have no idea."

"Yes I have," said John. "Many a time I did it to you."

They laughed together, heartily, long, and lovingly. "Oh, dear," she said. "Oh, dear me."

At the church and at the reception some of the Southampton regulars remembered John from the previous summer, but the vast number of guests from other places contented themselves with the comment that the groom was quite nice-looking, clean-cut, had an athletic build, seemed to be very much in love with Elizabeth, or was a dull bastard. Shorty Conners, the best man, and John's six ushers all had bad hangovers at the wedding. They had done their drinking as a unit and had had no success with Elizabeth's bridesmaids, not one of whom had ever heard of Spring Valley College and knew they were unlikely ever to see any of the ushers again. The invasion of Southampton by Spring Valley College was hardly more than a skirmish, and the invaders retired on Saturday night to nurse their wounds. By Sunday noon they had all gone. The rejection of John Appleton's friends could not have been accomplished more efficiently if it had been planned.

John Appleton's mother stayed in Southampton until the late afternoon train, and would be in Spring Valley before midnight. She had been no problem at all, and on the way to the station Amelia said: "Ethel, I hope you'll let us know when you're coming to New York."

"I could tell you that now, Amelia," said Ethel Appleton. "The last time I was in New York was when Charles was going overseas, in 1918. I never go to New York. Pittsburgh and Fort Penn, they're city enough for me. Maybe I could get you and Jarvis to come to Spring Valley."

"I'm looking forward to it," said Jarvis Webster. He lied quickly to cover Amelia's almost audible wince. "Your husband was in the army?"

"A captain. Boots and *spurs*, mind you. And a strap across his chest, crosswise. Never was a man more unsuited to a uniform. Those caps they wore. On most men they looked jaunty, they wore them at an angle. Charles wore his on the top of his head, straight, the same way he always wore his hats."

"The 26th Division?" said Jarvis Webster. "They were the New Englanders."

"Oh, no. He was given a commission, captain, to work on documents for a military history. He was familiar with German and French, although those weren't his languages. The war was almost over by the time he was sent overseas. He was over there for nearly a year. John was so proud of his father."

"I'll bet he was," said Jarvis Webster.

They had reached the Long Island station. "Oh, *they* were at the wedding," said Ethel Appleton, nodding toward a stylish couple on the platform.

"The Nortons. Yes, they were there," said Amelia Webster. "Shall we just wait in the car till the train comes? Jarvis, have you got Ethel's ticket?"

"I have it right here."

"Let's just wait here instead of standing on the platform." Amelia was not quite sure why she wanted Ethel Appleton and the Nortons kept apart, but at the moment it was what she wanted. "You'll be able to get a nice nap on the train," said Amelia Webster.

"Oh, I'm not a bit tired, and I love trains. I'll probably fall asleep after Philadelphia. Then I change again at Altoona and get the late train to Spring Valley."

"Are you being met at Spring Valley?" said Jarvis Webster. "It'll be quite late, won't it?"

"Old Frank Murphy, with his seagoing hack, as John always calls it. Frank drives the taxi. He'll be my reception committee, and I'll have to tell him all about the wedding. But a good soul, and must be worth a fortune but still meets all the trains. Frank's sister had a very serious operation last winter, and for a—"

"Here's your train," said Amelia Webster.

"Oh, well, it wasn't much of a story anyway, except for one funny remark Frank made," said Ethel Appleton.

The Websters' chauffeur opened the door of the Lincoln. "There was just the one suitcase, ma'am?" he said.

"That's all," said Ethel Appleton. "And thank you very much, Thomas. Say goodbye to everybody for me."

"I will, ma'am, and thank you."

"I'll take Mrs. Appleton's bag, Thomas," said Jarvis Webster.

"You won't mind if I don't get out, Ethel," said Amelia Webster.

"Oh, you stay right there. Goodbye, and many thanks for all you did and everything. Goodbye, Amelia. I'll write."

Jarvis took her bag and led her straight to the Nortons, reintroduced her, handed her bag to Norton, kissed Ethel on the cheek, and waited on the platform until the train had gone.

"I saw what you did," said Amelia, when he was back in the car. "What ever possessed you to inflict her on the Nortons?"

"Drop me off at the club, Thomas," said Jarvis Webster.

"I asked you—" said Amelia Webster.

"And I heard you. I always hear you, and I don't always like what I hear. John Appleton has rescued Elizabeth, and I'm going to be damned sure you don't do the same thing to Jean that you did to her."

"Well, then heaven help Jean if *you're* going to take charge."

"Not heaven, Amelia. You've got the entree there. But by Christ if Jean's going to turn out to be a little snob. Not if I can help it. The one that needs the help now is John Appleton."

"John Appleton is an extremely fortunate young man, and nobody knows it better than he does. He's got himself married to a pretty, rich, stupid girl, and he knows all that about her. You're responsible for this marriage. I wanted Elizabeth to marry one of the boys she grew up with. But you did everything you knew how to marry her off to this intellectual hick. Why? Because you wanted to oppose me. Very well, you've succeeded. And now Elizabeth is going to have to pretend she hasn't any money, because her husband hasn't any. She's never going to see her friends, and she's never going to fit in with his friends. A girl that's been very carefully brought up in New York society is going to have to spend her life with taxi drivers and their sisters. Thank God that train came along. Frank Murphy and his sister's operation. That's what Elizabeth is going to have to listen to. That, and whatever college professors talk about. Oh, you've done beautifully, Jarvis Webster. You really have. Now you'll get off at the club and get tight. Who with? Not a Frank Murphy. Oh, no. The same men you've known all your life. You don't want your daughter to marry her own kind of people, but you've never made the slightest effort to move one inch out of the same circle. In other words, you're a hypocrite."

"Well, if we're a sample of—"

"I knew you were going to say that. Blame *us* on the way we were brought up. Forget the good marriages and the nice people. Blame everybody and everything but yourself. And then after you've had ten Martinis blame me for letting my son drown."

"I've never done that."

"Yes you have. That was too good a secret for Rhoda Watley to keep," said Amelia Webster. "How are you going to get home? Do you want Thomas to come back here for you?"

"I'll get a lift."

"Then I'll let Thomas go. He hasn't had any time off since last Sunday. And please don't turn on the radio when you come in. You turn it on full blast and it wakes the whole household."

"Is there anything else you'd like to get off your chest?"

"*Is* there!"

"Goodbye."

She was sitting upright, drying her back hair with a dark blue towel. Her bathing suit was one-piece and of white wool, cut low in back. He lay on a larger blue towel, so high-piled that it was almost a rug, that covered an area of the pebbly, narrow beach. He had his head propped on one arm, and in his free hand he held a cigarette. It was a new pleasure to study her and her body. If he looked too long, passion would commence, and he did not want that now. He wanted to think what there had been, what there was in this body that she carried around with her. From where he lay he could not see her face or the front of her body, but he could see the line that began under her arm, down past the spread of her hips to the big towel, and there was a hint of her breast under her bathing suit. She went on drying her hair, and the act of drying her hair was a part of her other life, the life of ordinary acts and speech and words that were not a part of what he now knew. And that he alone knew. That to some extent not even she knew, since so much of what he knew was learned when she would let go. She would not care to know how she looked or sounded when she let go. In the calm person who was performing an ordinary act, the act of drying her hair, now rested, hidden or nearly hidden beneath a white bathing suit, an engine of such pleasure as he had never known. The same hips now squashed on a blue towel, the hands and arms rubbing the back of her neck, the breast that strained ever so slightly at the gently confining wool, the voice that was humming "Stardust."

She finished drying her hair and sighed from the small effort and lay back to take the sun. Now he could see the front of her body. She lay with her feet close together and her arms rigidly at her side. He put his hand on her knee and slowly moved it upward until it rested on top of the *mons veneris.*

"John?" she said.

"What?"

"Please?"

"All right," he said, and took his hand away. "It was just a caress."

"I know, dear, but I don't like it in public. What I really don't like is to start feeling that way and not be able to go on."

"Let's come down here tonight."

"I thought of that, too. But I'd rather die than have some of these French people see us. And they'd know that that's what we came for." She sat up suddenly. "Let's talk about something and get our minds off it."

"All right. What shall we talk about?"

"You're the brilliant one. You decide. And don't stare at my bosom."

"The buttons are there."

"I know they are, only too well, and they won't go down

if you stare at me that way. Look out at the blue Mediterranean. Wave to Africa. And light me a cigarette. How is our supply? Are we going to have to buy some more? Thirty cents for a pack of Chesterfields. It's robbery."

He lit a cigarette and passed it to her without looking at her. "Here," he said.

"Thanks," she said. "How far is it to Africa, I wonder."

"From here, oh, I'd guess about five or six hundred miles. Maybe more, maybe less."

"I have no idea. We went abroad that way one time. Past Gibraltar, and across the Mediterranean to—heavens, I don't remember where we landed. Naples, I guess. I was about eight, and my brother was four. Jean wasn't even born. We traveled in style, that time. Mother had a maid and Father had a valet, and a Mamselle for us, my brother and I."

"You always say 'my brother.' You never call him by name."

"I know."

"What *did* you call him?"

"His nickname was Dan, after Daniel Webster, but we never called him that at home. We called him Tony. I started that. Hamil-tony. Hamilton was his real name." She looked out at the sea, very soberly, then suddenly turned away. "He was sweet," she said, quietly.

"I've never heard you say that about anybody."

"Sometimes I feel like saying it about you. You're like him, in some ways."

"How?"

"I don't know exactly. But sometimes you remind me of him, a little bit. Some people never seem to worry about the future. They go from day to day. I guess you don't worry about the future because you know what you want to do, what you want to be. But Tony was like that, too. It isn't optimism, but it's thinking that things will take care of themselves. I don't know."

"How did he drown?"

She considered for a moment. "This is one of those things that married couples have to tell each other, I guess. I'll probably want to know things, too. About you, and your family." She paused again. "Five years ago this summer Tony was eleven. I must have been fifteen. That was the difference in our ages. Anyhow, this day it had rained all morning and part of the afternoon. It might have been the tail end of a nor'easter, which usually lasts three days. I don't remember. But Mother and Tony, as soon as it stopped raining, decided to go for a swim. It was pretty late in the afternoon and the red flag was still up at the club, although the storm was over, and the ocean had calmed down. This is the hardest part to explain, but Mother decided that instead of going in at the club, they'd use the Laidleys' beach house. We often did that. The Laidleys had a big house near ours, but they also had this beach house. They still have it. It's quite big and they often use it as a guest cottage. I don't know why Mother decided to go there instead of the club, except that you always had more privacy at the Laidleys' and actually Mother preferred it. And I should explain that we're all good swimmers. Mother is. Father. Jean and I. And Tony was faster in the water than any of us."

"Where were the other members of the family?"

"Father was at the Southhampton Club, playing bridge. Jean, I think, was having her supper. And I was at Marjorie Talcott's house. You met her. She was one of my bridesmaids. I got home at about six-thirty and Jean was the only one there, of the family. That was very unusual, and I suspected something wrong because the servants were acting strangely, and in any case Mother always got home around that time to be with Jean before she was put to bed. I asked one of the maids if there was anything wrong, and what I know now, of course, is that they'd been told not to say anything to Jean or me. But I wasn't home fifteen minutes before Marjorie called up and said how sorry she was. Sorry about what? That was the first inkling I had. And I knew what I had to do. I had to play mother to Jean and keep it from her.

"I have to piece it together, what happened. Apparently Tony and Mother had just been diving under the waves, but then Tony took a notion to see how far out he could go. Mother called to him not to go out so far, and he heard her the first time, because he stopped swimming and waved, but then he started swimming again and Mother called him again but either he didn't hear her or pretended he didn't. Mother said afterwards that he may have been challenging her to a race, and had waved to her to come out. But she stood on the beach and waved a towel, hoping he'd interpret that as a signal to turn back.

"As I said, he was very fast in the water and it suddenly occurred to Mother that he was out dangerously far. I imagine she was very cross, too. But then suddenly she couldn't see him, and for a moment she was panicky, but she got hold of herself and went in and swam out to where she'd last seen him. But he wasn't there. She kept looking back to the Laidleys' house to keep her bearings, but the sun got in her eyes. She had to decide whether to keep searching where she was, or go back for help. And that's what she did. She swam back to the Laidleys' and telephoned the lifeguard at the club, and the Coast Guard, and Father at the Southampton Club. It took them a while to get there, and they all arrived more or less at once. Father got a bathing suit and went out with the lifeguard in a rowboat, and the Coast Guard came in their motorboat. By that time the news had spread like wildfire, and pretty soon there must have been a hundred people congregating around the Laidleys' beach house. Mother went out and got in the Coast Guard boat to show them approximately where she'd last seen Tony. Actually she stayed on the boat till past midnight. Someone took some clothes out to her and she changed out there. She refused to leave. Father also got in the Coast Guard boat and two more boats came from the Coast Guard and several boys I knew were out there in their sailboats. But it was no use."

"Did they ever find him?"

"Well—yes. The next day some bunker fishermen found

him about halfway to Wainscott. They wouldn't let Mother see him. Father had to identify him—from the name tape on his bathing suit. That was the worst summer I ever spent in my whole life, and our family's never been right since."

"It must have been a really bad time."

"You've never seen a husband trying to console a wife but hating her and secretly blaming her at the same time. And a wife that didn't want his consolation and wouldn't try to console him. The only thing I ever heard her say— overheard, because I wasn't supposed to hear it—was 'Go away, Jarvis.' And he said, 'I wish I could.' Whatever he meant by that. There was no reason why he couldn't. He wasn't that much of a father or a husband, that we couldn't have gotten along without him."

"Maybe he couldn't get along without you."

"Men stick together, don't they?"

"I wouldn't say that. Not according to history."

"That's countries. Nations. But men always defend other men against women, when women criticize men."

"No, not even that. I happen to like your father."

"And not my mother."

"Don't make me say that, Elizabeth. You know all about that. More than I do. She didn't want you to marry me."

"She thought you wouldn't be good for me."

"Do you think I am?"

"In every way," said Elizabeth.

"Except the two things that mattered to her. Money, and social position. Thank God they didn't matter to you."

"They do. But they didn't matter enough to keep me from falling in love with you. But I love my mother, too, John. I think she's a wonderful and clever and beautiful woman."

"She is." He kissed her hand.

"What's your book?" she said.

"It's called *The War of Independence: American Phase.* Written by a man named Claude Van Tyne."

"The name of an Oriental shop. Incense burners and Japanese prints."

(75)

"It is? Well, we can burn incense to this man. He won the Pulitzer prize, and he's dead. In fact he died before they gave him the prize."

"Is it any good?"

"At this stage of the game, all histories are good. I have to think they are, because I have to read so many of them. Enough seriousness for today. Let's get some of that blue water on us and then go have a cocktail."

"I don't want to go in again."

He frowned. "Because we talked about Tony?"

"Oh, no. Only because my hair is dry and I don't want to get it wet again. I'm not affected by those things, that way."

In the Thirties many boys of the upper and professional classes were christened Peter. There were some named Peter Stuyvesant, some named Peter Cooper, even a few named Peter Bent Brigham. But most of the infant sons who were called Peter had no grandparent or maternal hero whose name had been Peter. It was a name that was extremely, if momentarily, popular among young parents of the day. The middle and lower classes had been abandoning the name in recent generations, and its new popularity was comparable to the revival of interest in various objects that had been unfashionable or common in the previous century. The Franklin stoves, the ships-in-bottles, the sconces and trivets that had once served useful purposes in the decades between Washington and McKinley now reappeared as Americana, and the name Peter was back in circulation.*

The naming of their first child, if a girl, was no problem to Elizabeth and John Appleton. Elizabeth liked her name, and John favored it for their daughter. He was equally determined not to call his son John, which he said was lacking distinction, or Charles, for the same reason. Elizabeth considered calling a son Hamilton, after her late brother, but Hamilton Appleton sounded like the beginning

* As an index, in 1957 there were seventy-three undergraduates at Princeton named Peter; in the 1929 class at Harvard College there was one Peter.

of a funny poem, and she refused even to discuss John's suggestion of Jarvis Webster Appleton. The expectant parents arrived at Peter in much the same way as a thousand other fathers and mothers: they wanted an old-fashioned name, unusual, and one that had not been in either family within memory.

The child was born in the Spring Valley Hospital, somewhat prematurely and in spite of arrangements for its birth at the Harkness Pavilion. The time was June 1934, and John Appleton, instructor in American history at Spring Valley College, had expected to take Elizabeth to New York after commencement and there await the birth of the baby. The pregnancy itself had been carefully planned and with complete success: they had put off starting a baby until John was finished at Harvard and settled in Spring Valley.

Amelia Webster, who had never flown, insisted that an airplane must be chartered, but there was no landing field within a hundred miles of Spring Valley that was suitable for the size aircraft she wanted. She therefore did not see the baby and his mother until the child was a full day old. She wasted no time on the amenities, and when John Appleton and his mother met her and Jarvis Webster at the Altoona station she said: "John? I didn't expect to see you here. Hello, Ethel."

"Oh, I didn't mind driving down."

"Not a question of your minding driving down. I fully expected you to be with Elizabeth."

"I *was* with Elizabeth, till two hours ago, and I'll be with her again in another hour," said John. "Hello, Mr. Webster."

"She's perfectly all right, and so is little Peter," said Ethel Appleton. "Both are doing so well."

"But it was a premature baby, and I wanted Doctor Doman to deliver it," said Amelia Webster. "Who have you got out here to compare with Doctor Doman?"

"Only a local young man, but he's had a lot of experience," said Ethel Appleton. "Don't be upset, Amelia. Everything is all right, as you'll soon see."

"And you're not *going* to see if you intend to barge in

and upset Elizabeth," said John Appleton. "This Doman may be the greatest doctor in the world, but Harry Jeffries was here and he did the job and he did it damn well."

"Now, John," said his mother.

"Yes, really? Who do you think you are, talking to me that way?" said Amelia Webster.

"You'll damn soon find out who I am and what I am. I'm Elizabeth's husband and the father of the baby."

"I suggest we get started and maybe the drive will . . ." Jarvis Webster left the sentence unfinished. He got in front with John Appleton and he and Ethel Appleton maintained a conversation as the car climbed the mountains toward Spring Valley.

At the edge of town John said to his father-in-law: "Do you want to stop at the house first?"

"I do not," said Amelia Webster. "And I'd much rather stay at a hotel, if there is one."

"There *is* one, and it's new," said John Appleton. "If that's what you want to do. But before you go in and see Elizabeth, I'm going to have a look at her first."

"That won't be necessary," said Amelia Webster.

"I say it will, and that's how it's going to be. I want to have you get this straight, Mrs. Webster, so there'll be no misunderstanding. I'm running this show, and I'm not going to have my wife a nervous wreck. You can see her for ten minutes this morning and ten minutes this afternoon."

"That's perfectly satisfactory, John," said Jarvis Webster. "We just want to see Elizabeth and the baby and let her know that we got here as soon as we could. And I promise you that we'll leave here the day after tomorrow."

"Don't make any promises for me," said Amelia Webster.

"That's exactly what I *am* doing, Amelia. And we're not stopping at the hotel. We're staying at John's house. Well, this is quite a hospital. Very modern and up-to-date."

"J. W. Framingham," said Ethel Appleton. "You probably heard of him in New York, Jarvis."

"The name has a familiar ring to it," said Jarvis Webster.

"Well, maybe not in New York, but around this part of the world," said Ethel Appleton. John entered the hospital and his mother filled the Websters in on the Framingham philanthropies until John returned.

"She's awake," he said. "You can see her."

"If we're a little over ten minutes—fifteen—but we won't stay too long," said Jarvis Webster.

The house at Harvard Road and Bucknell Street was generally considered to be as fine as any but the very finest residences in Spring Valley, but Amelia Webster gave it a low rating. "They paid eighteen thousand dollars for this house?"

"Don't pretend you think eighteen thousand is a lot of money," said Jarvis Webster.

"It is to *him*," she said.

"It's a well-built house. I've been having a look around, and they got a bargain."

"Everything's a bargain these days."

"You couldn't build this house for eighteen thousand today, let alone get a house and a corner location in a very desirable part of town."

"How do you know it's desirable?"

"Look at the other houses, and look at the people. In a town like this, this is the fashionable part. Look at the cars. And look at the dogs."

"What on earth have the dogs got to do with it?"

"In this block alone I've seen two Scotties and two Sealyhams. They cost money. A Lincoln. Two Cadillacs, and two Ford station wagons. And the women dress just the same as the women in any good suburb of New York. If they have a country club here, these are the people that belong to it. If we moved to Spring Valley, this is where *we'd* live."

"Thinking of moving here, Jarvis?"

"You know I'm not."

"I'm so relieved to hear that, because you wouldn't be very comfortable in a house that first of all has no maid's room, no laundry. The laundry has to be done in the cellar. There are only two bathrooms and no downstairs lavatory. The cellar is too small. It's already cluttered up with lawn mowers and garden hose and trunks. The big closets are in the wrong places, and if Elizabeth has any more children . . . But I notice John has a whole room to himself downstairs. With a baby in the house they're going to need a new hot water heater, and in 1934 they're *still* using a coal range. Would you like to know what else they got with this bargain? The wiring. One little lamp in the cellar, hanging from the ceiling. No extra outlet in the rooms on our side of the house."

"I don't see how they stood it," said Jarvis Webster.

"I'm *told* that you're creating a trust fund for the baby's education. *I'm* going to give Elizabeth some money to make some necessary improvements in this bargain house."

"You're waving a red flag in front of John's nose, but go ahead," said Jarvis Webster. "Not that you care, but I had a very good talk with the president of the local bank, a man named Brice Ditson. I know his younger brother. They think very highly of John Appleton in this town, and that was a banker's opinion. Ditson and his wife wanted to entertain us while we're here, but I told them we were leaving tomorrow."

"You're determined to leave, aren't you? All right, but if anything happens to Elizabeth or the baby . . ."

"What could you do? Suppose something does happen? To Elizabeth *or* the baby? What the hell could you do? Once before you waited a half an hour before sending for help."

"Oh, God, I hate you for that!"

"Amelia, your hatred of me began in 1908."

"It was never as great as it is right now."

"Then I'm about to make it a little greater. I've told John that he would be making a mistake to bring Elizabeth and the baby to Southampton. If he and Elizabeth are ever going to make a clean break from you, from us, this is the time. Until this child was born, or on the way, your trips to

Boston and Elizabeth's trips to New York didn't matter so much. But by great good fortune the baby was born here instead of New York. It almost makes me believe in God all over again. Divine intervention, you might call it."

"I wish you'd die."

"Do you know, I've wished it myself. But now that I have a grandson, I'd like to see how he comes out."

"You have a fourteen-year-old daughter of your own. You don't care how she comes out?"

"I care very much, but there I've been a failure. Elizabeth didn't even love me, thanks to you. But Jean loved me and now she has no respect for me, thanks to you. I don't think she has much respect for you, either, but that's no consolation. After Tony was drowned Jean might as well have had no parents at all. As that sanctimonious bastard says, she was the forgotten man. The forgotten daughter. The only one in this family that has any sweetness and niceness, and love, and God only knows where she got it from. Or how she held on to what she's got."

"So you'd like to have another try, at your grandson."

"No, I know enough now to keep hands off. But I'd like to be around to see that you keep your hands off. Off the grandchild and his parents' marriage."

Jarvis Webster's vigilance lasted a year, until Amelia got her wish. In June 1935, Jarvis Webster, in New Haven for his thirtieth reunion, collapsed in a meeting of the Death's Head Society, and died on his way to the hospital. He was buried in the family plot on Staten Island, and to the surprise of a few intimates, his wife was the lifetime beneficiary of his estate, which before taxes was worth close to two million dollars. On her death the principal was to be divided between the two daughters.

In his personal file at his office there was a letter to John Appleton, which read, in part:

I have left nothing outright to Elizabeth or to Jean. Thus they will have to go to their mother for money. Knowing, as I am sure you do, that Mrs. Webster and I did not have a happy marriage, you may wonder why I have given her this power instead of leaving the money to Elizabeth and Jean so that they would be financially independent of their mother. I did that for a reason. Aside from the fact that I do not wish to disturb or restrict Mrs. Webster's mode of living, I am also hopeful that Elizabeth will accustom herself to living within your income, without appeals to her mother. You have told me what that income is and I fully realize that by past standards, Elizabeth will face some hardships. Nevertheless I believe I am acting in her best interests and in yours. You are both young and have courage and strength. Later on, when you are older and all your expenses will be mounting, Elizabeth can count on eventually coming into control of her half of the trust fund of which her mother is now the sole beneficiary. I, of course, have no control whatsoever over Mrs. Webster's personal income, which is considerably less than the income that will go to her from my estate. She is free to do with that as she will and it is possible that she may give or offer to give money to Elizabeth from time to time. By so doing she would, of course, defeat the purpose of my will as I have explained it to you, but I know that you will be able to handle such situations as they may arise. It is foolish to pretend that Elizabeth will never have money, but I likewise consider it extremely unwise for a young couple to live beyond the husband's income. I have every confidence in you, my boy, and if I had been convinced that an alternate course would have put you and my daughter on the road to happiness, that is the course I would have taken . . .

In the summer of that year Elizabeth bought a little Ford sedan, which required a doubling of the space in the garage. The new car and the renovations to the garage were more than covered by the ten thousand dollars which Amelia Webster, in August, gave Elizabeth as a Christmas present. In September a daughter was born to the Appletons, and Amelia told John Appleton that she was putting aside ten thousand dollars for the child's education, as had been done for little Peter, for whom a trust fund of twenty-five thousand had been established. Amelia did not tell John that the money she had put aside had in reality been a cash gift to Elizabeth. Elizabeth kept this little secret from John, and in so doing she learned that it was not hard to keep from him things he did not want to know.

III

It was a historical fact that Spring Valley College was older than the town. The college came first, because the Everett brothers, Robert and John, in 1836 decided to camp for the night near a spring beside the corduroy road. In the morning they saddled their horses and were on their way up the mountain. But they had gone only a few hundred yards when they came upon a good-sized clearing in the otherwise thickly wooded forest. The clearing had not been made by the lumberman's ax; there were no lumberman's stumps. The brothers halted the horses and dismounted for a better look and an exchange of theories; and ultimately agreed, as New Englanders who had seen the phenomenon before, that the clearing, with its irregular contours, had been made by a forest fire caused by lightning. Nature had started the fire, and Nature had put it out. According to Robert Everett's journal, which reposes under glass in the college library, the brothers devoutly agreed that this was as far as they wanted to go; it was predestined. Behind them were tiny villages, each too small to have its own place of worship or school-house, but a church and school here, in the cabin they would build, was a beginning. There was water aplenty, meat on the hoof, meal to be had from the land they had passed. They built their first cabin in the approximate center of the clearing, and when that was done they called it a schoolhouse, because they correctly guessed that it would be easier to offer education to children than to preach religion to their parents. Down in the valley, four road miles from the clearing, lived two families with a total of six children, and they became the first students of the school. These six, later increased to ten, attended classes from April to November, the months when they could walk barefoot, and during which the Everetts' clearing was not isolated by deep snow. Between November and April the brothers would visit the families of the trappers and farmers whom they hoped to make, and in many cases did make, their parishioners. John Everett, the younger brother, married a widow with two children, and he became the clerical half of the two, remaining with the widow on her farm. Robert Everett continued as the schoolmaster. Two of his first students stayed with him through trigonometry, Horace, and the *Anabasis* of Xenophon, and they became traditionally the first alumni of Spring Valley College.

The name Spring Valley was an accident, so far as the town was concerned. The Everetts had privately used the name Spring Valley to designate the bottom lands, which had no name. They called their first cabin Spring Valley School, and when two families of trappers asked and received permission to build on the clearing, the settlement became known as Spring Valley, a technical misnomer, since the valley was at least a mile below the Everetts' cabin. (Even in the middle of the Twentieth Century the downtown section of Spring Valley did not reach the true valley.)

For some thirty years Spring Valley was little more than a college town on a mountainside, but after the Civil War, with the construction of a railroad branch to accommodate the timber interests, the town grew. It became a trading center for the farms to the south and east, a paper mill and then another were built at the lower end of town, and inevitably there were several lumber and planing mills. The Commonwealth put up a sanatorium for tuberculosis patients in 1907. From 1907 to 1914 the population and economy of the town remained fairly static, except where the steady growth of the college affected the size of the student body and the students' spending was reflected in the commerce of the town. But among certain families—holders of shares in the Spring Valley Power & Light Company—the increasing use of electricity for domestic and commercial purposes was noticeable in the size and number of automobiles and other luxuries and in residential renovation or construction. Spring Valley was said in 1914 to have more Pierce-Arrows per capita than any other non-suburban town of its size in the United States. In some cases the profit from Power & Light Company stock was diminished by the loss in the value of stock in the Spring Valley Traction Company, operator of the trolley line, although the Power & Light Company continued to receive Traction Company payments. By 1914 the town was a community with a character and a history. The population was slightly more than 6,000, exclusive of 700 students and semi-transient faculty. It was a prosperous community; there was no abject poverty, there was work for everyone who needed it. The population was more than 70 percent white Protestant, of mixed New England Yankee and Pennsylvania German stock. The mountain air was dry and clean, in spite of the paper and lumber mills. Local option had been defeated several times, but always threatened, and the saloons were kept a legal distance from churches and college property. Professional prostitution was nonexistent. Petitions in bankruptcy did not average one a year. The lyceum program at the college was an adequate substitute for a theater, and the picture shows on Friday and Saturday evenings and Saturday matinée drew a steady but not highly profitable patronage, principally from the undergraduates and children of grammar and high school ages. The homicide rate was a fraction over one in five years; the suicide rate about one in two years. The typhoid fever epidemic of 1912 caused eleven deaths and was responsible for some agitation in favor of a town reservoir to be built above the college campus, but within the borough limits. The opposition to this expensive project prevailed when the Board of Health traced the epidemic to a recently arrived chambermaid at the Valley Hotel, and the town continued to get its water from the county reservoir at Big Bear Gap. The money thus saved, plus a slight increase in the millage rate, paid for the hard surface paving of Hill, Main, and Everett streets, and for a time Hill Street was nicknamed the Speedway, although in 1914 no automobile could go the entire length of Hill Street, from the Pennsylvania depot to the campus, without changing gears. Nevertheless the smooth hard surface of the Speedway tempted motorists to try out their cars, and they became a menace, which in turn led to strict policing of Hill Street, which resulted in heavy fines, which supported a larger police force than was customary in towns the size of Spring Valley. The larger police force earned the town a reputation for extreme conservatism which was not lost on every incoming freshman class. To the students Spring Valley was a puritan town, a dull town, a cold town, but they respected its character. Acts of collegiate vandalism were rare, and there never was a town-and-gown riot.

The character of the college had been determined from the beginning through its Presbyterian associations, its sometimes tenuous connection with Harvard, and the high incidence of comparative wealth among its alumni, dating back to the middle of the Nineteenth Century. Spring Valley College was always said to be rich and small, small and rich, and was often mentioned in the category that included Trinity, Hamilton, Haverford, Hobart, Kenyon, and Knox. It had chapters of Delta Kappa Epsilon, Alpha Delta Phi, Psi Upsilon, Beta Theta Pi, Zeta Psi, Delta Phi, Phi Gamma Delta, and two local fraternities. More than twenty percent of every freshman class after 1900 was composed of boys from preparatory schools; Mercersburg, Kiski, Shadyside, Bellefonte, Lawrenceville, Blair, Culver, Staunton, Hill, and Andover. Most of the boys had had no more than two years of boarding-school after two or three years at their local high schools, but they had acquired the prep school finish and they set the social tone of the college. The coeducational aspect of the college was an embarrassment to alumni and students who wished to preserve its all-male character, but the trustees voted to admit women students in 1902, in order to qualify for a gift of two hundred fifty thousand dollars from a Cleveland alumnus who wished to honor his deceased mother. The trustees demurred in the hope of raising an equal sum among alumni who opposed coeducation, but the donor put an end to the trustees' delay by threatening to give the money to Western Reserve. The trustees then discovered a weakness in the deed of gift: coeducation was a condition of the gift, but nothing had been said about residence or non-residence, and until 1920 no boarding women students were admitted to the college. Among the social elite of the undergraduate body it was considered bad form to take a coed to a football game or a college dance, and the Greek letter fraternities passed a Pan-Hellenic rule which barred women students from admittance to the fraternity houses. The coeds came to be known as blue-stockings, blues, suffragettes, jennies, hens, and bimboes. They were also referred to as Kappa Chis, for Kotex; Maggies, for Margaret Stonebraker, in whose memory the coeducational fund was given; and Amazons. Until 1920 the women were outnumbered ten to one. In that year women were admitted as boarding students, and the college, in the minds of many, began to lose distinction. (Even Hobart, with its William Smith College, had evaded the coeducational designation.) In 1923, '24 and '25 Spring Valley College fielded a six-goal polo team that played, and lost to, Pennsylvania Military College, Princeton, Norwich University and several cavalry troop teams in the National Guard, but that was the last stylish gesture of the college. More and more alumni were sending their sons to Harvard, Yale and Princeton and to the New England prep schools. The Spring Valley chapters of Delta Kappa Epsilon and Delta Phi were withdrawn in 1926, and the percentage of prep school boys in the autumn of 1927 had dropped to ten. In that year the Spring Valley-Mount St. Joseph's game was attended by, among others, sixty-five alumni and forty-four undergraduates in raccoon coats; eight alumni in Lincolns, sixteen alumni in Cadillacs, three in Pierce-Arrows and one alumnus in a Rolls-Royce, but a good proportion of those alumni had been members of D.K.E. and Delta Phi, and while they had been invited to the post-game parties at Psi U. and Alpha Delt, many of them were heard to remark that this would be their last football game at Spring Valley. "Jap Framingham can have it for his very own," said one alumnus, speaking of Jasper W. Framingham, the college's principal benefactor. "It isn't the college I went to. This is too much like that one in *Good News,* you know that show in New York?"

"Well, the old dump can't compete with Princeton anyway," said a friend. "The boys all want to go East and when they graduate go down to Wall Street. Who is there in Wall Street that cares if you were a Deke and a member of Key and Dagger? Nobody ever heard of Key and Dagger outside of Spring Valley, and God, how I sweated over making it when I was here! In our day it meant something. Now you get it automatically for being captain of a sport or Phi Beta Kappa, no matter what kind of a guy you are. Frankly if I were going to college this fall, I wouldn't pick Spring Valley."

"Neither would I. I remember Witherspoon arguing that high school boys and poor boys generally would work harder. But it hasn't turned out that way. Brice Ditson, married to Evangeline Framingham, you probably know him—he told me he heard on good authority that they're worried about how many flunk out the end of first semester. The work's too tough for them. The high schools don't prepare them

(89)

for college. When you and I were here we had to have Vergil to enter. And solid and trig. And didn't we have to have two years of French?"

"Or German. I had German."

"Well, they haven't got anything like that now, and Ditson tells me that what they're really worried about is lowering the requirements and then losing standing with the Middle Atlantic Whatever It's Called."

"Association of Colleges and Universities or something on that order. I don't think it'll ever get that bad."

"You don't? Do you want me to name off for you some of the colleges I know that have disappeared off the map? What they're worried about is, according to Ditson, rumors get around about the standing, then they can't get good teachers, and when they can't get good teachers, the rumors turn out to be facts. I just hate to see it happen here, and I have nothing against poor boys. This kid that played end today, Johnny Appleton—"

"Prof Appleton's son."

"Yes. He's a poor boy. Old Prof has no money, and the boy's not only a hell of a good end but an all-around athlete and a good student to boot. Nice kid, too. But I was thinking today, it's almost unfair that a boy like that has to go to Spring Valley."

"Probably doesn't cost him anything."

"I hope not. A good athlete and a good student, and his old man went to Harvard. He could have got some kind of a scholarship to Harvard."

"Maybe he gets everything free here, and a Harvard scholarship would still cost the old boy more than he could afford."

"Well, it's damn unfair. I'd have helped him if I'd known about it in time, so would you."

"Yes, I'd rather have helped him than some of those on the team that I *am* helping. Maybe he'll get a Rhodes scholarship."

"From Spring Valley? There's never been one, has there?"

"Yes, we've had one, but I admit it's unusual."

"Well, I've got my boy entered in Williams for next year and your two went to Yale. I guess that's the real story, isn't it? You try to give your children the best you can, and the old alma mater isn't it. But we had some good times, and we weren't morons when we got out. Both my partners are Yale men and I never have to take a back seat to them, not when it comes to the classics. And this old place is where I got it."

"*De mortuis nil nisi bonum.*"

"You're damn right. I'm going to shut up and have a shot."

"I have some gin."

"Thanks, I have a bottle of prescription rye. *De gustibus non est disputandum.*"

"Hail to thee our Alma Mater."

The defection of so many wealthy alumni, as revealed by their sons' entering the New England colleges, had the effect of concentrating authority in the group who remained loyal, and the trustees, a self-perpetuating body, welcomed Brice Ditson to membership on the board. He was rather young—in 1931, the year of his election, he was thirty-three years old—and he was a Princeton man and the son of a Princeton man, but he was the son-in-law of Jasper Framingham, who retired from the board in 1930. Nothing that Jap Framingham could have done would more unequivocally have told the town and the college that Brice Ditson had made the grade.

Framingham's consent to his daughter's marriage to Brice Ditson had been the formality of a father's publicly acceding to his own secret wish. Evangeline Framingham had always been well liked by boys, but not for her beauty. She had well-defined masculine features; her father's mouth and chin, cheekbones and nose, like a caricature by Hugo Gellert. This head was set on an opulently female body that had been neglected by the opposite sex until Evangeline married Brice Ditson. Because she had been half reconciled to permanent spinsterhood, Evangeline was inclined to be philosophical regarding the childlessness of her marriage, especially since at least one doctor, Harry Jeffries, told her that Brice might be the sterile one. In truth neither Evangeline nor Brice was anxious for parenthood; Brice, in fact, did not like children at all and would shy away from them and their bubbling noses and damp diapers and fearful screams. He did not even like his brother, Porter Ditson, who was seven years younger, and apparently planned to go through life as a player of games, a drinker of whiskey, and a shirker of work.

No one in Spring Valley ever addressed Porter Ditson as anything but Porter. The members of the police force, the taxi drivers, the bartender at the Elks clubhouse, the hotel staff, garage mechanics, reporters on the Spring Valley *Leader*, the clerks in the stores, including those in the Ditson hardware store, all were on a first-name basis with him, and he with them. Among them were those who snickered at him, whose envy of the Ditson family was expressed in a contemptuous familiarity toward this one member of it. The score was evened by their nervous politeness to Brice Ditson, and for the most part the townsfolk addressed Porter with a casual affection. He did not go over their line, they seldom tried to go over his. On his way back to the hotel after a dinner party he would often stop in at the Elks clubhouse or Joe Weber's—the only speakeasy; students not admitted—for a nightcap. He would be wearing a dinner jacket, his special-body Chrysler would be parked where it could be seen and recognized by all. He would get his drink at the bar and take it to the pinochle game or, if there were no cardplayers, he would seat himself at a table and join in the conversation. He scrupulously observed the rule not to treat a beer drinker when he himself was drinking whiskey; beer was fifteen cents a glass and whiskey was fifty, and to return the compliment a beer drinker might have to curtail his own drinking. Sport, politics, machinery, building and highway construction, weather, accidents, sexual deviations, the Deity, and transportation were the conversational topics late at night at the Elks and at Joe Weber's. When the group was small the bartender or proprietor or steward would announce: "Who wants a little lunch?" The repast usually consisted of ham sandwiches, cheese sandwiches, and ham-and-cheese sandwiches, and when they had been eaten it was time to go home. Occasionally someone would say: "Who wants to get laid?" Four or five men would get in a car and drive to a roadhouse fifteen miles away, drinking from bottles on the way, talking or sleeping on the return trip. Sometimes Porter Ditson would go with them, sometimes not. But even when he did, even when they shared this intimate experience with him, the line over which neither he nor they would cross was there. One of his friends was Lamarr Holliday, partner and salesman of the Schumacher-Chevrolet agency, a widower in his middle thirties and a man who spoke in a perpetual growl. "Porter, I been noticing something," he said one night when they were temporarily alone.

"What's that, Lamarr?" said Porter Ditson.

"When we go for a hump, over to Chick Medina's?"

"Mm-hmm?"

"If Lew Jarrell goes along, you don't go."

"That's true."

"Why is that, Porter?"

"Are you asking me as a friend of Lew's or a friend of mine?"

"Well, I'm a friend of the both of you, but this is in cawnfidence. You never had any falling-out with Lew, not that I know of."

"Has Lew noticed it?"

"Hell, no."

"Well, since you've noticed it, you're right. I don't like to go to Chick's when Lew's along. As to why I don't like to, why are you asking me? How did *you* happen to notice it if Lew *didn't?*"

"Because I been thinking, *I* don't like to go when he's along. But I don't know why."

(93)

"Lew talks too much about it afterwards."

"You mean he spreads it around? Lew's a married man, he doesn't want that spread around."

"No, I didn't mean that. I meant on the way home. I really don't want to know what happened to Lew, but he insists on telling me. Then he waits for *me* to tell *him,* and I don't want to. So I don't."

"Yeah, I see what you mean. You know, Lew likes to be considered a friend of yours. He always asks where you are and all. You'd think he knew you better than any of the rest of us."

"Well, he doesn't."

"You don't mind if I get personal, Porter. But you're a funny guy. You go around with the Hill people, but I often think you have a better time with us."

"I do."

"Not that I ever saw you with the Hill crowd, but just a feeling I got. You know, I don't like that about Lew, either. It goes against the grain, with me. Every once in a while I feel like telling him to for Christ's sake shut up about it. We all got laid, he's not the only one. Yeah, and half the time I'm driving the car, the only one awake, and I get the brunt of it."

"I can imagine."

"Privacy. A man's entitled to his privacy."

"Right. And you can have it if you want it enough. Just don't let other people run your life for you. When they start that, just give them the air."

"Am I right, Porter? Is that what you did with the Hill crowd?"

"In a manner of speaking. To a certain extent. Independence is a very important thing."

"Yeah, as long as you don't get too much of it."

"Like everything else."

"You keep your independence by bumming around with us when you want to get away from the Hill crowd. And vicey versa. You're lucky. I don't have no other crowd."

"No other crowd, maybe. But you have yourself."

"Jesus Christ, Porter! I'm terrible company, for myself."

"Well, then maybe you don't crave independence as much as I do."

"Don't you ever get lonesome? I guess not."

Porter Ditson smiled. "Why do you think I need *two* crowds?"

"A funny guy, Porter. I'll be a son of a bitch if you're not."

IV

Elizabeth Appleton was not severely handicapped by her aristocratic appearance, her gentility of manner, or the fact that she was believed to have inherited money from her father. Her sweaters and skirts were of the finest quality, and she allowed herself the adornment of a cultured pearl necklace; but the faculty wives and the town hostesses saw the same costumes over and over again. Elizabeth's entire wardrobe was as familiar to the women she saw as the contents of their own closets. Her speech was that of her class, who were the products of certain schools and childhood associations. She dropped her r's, she pronounced *third* as *thidd*. (When Roosevelt spoke on the radio women in Spring Valley often remarked that he talked the same way as Elizabeth Appleton.) But faculty wives were keenly aware that while Elizabeth Appleton had a cultured accent, she made frequent grammatical errors. The belief that she had inherited money became in time a doubt that she had inherited as much as the original rumors had proclaimed. She had no live-in servant, she did her own cooking, and the two Appleton cars did not add up to one of the more expensive Buicks. She and John did not belong to the country club; they played tennis on the college courts. They took every advantage of the college Co-op. The original million-dollar estimate of Elizabeth's inheritance was revised downward to one hundred thousand dollars, and the Brice Ditsons, virtually the only Spring Valley citizens in a position to know the truth, had no comment to make, since they themselves preferred to live well within their joint income. The Appletons' contributions to Spring Valley charities, which might have been revealing, did not exceed a hundred dollars a year, and on the two occasions of faculty wives' attempting to borrow money from Elizabeth, one was a total failure and the other woman got the money she asked for—three hundred dollars to help pay a hospital bill—only after two days' deliberation by Elizabeth and the signing of a note by the woman's husband. Casual borrowing was thus permanently discouraged and while there were some women who said that Elizabeth Appleton was stingy, there were none who could say that she was careless or extravagant. Her money, such as it was, was not on display and therefore did not become a cause of envy. Shorty Conners, who had been John Appleton's best man, was the only permanent resident of Spring Valley, aside from Ethel Appleton, who had seen the Jarvis Webster establishment in Southampton; but Shorty's visit to Long Island had been brief, his impact insignificant, and the experience unsatisfactory. He did not want to talk about it, and indeed his college friendship with John Appleton did not continue through John's marriage, partly because John and Elizabeth had gone to live in Cambridge while John was getting his master's degree, but also because the two men seldom saw each other. Shorty was Town, John was Gown. Ethel Appleton's description of the Jarvis Webster cottage in Southampton was that it was a beautiful place, and she provided a detailed report of the rose bushes and the hedges, but in reply to questions Ethel Appleton said that the Websters' place was nowhere near as big as Jap Framingham's, or Charley Mossler's for that matter.

Elizabeth Appleton's campaign to vacate her place in fashionable society and achieve the appearance of simplicity was assisted by the notion, prevalent in the early Thirties, that after October 1929, all the rich were suddenly poor. In Spring Valley there was evidence to the contrary: J. W. Framingham was not poor, the Brice Ditsons were not poor. But they were Spring Valley people, not New Yorkers whose fortunes were made entirely in the stock market. Ethel Appleton's reference to the Jarvis Websters' "cottage" was a confirmation of this notion: perhaps Elizabeth Appleton's family had once owned a great mansion; but after 1929 they lived in a cottage that derived its beauty from the rose bushes and hedges rather than from splendor and elegance. In any event, Elizabeth had come from a place that a truthful Spring Valley resident had described as a cottage, that Elizabeth herself called a cottage. And whatever riches Elizabeth may have possessed in the past, her scale of living in Spring Valley did not indicate that she possessed them now. Actually no one knew the terms of her father's will, or had knowledge of Amelia Webster's gifts, and Elizabeth was in fact not an heiress until 1940, when her mother died. But by that time Spring Valley and the nation had the threat of war and a national election and shortages of matériel to talk about. By that time, too, Elizabeth Appleton had established herself as the hard-working, devoted wife of John Appleton; a handsome woman of thirty who was quite content to live in the shadow of her husband. The image was a fair one, especially since it was what she had been striving to achieve.

In 1940, at the age of thirty-two, John Appleton was made a full professor, the youngest in the history of Spring Valley College. The *Echo*, the college weekly, in its annual polls had already shown that for two successive years Appleton's History III had been voted the most popular course in the college curriculum. Along the way he had become a supporter of the New Deal, and in the autumn of 1940 History III was considerably enlivened by John Appleton's jocose comments on the speeches of Wendell Willkie and Senator Charles L. McNary. John Appleton spoke from notes, uninhibited by professorial style and interlarding his lectures with sardonic references to Commonwealth & Southern, Samuel Insull, Harrison Williams and, on one occasion, J. W. Framingham.

On the day after he made his reference to J. W. Framingham he was notified that his presence was requested in the office of President-Emeritus Witherspoon, "whenever you have a free moment," Witherspoon had said.

The old man sat back in his chair, with his hands clasped behind his neck and his reading glasses pushed back on top of his white hair. "Well, John, word reaches me that you're backing the winner," said Dr. Witherspoon. "I suppose I make myself clear enough, don't I?"

"Yesterday's lecture?"

The old man nodded. "Any repercussions?"

"Not serious ones, but I'm expecting some, naturally. I thought I'd be hearing from your successor."

"No, you're hearing from me instead. Prexy McAndrews thinks I can handle you better."

"Does he want to fire me?"

"Nobody wants to fire you, John. At least, nobody on the faculty. You're not going to be fired, not even by Brice Ditson. Put your mind at ease on that score. But I claim the various privileges of old friendship and advanced age, so I asked you to come here as much for my own enlightenment as anything else. Now I know you speak from notes and of course there's no stenographic record of your lecture. But *did* you call Jap Framingham a robber baron?"

"No sir."

"Well, then, did you mention him in a context that would leave that inference?"

"I know I never used the term robber baron."

"I'm glad to hear it. I knew Jap Framingham very well.

I didn't know all the convolutions and involutions of his transactions. But I knew the man. I wouldn't like to see manure thrown on his grave."

"I didn't throw any manure."

"I'm glad to hear that, too. Some of it might blow back on you, you know, and I wouldn't want to see that, either. You didn't know Jap Framingham. Not many people did. Your mother knew him, so did your father, although your father oddly enough was so engrossed in his own work that he hardly had any time for anybody but students and faculty. And Jap Framingham was much the same way about *his* interests. You might think that being one of the biggest benefactors of this college he'd have known your father better, but he didn't. He knew your mother because she was born and brought up in Spring Valley, and the town was one of his interests. If your mother were alive she could set you straight about Mr. Framingham. She would have told you, as I tell you, that it would have been impossible for Jap Framingham to take a dirty dollar. And yet I'm afraid that that's the inference a lot of your students drew from your lecture. That he was a crook."

John Appleton knew he was expected to make a denial. "I'm sure he was within the law."

"That isn't enough for me, John. When I was president of Spring Valley I had to break bread with a few men that I knew were barely within the law. But I never gave them my friendship. I never had them to my house for breakfast, as I did Jap Framingham many times. Sunday breakfast after church was when I'd have my friends to my house."

"Prexy, I notice you haven't given me any facts."

"No, I haven't. Not the kind of facts you may want. Nor do I intend to. But I am giving you something that I think is as valuable. And that is an opinion of a man's character, based on lifelong association. It wasn't only that Jap Framingham was legally within his rights. The tendency nowadays, especially among historians, is to be iconoclastic. Well, that word only means idol-smashing, so I'll choose another. Let's just say skeptical. Incredulous. But what I've noticed, John, is that whether you call it iconoclasm, or skepticism, or incredulity, it's all on the side of evil that the historians make their inquiries. I don't want you to reconsider Benedict Arnold and make him a saint. As far as I know, the judgment of history in his case was fair enough. But do we have to brush aside all the good things we know about George Washington and lick our chops because someone discovers that he had a mistress? The trouble there, John, is that iconoclasm unfortunately doesn't carry instructions on how to put the pieces back together again. You dirty a man like Washington, or Jefferson or Franklin, or in my time, Woodrow Wilson, and it's almost impossible to scrub him clean again."

"He shouldn't *be* scrubbed clean."

"Perhaps not. But the power of evil, the bad things, are so much stronger than the good. Dirt is dirtier than purity is clean, if you see what I mean. And I'll tell you something else, John. I knew Woodrow Wilson slightly. I visited Princeton several times while he was there. But I also had friends that knew him well. Do you know that those friends of mine don't even agree on the facts about Wilson? Those that were against him say certain things about him that his admirers say were just not true. A man can so infuriate people with his principles that they cheerfully lie about him. Of course a man can also dazzle people with his principles."

"Yes, I was about to say."

"Oh, were you? About whom?"

"Well, very respectfully, about your opinion of Mr. Framingham."

The old man laughed. "I don't think anybody was ever *dazzled* by Jap. I thought you might be talking about someone else."

"Who, may I ask?"

"Franklin D. Roosevelt."

"Are you against him? You voted for him twice."

"I'm going to vote for him again. And if we get in the

war I'd have no hesitancy in voting for him yet again. He's Uncle Sam, John. Till after this thing is over. He's great. Real greatness. But I don't trust him."

"Pardon me, Prexy, but how can you say that?"

"That he's great and that I don't trust him? Well, he's a liar. You know that. He's a brilliant opportunist. Dazzling, you might say. And as for his record, he's been very fortunate in his enemies. His opposition in his own country, during the depression, came from a lot of befuddled rich men. And his enemies abroad are two cheap mountebanks that an aristocrat like Roosevelt isn't a bit afraid of."

"Prexy?"

"Yes, John?"

"Iconoclasm is only for dead idols, then, eh?"

"Clever, but not clever enough, my boy. The living aren't really idols, are they? And while they're alive they can defend themselves. I said nothing, I hope, that would imply that I would silence criticism. I haven't even asked you to correct the impression you gave of my friend Jap Framingham. But I've probably read nearly everything you've read, John, and I'm more than twice your age. So I thought I'd take the opportunity to have another of those talks with you that I used to enjoy so much. However, you're a full professor now, and as we get older our arteries harden, so why not our minds? Don't let me keep you any longer. You must be very busy." The old man lowered his glasses and picked up the newspaper that lay on his desk.

"Goodbye, Prexy," said John Appleton.

"Goodbye, Professor," said the old man.

The interview had been upsetting to John Appleton, who had tried to anticipate the words the old man would use and had not even correctly anticipated his thoughts. He had gone prepared to defend his attack on J. W. Framingham, and Witherspoon had only offered a rather generalized defense of Framingham's character.

"I had a summons from old Prexy Witherspoon," he said when he got home.

"About the Framingham lecture?" said Elizabeth Appleton.

"Is that what they're calling it? The Framingham lecture?"

"Not yet, but they will," said Elizabeth Appleton. "What did Dr. Witherspoon have to say?"

He told her, and ended by saying: "I left his office feeling like a chastised sophomore."

"That's the way he intended you to feel. His sarcasm in calling you Professor. But he doesn't matter—"

"He does to me."

"I haven't finished. He doesn't matter as much as Evangeline Ditson. You didn't call her father any of those things, and you owe it to yourself, not to her, but to yourself, to say you didn't."

"What do you think I ought to do? Write her a note?"

"Go see her this evening, and make sure Brice is there."

He did not telephone in advance. He saw Brice Ditson's car in front of the Ditson house, parked his car, and rang the doorbell. Evangeline Ditson was shocked to see him, as Elizabeth had predicted. "Well—John—well, come in."

Evangeline and Brice Ditson were formal in their manner and instinctively took chairs together so that they faced him two to one. "You know why I'm here, I'm sure."

"Your lecture, I suppose," said Brice Ditson.

"Naturally. I brought my notes with me, and I can give you the reference to Mr. Framingham pretty nearly verbatim."

"No need to do that," said Brice Ditson. "The fact that you came here is practically a denial of the rumors we've been hearing all day."

"Our telephone's been very busy, I can tell you," said Evangeline Ditson.

"We would like to be told, by you, that you didn't cast aspersions on Mr. Framingham's integrity. His honesty," said Brice Ditson.

"Unfortunately I seem to have given the impression

that I did. Lumping him with Insull, and holding companies and power grabs. I probably shouldn't have done that, not the way I did."

"Probably? Why do you say probably? What are you here for if 'probably' is as far as you'll go?" said Evangeline Ditson. "If there is any doubt in your mind, I don't see the point of this visit."

"The point of this visit is to reassure you that I didn't impugn your father's honesty."

"Oh, fiddlesticks, John. If you called my father a crook, I want you to get out of this house and never show your face here again. If you have any doubts on that score, if you think he was *slightly* crooked, I don't want you in my house. Everybody knows you're a New Dealer. We've known it all along and we've had you in our house and gone to yours. But this is a different matter entirely. This is slandering my father—if you did it. The question is, did you, or didn't you?"

"No, I didn't."

"Well, then, correct the impression and the harm will be rectified. We don't care if you want to make your course a lot of New Deal propaganda."

"If that's the way you're rewriting American history, go to it," said Brice Ditson.

"Yes," said Evangeline Ditson. "Go to it, and welcome. Colleges like Spring Valley wouldn't exist if it weren't for capitalists like my father."

"Who were always very carefully watched by the Attorney-General," said Brice Ditson.

"Not always," said John Appleton.

"Well, with very few exceptions, and if the Attorney-General wasn't watching them, people like Senator Walsh and Norris were. La Follette and the rest of the Progressives, and Democrats and semi-Socialists. In any case, let's confine this discussion to Mr. Framingham and what you said about him. You've denied you called him a crook. Good. We have your explanation. All you have to do now is rectify the wrong impression you gave."

"*Have* to do?"

"Oh, not have-to-do in the sense that we are compelling you to. But this New Deal that you're so pleased with, I thought it was supposed to be founded on high principles. Ethics. Honesty. If that's the case you ought to be eagerly awaiting the chance to correct a rank injustice. It shouldn't only be a question of our friendship. In fact, we'd have appreciated it much more if you had made the correction first and *then* come to us."

John Appleton rose. "I'll make the correction. I'll prepare something and read it to my class, and send you a copy."

"Better yet, why don't you have it printed in the *Echo?*" said Brice Ditson.

"Is that what you want me to do?"

"Isn't that what you'd like to do, in view of how widespread the attack on Mr. Framingham's character is? The effect wasn't confined to your class," said Brice Ditson.

"I'll have to think about that," said John Appleton.

"All right, think about it," said Brice Ditson.

"Why are you so darn reluctant to admit you were wrong?" said Evangeline. "As Brice said, you ought to be eager to undo the damage. But instead of that you're going to *think* about it. I honestly don't understand why you came here. I'm not going to accept any half-hearted apology or explanation. *My father was not a crook,* and you damn well better not say he was. My patience is exhausted." She got up and left the room.

"She's very upset and has been all day," said Brice Ditson. "As a matter of fact, we heard about it last night, and I had to restrain her from going out to your house and telling you off. But that doesn't say I'm not with her one hundred percent. Why do you make these reckless accusations? You don't know a damn thing about business, and I'll tell you one thing you overlook. J. W. Framingham didn't *have* to be dishonest. He built up Spring Valley Light & Power from nothing, a few thousand dollars a long time ago. The company always made money, after the first few years, because electricity caught on *and* the company was well managed. If you'd invested a hundred dollars in the original company do you know what your stock would have been worth, if you'd taken advantage of stock dividends, et cetera? About five thousand dollars. When Ohio-Pennsylvania took over Spring Valley your original hundred dollars amounted to five thousand. More, actually, but that's putting it in the simplest possible terms. I just want you to know that Mr. Framingham didn't have to be dishonest, even if it had been in him to be. And have you any idea how much Mr. Framingham gave to Spring Valley College? Not only what he actually gave the college, but increases in the value of the stock he gave? And now I think of it, he didn't vote that stock. It was given to the college free and clear, without any strings. A crook wouldn't have done that, my young friend."

"All right, Brice. Tell Evangeline I'm sorry she was upset. Goodnight."

John Appleton went home, but not to bed. There was a message from Porter Ditson, asking Professor Appleton to telephone him at the hotel. "It's after nine," said John Appleton. "Do I have to call him tonight?"

"Get it over with," said Elizabeth.

"Did you speak to him?"

"Yes. He was very nice," she said.

"I thought you didn't like him."

"I don't approve of him. I never said I didn't like him. And heaven knows it was a relief to talk to somebody that wasn't either indignant or sort of gloating. You've no idea how much I've been on the phone today."

John Appleton was connected with Porter Ditson, who opened the conversation by saying: "This is Porter Ditson. I hear you've been putting the blast on old Mr. Framingham."

"That's the general impression. Why?"

"Well, it amused me, the old fart. I just thought I'd tell you so."

"Oh, thanks. I was hoping you might be able to tell me that he swindled widows and orphans."

"Afraid not. He may have, but I doubt it. No, I just thought he was an old horse's ass. Maybe if he'd been more of a scoundrel I'd be on his side. But he was holier than the Pope, and had just about as much fun. You know about the rule he put in at the country club? No booze after midnight Saturday. And I hope Elizabeth isn't listening, but thanks to him you have to drive thirty miles to get a piece of tail. And those dinners at his house. I don't think you ever went to one of them. You were spared that . . . Well, I heard about your little blast and I thought I'd have a chat with you. Nothing important. Unless you feel like having a drink. That's an idea. Why don't you come on down?"

"Well, thanks, Porter. I feel like having a drink, but I know what'll happen if I go to the hotel bar. I'll be pestered. Why don't you come out here?"

"Fine. You're sure Elizabeth won't mind?"

"I'm sure she won't."

"Have you got Scotch? That's all I drink, except Martinis, and I had an early dinner."

"We have Scotch. Come on out." John Appleton hung up. "He just wanted to chat. Be here shortly."

Porter Ditson arrived, hatless, wearing a very old polo coat, a double-breasted grey flannel suit, striped necktie on a blue shirt, and cracked patent leather pumps. "I brought this in case," he said, handing John Appleton a bottle of Scotch. "Also, I practically invited myself. How are you, Elizabeth? The old boy's been dumping the apple cart, eh?"

"Hello, Porter. Yes, a little excitement. How are you? We never see you."

"You don't get around to the right places, I guess. I *never* see you at the Elks, Elizabeth."

"No, I've never—"

"He's pulling your leg," said John Appleton.

"Can think of worse pastimes," said Porter Ditson. "I'm

not going to be any trouble, Elizabeth. Just as long as you
have some ice and plain water, and a chair to sit in. What
time do you want me to go home? You know this is only
about the third or fourth time I've ever been inside this
house."

"You've been invited oftener than that," said Elizabeth.

"Not much oftener. You have what, now? Two children?"

"Two. Boy and a girl. One of each," said Elizabeth.

John Appleton made the drinks, bourbon highballs
for himself and Elizabeth, Scotch and water for Porter
Ditson, and when they were seated and taking their first sips,
Porter Ditson said: "Maybe you'd rather not talk about it,
but I thought it was high time somebody went to work on
Mr. Framingham. You may have gone overboard—"

"How?" said John Appleton.

"Calling him—what was it?—a profiteer, you called
him?"

John turned to Elizabeth. "That's a new one," he said,
and then turned to Porter Ditson. "Porter, I had a pretty
gruelling session with your brother and Evangeline tonight.
I've decided to write a little statement for the *Echo*—"

"The college paper?"

"The college paper. It may not satisfy everybody. I'm
sure it won't, but it's all I'm ever going to say about my lecture."

"Oh, this is news to me, too," said Elizabeth Appleton.
"John hasn't had a chance to tell me about his meeting with
Brice and Evangeline."

"That couldn't have been much fun. Evangeline is hop-
ping mad and my brother is a study in cautious indignation.
Of course that doesn't come too hard. He's always a study
in cautious indignation. He's afraid people will think the
Ditsons haven't as much money as the Framinghams. And
he's right, they do think it. And *they're* right, we haven't. In
another couple of years the *Mosslers* will have more money
than the Ditsons. But Bertha Mossler hasn't got ten million,
and Evangeline has, so the Mosslers are never going to

snoot the Brice Ditsons, you may be sure of that. Unless, of course, Harry Jeffries gets rid of Frances and marries a rich widow from Pittsburgh."

"Is he going to?" said Elizabeth Appleton.

"Not that I know of. Harry is stuck with Frances. But if he did get rid of Frances, and found a rich widow, really rich, then the Mosslers and the Jeffries would be the new royal family."

"I can never think of Harry Jeffries and Bertha Mossler as brother and sister," said Elizabeth Appleton. "As long as I've lived here, I still think of Frances Jeffries and Bertha Mossler as sisters."

"Well, I see your point. They're both a couple of clods. They have that heavy, Cadillac look about them."

Elizabeth laughed. "I'm afraid that's exactly what I wanted to say, but I never would have thought of it. But do you think Harry has that same look?"

"Almost. But not quite. If he were a little more complacent he'd have it. But doctors never get enough sleep, I'm told, and that gives them all a drawn look. That, and I suppose worrying about their patients. And in Harry's case, worrying about that hunk of frustrated woman he's married to. I guess Harry has plenty on his mind. He got out of that last jam safely."

"I didn't know he was in one."

"The woman interne. You know. Richards? Williams? I always get those names mixed up. It was almost a repetition of Harry and Frances. You know, Frances used to be a trained nurse. Only this time instead of a nurse, Harry was bettering himself. A female doctor. I'm on the hospital board, only because Brice didn't want it. Well, in one of our informal meetings, which is where the work really gets done, we took up the matter of Harry Jeffries and Dr. Richards. I think her name *was* Richards. It wasn't a public scandal, but Charley Mossler had all the dope. He's very active on the board. He said the woman was throwing herself at Harry, which I guess was the way he heard it expressed by Bertha. So Dr. Richards was quietly told that she had better look around for another hospital. No problem. Shortage of doctors everywhere. No black mark on her record. Work satisfactory. Just decided she would like to do her next year in Southern California. It must be very convenient to have a brother-in-law on the board, but I don't know how many times Charley Mossler's going to be able to get Harry off the hook. I guess Harry is the leading surgeon in this part of the country. I don't know who's better. But doctors aren't the most un-jealous people in the world, you know, and there must be some of them quietly gunning for Harry. Personally, I don't mind Harry. I go to Frank Hopkins whenever I have anything the matter with me. I grew up with Frank and old Dr. Hopkins was our family physician and so far I haven't needed any surgery. If I ever do, and there's time enough, I'll have it done in New York. Friend there's a surgeon at Presbyterian, and if my ailment isn't his specialty, I'll at least be able to rely on his suggestion as to who *should* operate."

"Harry was my doctor for both children," said Elizabeth.

"A good obstetrician. That's what everybody says. I'm glad he turned out that way. But when he first started private practice as a g.p., when he had that little office on Oak Street, I dropped in one afternoon to ask him if he'd let me have a couple of prescriptions for liquor. I knew all the doctors in town, and they all gave me prescriptions in those days. Paid for them of course, and it didn't make any difference whether I was their patient or not. They just did it to be nice. So I asked Harry if he could let me have two prescriptions. They were for a pint apiece. Four Roses, I think was the liquor. Sure. He'd be glad to. Very pleasant. And I asked him how much I owed him. The usual charge was three dollars a 'script. He said I owed him nothing. Well, I insisted, and he insisted back. Then it flashed over me. Harry was up for the country club, and Brice was chairman of the admissions committee. 'Oh, this son of a bitch is trying to bribe me with two pints of liquor,' I said to myself. You don't belong to the club, so you don't know how much opposition there was. Not to Harry, but to Frances. And I knew it was on his mind, because he asked me how my golf game was, which was a stupid question because in those days I didn't play golf. I was only about twenty-four or -five. Tennis was my game. In fact, I thought I was pretty hot. Well, anyhow, I said I wouldn't accept the 'scripts unless he let me pay for them, so realizing it was an awkward situation, he took the money. But I never went back again. They got in the club, but only after a good long wait."

"Look," said Elizabeth Appleton.

Porter Ditson looked, and saw that John Appleton, who was sitting at his right, had fallen asleep. Porter reached over and gently took the nearly empty highball glass out of John's hand.

"Shall we let him sleep?" said Porter Ditson.

"Yes. Go on talking or he may wake up."

Porter Ditson smiled. "I may put *you* to sleep."

"No. It's just that he's really had a hard day."

"But so must you. Why don't I just go quietly and leave you two alone?"

"No, please stay. I'm having a lovely time."

John Appleton opened his eyes and took a deep breath. "Oh, I was asleep, wasn't I? Porter, I'm sorry."

"Perfectly all right, John. I was having such a good time with my monologue, I never noticed that half my audience was in slumberland. At least you didn't snore. And I was just leaving."

"No you weren't, but dear, Porter will forgive you if you toddle off."

"I even forgive you for falling asleep."

"Well, if you don't mind, I think I will climb the golden stairs. I know I'm not going to be any addition to the party. Goodnight, Porter."

"Goodnight, John. Get a good rest."

"Thanks, I'm pretty sure I will. Goodnight, Elizabeth, in case I'm asleep."

"I'll be quiet," said Elizabeth Appleton, as her husband kissed her cheek.

"Could I have just a half and then go?" said Porter.

"I don't want you to go. I'm having fun. I'm finding out more about Spring Valley than I ever knew. It's an odd town. There's the Hill, and the campus people, and the downtown. Our next-door neighbors are Hill people, but we're campus people. Really nothing in common except when one of our children breaks one of their windows, or their dog has her puppies in our garage, which happened last week. Things like that. Are we entitled to pick of the litter?"

"You've made a very good life for yourself, Elizabeth. And I'll bet it wasn't easy."

"No, not always. But I wouldn't change places with the girls I grew up with. Why do *you* stay here?"

"Money," said Porter Ditson. "I don't pay any rent at the hotel, for obvious reasons, and I get fifty percent off on my restaurant bills. I keep my car in the hotel garage, no charge. And fifty percent off there for gas, oil, and repairs. As you must know, Brice owns the hotel. So that takes care of what you might call necessities. Food and shelter. My income is enough to cover my clothes, club bills, and an occasional binge in New York. So forth."

"But you could do all that in New York if you had a job."

"I *had* a job, Elizabeth, and I *lived* in New York. But I have no ability, no special talent. And the worst thing of all, I have no ambition. If I'd stayed in New York, what would have happened? Back and forth to Wall Street. Marry a nice girl. Back and forth to Wall Street. Two or three nice children. Back and forth to Wall Street. Heart attack. Back and forth to Wall street, a little more slowly. 'Take it easy, boy. Just don't rush things and there's no reason why you shouldn't last another five or ten years.' *Jesus!* For what? The nice girl and the nice kids? Is that all I get out of the sixty or sixty-five years I have on earth? What can you see from a subway train? You don't want to look at the people. At least I don't. I did . . . My brother and my sister-in-law, and some of my friends, they're all

(112)

convinced that I have no ambition, and if you don't mind my saying so, they seem to imply that that's the same as being born a eunuch. Well, I know I'm not a eunuch, and I do have ambition, but it isn't *their kind* of ambition. Even when I was in love, twice, the lucky girls thought I was kidding when I said I didn't want to spend my life going back and forth to Wall Street. Their fathers did, their brothers did. The boys they knew did, if they weren't doctors or ministers, or in advertising, perish the thought. The girls thought I was an odd bird, too."

"Although not a eunuch."

"Why, Elizabeth," he smiled. "No. At least one of them knew better, so having made that statement I'll never tell you who the girls were. I'm sure you know them. It became a question of changing my whole life to accommodate some nice girl, how long would that have lasted? What kind of a husband would I have made, discontented and blaming it all on her?"

"Well, what *is* your ambition?"

"To live to be seventy-five."

"Oh, come now, Porter. That isn't really your ambition."

"Yes it is, Elizabeth. You got out of that rat-race, so you ought to be more understanding."

"I understand completely, but I don't believe that that's your ambition."

"Well, it is, though. The strongest thing we have in us is the will to live. Self-preservation. Right?"

"Yes, I guess so."

"Therefore, wanting to live to be seventy-five is a perfectly natural ambition. Natural, and logical. It is *not* logical or natural to live in a way that you know is going to shorten your life. So I don't. Fortunately I have just enough money to take care of my fairly modest needs. I have to save up to pay for my occasional binges in New York, and I do. But my binges aren't just going to New York and getting plastered for a week. I could do that here, but I don't. I drink every day of my life, but I almost never get drunk.

Actually I take very good care of myself. I get some exercise every day. Golf. Tennis. Skating. Shooting pool at the Elks club, or just walking. I go to church on Sunday, and I read anywhere from fifty to a hundred books a year. The Pittsburgh and New York papers. *Time* and *The New Yorker* and *The Saturday Evening Post.* And I suppose I know more people in Spring Valley than anyone else in the town. Do you realize that? Do you know anybody else that belongs to the Elks? I'll bet you don't. Mind you, I don't get invited to be a pallbearer when a brother Elk dies, but I go to his house to pay my last respects. I did that last week, and on the same day I got a free lunch at the hospital board meeting. Very little goes on here that I don't hear about, and I hope to continue for forty more years. I had to register for the draft, and they still might take me, although I'll be thirty-six any minute now. But unless we get into the war, I'm not going to enlist or anything like that. Self-preservation."

"What about self-preservation if there *is* a war?"

"Thought it all out. It might seem logical to be a conscientious objector, is that what you mean?"

"Yes."

"Well, it wouldn't be. In the first place, my own self-preservation is affected by what happens to the country. If we're at war, I'm at war, and I owe it to myself to help fight the enemy. Our enemy, my enemy. Then there's another personal reason. If we were at war and I wasn't in it in some capacity or other, that would bother the hell out of me."

"Why?"

"That's something I've never tried to explain to anyone else. To put into words. But here goes," he said, and took a swig of his drink before going on. "Independence has a great deal to do with the way I want to live my life. I guess that must be pretty obvious if Brother Brice is continually harping on it. Too damn independent, he says. But it isn't independence by itself. My particular independence is really an outgrowth of this self-preservation thing. People don't know about the self-preservation thing except you, now that I've told you. People only see the independence, going it alone, my own way. They think the independent way of living is a thing in itself, but it isn't. But following my instinct for self-preservation to the extent that I do, that looks like independence. Do you follow me?"

"Yes, I guess I do. Yes, I do, so far," said Elizabeth Appleton.

"Well, then, if we were at war, and I stayed out of it, that would worry the hell out of me. Not because I wasn't going along with the common herd. No. But because by not being in it, I would be dependent on those who *were* fighting the war. That would mean sacrificing my independence, which in turn would be very damaging to my policy of self-preservation. It could mean, of course, that by getting in the war I would give up my ambition to live to be seventy-five, but here the circumstances are beyond my control. The war would be like—well, as if I were waiting for a train at the Pennsy depot and just as it pulled in, it jumped the track and put an end to me. Did you ever read a book called *The Bridge of San Luis Rey,* by Thornton Wilder?"

"I think we read it in school."

"The bridge collapses. Why did those particular people happen to be on the bridge? Well, why would I happen to be at the station when the train jumps the track? You see? A lot of things I can't control, and I know that. But it doesn't keep me from having that ambition, to live seventy-five years."

"This is almost as if I'd never really met you before, Porter."

He nodded. "Independence? Why do I see so many people if I'm so independent? The answer of course is that I'm not really independent at all. The way I live just makes it look that way. But I like the way I live. I'm never bored. The little things I do, my private little schedule of unimportant things, they keep me busy and amused. You know one of the worst things I noticed in my brief time in Wall Street?"

"What?"

"Seeing a guy in a big office, sitting at his desk, and staring out the window. Daydreaming. A thousand miles or a hundred years away from what he was supposed to be doing. Then snapping out of it when the phone rings and Miss Hammacher says Mr. Schlemmer of Cities Service is on the phone. The worst part of it all was that the guy probably didn't really dream about anything. He was dreaming about nothing. And that's what his ambitions amounted to. Sure I could have stayed on, and made a little money, and all the rest of it. But I never would have made as much money as Jap Framingham, and anything less is too little. If you can't be Jock Whitney, at least you don't have to be Charley Mossler. Did you ever know a fellow named Lex Porter?"

"Met him. Is he any relation of yours?"

"Very distant. I know it, but he doesn't. Well, he's a bum, too. But a very different kind of bum. He was a big hero in World War One and he's never done anything since. He's running a ranch in Colorado. But where he and I are different, he put all his ambition into the war and came back with a chest full of medals. And that was it. Whereas I have a long-range ambition that's the direct opposite of his. He got into the game of killing people for the fun of it, not for self-preservation, but for the fun of it. And I'm sure it was fun. When I was playing hockey I was just as murderous as Lex Porter. And if a puck hits you just right, it's bye-bye. Here on the temple."

"Why did you play hockey?"

"Oh, that was before I developed my theories about self-preservation. You don't spend much time *thinking* about playing hockey. It's a game, and if you play it well enough, you make the team. If you don't, you spend the winter playing squash. Now, when I go to New York, I always go to the Garden at least once to see the Rangers play. I haven't the slightest interest in whether they win or lose. I just go and watch the guys that play my position and compare them with myself. And wonder what ever made me think I was so hot."

"You obviously love the game, Porter."

"I did, but even if I had the wind and the legs, I wouldn't play it now, you can be damn sure. Look at this." He raised his right trouser-leg. "Sixteen stitches."

"Through those thick stockings?"

"I wasn't wearing them. It wasn't even a regular match. Just skating on the lake and using a tobacco can for a puck. Sticks we broke off trees."

"Did you stop playing?"

"No. I played in two more matches that year, then I retired from college after a little heart-to-heart talk with Dean Gauss. 'Diston, I'm afraid you got all you want to out of Princeton.' 'Dean Gauss, I think you're right.' We understood each other perfectly. I got a room at the Allerton House and a job as a customer's man. Went to a lot of parties. Quit the job, went abroad with two friends of mine. Came back and got another job. Went to a lot more parties. Fell in love twice. Lost a lot of money, and came home. And here I stay. But not literally, here. I've stayed too long and talked too much, and you want to be with John. Thank you very much, Elizabeth. Do you and John play bridge?"

"I'm afraid we don't. John never learned, and I haven't touched a card in years. Why?"

"Oh, I was going to say, if you're ever looking for a fourth. I sometimes play with some faculty people. Professor Hillenketter plays a good game."

"So I've heard. He's been coaxing us to take it up."

"And that young couple, the Leslies. Roy and Mary. She's better than he is."

"She was very bright in college, I know. Hard to believe, isn't it?"

"Not really. *You* combine looks and brains."

"Thank you, Porter. So do you, for that matter."

"Well, now."

"In fact—this may seem rude, but it's meant as a compliment—tonight's been a revelation to me."

"Then this is the right moment to leave, before I disillusion you."

John Appleton was asleep, but even though he had been very tired, he had put out his clean shirt, underwear and socks for the morning, folded his slacks over the back of a chair, put his razor, brush, and shaving cream in their proper places on the bathroom shelf. He lay on his right side, and his shoulders and back looked bigger than usual. He seemed older than Porter Ditson, and he was younger; he seemed husky and thick, in contrast with the wiry slenderness of Porter Ditson. She was glad he had not been there to hear the rambling utterances of Porter Ditson. She had enjoyed Porter, and John Appleton's comments would have made her feel that it was unintelligent to enjoy them. In the morning, during their hurried breakfast, John Appleton would ask her what she and Porter Ditson had talked about. She would not tell him.

V

Elizabeth Appleton had been flattered by Porter Ditson's estimate of her as a woman who combined intelligence and attractiveness; but the compliment, on reflection, was less valuable than it would have been had it come from a man whom she was in the habit of respecting. Her intelligence, or rather, her intellect, she had appraised with some honesty; her appearance, which she never called her beauty, was as honestly appraised, and there was no doubt in her mind that if she was a combination of beauty and brains, the beauty was predominant over the brains. She possessed a mentality that was part shrewdness, part curiosity, and the rest was information that had been provided by her schooling, her social-economic background, and her sex. Most of her mental exercise was related to her life as wife and mother; American history bored her, in spite of her willingness to look up facts and dates for her husband's lectures and her accuracy in copying them down. She made no attempt to retain the information that she briefly handled during these chores. She had not, in truth, learned very much new as the wife of a college professor that she would not have learned as the wife of any other man. She would just as efficiently have studied actuarial tables for a husband who was an insurance agent, recorded chemistry experiments for a husband who was in that line of endeavor.

But she knew that she was a good-looking woman. As a young girl she had felt to the point of embarrassment the admiration of boys and men who saw her in a bathing suit or a tennis dress, and in her present life, in which her everyday costume was skirt and sweater, she was accustomed in every brief conversation to the man's glance dropping toward her bosom. There was a power in the attractiveness of her body that she did not care to use, since the use of it implied intimacy with the man, and she was more resentful than not when men allowed themselves the intimacy of an intimate glance. She was a woman and had a woman's ideal body, but she did nothing and wore nothing that was provocative, and she had an angry contempt for every man who stared.

She liked Porter Ditson because he had not stared, and because he had twice in the same conversation divided his compliment between her mind and her body. Since she had had no respect for his intelligence—and in the politest possible way had told him so—she could not treasure his words of praise for hers, and she knew that he would not have flattered her if she had been plain or ugly. But he had deliberately or otherwise given her the compliment within a compliment of saying good things about her "appearance" while seeming to mix the compliment to her appearance with a tribute to her intelligence. As a consequence, she did willingly absorb the compliment to her appearance and thrilled to it, while rejecting his compliment to her brains. For weeks she would stir in recollection of what he had said to her, stir pleasantly, and want more.

If John had paid a compliment to her appearance—

and he often had—he would not have coupled it with a compliment to her intelligence. His compliments to her intelligence had always been, and always would be, separate from words of admiration for her breasts, her lips, her legs, her eyes, her hair, her nose. John's compliments of a physical nature were made in bed, or preceded their going to bed and were therefore to be expected in much the same way that a kiss could be expected to be followed by the ritual pressures on her breasts. In such cases the compliments were sincere enough, genuine enough, but always closely related to the act of physical union. His compliments to her intelligence were daytime compliments, kept apart from her identity as a desirable and desirous woman, spoken usually in a tone of judgment and passed down to her as from authority to clerk. That being the case, the woman herself kept such compliments apart from the rememberable and remembered things he would say about her face and areas of her body. But she continued to remember that Porter Ditson had complimented her, long after she had dismissed from her memory the actual words that apportioned the recognition of her diverse attributes.

Some of the effectiveness of what Porter Ditson had said was due, of course, to the surprising fact that he had said it. She had spoken the literal truth in telling him that it was "as if I'd never really met you before." Porter Ditson had already returned to Spring Valley when John and Elizabeth Appleton went there to live, and except for the fact that he had mentioned having met her father, he had made no special impression on her in the first meetings. When she had had an opportunity to meet and observe the undergraduates and recent alumni of Spring Valley she saw that Porter Ditson was obviously not a local product. At the college "formals" that she and John chaperoned, none of the boys wore pumps; but Porter Ditson wore pumps on nearly every evening occasion, black tie or not, just as Jarvis Webster did and dozens of the young men she had known in New York. In a year or so of encountering Porter Ditson at Hill parties and on various tennis courts Elizabeth Appleton categorized him as an idler whose chief distinction was that he was in Spring Valley instead of in New York, where he would have been one of several thousand unremarkable young men who attended the deb parties and frequented Dan Moriarty's speakeasy. On one of her earliest encounters with Porter Ditson, but after she had begun to label him, Elizabeth Appleton had an irresistible opportunity to take him down a peg or two. "You know, Mrs. Appleton," he said. "I think I went to your coming-out party. Was it in 1928?"

"Yes, but you weren't there," she said.

"Are you sure?"

"Oh, yes, I'm sure. At my party there wasn't a single crasher, not a one."

He did not give up. "How do you know I wasn't invited?"

"Because my party was a dinner dance and I knew every boy and girl there. Every single one. There were eighty-two places and eighty sat down. One boy and one girl couldn't come because their mother died."

"Then I must be wrong."

"I'm afraid so. I did have a big party in the summer of 1930, but I'm almost positive you weren't at that one. I think I'd have known because John was at that party and he'd have mentioned that another Spring Valley boy was there."

"Did you go to the famous Stipplebird party?"

"No. My mother was very much against my going to the parties of girls I didn't know. I heard all about it, though."

"Weren't you sorry you didn't go?"

"Not a bit. I didn't like Viola Stipplebird."

"I thought you didn't know her."

"Oh, she got on committees. I knew her *that* well."

"I liked Viola. I liked Phil, too. Her brother. All that was the old man."

"Well, then you *should* have gone to her party."

"I still have the silver Dunhill lighter we got."

"You wouldn't have got one at my party. Maybe that's

why you don't remember it. That, and just not being there. All that expense parents go to and a few years later nobody remembers whether they went to Susie Jones's or Sally Smith's."

"I did go to Sally Smith's. It was at the Allegheny Country Club. Emil Coleman played. The place was decorated to look like a steamship. And the waiters were all dressed to look like French sailors. It was supposed to be the *Ile de France*. You see, I do remember."

"I didn't mean any particular Sally Smith."

"I know you didn't. However, I didn't go to Susie Jones's."

"How do you know you didn't?"

"You know, you have a point there. Give my regards to your father when you write to him."

"I will, and you give mine to Viola Stipplebird."

Three years after the preceding conversation Porter Ditson wrote a note of condolence to Elizabeth Appleton on the death of Jarvis Webster, and the notes that passed between them at that time typified their relationship:

Dear Elizabeth:
Please accept my sincere sympathy on the death of your father. As you may recall, I met him several times while I was living in New York. He was very kind to me and I am sure his loss will be felt by his family and many friends.
Sincerely,
Porter Ditson

Dear Porter:
It was very kind and thoughtful of you to write when my father died. Please forgive my delay in acknowledging your note. Now that things have settled down a bit perhaps you will come out and have a quiet dinner with us some evening in the near future. Thank you for writing. John joins me in best wishes.
Sincerely,
Elizabeth W. Appleton

From time to time—when it was, as it were, his turn —Porter Ditson would come in for his share of unfavorable criticism for the futility of his manner of living. The criticisms, however, were brief, since he had not been involved in trouble or scandal that might have dramatized him and his habits. He got about so much that he was not even mysterious. He continued to be welcome in the social life of the Hill, he took part in a few community enterprises, he was predictably at the country club on certain days in certain seasons, and his succession of quickly identifiable automobiles could still be seen parked at the Elks clubhouse and Joe Weber's saloon. At the time of his surprise visit to the John Appletons he was saved only by his being a Ditson from becoming a nonentity, and he was not quite old enough to be considered a town character. He was neither tragic nor comic but only, in the view of his brother and sister-in-law and their friends, an occasional source of minor irritation. In the view of John Appleton he was "a harmless nitwit," not even worth the full fury of his New Deal scorn. Likewise, to the study group of the Communist cell at Spring Valley College and in the town Porter Ditson was not worth proselyting. As a Ditson and a Framingham in-law he had been under the Party scrutiny, but their severely realistic judgment was based on a well-prepared dossier covering his habits and utterances, and bafflement over his Epicurean nonconformism, which was complicated by his going to church every Sunday when there was no real reason to do so. The party members at the Spring Valley public library and the depot newsstand reported on his reading habits, which were discouraging, and the tailor who pressed his clothes had got very unsatisfactory answers to his political feelers. To him Porter Ditson was a *schnuck*. Elizabeth Appleton was the only living soul to whom Porter Ditson had confided that he had an ambition.

For more than two months, then, Elizabeth Appleton respected a confidence by thinking of it less as a confidence than as a compliment. And the conversation in which the confidence and compliment were contained was itself a secret from her husband, a not very important secret, but not an insignificant one; not a significant one of itself, but because it was one item of an increasing quantity of withheld information that had begun with her taking money from her mother. Once it had been a matter of not telling her husband things he did not want to know; now it had become a matter of not telling him things she did not want him to know.

The scene with her husband from which she would come to date the first year of her discontent took place during the Christmas holidays of 1940. Except for the administrative staff the campus was deserted, and married members of the faculty mingled socially with the Hill set. A very few—the John Appletons among them—were invited to the annual big dinner dance at the country club, to the Brice Ditsons' New Year's Day at-home, and to the other big party that was not a fixture on the Spring Valley social calendar, but that someone was sure to give. This year the host and hostess were the very young Roy Leslies, who gave the party as a pay-back for the entertainment they had received during their first year of marriage, and because there was an over-all sense of foreboding that was based on the fact that already many of their contemporaries were in military service. "We'll start by inviting everybody that's liable to be drafted," said Mary Leslie. "Then we can decide how many of the older crowd we can have."

Elizabeth Appleton, thinking along the same lines, decided to have a dinner party before the Leslie dance. The first name she put down was Porter Ditson.

"What made you start out with him?" said John Appleton.

"Because I'll bet he'll be drafted soon."

"He's safe. He's just turned thirty-six."

"Well, I want him anyway," said Elizabeth.

"If you can get him. A social butterfly like Porter, you won't find many of them in Spring Valley."

"A social butterfly is just what we want, although I happen to think that there's a little more to Porter than that. But I do hope we can get him, because the few parties we have are apt to be heavily intellectual—face that."

"Wait a minute. That's quite a remarkable statement you slipped in there. Where did you get the idea that there's more to Porter Ditson than just the social butterfly? I've known him all my life and I've never seen anything else. And when did *you* change your mind?"

"Fairly recently, I'll admit."

"The only time you had a chance to talk to him was that night after I excoriated J. W. Framingham."

"Yes, and fell asleep while Porter was talking."

"Did I miss anything? I must have. Tell me all about it. Unless of course you're having a secret love affair with Porter."

"I thought we never made jokes about those kind of things," said Elizabeth Appleton.

"That was because we didn't want to have silly quarrels over women students. I hope you don't mind if I make a feeble attempt at humor about Porter. Porter Ditson is exactly what you gave up when you married me."

"Yes, but don't forget, he was exactly what I'd always known till I met you."

"Well, you're not trying to tell me—no."

"No. I want to have Porter for our dinner party, and unless you want to make up the list, and order the food and seat everybody and all the rest of it, please don't complicate things any more than you have to. You'll probably fall asleep anyway, before the night's over."

"Is that why you want to have Porter?"

"It wasn't my original reason, but since you mention it, yes. I'm going to buy a new dress and I intend to have a good time."

"I'm sorry, Elizabeth. I want you to have a good time, you're entitled to it. I'm not jealous of Porter. I just don't think he has very much to offer, but for a party like this, and Mary's dance, I guess he's ideal."

"Even you must get a little tired of the same old faces. I wish we didn't have to have any faculty people, but then I suppose there'd be a lot of hurt feelings. So we'll have to have the McAndrews and the Boalses and Dr. and Mrs. Chung and Frank and Hessie Hopkins. Do we absolutely have to have the Chungs? She's sweet and pretty, but honestly, John, she *doesn't* speak English and none of the others speak French too well. I speak pretty good French and she speaks it with a Chinese accent."

"They're going to be away."

"Thank God. I can invite them and get credit, and then with any luck get two people that will be fun to have."

"Like Porter Ditson."

"Why did you say that?"

"Well, you make me think that all the parties we've had in the past ten years were an ordeal for you. And it's just coming out."

"First of all, we haven't had that many parties. And in the second place, can't we have one party that isn't just a lot of people saying how wonderful Mr. Roosevelt is?"

"We could join the country club and hear just the opposite. To my untutored ear they're just as boring as my friends are to you."

"You know perfectly well I voted for Roosevelt, even if my heart wasn't in it. And if it comes down to that, my mother and father *know* the Roosevelts and none of these friends of yours do. My uncle was in the same class *and* the same club as Mr. Roosevelt at Harvard, long before any of your friends ever heard of him."

"Bet your uncle doesn't see much of him nowadays."

"Mr. Roosevelt can be thankful he doesn't."

"And I'll bet he is, if he ever gives it a thought."

"This isn't getting our list made up."

"No, but other things are coming out," said John Appleton. "Things that are a hell of a sight more important than a party."

"Well, what do you want to do? Help me with the list, or start rehashing our life? I've always gone along with you in everything you've wanted to do. Isn't it permissible for me to have my private feelings, my own opinions? Especially

(127)

about people. The trouble with you is that you're lazy. You're mentally lazy. You can only stand people that agree with you."

"How long have you been feeling this way?"

"Ever since we've been married. When we lived in Cambridge you never let me see Boston friends of mine. And this is the only other place we've ever lived. Now you object because we're having one party that's the kind of party I'd like to give. One party in almost ten years. And your real objection is to Porter Ditson, because all the others are your friends too. Porter just happens to be the only one in town that is anything like the boys I grew up with, and that's why you resent him."

"My objection to Porter Ditson is that he's a light-weight."

"Then I'm a lightweight, too. If you're not going to be any help, go to bed."

Elizabeth Appleton thereafter left him so completely out of the planning for the party that when the guests began to arrive he did not know who was coming or how many. Nearly three weeks had passed between their conversation and the night of the Leslie dance, and in that time he had not gone to her bed, she had not gone to his. As they were dressing for the party she said: "Will you zip me up, please?"

"Is this your new dress?" he said.

"Yes."

"Very nice," he said.

"Thank you." She did not turn to display it. She looked at herself in the mirror, frowned a little, then reached into a drawer and took out her jewelry case and from it brought out a diamond necklace and a large diamond ring that had belonged to her mother. She had often in the past got to the point of taking the necklace and the ring from the case, but had always decided against wearing them. Now she put them on and drew back her shoulders and took a deep breath. The action extended her breasts and he moved close to her and from behind put his hands over them.

"Don't, please," she said.

"Oh, all right," he said. "I'll go down and start the Martinis."

"You won't have to. I've engaged a man to serve drinks."

"A man to serve drinks? How many are coming to this party, for God's sake?"

"Thirty-one."

"Thirty-one? Where did you get a bartender?"

"From the Elks club."

"Well, I guess I don't have to ask who got him for you."

"Porter Ditson got him for me."

"Maybe he'd better sit at the head of the table, too."

"For all the help you've been, yes. But it's going to be small tables. Our table isn't large enough for anywhere near that many people. Neither is our diningroom."

"Where did you get the plates and the silverware? From the caterer? I assume you're having a caterer."

"There's a caterer, but I have enough plates and silverware. I've just never had the chance to use them before."

"You're going all out tonight, aren't you?"

"Not really. We have things in storage that you've never seen."

"You probably have forks that I don't know how to use," said John Appleton.

"Just watch me, if you're in doubt," she said.

"That might be a very good idea," he said, so meaningfully that she laughed at him.

"Good heavens," she said.

Her dinner party was a great success, particularly so because on an impulse she had invited Roy and Mary Leslie, and to her astonishment no one else had invited them to the dinners that were to precede their dance, most likely in the belief that the Leslies would be having their own dinner party or that "someone else" would ask the principal host and hostess of the evening. Mary Leslie had accepted immediately, whereupon Elizabeth Appleton chose her other guests from among the younger married group. With the Leslies as her guests, her party automatically became the principal prefatory dinner, a fact of which Elizabeth and all her guests were snugly aware. The Leslies left at ten o'clock to receive at their own party, but it was tacitly conceded that the dance did not really begin until the Appletons' party arrived. Spring Valley was seeing an Elizabeth Appleton they had not seen before; stimulated, radiant, beautifully dressed, impressively bejewelled, and new.

"You're the belle of the ball, and no two ways about it," said Porter Ditson.

"I feel like the belle of the ball," said Elizabeth Appleton.

"Couple of people asked me if you were tight."

"Tell them I am. It's a better explanation than the real one."

"Oh? What is the real one?" said Porter Ditson.

"If I ever tell anybody, it'll be you."

"Well, God *damn* it, Elizabeth, if it was anybody else I'd say you were flirting. Are you flirting with me, Elizabeth?"

"Of course I am, Porter. You're responsible for the way I am tonight."

"Now I'm being had. How am I responsible?"

"You got me tight."

"I got you tight? I'm beginning to think somebody did, but when did they have time?"

"This took quite a long time."

Someone cut in and Elizabeth was disappointed, then relieved, that Porter Ditson did not dance with her again. The dance ended at three o'clock, a late supper was served at the Brice Ditsons', and John and Elizabeth Appleton got home shortly before half past five.

"Will you unzip me, please?" she said.

"I'd be glad to," he said, and did so.

"I don't think I've had a better time ever, anywhere," she said. She hung up her new black satin dress and stood in her black satin shoes and panty girdle with her arms folded in front of her breasts.

(130)

"Do you want to come to bed with me, just the way you are?"

"I'll have to take *this* off," she said.

"Yes, I guess you will."

She lay in his bed and looked up at the ceiling. He was eager for her and wanted her without much delay. She reached over and snapped out the light and accommodated him, but that was what it was. When it was over for him he said: "You didn't, did you?"

"No," she said. "I don't always, you know that."

"Nearly always. What was the matter?"

"Nothing the matter. I enjoyed it." She went to the bathroom in the dark, and when she came out she was wearing her nightgown, as he could see by the light from the bathroom. "Goodnight," she said. "Oh, I have to take Peter to the dentist at eleven, but I'll try not to wake you."

"You're not going to get much sleep."

"I'll sleep like a top. Goodnight."

In the time it took him to smoke a cigarette she was deep in sleep. He had not possessed her, he had not approximated for her the excitement she had induced in him, he had not entertained her to the degree that the evening had entertained her. Any man she had danced with, or all the men she had danced with, had done more for her lubricity than he in bed with her had done. They had brought her to the state of willingness, and she had accepted his necessity, but there had been no urgency to her actions and no demand for his climax that always—*nearly* always—sprang climax for her. Nearly always was always, except when she was worried about one of the children, and such was not the case in this early morning. She was not thinking about Peter and the dentist; she was thinking about herself and quite possibly no one else.

Elizabeth Appleton's brief emergence from the life she led as a tweed-skirted faculty wife was followed by some invitations that would have established her in the Hill crowd. But Elizabeth had always known that there was a place for her in the Hill crowd; their discovery of her social value may have been news to them, but not to her. Spring Valley society was no substitute for New York, even in the unlikely event that she could persuade John Appleton to take part in the local activities. But shortly after college reopened John said: "Rupert Hillenketter asked me today if I'd mind if you made a fourth at bridge. Has he said anything to you?"

"Not a word. I haven't played in years. You know that."

"Where did he get the idea that you're a shark?"

"He couldn't have that idea, because I never was. My mother and father were quite good. Among the best. Father especially, but I don't see how Professor Hillenketter would know that."

"Did your father ever play in any tournaments? Rupert might have seen his name in that connection."

"You mean with Culbertson and Mr. Vanderbilt? No, he was never that good. He played at the Regency Club, but I don't think he was a member. And when I say Father and Mother were among the best, I meant among their friends, not with the professionals."

"Well, what shall I tell Hillenketter?"

"Tell him I haven't played in years, and I never was in the same class with my father and mother. I used to irritate Father because I bid too conservatively. The fascination of contract over auction was in the rewards for game bids, and—"

"It's gibberish to me. If you want to play, it's all right with me."

"Well, that's really what he wanted to know, isn't it?"

"Yes, but I thought I'd give you a chance to duck it if you didn't want to play."

Rupert Hillenketter was in his middle fifties, the last— or the first—Spring Valley faculty member to wear a beard. He had a room at the Faculty Club, a small white house just off campus that had once been the Spring Valley home of Hillenketter and his wife. Upon her death in 1916 he arranged with the trustees to deed the house to the college for use as a faculty club, with the proviso that he be allowed to live there rent free so long as he would be a member of the faculty, and during his retirement. The arrangement was highly satisfactory to Hillenketter and not burdensome to the college. The dues were kept at a minimum—ten dollars a year in 1916, twenty-five dollars a year in 1940—and it was a convenience for the men teachers, although annually there were murmurs among those who regarded membership as compulsory instead of voluntary. But it was a pleasant little place, thanks to the management of the club, which was performed by Hillenketter. He hired the staff—a Negro cook and a Negro house boy—and wrote the rules and watched accounts, and at the end of the year he covered the usual small deficit. Hillenketter had a private income; that much was known. The amount of the income was not known, even to officers of the Spring Valley Bank & Trust Company, where he maintained a checking account. From time to time he would deposit cheques for varying sums drawn on a bank in Chicago to supplement his deposits of faculty pay. Since the Chicago cheques were for as little as fifty dollars and as much as one thousand, and the deposits were made with no regularity, the only information available to the Spring Valley bankers was that Hillenketter was a man of independent means, which everyone knew in any case.

He had no car, but he used taxis frequently. He had not changed his style of dress in thirty years, but it cost money to have a Chicago tailor duplicate his four-button suits of 1910; his stand-up collars came from New York; his high-laced shoes from a factory in Brockton, Massachusetts. He was the only member of the faculty who patronized the manicurist in the hotel barber shop, and the only one who would openly admit to a valuable collection of pornography, which he justified as required reading in his field. "I'm told that the most complete collections are in Vienna and at the Vatican, but I'm *persona non grata* at the Vatican, and I couldn't possibly meet the prices they get in Vienna," he would often say.

As a campus institution he was as essential to Spring

Valley College as a winning team, the alma mater hymn, the Phi Beta Kappa charter (which for so many years had been denied the vastly larger Penn State College), the tenuous Harvard connection, the old reputation as a rich man's college, Spring Day, and the indigenous slang terms for women, toilets, and certain buildings. As he strode across the Quadrangle he would be pointed out to visitors and parents, a bearded eccentric in 1910 clothes and carrying a silver-mounted cane. "That's Prof Hillenketter. He's a screwball but what he doesn't know about psychology—*boy!*" they would say, and except for the word screwball students had been saying much the same thing for three decades. Students who bothered to look him up in *Who's Who in America* and, with pride, found that he not only was listed but took up half a column in that volume, closed the book with new awe and respect for Hillenketter, especially since neither Prexy Witherspoon nor Prexy McAndrews occupied so much space, and J. W. Framingham was limited to twenty lines. Hillenketter's sketch included the German and English titles of monographs he had translated, the many learned societies to which he belonged, professional offices he had held, the foreign universities he had visited, as well as the titles of the many papers and the one book (*Recognizing the Obvious: A Psychological Study of Modern Psychology;* pub. 1926) of which he was the author. He was a well-documented celebrity, and what was more he had the appearance and the manner of one.

He could be very scornful of a student or a colleague who questioned any statement, and while his sarcasm made him no friends, it tamed his students and discouraged his colleagues. There could be no criticism of the preparation of his lectures, which in their final form consisted of excerpted material from all the greats in the field, and Hillenketter's own comments for or against. The eclectic method, as he termed it, was the only proper one to follow in the teaching of psychology to boys and girls who were only a couple of years out of high school. If it created or stimulated a genuine interest in the subject, that was precisely what every worthwhile teacher hoped for, and students who had been thus stimulated were encouraged to go on to graduate schools. If on the other hand a student was going through college with no more than a general culturization in mind, it was as foolish to go deeply into the subject as for a math teacher to give an advanced scientific course to boys and girls who had had difficulty with solid geometry. Since it was a simple fact that most undergraduates at Spring Valley were there to acquire a general culturization, it would be unfair to *them* to change his lecture policy, and accordingly Prof Hillenketter made very few changes from year to year. By following this policy he was able to polish up his old stand-bys, as he called his set of lectures, but that was not the only advantage of the policy: after so many years he was also able to recognize the papers turned in by his students. Students do not differ much year by year, class by class; the same lectures could be counted on to produce the same mixed reactions. The politely skeptical, the lazy, the hard-working dullard, the quick assimilator, and all the others turned up each year, saying the same things. Prof Hillenketter found this so true that he had to read only a page—and sometimes not even that—to know what a student had written on a given topic. This made the marking of papers much simpler for the professor, and gave him time for other things.

He had his long walks, his Philharmonic on Sundays, his books, his attention to the details of the Faculty Club, and his surprise visits on his more interesting students, who were not necessarily always his brightest students. He also took extremely good care of his health. The death of his wife in 1916 had been a shocking experience and had taught him the lesson that he urged upon all his friends. Only a few now remembered Sarah Hillenketter and her death by poison self-administered. "She was sure she had consumption, as we called it then," he would recall. "And the thought of a long, lingering illness from a wasting disease—it was more than she could bear. I was away at the time, or I might have been able to reason with her. But no. You know why I am doing this,' she said in her note. And indeed I did. That was all she said. All she could bring herself to say. And the real tragedy was that it was all up here." He would tap his head. "Her lungs were perfectly healthy. They did a post-mortem because it was a suicide, but I could have told them that it was a psychoneurosis. The truth is that I married Sarah to take care of her, but she needed more care than I could give. A young instructor just beginning to make his way." To reassure himself on the question of his own health, Professor Hillenketter had a thorough two-day checkup at the hospital once a year, and Harry Jeffries was the man who supervised it. "At one time I knew all about Harry, and now he knows all about me," the professor would say. "Harry was one of my guinea pigs years ago, and now he knows all my secrets." The lesson he urged upon all his friends was to have no secrets from themselves; to have periodic medical checkups so that they would not worry over illnesses that did not exist. If possible, they were to have the examinations supervised by Harry Jeffries, but Harry was such a busy doctor, practically a specialist now, and could not accept all the patients Prof Hillenketter sent to him. It could not be said that Harry Jeffries was ungrateful for all that his former teacher had done for him. Harry Jeffries' confidential files were always available to Rupert Hillenketter, a small enough repayment, especially to a man who not only had been kind in the past but also was helpful in the present, when examinations of the more interesting patients disclosed problems that were not entirely of a medical nature. Rupert Hillenketter was generous with his comment and his advice, thereby giving Harry Jeffries the full benefit of his professional experience in a field with which Harry was understandably unfamiliar. Many interesting problems and situations occurred in Harry's own field of gynecology and obstetrics that called for an outside opinion, and as Hillenketter said, "I like to think we work as a team." The teamwork, however, was of a confidential nature. Hillenketter wanted none of the credit, and insisted that his name be kept out of the discussions between Harry

Jeffries and his patients. "My reward," he told Harry Jeffries, "is in the study of these cases, and I only wish I had more time to give them."

Rupert Hillenketter's efforts to make a Jeffries patient of Porter Ditson were a complete failure, but in many other respects the professor and the gentleman of leisure were in accord. Like most citizens of Spring Valley, Town and Gown, Porter Ditson was impressed by Rupert Hillenketter's intellectual attainments. Like most citizens, Porter Ditson took the attainments for granted; he did not for a moment question the standing of a man who had been teaching psychology for thirty years. He was flattered, too, by the professor's interest in his own activities, and he was evasive only when the professor seemed to be on the verge of inquiring into his sex life. But the professor had never been too inquisitive; it just seemed that occasionally they were only one or two questions away from an overt discussion of Porter Ditson's relations with women. It was one thing to go to a whorehouse with the fellows from the Elks; it was something else again to talk about it later with a man of Professor Hillenketter's stature. Porter Ditson refrained from expressing any but the most superficial comments on women, to Hillenketter and everyone else. The borderline of intimacy that he maintained with his downtown friends would have been violated irreparably by comments on women, and this habit of reticence was easily repeated in his conversations with Hillenketter, since he had no curiosity about Hillenketter's relations with women and sought no exchange of information.

Hillenketter, although twenty years older than Porter Ditson, was less sure of himself in areas where the younger man was by nature at ease. Hillenketter dressed up as an old school gentleman and controlled his speech and added unnecessary bows and swept his hat toward the ground and patterned his manners after those of his favorite actors, who were William Faversham and George Arliss. He owned a monocle that he employed in the restaurants of Boston, New York and Philadelphia, where he referred to his suitcase as a portmanteau, to the confusion of the modern bell-boy. But the younger man was tolerant of Hillenketter's personal style in clothes and manners; at Princeton there had been professors who were just as screwball. Moreover, Porter Ditson was conscious of his own status in the Spring Valley community and while there were no points of actual resemblance between his actions and attitudes and those of Hillenketter, they were two men who stood apart from all the others. They had *that* in common, and it was enough for their association.

They also had the game of bridge, which in Spring Valley was the principal social pastime. The winter usually came suddenly and lasted late in the mountains, and there were a dozen bridge-playing groups that met regularly from early November to April. The game would start at eight and seldom would continue past ten-thirty, the customary hour for sandwiches and coffee, sandwiches and beer, a salad and coffee, cold cuts and beer. The same people as a rule played with the same people, but Rupert Hillenketter liked to alternate his guests and to introduce new ones when he was host. His evening was Tuesday, when there were almost no casual visitors at the Faculty Club and the resident members would yield the small sittingroom. A little before or a little after ten-thirty, if he was dummy, he would go to the kitchen and put the water on to boil; if he was to play the hand, he would turn it over to his partner. At ten-forty-five if the rubber was not completed, play would have to stop because of the club rule that ladies must be off the premises at eleven.

Elizabeth Appleton's previous visits to the Faculty Club had all been in daytime, for faculty teas and the like. (John Appleton had been one of those who thought they could find a better use for fifteen or twenty dollars than to pay it in dues for a club they seldom used.) It was rather strange, she thought, to be driving up to the club, alone and at night, and ringing the doorbell.

Hillenketter opened the door. "Dear Elizabeth, welcome to these hallowed precincts, and you're so punctual.

I *like* that. Let me take your things. I see you drove yourself. I neglected to tell you that Porter Ditson volunteered to bring you here. Oh, I didn't neglect. I purposely didn't tell you because I thought I detected a slight lift of the brow when I informed John that my other guests would be Porter Ditson and Mary Leslie. Needless to say, he was not concerned about your playing bridge with Mary Leslie. Or with me, for that matter."

"Oh, Professor, John isn't jealous of anybody, and needn't be," she said. "It's so peaceful and quiet here."

"It is most of the time."

The others arrived a few minutes later, and the bridge game commenced. They played for a tenth-of-a-cent, and at ten-thirty-five the winners were Mary Leslie and Elizabeth Appleton. "I had all the cards," said Elizabeth. "I've never seen such a run of luck as I had tonight."

"Takes more than the cards to win in this game," said Porter Ditson. This was as close as he came to a criticism of their host, who had cost himself and Porter Ditson a great number of points by throwing away a small club that was his only reëntry into dummy, thereby being set four tricks, doubled and redoubled, both sides vulnerable. It was the only serious misplay anyone made during the entire evening, and the stillness at the end of the hand was a painfully awkward thing. The loss had, in fact, been anticipated; all three players showed their mystification when Hillenketter discarded the small club, and Mary Leslie made good four diamonds that swept dummy of his valuable clubs.

Hillenketter's only comment was: "I should be punished for that. Well, as I look at the score, I am. But I'm most dreadfully sorry, partner."

"Don't give it another thought," Porter Ditson had said.

Hillenketter brought in the refreshments on an old-fashioned teawagon. "Those are watercress, and those are tomato. There's beer in the icebox, but on such a cold night I'd rather send you away with some hot coffee. Can we do this again next Tuesday? The same four? I'd like to redeem myself for that stupid misplay. Not in your eyes,

Porter, or yours, Mary Leslie. You know I rarely play so badly. But I have to prove myself to Elizabeth. And by the way, Elizabeth, you have a really fine card sense."

"She has," said Porter Ditson.

"Yes," said Mary Leslie. "If you'd left me in that five diamond bid instead of switching to five hearts—that was brilliant. And you played it beautifully, Elizabeth."

"I'm afraid it was beginner's luck. I really haven't played in years."

"But you must have followed the game," said Porter Ditson.

"In the newspapers. I do the bridge problems in the morning after I've taken the children to school. But I'm nearly always wrong."

"You damn well weren't tonight," said Porter Ditson.

"Well, shall we say Tuesday next?" said Hillenketter.

"I'd like to," said Mary Leslie.

"So would I," said Elizabeth Appleton.

"And you can always count on me unless I'm out of town," said Porter Ditson.

The foursome remained the same for two more meetings; on what would have been the third renewal of the Faculty Club bridge game Rupert Hillenketter (and John Appleton) had to be at a monthly meeting of the faculty advisory council, and Mary Leslie invited Elizabeth Appleton and Porter Ditson to play with her and her husband. Elizabeth telephoned Student Employment and got a girl to watch the children, and at a quarter to eight, as she was about to leave the house, Porter Ditson appeared. "Some desperate prisoners have escaped from Bellefonte, so I came to take you to Mary's."

"Is that true, Porter? I haven't had the radio on," said Elizabeth.

"Not a word of truth in it. I came because I wanted to," he said. "As a matter of fact we could walk to Mary's if you Hill people would only shovel the snow off your sidewalks."

"We pay a senior to do it, but he didn't show up today," she said, and got in his car.

They proceeded slowly. "You're not worried about my driving, I hope. I've got chains on."

"No."

"Then why so silent? Are you thinking about John? He won't like this, will he?"

"No."

"It's time he was given something to disapprove of."

"Is it? Why?"

"Because I'm in love with you, and you're a little in love with me."

"What's that got to do with giving John something to disapprove of?"

"Because he's so damned complacent that if anything comes of this it's his own fault."

"Well, nothing's going to come of it, and we both know that."

"Is 'we both' you and I, or you and John?"

"You and I."

"I could stop this car this minute, on Bucknell Street at ten minutes of eight in the evening and something would come of it."

"But you're not going to stop this car. We have to be at Mary's in ten minutes, and if we weren't there at quarter past eight she'd telephone my house. If we were later than that we'd start a scandal."

"That was an optimistic shot in the dark, my saying you were a little in love with me, but it's true, isn't it?"

"Yes, I guess it is. But as long as it's only a little we can keep it under control. I thought you were in love with Mary."

"I could love Mary, and I do, but Mary isn't in my thoughts day and night, the way you are. It may be a little with you, Elizabeth, but not with me. I've never felt this way before. The other times I was in love, twice, they were kid stuff."

(141)

"One wasn't."

"Yes it was. The sex was kid stuff. I don't mean—a lack of proficiency. I just mean that the girl and I got in bed together because the opportunity presented itself. As far as that goes, the other girl and I were just as rooty for each other, but the opportunity didn't present itself."

"I don't want to have an affair with you, Porter."

"I know that. I know what you want. But you've *been* that for ten years, and now you know it isn't enough for you. You're just about ready to have an affair with somebody."

"Is that another shot in the dark?"

"No, this time it isn't a shot in the dark."

"Did Professor Hillenketter tell you that?"

"I've never discussed you with Hillenketter. Your bridge, your personality, yes. But to discuss you with him, it would be like my lifting your skirt to show him—"

"Please don't, don't say any more."

"All right."

"As it is, I'm not going to have my mind on the cards tonight."

"Just keep track of trump. That's the kind of bridge Roy plays. He'll start yawning at half past nine."

"Porter?"

"What?"

"Don't try to make love to me on the way home?"

"Why?"

"*Do* you love me?"

"Yes, I do."

"Then, I'll tell you why I don't want you to even try to make love to me. I might let you. I very easily might let you. But—"

"Say it, Elizabeth. Tell me."

"It isn't easy to say. Oh, all right. You see, I know after ten years when John is going to get in bed with me. I know it all day. And he's going to tonight."

"Jesus, Elizabeth! I wish you hadn't told me that."

"Well, I know he will, tonight, and if I did with you, I couldn't with him."

(*142*)

"Don't worry. Now that you've told me that, I couldn't make love to you. I'd feel that it was just a dress rehearsal. Undress rehearsal is more like it." He spoke bitterly.

"Don't be cross with me. This is how it would be if it ever did get out of control. There would be times."

"When you'd go to bed with me and then go to bed with him?"

"Yes. I think you'd better forget about the whole idea of being in love with me."

"Take my word for it, Elizabeth. I didn't wish this on myself."

"I didn't either—although I guess maybe I did. I guess this is exactly what I've been wanting, ever since the first night we played bridge. Oh, who knows when these things start?"

"I do. It started for me the night I went to your house, the time John was attacking old Jap Framingham. I've thought about that visit of mine. I didn't go to your house to talk to John. I really went because I thought you might be in a little trouble. Maybe I've always been in love with you. Maybe it didn't start that night at all. I know that it was you I wanted to see. Well, here we are . . . And *where* are we?"

The bridge game was a desultory one, with several long conversations between hands that had nothing to do with bridge. Roy was almost certain to be drafted in the very near future, and he had been investigating all the possibilities of obtaining a commission. He was twenty-two years old and he had dropped R.O.T.C. in college after one year, but he had a first cousin who was a West Pointer and a Regular Army captain whom he was waiting to hear from. Roy also had heard that the quickest way to get a commission was to join up with the Canadians, and the Representative for their Congressional district was a friend of Mary's father. On the other hand the war scare might turn out to be a false alarm, and he might get a commission and find that he was stuck for three or four or five years' army service, which would be a hell of a damn nuisance.

(143)

"God, they're young," said Porter Ditson, as he and Elizabeth started for home. "Would we have been that young if we'd gotten married?"

"You would have. I don't know, I guess I was as young as that. Of course I was."

"You're going home to your husband now, and he's going to get in bed with you."

"Are you trying to make me unhappy, Porter? I'm very sorry I told you that. I've never told a single soul anything like that about my marriage. I don't know why I told you."

"Do something for me?"

"What do you want?"

"Go home and don't go to bed with John."

"You have no right to ask that."

"I know I haven't. Not what you call a *right*. But I would like it if you'd say you weren't going to bed with him tonight. This is the night I told you I love you. Don't let him—well, just don't *let* him tonight, while you can still practically hear me say I love you. Can't you put him off for one night?"

"You've made it almost impossible for me to do anything else. All right, I won't sleep with him tonight. But that's all I can promise."

"That's all I asked."

"But it isn't all you're *going* to ask."

"No, but I can go away for a couple of weeks."

"Please do, Porter. That's a fair exchange. I'll tell him I'm tired tonight, and you go away for a while."

John Appleton was in his study. He called out, "Elizabeth?"

"I'm home," she said. She paid the girl from Student Employment and went back to the study.

"Game over early?" he said.

"Not much of a game. Mostly Roy talking about getting in the army."

"I was all confused when I got home, and both cars were still in the garage."

(*144*)

"I know. Porter stopped for me," she said. "And of course brought me home."

"Well, I guess I'll have to get myself a girl friend for Tuesday nights."

"You mean a girl friend like my boy friend Porter?"

"What else could I mean?"

"Just wanted to make sure," she said. "You could learn to play bridge. You were invited before I was. Professor Hillenketter spoke to you, not to me."

"Knowing I didn't play. I wouldn't put it past him."

"What wouldn't you put past him?"

"To put you and Porter under the microscope together to see what happens."

"Well, he can't be very pleased with his experiment. Nothing *has* happened."

"Oh, he can wait."

"Is that what you're doing, John? Waiting? All you have to do is say you want me to stop playing bridge, and I'll stop. But you have to give a reason. If you can't think of a better reason than Porter Ditson, I may *not* stop."

"Let me ask you this. Will you have sense enough to stop?"

"Stop what, and where?"

"Stop this seeing Porter Ditson every week, before you go to bed with him, that's what I'm talking about. You're getting bored and I've noticed it, and when a woman like you gets bored, a social butterfly like Porter Ditson comes in mighty handy."

"I'm good and bored with this conversation. Will you remember to turn down the thermostat? I'm going to bed."

She kept her promise to Porter Ditson, but in so doing she acquired a new feeling of neglect and loneliness: Porter Ditson was away somewhere, and her husband, who was not away, whom she had slept with hundreds of meaningless times, might as well have been away, for all the sexual companionship he provided. On the next Tuesday night she did not go to the Faculty Club.

"You're not going out tonight?" said John Appleton.

"Does it look that way?" she gestured toward her sewing basket with its contents of children's clothes and two shirts of his.

"How long can you hold a grudge, anyway?" he said. "You aren't staying home to please me. You're doing it to show how mad you are."

"You've got what you wanted. It's Tuesday night, and I'm home."

"I didn't get what I wanted. I happen to know that your friend Mr. Ditson is out of town. Is that news to you?"

"No. Professor Hillenketter told me he was away."

"Then I didn't get what I wanted at all. It would have been a damned sight better if you'd played tonight, when Ditson wasn't there."

"You're much too hard to please. The way you're going on, I should be off somewhere with Porter, having a gay old time in Palm Beach."

"Is that where he is?"

"I haven't the faintest idea. I *do* have the faintest idea. He's in New Hampshire, skiing."

"I hope he breaks his leg."

"That's dear of you."

"The question is, how much longer are we going to go on like this?"

"Exactly. If I *had* slept with Porter you couldn't have made more of a fuss. Actually he's never even held my hand."

"Maybe not, but—"

"No maybe about it. Get it straight. He hasn't even held my hand."

"All right, he hasn't held your hand. But we're fighting over him. He's kept us out of the same bed for two weeks."

"Precisely. It all started over nothing. I can't remember what. But it's something now." She looked up from her sewing. "You're the history expert. What's the history of this?"

"I don't care what it is. I just want it to stop. If you want me to apologize, I'll apologize. If I was unreasonable, I'm sorry. This is no way to live."

She looked away from him. "No, it isn't," she said.

He left the room, but a couple of hours later he followed her to their bedroom. He got into bed with her and held her for a while without making any erotic gesture. They waited in the dark, and then it was she who touched him. "I've missed this," she said.

"I've been going crazy."

She had no love for him, but he could not know that from what she did. All the things that excited him she did eagerly, to bring him to such excitement that he would not notice the lack of tenderness. She was willing to appear to be overcome by desire for him, to keep him from thinking and noticing that everything she did might easily be done with someone else. For her it might as well have been someone else, and at the last moment it was.

He went to sleep happy and proud, and she lay awake, for the moment content but as surely Porter Ditson's mistress as if the fact had been certified by events yet to come. Already Elizabeth Appleton was beginning to know that she wanted tranquillity at home, that it was an essential to the pleasure of meeting her lover. The real deception of her husband was in leading him into self-deception, which she would repeat whenever he wanted her. She had learned, she had shown herself, that making love with John could be done with a purpose, which was to ensure an orderly, placid home life, symbolized and climaxed by such pleasures as they had shared this night. She looked over at the sleeping man and had a whimsical impulse to thank him for establishing peace again and thus clearing the way for her adventure with Porter Ditson. It came back to her now that she had known for years that John Appleton was a master at self-deception. He could be totally incurious about what he did not want to know.

In the morning she wrote a one-line note to Porter Ditson which said only: "Don't stay *too* long." She mailed it without signing it, and on the second following day Mary Leslie telephoned her and said: "Porter's back and he's looking for a bridge game."

"Let's have it at my house. You and Roy and Porter," said Elizabeth Appleton.

"Are you sure you want Roy? You don't have to be polite about his bridge," said Mary Leslie. "What about the professor?"

"I can have him some other time. You and Roy come, and will you tell Porter?"

"I think you ought to," said Mary Leslie.

"All right."

To John she said: "Mary called. Mary Leslie. I've asked her and Roy and Porter to play bridge here. Why don't you sit and watch us and we'll explain the game to you. You've got to learn sometime. If you go in the army you'll wish you had learned."

"If I go in the army, it'll be the navy."

"Well, I'm sure they play bridge in the navy."

"No thanks," he said. "But I'm glad you asked me."

"I thought you would be. I want to get any funny ideas out of your head."

John Appleton was on hand to greet his wife's visitors. He lingered only long enough to see that there were cigarettes and ash trays, then went to his study. He rejoined the foursome when refreshments were being served, and stood with Elizabeth at the door when the guests left.

"Porter's just as tanned as if he'd been in Florida," said John Appleton.

"I guess he never really loses it. If he isn't playing golf or tennis, he's skating or something out of doors."

"Roy could use some of that color."

"Or some of Mary's rosy cheeks. She's terribly pretty, and she's so bright."

"Well, she had a damn good history teacher."

"Of course she did. Are you going to work late?"

"Another hour or so."

"Well, I'm off to bed. Goodnight," she said. He kissed her cheek. She was at ease and friendly toward him; Porter was still in love with her. They had not even needed the one exchange of frank looks and briefest of nods they had managed during the evening. But they had had them, and now she was sure.

In the morning she telephoned the hotel and asked for Mr. Ditson. "I think he's in the Coffee Shoppe," said the operator. "I'll try him there . . . Helen, is Porter Ditson there? I have a call for him."

Helen, presumably the Coffee Shoppe cashier, said: "He's here . . . Porter, it's for you."

Porter Ditson came to the telephone, and Elizabeth Appleton could tell that the switchboard operator was listening in.

"Hello," said Porter Ditson.

"This is a friend of Oswald Jacoby's," said Elizabeth Appleton.

"Who? Oh, I see. Yes, I recognize your voice."

"Why don't you drive out this way in about half an hour? Can you do that?"

"Of course."

"I'll be in my car. That's all I can say now." She hung up, and a half hour later she was in her car when he drove past her house. She started the car, overtook him, and he followed her for five miles before she stopped at a gas station, told the attendant to fill the tank, and asked if she could leave her car for about an hour. She then walked to Porter Ditson's car, where he had parked it a short distance beyond the gas station. She got in quickly and said: "Very smart, but let's get away from here. I told the man I'd leave my car there for an hour. How are you?"

"I'm fine."

"We won't be able to stop anywhere, but we can talk."

"Look in the glove compartment. There's a pair of sun glasses. Nobody will recognize you."

"Splendid. The man who thinks of everything."

"I got them for skiing."

"No, you got them because you knew I was going to need them. You had it all planned out."

"That's right. I had it all planned out. I wish I did have it all planned out. I still haven't even kissed you, and yet we're as close as if we were in bed together."

"I know. I feel so young and in love, I'm light-headed. Say you love me, Porter."

"I love you."

"That's our first kiss. Say it again."

"I love you."

"That's something else."

"Undressing you?"

"Yes, if you like. I was thinking I was already undressed, but your way is better. No, it isn't. I know you're excited, and I am too, and it's not going to do either of us any good today."

"The world is full of places to go to."

"Yes, but not full of excuses for going there."

"You can't make up an excuse to go to New York?"

"I've racked my brains. It isn't only John that we have to be careful of. It's everybody that knows you or knows me. And you know so damn many people in Spring Valley."

"If I telephone you in the next few days and tell you to meet me in a certain place, will you trust me? Will you just take for granted that I know it's safe, and go there?"

"I wish we could go there now. Yes, I'll trust you, unless I have a very good reason for not. It isn't that I wouldn't always trust you, but I might know some reason for not going there that you wouldn't know."

"This place is perfect. If it works out."

"Do you want to tell me what you have in mind?"

"All right. Evangeline's."

"You're the light-headed one. Evangeline isn't only the worst gossip in town. She's a snooping gossip. She tries to find out things about people that have never been talked about. People like me."

"That's why her house is so perfect. They're going

away next week. Florida, for two weeks. The house will be absolutely empty. Both servants are going away, too. My idea was that you would call Evangeline and volunteer to go in and have a look at the house to see if everything was okay. Pipes not frozen. Gas turned off, et cetera. And I could meet you."

"Oh, Porter, it's *such* a bad idea. In the first place, why would I suddenly volunteer to have a look at the house? That's the first question Evangeline would ask herself, and that's what makes it a bad idea. But I've been thinking, has Brice got someone living up at the camp?"

"A caretaker and his wife, and anyway it's forty miles away, of which ten miles are off the main road. Snow all winter. And that road is never cleared more than one car wide."

"No good . . . John is going up to Ithaca on the twenty-third and twenty-fourth of next month. A conference of history teachers. Can you wait that long? I'm not at all sure I can, but we'll have to."

"Where would we go then?"

"My house."

"What about the children?"

"After they were asleep."

"I still think Evangeline's house has the best possibilities. How would it be if I asked her to let me stay there while I had a painting job on my rooms at the hotel?"

"Everybody would know you were staying there, and the servants would be there. I couldn't go there at night, but you *could* come to my house at night. In fact you'd have to. On the twenty-third of next month you come to my house at eleven o'clock. The whole house will be dark, but I'll leave the kitchen door unlocked and I'll be waiting for you there, in the kitchen."

"All right. But I might as well tell you, I've just had a very devious idea. I'm going to work on it. In fact, I'll tell you what it is so that you can work on it too, in your own way."

"What is it?"

"Well, I keep going back to Evangeline, and I have a hunch. Do you like Evangeline?"

"Yes, and she likes me."

"I know she does. And she really hates John. She'll never forgive him for that lecture. I know. She never forgives anybody, and I've heard her when John's name comes up. Granted that she's the worst gossip in town, and a snooping gossip, in a strange way I would trust Evangeline. Do you see what I'm driving at?"

"Yes. But I don't want *anybody* to know about us."

"Neither do I, but the only two people in town that I'd trust are Evangeline, and Mary Leslie."

"Mary Leslie? Why have you any special reason to trust her?"

"I have no reason. It's the same reason that—if you were in some kind of trouble and there were a lot of people standing around, an accident, for instance. What would make you pick one person instead of any of the others? I've always felt that way about Mary, ever since she was a kid of sixteen."

"Why didn't you marry her?"

"Oh, no. I know a lot of people like Mary's family, but I wouldn't want to go there for Sunday dinner the rest of my life."

"You're as much of a snob as I am."

"Much more of a one than you are. I've lived here all my life, and I see people like Mary's father every day. But I'd never go to his house, and he'd never think of asking me. If Mary had children and I had children, they'd play together. And I go to Mary and Roy's house and have a perfectly pleasant time. But I'd have a terrible time at B. F. Phillips's house. On the other hand, I often have a beer with him at the Elks, and we get along fine. But I'll give you another illustration of snobbishness. B. F. Phillips and four friends of his have lunch at the Coffee Shoppe every day, and if I ever sat down with that group I'd be no more welcome than the guy that I buy papers from at the station. I consider myself an authority on the whole subject of snob-bishness, and I'm in favor of it."

"I guess I am, too, although I spend most of my life pretending that I'm not. Anyway, I'm glad you didn't have an affair with Mary Leslie. You didn't, did you?"

"No. I had an affair with Evangeline, though."

"*What?*"

"I certainly did."

"How could you? I don't believe you. I don't believe you for a minute."

"Well, I had sexual relations with her. I was thirteen and she was about seventeen or eighteen. When you were that age didn't nasty little boys make passes at you?"

"When I was younger than that my brother and friends of his used to try to lift up my skirt."

"That's what I did with Evangeline."

"But did she—cooperate?"

"Not exactly. She struggled, but she always let me get my hand on it. When I realize what a strong girl she was, I consider that cooperation, therefore I had sexual relations with her, and as much of an affair as I'd had up to that time."

"Where did this happen?"

"Oh, in the Framinghams' yard. Once at a party at our house, Brice's birthday party. In swimming up at the camp."

"I'm still shocked."

"Well, don't be. I've known very few girls that didn't have similar experiences, and very few boys. And the point of telling you now isn't to shock you, although I admit I said it the way I did to shock you."

"And you succeeded."

"The point is now that Evangeline, much as she dis-approves of the way I live, she doesn't dislike me. She was a very plain girl, and not many passes got made at her. I'm sure she and Brice were both virgins when they got married, and I'm sure she never told Brice about his naughty little brother. That's something Evangeline and I have kept secret, and now that we're both older it's rather nice to remember. No harm was done, and Evangeline was flattered. And I got a kick out of it. You know, for a boy of thirteen a fully developed girl of seventeen or eighteen is a grown woman. And she was."

"I begin to see what you have in mind."

"Of course you do. There's another thing. Evangeline is terribly impressed by you. Let's be frank about it. Your society background."

"Oh, I've always known that."

"As far as Evangeline is concerned, you and she are the *crème de la crème* of Spring Valley. It happens to be true, of course, when you come right down to it. And I know this, if Evangeline ever had the opportunity to have an affair with somebody and needed a friend, the only person she'd even consider would be you. In such matters you can do no wrong. In a lot of other matters, too. That time John attacked old Jap Framingham, for instance, Evangeline said in my presence that she would bet anything that you weren't in favor of John's New Deal line."

"I'm not, but I'd never say so."

"Evangeline knows that, and is very sympathetic."

"Do you want me to tell her that I'm having an affair with you?"

"I don't want you to rush home and call her up, but if you want to sound her out, you'll find her cooperative."

"She won't want us to use her house. That you can be sure of."

"Maybe not. But she'll cover up for you. You sound her out, and meanwhile I won't say anything to her."

"No, don't you say anything."

He lit a cigarette. "You don't smoke, do you?"

"No," she said. "Not any more."

"It's one of the little things I know about you. There are so many that I don't know."

"I know."

"And there's one big thing I do know."

"What?"

"That you have no intention of leaving John. That's a proposal, in a roundabout way."

"No, I won't leave John. What you and I have is ours. I love you, I want you. But I've always admired my father and mother for sticking it out, even though they hated each other. Actively hated each other. I don't hate John, and he at least thinks he loves me."

"Yes, I'm sure he does."

"I know now that I shouldn't have married him, but all the things that are wrong with our marriage are my fault. Some of the things that I don't like about John are my fault, too. Money is one of the troubles. He must know that even though we live modestly, we couldn't do some of the things we do if I didn't pay for them. That's bad, and I'm responsible for that. I took money from my mother while she was still living, and paid for things that we couldn't have afforded on John's salary."

"Then he's been kidding himself. That's not your fault."

"Pretty much my fault. He's weak, and I found it out a long time ago. He doesn't like to oppose me, and he knew that if he asked too many questions he'd have to oppose me."

"What if you told him you were in love with me?"

"I never would. At least not until he's done something so, uh, outstanding that I wouldn't destroy his masculine ego. I've learned that much about him, or about the masculine ego."

"Maybe you'd better not tell me."

"You haven't got it. Not a typical masculine ego. John when he was younger liked to show his muscles. I mean that literally. When we were first married he was always showing how strong he was."

"He was a damn good athlete."

"And he liked to show off how much he knew, too. But it was the same thing as showing his muscles. Now that he isn't a big football player he has to be the big man on the faculty. Two years ago, when his course was voted the one the students got the most out of, he said he hadn't been so pleased since he won his first letter *in high school*. Did you know his father?"

"Not very well."

"He's told me a lot about his father. Things that would be fascinating to somebody like Professor Hillenketter. John admired his father, but Professor Appleton must have been very cold."

"No, I don't think so. Aloof, reserved, but not cold."

"I see. The reason I wondered was that he never would praise John, whether it was for studies or athletics. All the compliments came from Mrs. Appleton. Professor Appleton seemed to think that if you did something well, that was satisfaction enough. For instance, when John made Phi Beta Kappa he asked his father for the ten dollars to buy a key. 'You can have mine. I never wear it,' the old man said. *And* didn't see why John would want to wear his own. 'We know you're a Phi Beta Kappa, but why do you want strangers to know it?'"

"So I imagine Mrs. Appleton gave him the money."

"No, John made money in college. He bought his own, but he thought his father could at least have bought that. Then the old man did give him ten dollars, but told him to buy something that wasn't for show."

"He wasn't an old man, you know. He was a queer duck, but he died quite young. He had cancer, and he got old-looking but he was much younger than you think."

"Well, of course I never saw him, and the picture they always used in the yearbook must have been taken in 1890. Anyway, John needed praise, compliments, and his father never gave them."

"He got plenty elsewhere."

"But not from his father, and that's why he needs more from outside sources. And also why he couldn't stand it if I destroyed his ego. He'd collapse like a toy balloon. He hasn't got what you have."

"What have I got, besides a strong urge to take you to Tahiti?"

"Dear. You have whatever it is, confidence, self-confidence, that makes you totally un-dependent on people praising you. You don't need applause. Far from it. You fly in the face of popular opinion. Oh, my. Listen to me. But it's true. You're sure enough of yourself to not do what everybody says you ought to do. Have a job. So forth."

"That's because Brice and I were raised by an uncle and aunt. I was thirteen when my father and mother died. They both died in the flu epidemic, and my uncle and aunt were so kind to the little orphan that I was hardly ever punished for anything. I grew up with practically no discipline. It's quite surprising that I turned out as well as I did."

"And so modest."

"I'm modest, but I'm not a damned fool. What I said still goes. It's surprising that I didn't get in more trouble, or that the insufferable little prick that I was didn't get his block knocked off. Brice was older, and he was unhappy after my father and mother died, but I got over it very quickly. And the way kids know things, I knew that people would take a lot more from me than from most kids. I was a little prick."

"Can't you think of something else to call yourself? We have to be getting back. I have to get my car at the gas station, and then go back and stop for the children at school."

"All right," he said. "Are the children the real reason why you won't leave John?"

"They're part of it, but they're young enough now, right now, so that they're closer to me than they are to John. They'd get used to different conditions. But no, John is the one I can't destroy, and that's what it would be now. Destruction. Losing the children would be part of the destruction, but *everything* would be part of it. Me. The children. The house. The scandal. The public disgrace of showing him up. He might even kill himself."

"Yes, if you're right about everything else, he might,"

said Porter Ditson. "I could very easily understand that. If you took everything away from him, he wouldn't have anything left, would he? You see what I mean."

"If he had only himself. Yes. Some day he'll have, or do, something, I hope. Then I can leave him, or I can tell him that I love you. But not till then. Until then I'll be your mistress, and love you as much as I do now. Which is more than I ever loved him. Stop the car."

He did so and she kissed him.

"That's all love," she said. "I want you to know that, that I love you and want you terribly. Because you don't know how difficult it's going to be. You haven't thought about that, but I have. And it may get to be more difficult for you than for me. I don't envy you your freedom."

"I was just thinking about that."

"I can keep busy."

"I know. Three people need you."

"And you need me and I won't always be there. And I need you, but that won't come first. I can write to you, but you can't write to me. You can always talk to me, though. No, I guess not. Not every day. But some days. You can telephone me in the mornings, between nine-thirty and eleven-thirty. Maybe twice a week? Mondays and Thursdays?"

"Yes, from the phone booth at the station."

"And there'll be the twenty-third and the twenty-fourth of next month, and every time after that that we possibly can. We need a friend, but I don't think it's Evangeline and I know it isn't Mary Leslie."

For nearly a full month her affair with Porter Ditson was kept alive by the excitement of anticipation, with little notes to him, brief telephone calls from him, two evenings of bridge when she could see him in the watchful presence of two other people. She found that she could take pleasure in John's visits to her bed, in her visits to John's bed. She was discovering that during the more than ten years of their marriage she had unknowingly acquired a habit of periodic sexual need in which her husband had been the partner. But because he had been the only partner did not mean that he was the indispensable partner. In this new discovery she realized that John himself was a habit, and that for an undeterminable length of time she had most enjoyed the sexual relation with him when personal romance had been absent from their love-making. The element of love had, for this undeterminable length of time, been a disturbing factor, and she realized retroactively that love in the form of passion had vanished; that John's occasional efforts to speak of love and to be unusually tender had actually vexed her, for the reason that—she now knew—she was out of love with him. She loved him as a figure in her daily life, as the formal husband and formal father of their children, but she did not love him when he made tender love. She liked him when he was the instrument of her pleasure. He was a man whom she took between her legs and who could produce in her the fullest excitement and a glowing relaxation that she had never known with anyone else. But personal desire uniquely of him no longer existed.

The anticipation of love-making with Porter Ditson was already a part of an adventure. Their one kiss had not been part of the adventure. The adventure would begin on the twenty-third of the month, and every bit of it would be new and adventurous. What would he like? What would he want? How would he surprise her? She could not recall asking herself such questions in the beginning of her life with John. The mystery itself and the mysteries themselves had all been one when she married John, an altogether thing that was an experience of life that she did not consider in its details. The reason was her ignorance of herself in circumstances of such intimacy, with no precedent or recollection to go by. But now she knew a great deal about herself and, through the years with John, about men. She had learned about the functioning of a man. She had read a great deal in sexual case histories, and what she had not understood she had asked John to explain to her. Men thus became for her creatures of varying attractiveness who resembled or differed from the only partner she had had in the practice of sexual pleasure. Until, that is, she fascinated herself with her curiosity about Porter Ditson, which had steadily become so obsessive that in comparing it with her life with John she recognized it as love. The neat small things that she approved of in Porter Ditson—his looks, his manners, his clothes, his conversation—had always been part of him, but accidentally she had not been aware of them until accidentally she had been made aware of them, at a time in her life when her marriage was stolid. She now realized, too, that only the renewals of sexual pleasure had enabled her to endure the tedium of housework, attending to the children, the fact of being thirty years old, and the restricting existence of life with John Appleton. The moment had come for something bright and new, and she was happy that it was Porter Ditson. On the afternoon of the twenty-third she packed John Appleton's bag and waved to him as he drove away. When the children had been put to bed she took a long, warm bath, put on her best negligee, and waited in the darkened kitchen.

"Take my hand," she said. "We go down this hall, turn right and up the stairs. There are thirteen steps. Very lucky. Then we go left through the guest-room, then the bathroom, then my room."

"Can't we have any light?"

"In the bathroom, but nowhere else."

"I want to kiss you here."

"All right, but only for a minute. Give me your hat and coat. I'll put them here on the kitchen chair. My eyes are used to the dark. I've been sitting here." She embraced him. "Now let's go."

She led him to her bedroom. "I'll put on the bathroom light and leave the door open an inch or two so you can see." She did so, then sat in bed in her negligee while he undressed. He sat beside her on the edge of the bed. "Do I have to take this off?" he said, touching her negligee.

"There's nothing to it," she said, and opened it.

"I thought you had a nightgown underneath it."

"No. Don't let's talk any more."

"No," he said.

They were quick and unfamiliar with each other, but

she was more than ready when he entered her. "Hurry," she said, and hurried him. "Oh, lovely," she said. "My darling."

He lay with his head on her chest and she put her hand on his head and smoothed his hair. He kissed her.

"Nobody can ever say I haven't kissed you three times," he said.

"No."

"Now we're lovers."

"My life and your life," she said. "And nothing can ever change that. We can lie about it, and we can both wish we hadn't ever done this, but we can't change it, can we?"

"We won't want to. We may have to lie about it."

"The way I feel now, I don't think I could lie about it," she said. "I don't want to deny it. Was it good for you?"

"Wonderful."

"I'm so glad. I'm so glad for myself, too. You were just right for me."

"Was I?"

"Oh, yes. To think we've been in this same little town all these years. But I don't know why I say that. I've lost all sense of time. And people. And the world."

"It's wonderfully quiet. Listen. A bus. I can hear a bus."

"Do you want to sleep?"

"No, I'm not a bit sleepy," he said. "I want to examine you."

"What do you mean? What for?"

"Admiringly. I was too excited to before."

"All right."

He looked at her and caressed her. "I knew all this, but seeing's believing."

"How did you know?"

"These couldn't be anything but real."

"You like them, do you?"

"I love them, but I would anyway. But they're remarkable for somebody that's had two children, and played a lot of tennis."

"They were a lot smaller when I was playing tennis."

(*161*)

"They're just right, now."

"I'm glad you think so."

"How do you look standing up?"

"Do you want me to stand up? Suddenly I'm embarrassed. Don't make me stand up. I will if you want me to. I'll do anything you want me to."

"How do you know that?"

"Because I don't think there's anything you'd want me to do that I wouldn't love to do. I'm in love with you. You're everything I'd hoped you'd be."

"You are, too, Elizabeth."

"Will you come back tomorrow night?"

"Of course I will, if you let me. But is this the gentle nudge?"

"Yes. Tonight is the beginning. We had to have this beginning. But now we're lovers, and I'm beginning to get just a little nervous. Not much, just a little."

"All right."

"I want to talk to you while you're getting dressed. I've been thinking."

"What?" he said.

"I've almost changed my mind about Evangeline."

"Have you sounded her out?"

"No, but I've made a point of running into her since she got back from Florida. And this is what I've almost decided. I think I'll ask her to go to Pittsburgh with me."

"I have something to tell *you*. I had dinner there last week. Brice had some work to do, and Evangeline and I were alone for a while. She said I've changed lately, and was it on account of a girl, and I said yes. Naturally the gossip in her wanted to know who, but I wouldn't tell her. 'Then obviously she's married,' she said. 'Are you having an affair?' And I said no, but I was in love. She thought a minute and then she began listing names. Mary Leslie. A girl in Pittsburgh that I actually did have an affair with about five years ago. Stella Hopkins, Frank's wife. And then you. 'Don't tell me those bridge games are bearing fruit,' she said. I said I wouldn't say yes or no about anybody. 'Then I'm sure it's Elizabeth. Well good for her,' she said. Then she said, 'If I can help, you can trust me, but she's not going to marry you.' "

"That's amazing. But it explains why she's been so—I don't exactly know how to put it. Solicitous. Then I will ask her to go to Pittsburgh with me, and if she starts trying to pump me, I'll admit it. But I won't tell her about tonight."

"No, let her think she engineered the whole thing. But she'll be a good friend. She's the one we need. I know her. She won't even tell Brice."

"Good God, I hope not," said Elizabeth Appleton. "I can just see your brother trying to keep that secret. John would take one look at him and say, 'What the hell's the matter with Brice Ditson?' "

"She won't tell him. I've had to borrow money from Evangeline on several occasions, and she's never told him, not even when I paid it back."

Elizabeth stood up. "Your mistress," she said.

"You make me want to stay."

"I want to be sure you come back tomorrow." She put on her negligee.

"You can rest assured."

"I have to guide you down the stairs."

"Thirteen steps," he said.

"You remember."

"I'll remember everything."

"So will I. Maybe tomorrow night you can stay longer, but you understand about tonight. I wanted to be in bed with you and be your mistress, and now I am. But I don't think I'd be very good if you stayed. I know I wouldn't. To-morrow, other nights. And maybe a whole day and night to-gether in Pittsburgh. Maybe sometime a week, I don't know how, or where. Are you ready?"

"Let me kiss you," he said.

He took her in his arms and opened her negligee.

"You see I'm willing," she said. "You have to decide."

"I know. It isn't fair," he said. "Is it?"

"If you don't let me go, in a second it's going to be too late. Oh, I want you so."

He moved away from her. "I'll go," he said. "Lead me."

"I love you."

"I love you, Elizabeth."

"Come on," she said, and took his hand in hers. They went to the kitchen and he kissed her again and left. She locked the door and watched him until he was lost to her in the dark of the Bucknell Street trees. Then she went to her room and did the practical things that had to be done by a woman who had a part-time maid coming in the next day.

It was a two-hour trip to Pittsburgh in Evangeline's car. The car was a black Buick limousine, one of three chauffeur-driven automobiles in Spring Valley, and a bit of ostentation that Evangeline forgave herself because she did not drive well and because she was, after all, a Framingham and that much was owed to the position her father had occupied in the community. She could have had a Rolls, she could have had a Cadillac, but as Brice shrewdly pointed out, the difference in price between the Buick and a Cadillac in effect gave them the chauffeur's services without cost for a year. No one in Spring Valley had ever owned a Rolls, and the Brice Ditsons did not go to the big cities often enough to make that much of an assertion worth while. (If anyone else in Spring Valley had bought a Rolls, everyone in Spring Valley would still know that the Brice Ditsons could afford two of them.)

It was a bit of old times for Elizabeth, riding in a limousine, her legs covered by a grey laprobe that had the monogram EFD in the center, the car moving at the steady pace that a well-trained chauffeur maintains, the chauffeur knowing precisely what was expected of him so that no communication between him and his mistress was necessary from the moment they left Elizabeth Appleton's house to their arrival at the hotel in Pittsburgh.

"Have a Life Saver," said Evangeline, as they got under

way. "Peppermint. I've given up smoking again. You never smoke, do you?"

"No, I never have, really. When I was trying to be a tennis player I was told that smoking would hurt my wind. Then when I married John he used to light cigarettes for me and hand them to me, but I never inhaled, and after a while I stopped entirely. I guess he stopped lighting them for me," she said, smiling.

"They do stop doing those little things," said Evangeline. "But I suppose they do other things that make up for it. Although I must say for Brice, he hasn't let being married cause him to neglect his manners. Both those boys, Brice *and* Porter, had good manners instilled in them at an early age. Although Porter was quite a wild one when he was younger. But they've always had nice manners, both Ditson boys."

"Yes, and it's important, I don't care what you say. I hope Peter learns, although some of those children at Model School are growing up like young hyenas. Progressive education."

"Yes, and why on earth they call it progressive is beyond me. What's that word that's almost vandalism but not quite. Vantastic. Vana-something. Anavastic. *Atavistic!*"

"Atavistic, that's right. Going back to the ape."

"Yes, reverting to type. Schools nowadays. Although I suppose I shouldn't criticize education, not to the wife of an educator."

"Oh, I criticize it myself. Not all the time, but when it gets too much for me."

"Peter is what? Six?"

"Almost seven."

"Are you going to send him away to prep school?"

"I certainly am. My father left money for his education but I would anyway."

"Then what? Isn't John going to want him to be the third generation Appleton at Spring Valley?"

"That's a long way off. And of course actually he'd only be the second generation. John's father went to Harvard.

And so did John, for graduate work. It works both ways, I guess. Third generation Harvard or third generation Spring Valley. No, I guess it would be much more than third generation Harvard. A long line of Appletons went to Harvard."

"What do you really think of Spring Valley nowadays?"

"The college?"

"Yes."

"Well, of course I never knew it when it was supposed to be—when it had a different kind of reputation. To tell you the truth, I'd never heard of it at all before I met John. But in those days I didn't even know where Dartmouth was. I've learned a lot since then, at least about colleges, and teachers."

"I'm glad my father isn't alive to see what they're doing to Spring Valley."

"Who?"

"Well, frankly, the faculty. They don't seem to feel that they owe a thing to the people that *made* Spring Valley. Spring Valley wasn't meant to be another Oberlin, or that other place, Antioch. But that's the kind of place the faculty want it to be, and that's what it's becoming. I'm not going to leave any money to Spring Valley. Why should I? Men like my father poured money into Spring Valley and asked nothing in return but a college that would compare favorably with Hamilton and Haverford and Kenyon. And that's what it was. The records show it. It had a reputation as a rich man's college, but what of it? It had a much higher standing when it was a rich man's college than now. And I've never yet heard anybody complain about Harvard because it was a rich man's college. Or Yale. Or Princeton. A degree from Spring Valley used to mean something, rich man's college or not. The entrance requirements were tougher, and those so-called rich boys didn't last long if they didn't study. Men like your father-in-law didn't care whether a boy was rich or poor. If a boy didn't earn a passing grade, he didn't get it."

"I don't think John passes students that should flunk."

"Perhaps not. But why are there only eight—I think

it's eight, maybe nine, but not ten—eight or nine sons and daughters of alumni in this year's freshman class?"

"I don't know. I didn't know there were that few."

"*I* know why. The trustees sent out a questionnaire to alumni of about twenty-five years ago. They got replies from about fifty percent. It was a long questionnaire, but a pretty good one. One question had to do with why alumni hadn't or weren't going to send their children to Spring Valley. Had the college deteriorated, and if so why? Social standing? Educational standing? Limited facilities? Geographical location? Faculty standing? Then there was a space to answer in detail. The amazing thing was how many people marked both social *and* educational standing, and they blamed two things. Coeducation, and too many New Dealers on the faculty. Haven't you seen one of those questionnaires? Or the report on it? It was confidential, but I'm sure John must have seen it."

"He said something about it, but I never saw the report."

"We heard that the faculty wanted to send out a questionnaire of their own, to alumni of the past five years, but I haven't heard any more about that."

"They talked about it, but John was one of those that advised against it."

"Why?"

"He said that five years was too soon for them to have a perspective."

"Oh, I don't agree with him. I wish they *had* sent it out. They might find out that Spring Valley is at an all-time low, in social and educational standing. And from young men and women that were learning it the hard way, looking for jobs. Oh, well, it isn't really our problem, is it?"

"It is mine, as the wife of a professor."

"But it isn't a problem you can do anything about. I wouldn't like to try to change John's mind, once it's made up."

"I don't often try, and never about things that have to do with his work."

"Naturally I'm thinking about that famous lecture, when he said those awful things about my father. He didn't want to make a retraction, and when he did it was so carefully worded that no one reading it would think he was taking anything back. But I didn't pursue the point. I lost my temper once, and as Brice said, 'If you want to keep up your friendship with Elizabeth, you'll drop the whole matter.'"

"John was genuinely sorry about that. He said to me, if he apologized too extravagantly, it would be a defeat for academic freedom."

"Well, of course, if academic freedom means the right to say any damn thing whether it's true or not. Oh, let's forget it and enjoy ourselves. You were on the spot, as they say, between being John's wife and one of my best friends. You are, you know. I never feel, with you, that you're being nice to me because my father was J. W. Framingham. And yet I'm always conscious of that in Spring Valley. When I was a girl and starting to go to parties I always knew that I was a duty dance. I wasn't pretty and I wasn't very good at sports, and you're both, so you don't know what it means to come home from a dance and cry yourself to sleep. The thing that made me fall in love with Brice was one night he said to me, 'Vangie, you're almost as homely as I am, and we might as well make the best of it.' I was so shocked I didn't know what to do, but then I looked at that sad little smile and suddenly I realized that this was someone I could love. My whole life changed in just that minute. We know what we are, Brice and I."

"You're two very sweet people," said Elizabeth Appleton.

"We're two very lucky people, and I'm the luckier of the two, because it took a very honest boy to say that to me. I really and truly hate to think what would have become of me if it hadn't been for Brice Ditson. When Brice asked my father for his consent to our marriage, Father said: 'Where do you intend to live?' and Brice said, 'Right here in Spring Valley.' And Father said: 'That's all I wanted to know. My bless-

ings on both of you.' My father was always afraid that someone would marry me for my money and take me off to New
York and Palm Beach and that life. And I'd have gone, too.
But this is my home, with all its faults, and it's Brice's home.
And even Porter's. You'll never hear Porter say so, but he
loves Spring Valley." Evangeline turned to look at Elizabeth
and their eyes met, and Elizabeth quickly faced forward.

"Are you the girl?" said Evangeline. "You are, aren't
you? You don't have to tell me."

Elizabeth nodded. "Yes."

"I'm glad it's you. The change that's come over Porter,
it couldn't be an ordinary girl, and when he admitted that
he was in love but wouldn't tell me who, I narrowed it down
to about three, and then I eliminated the others. Is there
anything I can do, can I help you?"

"I don't know. It's very recent."

"You're happy, I hope. I know the obvious difficulties,
but one of the reasons I guessed you was because I haven't
liked the way you've been looking lately. Having no children of my own, I'm a sort of self-appointed mother hen to
a lot of my friends. Brice says I overdo it. But for about a year
you've just been going through the motions, and if it hadn't
been Porter it was going to be somebody. And I'm glad it's
Porter. In the family."

"But please don't tell Brice," said Elizabeth. "Not that
there's very much to tell."

"Maybe not yet, although I doubt that, Elizabeth. Two
such attractive people, sex is bound to happen. *And should!*
What are people attractive for, anyway? But I won't tell
Brice. You could trust him, but I guess you just don't want
people to know. It ends with me, Elizabeth."

"Thank you, Evangeline."

"Thank *you* for taking me into your confidence. It's a
great compliment, and a kind that I appreciate." Evangeline
Ditson was silent for a moment, her jaw set, sitting erect,
looking to right and left as the car passed through a town.
The only thing missing was the royal wave, although by this

time the car was out of the Framingham domain. Suddenly Evangeline leaned forward and lowered the glass partition. "Norman, have you any cigarettes?"

"Yes ma'am." He handed back a pack of Camels. She took one and returned the pack, and raised the partition. She lit the cigarette from the electric lighter at her side.

"Have to have a cigarette for this," said Evangeline. "You know there's another man in this town that's in love with you."

"No, I don't know."

"No, I don't think you have any idea, but he is. And he has the opportunities—it's Harry Jeffries."

"Good Lord." Instinctively she smoothed out the lap-robe, and hoped that Evangeline would not notice, but Evangeline noticed.

"That's what I meant by the opportunities," she said.

"I'll never go to him again," said Elizabeth.

"Why not? If he's behaved himself so far, it wouldn't be fair to change doctors now, and anyway, forewarned is forearmed."

"I know, but considering what he has to do, I'd be too self-conscious. Why are you telling me now, Evangeline?"

"Because I particularly hope you don't change doctors now. I had to tell you, because it's my duty as a friend. This is the mother hen talking. Elizabeth, you're about to embark on a love affair, probably your first if I'm any judge."

"It's my first," said Elizabeth.

"I know you'll be careful—discreet is the word in such cases. But no matter how discreet you are, if there's somebody looking for a slip, somebody suspicious, you may betray yourself in some small thing. Frances Jeffries is looking for a slip."

"Surely not looking at me."

"At every woman in Spring Valley, all Harry's patients, nurses, every person who wears skirts. She doesn't suspect you, Elizabeth Appleton. That's quite true, but you may do something, I don't know what, but something, that would be connected with you and Porter. And Frances, if she found out about it, might connect it with you and Harry. Do you see what I mean?"

"I guess I do. If I went away and Harry Jeffries went away at the same time."

"That's a good example. Yes. And if you stopped being a patient of Harry's, that would make her suspicious. I know, because that very thing happened once. Frances found out about one of Harry's girl friends because the girl friend made such a big point of not seeing Harry at all, out in the open. Frances is coo-coo, but she's smart, crafty. And it isn't love for Harry. It's insane hatred. So you go on just the way you always have, being a patient of Harry's, but now you know he's in love with you, be extra careful, or you'll get blamed for an affair with the wrong man."

"Naturally you're sure about Harry. That he thinks he's in love with me."

"Oh, I'm sure."

"He told you?"

"No. That isn't the kind of thing Harry would ever tell me. Harry spends a lot of time trying to convince me that he's the soul of uprightness. There are a lot of things Harry has his mind set on, things like getting on the bank board and the alumni trustees. He'll get there, but they may take some time. Harry's a Presbyterian now. Used to be a Baptist, and Frances used to be a Lutheran. Both Presbyterians now. And he's hinted to Brice that he'd like to get in the Duquesne Club—where he hasn't a chance. Oh, Harry's longing for respectability, and in the course of time he'll get some of the things he wants. The next vacancy on the bank board, and in four or five years, the college trustees. It isn't really philandering that Harry does. Actually there isn't much philandering in Spring Valley, compared to some places. But everybody's nervous about Frances. Harry's a man, and he has to have somebody he can sleep with, but it's as though people were waiting to see what happens when Frances explodes. As a matter of fact he was protected by Brice and some others during that episode with the woman doctor. They didn't want to have a big blow-up at the hospital, and they eased her out of there before Frances started shooting."

"Shooting?"

"Maybe not shooting, but I think she's capable of it."

"I don't want to go near Harry Jeffries."

"Forewarned is forearmed."

"You still haven't told me why you think he's in love with me. He's never given me any inkling of it."

"I saw him dancing with you at Mary Leslie's party, then somebody cut in and he went over to the stag line and I kept watching him. His expression was like a schoolboy in love. Not lecherous. Exalted. I've never seen him look that way, and I've known Harry all my life. You were different that night, too. Maybe that had something to do with it. Were you nicer to him that night?"

"I was nice to everybody, I was having such a good time. Except to Mr. John Appleton."

"That didn't escape me, either. In my little notebook, if I kept one, I'd put that down as the date when you began to be in love with Porter."

"No. I think more accurately that was the night I wasn't in love with anybody. I probably don't know much about love, but I think that there's a wonderful time when one love is finished and another hasn't started and a woman is momentarily free . . . You may not agree with that."

"I don't believe I do. I'm too dependent on Brice to even think about not being in love with him. And yet I can see how that would happen with you. You never *were* dependent on John."

"At first I was, then conditions were reversed and he became dependent on me. Too much so, and didn't dare admit it to himself. The more dependent he got, the more dominating he tried to be. Not cruel, and not bossy, but so damned superior. When he wasn't superior."

"This is what I call a good time."

"A good time to what?"

"Not a good time to do something. A good time I'm having. I love to know everything about my friends. What makes them tick. And just plain gossip. Brice says I'm a female Walter Winchell, but he's wrong. I don't follow Walter Winchell or Drew Pearson. I don't know the people they write about, and I couldn't care less. But I want to know everything about my friends."

"Is there anything I've left out?" said Elizabeth, with a smile.

"There is, and always will be."

"There has to be," said Elizabeth.

"Of course," said Evangeline. "But it would be the easiest thing in the world for you to telephone Porter when we get to Pittsburgh. We'll be there in time for lunch, and I hope you're having it with me, but I could find plenty to do all afternoon. By myself. I wouldn't even have to see Porter, and I wouldn't have to see him tomorrow afternoon either."

Elizabeth knew that a failure to take advantage of Evangeline's offer would imply a lack of confidence in her. She therefore telephoned Porter Ditson, and for the two afternoons in Pittsburgh she had the suite to herself—with her lover. On the return trip to Spring Valley Evangeline said: "Now I'm in this almost as deeply as you are."

"Not *quite*."

"Very nearly. Brice would disapprove of what I've done, and heaven knows John Appleton would."

"If you look at it that way," said Elizabeth.

"There isn't any other way *to* look at it, is there?"

"Porter and I don't look at it that way, Evangeline. We consider it a great act of kindness, and you're never going to be implicated."

"I've always had a soft spot for Porter. I really think of him as my kid brother, slightly crazy but terribly charming, the way crazy people are apt to be. That isn't the way you think of him, but it's the way I do. And as far as you're concerned, when we get home people are going to ask you if you spent all your time in the beauty parlor. What love does for a woman—I must say."

"Yes."

"Why is it a fair-haired blue-eyed girl can look so innocent? You do, you know, even to me, in spite of my knowing that you're a femme fatale. That's admiration, by the way, not disapproval."

"You had me frightened. I thought you'd suddenly regretted being a conspirator."

"Not a bit. And as I said before, I'm in it as deeply as you are. An instigator. I think I would have made a good hostess in the days when women had salons. You know. Ambassadors coming to tea and meeting their lovely ladies. Dolley Madison. Can't you just see me?"

"I can, very easily," said Elizabeth.

"Well, I'm enjoying my first experience so much, who knows? Can you imagine a salon in Spring Valley? Can't you just see Harry Jeffries meeting Mary Leslie?"

"Harry Jeffries and Mary Leslie?"

"Oh, there's nothing there. Little Mary Phillips Leslie has a good thing and she knows it, and luckily she happens to be crazy about my Cousin Roy. Why, I don't know."

"I just realized that only ten years ago I was in much the same position as Mary Leslie. What happens, I wonder?"

"There are as many answers to that as there are people. If you want to know what I think, it's the rules men and the church make for women regarding sex. They try to insist on women being monogamous, and we're not. And I don't really mean monogamous, because that means marriage. I'm in favor of monogamy. But I honestly don't think a woman can restrict her entire sex life to one man. I do, but other men aren't interested in me. But tell me this, Elizabeth—that is, if you feel like telling me. Did you ever find that you were looking at a man and just wishing you could go straight to bed with him, no marriage, no ties, no love. Just plain, unadulterated sex."

"Yes. When I caught myself I'd deny it to myself, but it certainly happened more than once. Especially when I was first married."

"When you were first married?"

"Yes. And in love with John. On our wedding trip. Suddenly there was so much sex in my life, after years of practically none at all, that every time I saw a man in a bathing suit—oh, dear."

"Go on."

"Well, we spent a couple of weeks on the French Riviera, and those men rolled their trunks down, and up, so that they all but showed everything. It was like suddenly being alone in a men's gymnasium. And it wasn't only on the beach. A man dancing the tango, I'd actually become jealous of the girl he was dancing with. I was glad when we got home and started a normal life."

"You got over it?"

"Not completely. But at least John started to work, and I was busy with our apartment in Cambridge, and I had other things on my mind besides sex. I think honeymoons are awful. A girl that's well brought up is supposed to be protected from sex, but then as soon as the wedding is over she's suddenly dropped into an atmosphere that's like a French whorehouse."

"Have you ever been to one?"

"We almost went to a peep-show in Paris, but at the last minute I backed out. I'm glad I did. I don't know what would have happened, that on top of everything else. I could go to one now and think nothing of it. Or at least it wouldn't upset me."

"We went, Brice and I. In Berlin, about ten years ago. I guess it wasn't much, by their standards. A man and two women, and two men and one woman. And a girl dressed as a man with another girl. Except for the girl dressed as a man, all the women were obviously acting. They were bored. I said that to Brice and do you know what he said?"

"What?"

"He said the men were bored, too. Bored stiff."

Elizabeth laughed. "Brice said that?"

"My Brice, believe it or not. He has a very dry sense of humor."

"Well, you'd never see anything like that in Spring Valley."

(175)

"Oh, don't fool yourself. One of the fire companies had a stag smoker about two years ago and the police raided it. They arrested four women from out-of-town. It was hushed up in the papers, but it was generally known."

"I never heard a word about it."

"They were all Town men. No students."

"Didn't they arrest the men?"

"They never do. They were going to arrest the man from out-of-town that brought the women, but he climbed out a back window and got away."

"Gallant gentleman," said Elizabeth. "Was Porter there?"

"You ask him. I'm glad you asked me, though."

"Why?"

"Because you sounded like a wife, and that means you really are in love with him."

"Oh, I'm afraid there's no doubt about that."

"Don't be afraid," said Evangeline.

VI

John Appleton looked out the window. "This place reminds me of home," he said.

"Where is home?" said the girl.

"Didn't I tell you? Spring Valley, Pennsylvania. I thought I told you."

"Spring Valley? Pennsylvania? It sounds pretty corny to me. Spring Valley. You have the nerve to compare San Francisco with a place called Spring Valley? San Francisco is one of the most glamorous if not *the* most glamorous city in the whole United States."

"Come here a minute," said John Appleton.

"What for?"

"I want to show you something."

The girl got up, carrying her highball, and stood beside John Appleton. "All right, what do you want to show me?"

"Look out the window," said John Appleton. "Tell me what you see."

"I see a couple of houses."

"What else?"

"Some cars. What am I supposed to see?"

"A couple of houses and some cars, on a steep hill. I might just as well be looking at Fourth Street, Spring Valley, Pennsylvania."

"Well, if you'll put on your coat and fix your tie we can go up to the Mark and it won't remind you of Spring Valley."

"I have to wait here for a phone call."

"Well, then don't complain."

"I wasn't complaining. I just pointed out an incontrovertible fact. That from this window San Francisco might as well be Spring Valley."

"Incontrovertible," said the girl. "Say, what do you do in civilian life?"

"Me? What do I do? I'm a hypnotist."

"Says you. You no more look like a hypnotist than Orson Welles."

"Orson Welles looks like a hypnotist."

"Maybe he does, but you don't look like Orson Welles. My point is that you don't look a bit like Orson Welles. What ever gave you that idea?"

"What do you do in civilian life?"

"I'm *in* civilian life," said the girl.

"All right. What do you do?"

"I'm a receptionist. I told you that."

"Where do you receive?"

"Is that supposed to be a crack?"

"It wasn't meant to be. I just wanted to know where you work."

"Rainsley and Wood, members of the Stock Exchange, Board of Trade, and the Los Angeles Stock Exchange."

"What do you do there?"

"I'm a re*cep*tionist, silly."

"I know, but what does that consist of? Do you have to run a switchboard?"

"Certainly not. I should say not. For your information,

Lieutenant Whatever Your Name Is, Rainsley and Wood have eight switchboard operators in two shifts. One of the oldest firms in San Francisco."

"What does your husband do?"

"My husband? He's a war correspondent for the Associated Press."

"Oh, where is he?"

"Why should I tell *you?*"

"Don't, if you don't want to."

"He's in England, the son of a bitch."

"Why is he a son of a bitch?"

"Because I know what that son of a bitch is doing in England. He's screwing every English dame that he can get his hands on."

"Don't believe everything you hear."

"I didn't hear it, I just know it."

"Then you don't know it, you're just guessing."

"Don't you tell me about that son of a bitch. I know all about him. You and I have another drink coming."

"All right." John Appleton poured bourbon in their glasses.

"Have you got any more cigarettes?"

"Sure."

"I smoked all mine. Are you sure you have plenty?"

"Sure. You keep this pack. I have some more in my bag."

"My boss gets a carton a week and he doesn't smoke, so he gives them to me. I have the nicest boss in the world, bar none."

"I know. He introduced me to you."

"That's right, he did. Where did you know him?"

"I didn't. We're both Betas and I had a letter of introduction to him."

"My husband was an A.T.O. at U.C.L.A. Before I met him I used to go out with a Beta. He's the one I should have married. When are you shipping out, do you know?"

"You know I couldn't tell you that."

"I don't want to know exactly, but just give me a rough idea. A week? Two weeks?"

"Around there somewhere."

"Do you mind if I ask you something awful?"

"Go ahead."

"Did you screw me?"

"Yes."

She nodded. "I wasn't sure. That's been bothering me. I kept looking at you and trying to get up the nerve to ask you if you did. You did, huh?"

"Yes."

"When?"

"A little while ago. About an hour or so ago."

"Thank you for telling me. I was pretty sure, but I wasn't positive. With all my clothes on?"

"That's the way you wanted it."

"I don't usually. I wonder why I did that."

"It was the only way you would."

"I've got nothing to be ashamed of, I wonder why I wouldn't take my clothes off. *You* don't like it that way, do you?"

"That's not the way I prefer it."

"Neither do I. I must have been looping."

"You had a lot of Martinis."

"Where? We must have gone to Angelo's. That's right, we did. We went to Angelo's. I don't think I ate any lunch, did I?"

"All you ate was a bread stick. Don't you remember any of that?"

"No, should I?"

"That's what got us together. You pretended the bread stick was something else."

She nodded. "It does remind me. Then I came here and went to bed with you and then what?"

"You went to sleep."

"You mean I passed out is what you really mean. Don't be so damn polite."

"All right, you passed out. Then we had the coffee."

"Yes, I can see the coffee. It's coming back to me. John. Your name is John."

"John Appleton."

"You know, you're pretty nice, and I don't only mean your looks. I don't give a damn about a man's looks."

"Thank you, you're not bad yourself, Emily."

"Oh, you know my name, huh?"

"Sure."

"What else do you know about me?"

"Well, I'd like to know more."

"You will. What do you say we just take everything off and stop this silly chatter?"

"I'm for that."

She watched him as she undressed. "You know, you've got a terrific build."

"So have you. Terrific."

"Come here. I'll bet you were an athlete."

"I was."

"Are you married?"

"Yes."

"Forget it, so am I. Oh, honey, you are really something. You and I have been wasting a lot of time, haven't we? You just lie here and be comfortable, and I will really make you know it, huh?"

"You do that."

"There's nothing I like better. My, what a boy."

It was a week before he was given his travel orders and he was with her every night. As a city San Francisco had no meaning; it was a state of mind and body that was part of the Navy, of the Navy in the Pacific Ocean, of time immeasurable and out of his control. The girl Emily was twenty-six years old, who in the week he spent with her never finished a meal, who drank anything that was available in the 12th Naval District, and gave him a bottle of bourbon wrapped in a brassière on their last night together. As gunnery officer on a reefer he was able to see her half a dozen times in the last two years of the war, but when he telephoned her in July 1945 the telephone operator at Rainsley & Wood told him that Emily had resigned her job and had joined her husband in New York City. Through the influence of the Brice

Ditsons, Elizabeth Appleton was able to join her husband in San Francisco.

For them both it was to be a new start. They had last been together in '43 in New York City. John Appleton, lieutenant USNR, thirty-five years old, Bachelor of Arts, Master of Arts, full professor, former athlete, excellent physical specimen, married to a woman of independent means, father of two children, respected by neighbors and associates, well adjusted psychologically, loyalty to his country unquestioned, eager to do his part to defeat the Axis powers, and with a good record at gunnery school, spent six months in and around New York while the Bureau of Personnel tried to make up its bureaucratic mind whether to use him in Bu-Pers, to place him in the Office of Naval Intelligence, to assign him to a coaching staff at one of the Pre-Flight football installations, to put him through an instruction course and make him an instructor, to release him to OSS, or to let him have a berth as Guns in a ship. For nearly six months he waited, and on two occasions Elizabeth went to New York in the belief that he was to ship out, only to have his orders changed both times. "What in the name of God are they fiddling around for?" he said. "I don't know whether I'm going to be in a gun tub or teaching officers' kiddies their ABC's. I'm getting so I don't care, either, just as long as they make up their minds." It was a rasping experience for him and for her. There was an approximation of the old love when she made the first trip to see him off; she could not simulate it the second time, although she tried. The third time he was given his orders he telephoned her. "I think this is it," he said.

"Then I'll leave this afternoon."

"No. I don't want you to. Let's remember not the last time but the time before."

"But I want to come."

"All right. God knows I want you to, but don't think of it as a farewell. Just come and we can at least sleep together."

In that frame of mind she went to New York. They had dinner, saw Ethel Merman in a not very good show, and walked crosstown to their hotel. They undressed and went to bed and talked, as they would and often had at home; and then they made love precisely, bringing each other to their recognizable signs of advanced preliminaries, to the ultimate closeness, and to simultaneous climax. She lay awake for a while, thinking that this could have been—if she had kept count—Number 3,152. It was satisfactory, satisfaction, and meaningless. They had given each other a pleasant time, and only in the morning did it become memorable: he had gone without waking her, leaving a note that said: "This is it. I love you. Will send mailing address. John."

It was wartime, and in Spring Valley the comings and goings of men and women were less subject to scrutiny than in the days of national peace. Porter Ditson was a captain in the Army Air Force, stationed for eight months in Miami, and sent back to Middletown, Pennsylvania, to sit out the war. "They apparently heard what I used to say about self-preservation," he told Elizabeth Appleton.

"You don't really think that. John said the Navy must have heard of his New Deal lectures and decided he wasn't a good security risk. But look where he is now."

"Have you any compunctions about us?"

"Wouldn't I be a *real* hypocrite if I had? This is just what I want. Have *you* any compunctions about us?"

"Not about us. But I hate to think that what I'm doing is all I'm good for."

"If you were sent overseas you wouldn't be flying. You're an old man of thirty-eight."

By bus and train they were only two hours apart, and Porter Ditson had an apartment in Fort Penn that he sometimes lent to some of the officers from the base, but that he refused to share on any other terms. "I want you to know in dollars how much you mean to me," he told Elizabeth.

"How much?"

"A gentleman from Hollywood offered me a thousand

(183)

dollars a month if he could live in this apartment with me."

"A thousand dollars a month is a lot of money, but I'm glad you think I'm worth the sacrifice."

"It's really one hell of a note, isn't it, when you stop to think of it," he said. "This God damn war, with all its misery and inconvenience, it was actually made to order for us."

"Yes, and the worst of it is, I can't work up a guilty conscience. Do you think I would if John were in greater danger?"

"He's still in some danger. A Jap submarine."

"Not very much danger. He says so himself. All the Japanese submarines are far west of where he is."

"What happens when the war's over? Will you divorce him? By that time you'll be more my wife than you've been his."

"I'll never be your wife. You don't want a wife. You want exactly what you've got, so don't trifle with your luck, Mr. Porter Ditson."

"Suppose the war lasts five more years? Will you get a divorce then?"

"I'll be even less likely to then. The children will be fourteen and thirteen, and I'll be thirty-eight and you'll be forty-three. The children need a lot of help at that age, and I won't be young any more, and you'll be too much of a confirmed bachelor. Don't talk about divorce, Porter. When you get tired of me, I'll have John and the children for my old age. I'll have had my fling."

"Is that what we are? Your fling?"

"Don't ask too much. I love you and I've proved it in every possible way, but what else is it but a fling, in all honesty?"

"Suppose John has found himself a lady friend in San Francisco, or Honolulu?"

"Well, I certainly hope he has. At least one. I hate to think of the alternatives. He isn't as exciting as you are, but he has to have sex, and I think it would be just fine if he got himself a girl."

"Don't ever say that to him. He'll know right away that

you and I, or you and somebody, are having sex. By the way, what *does* he think you're doing?"

"I wonder. There must be thousands and millions of women that aren't having any sex. I don't know that I could, now. Before you and I, I suppose I could have. But you really taught me what it could be, and how much I need it."

"Then if by some chance I should be sent overseas, you would find somebody else?"

"You want an honest answer, of course."

"I have the honest answer. Yes. Who would it be?"

"I suppose it would be Harry Jeffries."

"Good God, Elizabeth! You come right out with it. Do you want to sleep with Harry Jeffries?"

"No. I don't want to sleep with anyone but you. And don't intend to. But if you go overseas, there'll be somebody, every once in a while. It could be Harry Jeffries."

"Then why hasn't it been so far? What's to stop him when you get up on that table and give him a bird's-eye view?"

"Me."

"Do you get a kick out of having him prying and probing?"

"Don't say things like that. It's very rude, and very damned ignorant. Harry always has a nurse in the room next to the room where he examines you. If a woman wants to let Harry do it to her, that's one thing. But if she doesn't want him, all she has to do is raise her voice."

"You overlook one possibility. What if the woman happens to be someone like you, that would rather let him go ahead than make a fuss?"

"I don't think I'm that much of a lady, if that's what you mean. He'd certainly be taking an awful chance, if it was me. Anyway, a doctor's office isn't conducive to romance."

"His is."

"But not to me. I've never done it except in bed. Well, once. The very first time. But never since then."

"Now wait a minute."

"No, I know what you're going to say. That was heavy

(185)

necking. But I'd always rather have the real thing, and that means bed. B, e, d. Bed. What are you so jittery about to-night? I've come all this distance just to be with you. Do you wish I'd stayed home?"

"Don't talk nonsense. Of course I don't."

"Well, then be nice to me."

"How can I be nice to a woman that would go to bed with a lunkhead like Harry Jeffries? That would even think about it?"

"My thoughts, since I met you, since you've taken charge of my sex life, would probably shock Rupert Hillenketter."

"But he'd sure love to hear them."

"Well, he sure ain't going to, honeychile," said Elizabeth.

On the flight to San Francisco the weather was bad all the way, as though the God in whom she firmly but sporad-ically believed had arranged to frighten her for her compla-cent adultery, and to warn her that the affair with Porter Ditson must end. But she knew that much the moment she fastened her seat belt for the takeoff. It came to her with a stabbing sensation that she was going back to a husband who had never known she had been away, that she had parted with her lover without telling him it was a final parting, that the finish to the affair must be something he would have to infer, that it was a cowardly way to end it and an ungrace-ful, ungrateful way. The airplane jumped and dropped and she could feel stresses and strains and a baby cried and passengers who had been brave in the beginning now no longer smiled. Elizabeth Appleton finally gave herself up to an unfamiliar sensation of total fear, in which she wept quietly for her motherless children, forgave the stupid man who was their father, and asked that when death came, it would come quickly. Refueling stops were made at Chi-cago and Denver, and passengers were instructed to re-main in their seats, but a wailing woman demanded to be let off at Denver, necessitating additional delay. Her place was taken by a new passenger, a grinning sailor. Ten min-utes out of Denver he was airsick.

For most of the next hour it was like being on a tree swing, being pushed out of control by nasty boys who would not let her get down. The sixtyish man in the seat at her left had not spoken to her during the flight, but had sternly looked straight ahead, with a set frowning expression of disapproval. At last he spoke. He leaned toward his right, still looking straight ahead, and said: "You and I are going to have to be the calm ones. Do you know any first aid?"

"Yes," she said.

"If we hit, the worst danger is fire, an explosion. I was in one once."

"A crash?"

"Yes. You take care of the young woman with the baby. Drag them away if you have to."

"If I can," said Elizabeth Appleton.

"Well, that goes for all of us. If we can. But I'm telling you what's best. Don't bother with me, or *any* old people. If I'm all right, I'll take care of the soldier in front of us. If you save the mother and baby, and I save one, that's all we can hope for. That's the best we can do."

"All right."

"What's your name?"

"Elizabeth Appleton. Mrs. John."

"Patrick J. Kelly. Retired police sergeant. New York Police Department. When you know trouble may be coming, have a plan. That way you don't go running around haywire. Noticed you getting on at Pittsburgh and figured you for a dependable young lady."

"Thank you, Mr. Kelly. I'm glad you're here."

"Well, I wish we were both some place else. I been saying my beads since we passed over Columbus, Ohio." He took his hand out of his coat pocket and showed her a small black rosary. "You're not a Catholic, of course."

"No, I'm afraid not."

"Well, Mrs. Appleton, we're out of trouble!" said Kelly.

"What makes you say that?"

"The pilot just switched off the No Smoking sign. Let me offer you a cigarette."

"Thanks, I don't smoke. But the Fasten Your Seat Belt is still on."

"The No Smoking sign is what counts. We're out of it. The real trouble is past." He was relaxed and smiling as he lit a cigarette. "Going to join your husband in San Francisco?"

"Yes."

"Navy, I suppose."

"Yes, he's a lieutenant commander."

"I was with the old 69th in the first war." He touched his left lapel. In the buttonhole was an enamel miniature of a ribbon.

"What is that? I don't know one from the other."

"It's a good one. The D.S.C. Distinguished Service Cross. My mother, rest her soul, she wanted me to be a priest. I've a sister a nun, one brother a priest, two uncles in the priesthood, another brother a doctor, and another brother a city magistrate. But with all those peace-loving relatives, I went on the cops, and then went overseas in the first war. All my life I been mixed up with crime and violence." He pulled up his left sleeve and showed a five-inch scar. "Disarming a jealous husband with a razor." He rubbed another scar under his right ear. "Creased with a slug from a Browning automatic. Surprised a young lad holding up a candy store on Tenth Avenya. My Purple Heart souvenir I can't show you. It would of been the ir'ny of fate to get it cooped up in an aeroplane. But at least a beautiful young lady for my last memory in this vale of tears. And a courageous as well as a beautiful one."

"Thank you. Not a bit courageous."

"I didn't say you weren't frightened. That's where the courage come in. And, for that matter, the lady. That one that got off at Denver. Wouldn't she of been a fine one to have around in case we hit? Oh, you were frightened, and the tears were surely for your husband and children?"

"You saw the tears?"

"Mrs. Appleton, I been with you every minute of the way. I left you with your own thoughts till I re'lized where we were and decided to prepare you. The Rocky Mountains.

You're a New York girl, even if you did get on at Pittsburgh?"

"Born and brought up in New York."

"Did you ever go to Miss Spence's Finishing School? I used to help them cross the street when I was in that precinct."

"I went to Miss Chapin's."

"No, I had Miss Spence's on my post. Miss Chapin's, wasn't that over on Fifty-seventh?"

"Yes."

"What was your name then, if you don't mind me asking."

"Elizabeth Webster."

"Wait a minute. Give me just a—*Jarvis* Webster. Was that your father?"

"Why, yes. Did you know him?"

"No, but the Webster house on the north side of Fifty-sixth between Madison and Park. Iron grillework on the ground-floor windows and the service entrance you went under the stone steps. The butler was a fellow named Tom Something. Yes, and he drove for your father, too. What ever became of him?"

"He's still alive. I get Christmas cards from him. He's retired, but he helps out at parties. He lives on East Eighty-something Street, very far over. Thomas Rensingham."

"Yes, it wasn't an easy name to remember, although it would of come to me. Your father passed on, I suppose?"

"Yes, and my mother."

"I was upstairs in your house only the one time, a burglary scare."

"I don't remember. My father sold the house and we moved to an apartment."

"Well, this is a real treat for me. Those were good days, Mrs. Appleton, no matter what they say. There was one thing and another thing and there was this and there was that, but there was more respect for the law, and a sense of decency and right and wrong. There was no Adolf Hitler, only the Kaiser, a misguided fool with a withered arm. And we'd Socialists then and your Emma Goldmans and the like of them, but you could trust the people in your own government, which is more than can be said for the Communist rats you hear about. Now you've wireless operators in the Merchant Marine that won't take an SOS if it wasn't sent by a member of the union . . . What would we of been in Ireland? Cutting peat, perhaps, or tending sheep. And facing starvation half the time. And instead I've a brother a priest, a brother a successful physician in Mount Vernon, New York, and a brother a graduate of Fordham Law, a city magistrate on his way up. And as for me, I've me pension and a job, put my own two boys through Fordham and my daughter through New Rochelle. One of the boys with the Marines in the Pacific, the other flying a B-24 in the European Theater. And from what? From my father landed here barely able to read and write and learned the plumbing trade, worked hard and lived to see one son ordained and the others getting two degrees apiece. No, now I exaggerated there. My Dad passed away before Jerry got his M.D. But is it any wonder this family is ready and willing to lay down their lives if necessary for the U.S.A.? Ireland's in our blood and will always be dear to us, but this is where we learned to hold our heads up. Here's a picture of Gerald, as you can see, the one in the Marines. And this is Des, short for Desmond, taken in England last year."

"Oh, they're good-looking boys."

"Boys no longer, Mrs. Appleton. They went away boys, but both are married men now." He put the snapshots back in his wallet. "It's to have a talk with the wife of one of them that I'm taking this trip. Why have I been running off at the mouth so with you? Is it because we were in danger together? That's the reason, I suppose. In police work you learn to button your lip, but when it's over I talk as if next Tuesday they were going to pass a law against conversation. With you, though—I don't know. Maybe when I saw those little tears I knew you were a woman with heart. And you being on your way to meet your husband, the lieutenant commander. After how long?"

"Two years."

"Two years. Well, it's three for this girl. My son's wife. What is there in the young today, Mrs. Appleton, that there's all this impetuosity? She knew she was marrying a marine. Partly, he's to blame, I admit. I didn't marry till after I got home from France in 1919. He didn't know her very long, but she seemed a nice Catholic girl from all his descriptions and the photographs we got. Once I sent her the money to come and live with us, but she changed her mind and never another word about the money. She has a job in a war plant, too. But I don't mind the money. It's this boy having to write to me and ask me to find out why she stopped writing to him. I guess I know what I'll find when I get to Oakland. I guess I know."

Instinctively she put her hand on Kelly's hand. "But you may be wrong. And even if you're right, you can't tell your son."

"Do you want me to lie to him?"

"What's one lie in the world today?"

"But that's one of the things I'm against. The lies and the cheating."

She removed her hand. "Ask your priest. I don't know anything about the Catholic religion, but no minister would let you tell your son the truth, if the truth is what you think it is. Especially when it's two Catholics, that don't believe in divorce. If I were you, Mr. Kelly, I'd stay out of it. See the girl and talk to her, but if it isn't hopeless, try to persuade her to write your son a letter that will explain why she hasn't been writing him."

"You mean let her tell the lies?"

"Or let her tell the truth. No. Don't let her tell the truth now. Let her lie her head off till he comes home, and then they can settle it between themselves. But you stay out of it."

"What if she won't write the letter?"

"Does your son know you're going to see his wife?"

"No."

"Then you just have to make up a story that you were too busy, or you couldn't find her. That wouldn't be so good, either. That you couldn't find her. Just tell him you're too busy. If it's what you think or suspect, it's happening all the time."

"Gerald's a decent boy, never fooled around with girls. Des was the ladies' man in the family. You could tell that from their pictures."

"All the more reason for not disillusioning him now. But if he's going to be disillusioned, don't you be a part of it. There are some lies that *have* to be told, Mr. Kelly."

She had an irresistible impulse to turn toward him, and when she did he was studying her like a detective.

"I see," he said.

And she knew he had seen, everything.

"Well, now you've had enough of my troubles. Wouldn't you like to catch a wink of sleep? I'll get one of those blankets up here, and you stretch out."

"Thanks, I think I will take a nap. And I *hope* everything comes out all right."

"I hope that, too, Mrs. Appleton."

Presently she slept, exhausted from fear and emotion, and she did not speak to Kelly again until a few minutes before they were to land.

"Can I give you a lift in to San Francisco?" he said. "If you wouldn't mind riding in a police car. A friend of mine is meeting me, but there'll be plenty of room."

"No thank you, Mr. Kelly. I'm being met."

"Well, then I guess this is goodbye. We never thought we'd be here, either, did we?"

"I'd given up, but here we are. Good luck, Mr. Kelly."

"And the same to you," he said. "I mean that. You're a good-hearted woman."

"Thank you. Will you take that into account?"

He laughed. "You've a sense of humor, too," he said.

She was not met at the airport, nor had she expected to be. She saw Kelly in his tan gabardine rain-topcoat being greeted by a man of almost identical age and build in a tan gabardine rain-topcoat and the two men being whisked away in a black and white police car. For a while, listening to Kelly, she had thought she was learning something; but he had not taught her anything she did not already know. The idea of lying to save a marriage was not new to her, nor was her dislike of lying and cheating. Three thousand miles behind her was the man whom she already thought of as her former lover, who had given her the only novelty and excitement she had known in her life, and had given it in exchange for the novelty and excitement he found in her. He was miles and a timeless period away from her, and permanently so, and yet it was still too close and too soon for her to consider her decision from the standpoint of love. For four years she had been Porter Ditson's mistress, and if death had come to John Appleton, she would have become Porter's wife. But she had not loved Porter Ditson so strongly that she had at any time wished for John Appleton's death. In the beginning they had spoken of love and were convinced of the authenticity of their love, and they always, at every meeting, at least once made the simple declaration. But in their desire for extreme discretion—their secret had never got beyond Evangeline—they seldom met oftener than twice a month, and the one urgent and essential reason for their meeting was sex. Sometimes something would be worrying her, and she would tell him about that; sometimes she would have something amusing to tell him, and she would tell him. But her worries and her amusing anecdotes, and his concerns and chatter and philosophizing, and their talk of their love, all were fitted into their meetings before or after the time they could allot to sex. They would not waste a time together when she was due to have a menstrual period, and it was significant that they considered a meeting without sex a wasted time. Their reward for taking chances was sexual pleasure, and the pleasure was great enough to justify taking the chances.

Elizabeth felt loyalty and possessiveness for Porter Ditson more deeply than she had ever felt either for John, or so she believed; but the circumstances of her love affair forbade demonstrative loyalty and pride and possessiveness, and after a while they ceased to be factors in her relationship with Porter. Since she could not publicly avow her pride in him, her pride in him atrophied. As to her possessiveness, it was one of the sensitive areas of their relationship. Porter Ditson was aware that she continued the sex relationship with John—unlike John, he did *not* refuse to know what he did not want to know—but he maintained an almost haughty silence on the subject, so that her connubial bliss with her husband was made to seem no more romantic than a bowel movement. During the years of their affair Porter had never invoked his plain right to sleep with another woman since she was sleeping with another man, and the fact that he neither invoked the right nor made any claim to nobility for not doing so, was almost the nicest and best proof that he loved her. Her only proof, of course, was that her reputation was at stake every time they met. In truth, it was more convincing proof to Porter than to Elizabeth herself.

The affair had always had a tentative or a temporary aspect. They discovered that by exercising some caution they could meet as easily in Porter's room at the Spring Valley Hotel as anywhere else. Elizabeth would go to the hotel beauty parlor on the ground floor of the hotel, then descend to the basement, where the ladies' room was situated, and there take the self-service elevator to Porter's floor. Their only close call came when Brice Ditson once appeared unexpectedly and unannounced, and Elizabeth had to stand naked in Porter Ditson's clothes closet until Brice left twenty minutes later. "The only thing I was afraid of was that I'd sneeze," said Elizabeth.

"I kept half-hoping he'd find you. It would have done the poor bastard a world of good."

"Well, if I'd known that I'd have pranced right out."

"He has nothing like that at home."

She would remember such things, as she remembered them now in this mood of renunciation. She stood in line for a taxi and shared one with two ensigns in new blues and wearing new wings. They were polite and helpful to this woman of thirty-five.

There was no trouble about her reservation and she went to her room and had a bath and changed to a dress. The nap on the plane had made the difference between a sleepless night and some rest and she was full of nervous energy. There was no point in sitting alone in her room and she went downstairs to wait in the lobby until she could have lunch. Even though it was not yet eleven o'clock in the morning, the lobby was an exciting place. It was predominantly a Navy crowd, in all the blues, tans, greys and greens of Navy uniforms, and the women were dressed for San Francisco—wearing dresses and carrying coats. There was none of the dirt of war, the uniforms were clean and brightened with ribbons, and because of the time of day and the drinking-hour regulations peculiar to the area, the excitement was not alcoholically produced. In the crowd Elizabeth Appleton recognized two officers whom she had known in her debutante days, and three younger men who had been students at Spring Valley. With her hand she made a mask that covered the lower half of her face so that she would not be recognized; she wanted to enjoy the excitement of the whole crowd and not the amenities of brief reunions. The special quality of the crowd was hurry, the knowledge that the war would soon be over. The Germans had already surrendered, the Japanese had surrendered Okinawa two weeks ago, and every day it was expected that Tokyo would begin to get the saturation bombing that had been visited on the German cities. No one in this hotel lobby knew that a far more devastating weapon had recently been exploded in the New Mexico desert, but everyone had heard rumors of an improvement on the fire bombs that had been used in the earlier attack on Tokyo. A man hurrying to keep a date with his girl was also in a hurry to take part in the victory that everyone could feel was near.

"I don't believe it. *I* don't *believe* it."

Elizabeth turned, the words had been unmistakably spoken to her.

"Why, Shorty. Shorty Conners," she said

He bent down and kissed her cheek. "How are you, Elizabeth? You came all this way to see me?"

"Well of course I did, but it was supposed to be a surprise," she said. Now she saw that he was supporting himself with a hand crutch. He was wearing Marine Corps greens, was a major, and had a row and a half of ribbons. "Here, share half of my chair."

"No thanks, it's too damn much trouble getting up. Where's Appie?"

"Appie. I haven't heard that for so long. He's here, in San Francisco, but I haven't seen him yet. I just got in this morning and I'm to wait here for him."

"I knew he was in this part of the world, but I've never run across him. How are the children?"

"The children are fine, thanks. Naturally they wanted to come, but I never would have got here myself without help from the Ditsons. You remember Brice Ditson."

"Oh, sure. And Evangeline. And Porter. My wife is here, somewhere. Buying out Gump's, I guess."

"What are they?"

"It's a store. Is this your first time here?"

"I've never been west of Chicago before yesterday."

"Will you have lunch with us? I'm married again, you know, or maybe you didn't. Irma and I got divorced before the war and I married again, a Youngstown, Ohio, girl named Sophronia Venizelos. Just don't say anything about the Greeks having a word for it. They have, but she gets a little tired of it. Not that you would."

"I'm not that quick, anyway. Have you any children by your second wife? Sophronia?"

"No. Three by Irma. You knew that, because you sent presents when they were born. Sophie and I didn't want any till after the war was over, which ought to be any minute now. A little late for me, but those things can't be helped." He swung his right leg forward. "This is a phony. I use it to smuggle cigarettes out of the hospital."

"I hadn't heard a thing about it, and John hasn't either,

or he'd have told me. Do you think we ought to try to get a table now?"

"All right. Not that I have any trouble. Sophie says a few magic words in Greek, and you'd be surprised how many French headwaiters have studied Greek. Phony bastards. Pierre. René. Zhohn. But they know me here."

A queue had been formed at the entrance to the dining-room, but the maître d'hôtel held up a finger and said: "Your table, Major Conners. This way, please, sir."

"Will you tell him that I'm expecting a telephone call?"

"Mrs. Appleton, Mrs. John Appleton, now write that down, André. Mrs. Appleton is expecting a phone call. Will you be sure it doesn't get lost in the shuffle?"

"Absolutely, sir," said André, and left.

"We can't have a drink," said Conners. "Oh, here's Helen of Troy. Watch the act she puts on. She's jealous as hell, but tries to pretend she isn't . . . Hello, honey. I'd like you to meet a friend of mine, Victoria Vanderbilt, from New York."

"Oh, how do you do? Is it Miss Vanderbilt, or Mrs.?"

"It's Miss," said Conners. "Vic's been married so often she doesn't even change her name any more."

"Oh, stop, Conners. You had me believing it for a minute, but you always put it on too thick. If this joker won't tell me your name, what is it?"

"Elizabeth Appleton. Shorty was our best man."

"I know. I should have recognized you from your picture. We have a picture of you and your husband the day you were married."

"Oh, that was fourteen years ago. I don't blame you for not recognizing me."

"You haven't changed. Is your husband here?"

"Somewhere in San Francisco. I just got in this morning and I'm waiting to hear from him."

"I've been out here for three months. The town is full of creeps now, but I'd like to see what it's like after the war. I want Conners to go into business here."

(*197*)

"Anything looks good after Youngstown, Ohio," said Conners.

"Pittsburgh doesn't. I don't want to go back there," said Sophie Conners.

"Well, that's where we're going."

"All right, Major. That's where we're going. Your husband teaches at Spring Valley? I almost went there, but I went to State instead. A girl friend of mine went to Spring Valley. Kay Pappas."

"Another Mexican," said Conners.

"I remember her name," said Elizabeth Appleton.

"Oh, come off it, Elizabeth."

"I do. I don't remember her, but I remember the name, because I helped John keep his records, and I had to write all the names several times a year."

"Well, my father never heard of Spring Valley and he *had* heard of Ohio State, naturally. I love your ring. May I see it? Don't take it off, but just let me look at it."

"It belonged to my mother."

"Why don't you get me one like that, Conners?"

"I will, when your old man dies and leaves me all his theaters."

"I'll speak to him about it," said Sophie Conners. "It really is a beauty, the setting is so unusual."

"Yes. The rubies were in a necklace that Mother had broken up. So was the diamond. Two diamonds and four rubies. My sister has the other diamond and two of the rubies."

"I'm almost positive I've seen you in Pittsburgh. Do you go there much?"

"Well, fairly often."

"Where do you stay? The William Penn?"

"I have stayed there, yes."

"Your sister is quite a lot older?"

"No, younger. You must have seen me with a friend of mine. Shorty knows her. Evangeline Ditson."

"I'm sure I've seen you."

"What were *you* doing in the William Penn?" said Conners.

"Well, frankly, I was probably waiting to meet you. It was before we were married," said Sophie Conners.

Elizabeth experienced a retroactive dread of being discovered by Shorty Conners, who could so easily have seen and been unseen as she went to her room and as Porter Ditson went to his. And Shorty Conners would have very realistically formed only one opinion of the coincidence. He still could, if he would now recall having seen Porter Ditson, and she was determined to impress upon him that she had always been with Evangeline. "For a while Evangeline used to treat me to a trip to Pittsburgh every two or three weeks," she said.

"Well, at least you can be damn sure Evangeline wasn't using you to cover up. Not Evangeline Framingham Ditson. That's the horseface of the world, if you don't mind my saying so."

"Oh, she isn't that bad, Shorty. And she's really very kind. And a very good friend of mine, so don't talk that way about her," said Elizabeth. "Also, it was very pleasant to ride in a limousine with a chauffeur."

"You probably had one long before the Framinghams did."

"But never in Spring Valley," said Elizabeth. The danger point had been passed.

"How is old Prexy Witherspoon? Is he still around?"

"No, he died during the first year of the war."

"Prof Hillenketter still snapping the Amazons' garters?"

"I have no idea. He's still there."

"Porter Ditson? Speaking of the Ditsons."

"He's in the army. The last I heard, he was stationed at Middletown, but he may have moved since then. This can't be very interesting for you, Mrs. Conners."

"I don't mind."

"You don't have to any more," said Conners. "Look who's in the doorway."

They turned and saw John Appleton in conversation with the maître d'hôtel.

She stood at the window in her best negligee, a special present from Evangeline Ditson, and made a laughing sound.

"What's funny?" he said. He was lying on the bed with his hands clasped behind his head.

"I was just thinking, I've heard so much about San Francisco, but looking out this window, all I'm reminded of is Third Street, Spring Valley."

"Fourth Street," he said.

"Oh, you thought of it, too?"

"Sure, lots of times. I guess all hilly towns are alike, to some extent."

"Spring Valley never reminded me of Rome."

"Just wait a few thousand years," he said. "What would you like to do this afternoon? I have to be back on the ship by seven."

"Then let's just stay here," she said.

All was well, all had gone well. The presence of the Connerses had made for some awkwardness in their first greetings, but the awkwardness had given Elizabeth and John Appleton some diversion from the searching, questioning first glances that they would have exchanged if they had been alone. There had been a great deal to talk about, and the Appletons and Shorty Conners made it a Spring Valley reunion while Sophie Conners watched and listened.

"What did you think of Sophie?" said Elizabeth.

"Good-looking girl. Hasn't much to say."

"She has, but we didn't give her much chance."

"She's not going to put up with Shorty."

"Why not?"

"She doesn't have to. When he takes off that uniform, with all the chicken salad."

"No, they were married before he had a uniform," said Elizabeth. "She stands up to him, but she's still fascinated by him."

"Well, maybe," he said. "He always was a great swordsman, and maybe that's what she wants."

"I might say, who doesn't? I feel wonderful."

She was speaking truthfully, and the unexpected euphoria was not entirely physical. The tenderness of his lovemaking was not objectionable now as it had been in recent years; she wanted him to be sentimental for the very reason that sentiment had been lacking in their marriage, and if this was to be a new start, the things the marriage had lacked must be supplied. She was at ease with him because he had not been inquisitive and she had not been compelled to outsmart him. The encounter with Shorty Conners had helped to make it a sentimental occasion, an occasion for sentimental reminiscence and thus a reminder of the distant past; but, for her, it also was a convincing augury of the regeneration of her marriage. Shorty Conners was a man of no intrinsic interest, an aggressive second-rater whom she had long ago suspected of being extremely envious of John Appleton. But he had been best man at her wedding, by invitation; this time he was present by accident and she accepted the accident as fateful.

Nothing in John Appleton's behavior had enlightened her in the matter of his faithfulness to her, which was as she wanted it. She most positively did not want him to confess to infidelity and to make excuses for it. She did not want to trade guilt with him. If he had had other women, she was willing to trade his unspoken lie for her unspoken lie; and it suited her, as it seemed to suit him, to trade an untested trust. She slowly walked to the bed and sat on the edge. She took his hand and held it to her breast. They smiled at each other in the easy, nearly calm communication of pure sensuality. She looked down at his hand on her breast, and at the right moment they smiled again and she lay beside him. "This will be one to remember," he said.

"Anything," she said.

They had three days together. "I don't get to San Francisco as often as I used to. We don't go to Pearl any more. We go to Guam. But this is going to be over soon, everybody says so. I just wish I had a good medal."

"Why?"

"Points. If I had the Navy Cross or the Silver Star I'd be getting out quicker. However, if it looks as though I might be stuck here, you can come out again."

"I'll come out any time you say."

"This has been wonderful, everything I hoped it would be, but I haven't told you a fraction of what I wanted to tell you. For instance, I'm not sure I want to go back to teaching. Not right away. I'd like to do some writing."

"Whatever you want to do. But there's one thing you mustn't overlook. McAndrews will retire in five more years, and I'll bet you could have that if you wanted it."

"I want it, but I haven't made up my mind whether I want it enough."

"In 1950 you'll be forty-two. I know you won't want to stay president of Spring Valley for twenty years, but you wouldn't have to. You could leave any time you felt like it, when the right thing came along."

"I'll give it my best thought. I have plenty of time for that, God knows. We fire the fives and the threes on one day, on the way out. On the way back we don't fire them at all. My men spend their time squeezing blackheads. I spend mine rereading de Tocqueville. Maybe I'll finish his book for him. Not really."

"I want to ask you something."

"What?"

"Do you want to start another baby? We haven't, you know, but I would if you wanted one. Thirty-five isn't too old."

"Christ, no."

"Do you mean Christ-no, it isn't too old, or Christ-no you don't want to start one?"

"Both, I guess. I know it isn't too old. You don't look thirty. But we have a boy and a girl. We don't want any more, do we?"

"Not unless you do." She was disappointed at the positiveness of his answer. She had been entertaining the notion that a new baby might put a signature to the new start, but she consoled herself with the reminder that for him no new start was necessary.

"Anyway, not for a year. I like your figure the way it is."

"Frankly, so do I," she said. "And we ought to do more socially when you get home."

"Oh, do you ever see Porter Ditson, speaking of social life?"

"No, I don't even know where he is," she said. "I know he's a major, but that's about all I do know."

"Well, he can't pull rank on me, at least."

He shipped out the next day and she returned to Spring Valley. There was a note for her from Porter Ditson.

Elizabeth: I want you to marry me. If the answer is no, I will never speak of it again, nor will I make any effort to see you. Take as long as you like to decide, but above all don't let the fact that you have always said no influence your decision now. I have not been able to make up my mind whether your abrupt and silent departure is your way of writing "finis" to us. At all events, please consider, and then let me know. I love you and always will.

Porter

She went to the telephone booth in the Pennsylvania depot and sent him a telegram. It contained the one word *Finis*.

VII

❀

In 1932 Bruce Clanronald McAndrews had won out in an
easy contest over two worthy prospects. The Spring Valley
trustees decided that one gentleman had too much theol-
ogy in his background; and the other gentleman did not
measure up in personal interviews. B. C. McAndrews was
safely Presbyterian, and with his iron-grey, crew-cut hair
—he was only forty-four at the time—he imparted a sense
of honesty, wisdom, strength and intellect that the trustees
unanimously agreed was exactly what they wanted. His
qualifications were almost too good to be true: he was a
small-college man—Dartmouth '10—and a Rhodes scholar,
track man, Phi Beta Kappa, war veteran, husband of a
Wellesley graduate, father of four children, Ph.D. (Harvard), and had a clean record as teacher and administrator
at Wesleyan, Rutgers, and Princeton, with the emphasis

on the administrative side. Looking at him you could almost see him drying his hair after his morning cold shower and losing no time in trivialities as he buckled down to the day's work, and yet he did not give that undesirable impression of the go-getter. "Quiet strength, with no frills," was one trustee's summation for himself and his colleagues. They liked his frankness, too.

"I'm not the scholar that Dr. Witherspoon was and is," he told the trustees' committee-of-the-whole. "But I know that if you were looking for a scholar, you wouldn't have to leave your own campus. You have good men right at home. My Ph.D., as you undoubtedly know, was in the field of political science. But not because I had an all-consuming interest in the field. Not at all. I have almost no interest in political science now. My lifework is in the administrative end of education, both high policy and the kind of personnel work I've been doing in my various posts. Naturally I've been approached by other colleges before you gentlemen asked me to meet with you today, and at this very moment I have under consideration, serious consideration, two other posts. However, one of them is at a large university in the Middle West, and I know that I'm going to say no to that. I want to stay in the East, and I want to identify myself with a small college. The other offer *is* the presidency of a small college, a good one, in character very much like Spring Valley. The money and the perquisites are about the same. I've promised to let the other college know at the end of this week, so it becomes a question of time, doesn't it? I know you hadn't planned to make your decision today, but since you know all about me, and since I've now met all of you face-to-face, I'm afraid I'll *have* to have your decision today. I'll leave you for a while, an hour, and you can decide among yourselves whether you want to extend a formal invitation to me to become your president. If you do so, I can tell you now that I shall accept. If you decide that I'm hastening your decision—and I admit I am —then we can part company with no hard feelings, and I will take the other offer."

The meeting was taking place at the Rittenhouse Club in Philadelphia. McAndrews went out for a walk, promising to return within the hour, but he had hardly closed the door before Jasper W. Framingham spoke up. "That's our man," said Framingham. "You all saw what he did, of course. In about three minutes' time he completely reversed our positions. That is, instead of us considering him, what it amounts to is that he's considering us. And he did it without any arrogance. It isn't often a fellow can say take-it-or-leave-it without antagonizing you, but that's what McAndrews has done. I'm for him."

"My only misgivings," said someone. "I don't consider Wesleyan and Rutgers and Princeton small colleges. Or Dartmouth. The Harvard degree I don't mind. I like that. It continues the old Harvard connection at Spring Valley. But I wish Dr. McAndrews could have been a, well, say, a Haverford man."

"Well, he isn't," said Framingham. "And don't forget, we're getting an Oxford man and Oxford isn't small. You can't have everything, but this fellow comes pretty close to it. I move we get this thing settled without further delay. We don't want to lose this fellow just because he's *too* good. That doesn't make any darn sense whatsoever."

McAndrews went back to Princeton in triumph, and seeing John Grier Hibben waiting at the station in his Pierce-Arrow he waved to Hibben as one college president to another. Hibben did not see him.

McAndrews, his wife, and his four children were already installed at President's House, Spring Valley College, as John Appleton was getting ready to take up his new duties as instructor in history. The first meeting of Elisabeth McAndrews and Elizabeth Appleton established a relationship that did not get off to a good start and through the years never got any better. It was at one of the series of faculty receptions that Bruce and Elisabeth McAndrews were compelled to give.

Elisabeth Ridgeley McAndrews at forty-four was a dumpy little woman who after the birth of her first child never regained the cuteness that had made her attractive to Bruce McAndrews. She was quite conscious of the fact that her husband, with his flat belly, his sparse frame, and the oddly youthful-looking short grey hair, had stood the years with very little damage to his appearance. They were the same age exactly, but in the past ten years it had not been lost on Elisabeth McAndrews that people meeting her for the first time would immediately wonder how much older she was than he. This had been particularly notice-able at Princeton, and she left there with no regret. She arrived at Spring Valley determined to associate herself with women who were unmistakably older, so that the contrast was in her favor; and with women who were many years younger, so that she would partake of some of their youthfulness.

Elisabeth McAndrews was then just twice Elizabeth Appleton's age and three years younger than John Apple-ton's mother. "You and I," said Elisabeth McAndrews, "are the pea-green freshmen. This *is* your husband's first year on the faculty, is it not?"

"Yes," said Elizabeth Appleton.

"And did you meet as undergraduates?"

"Did I go here to college? Oh, heavens no. I didn't go anywhere. I went to a school in New York and that's all."

"Really? Where?"

"Miss Chapin's. I don't suppose you ever heard of it. Most people here haven't."

"Of course I've heard of Miss Chapin's," said Elisabeth McAndrews. "It's a very well-known school."

"Not here. How did you know about it? Are you a New Yorker?"

"No, but you don't have to be a New Yorker to've heard of Miss Chapin's. And Miss Spence's."

"They've *heard* of Miss Spence's. They always say 'Is the school you went to *like* Miss Spence's?' I'm glad *some-body's* heard of the school I went to."

"Then how did you meet, you and Mr. Appleton? Your husband's father was on the faculty here, I believe."

"John was tutoring a boy in the place where my family spend the summer."

"Oh, where was that, on the Cape by any chance?"

"No, a place on Long Island. Southampton."

"Oh, of course. Where Nicholas Murray Butler goes."

"Yes, he goes there."

"I had the great pleasure of sitting next to Dr. Butler at dinner two years ago. He *is* a fascinating man."

"I suppose he is. My father calls him Nichulas Miraculous, I don't know why. That's what everybody calls him."

"What does your father do?"

"Well, I guess you'd call him a stockbroker. He has an office in Wall Street."

"I see. And your mother? Is she a New Yorker?"

"Yes, both of them are, my father and my mother. They haven't been here yet, but when they come I hope you and Dr. McAndrews will meet them."

"I'm sure we'd love to. I have met your mother-in-law. She's a sweet little woman, isn't she?"

"Why yes. It's funny you should say so, though."

"Why?"

"Well, I guess it isn't *funny*, but I was thinking how much you remind me of her in certain ways."

"Oh, really? Now I don't see that at all. Isn't that strange, now?"

"I guess it's that generation. You all seem so much *nicer* than my generation."

"Oh, well, now isn't that nice of you to say so? It isn't true, of course. We're just like any other generation. Does your mother remind you of Mrs. Appleton?"

"No, but Mother—well, I guess I'm getting into deep water here."

"Not a bit. But will you excuse me? Some people I haven't met."

As a true snob Elisabeth McAndrews could not admit to having been snubbed by the twenty-two-year-old wife of the youngest member of the Spring Valley faculty, but there was no doubt in her mind that Elizabeth Appleton had been trying to put her in her place. In this she was attributing to Elizabeth Appleton a great deal more guile than the younger woman then possessed, but with the passing of the years Elizabeth Appleton's dislike of Elisabeth McAndrews became positive enough to make her satisfied with the antipathy she had accidentally created at the start. As John Appleton advanced in faculty standing, Elizabeth Appleton allowed her outward manner toward Elisabeth McAndrews to become more casual. Other faculty wives likewise treated Elisabeth McAndrews with no more deference than her husband's position demanded, and in 1942, after her youngest son was drafted, Elisabeth McAndrews paid the first of a series of visits to a rest home. Her problem was alcohol.

Bruce Clanronald McAndrews' problem was not alcohol, nor did he appear to have any problems that might develop into the alcohol problem. At forty-four he could look back upon the preceding twenty-two years, and think of the second half of his life thus far as a time of industry and struggle; he could look forward to his remaining years as a reward for his self-discipline, his conscientiousness, his self-abnegation. He had always kept out of trouble of whatever kind, antagonizing almost no one, and remaining true to his Yankee-Scots heritage by refusing to show off. He was known for his dependability, and he was aware of the recurrence of the word in his record. On several occasions while serving as an administrator he had been called upon to fill in as substitute teacher, and in each case his performance had been conscientious, self-abnegating, and adequate. The brilliance, and the reputation for brilliance, he was satisfied to leave to other men, for he had observed that brilliant teachers do not become college presidents, and college presidents last forever. It had all worked out according to plan, and at forty-four he could foresee a life of honorable occupation, honors, and solid financial security.

Bruce McAndrews was worth more than forty thousand dollars, representing his savings and several legacies from relatives. Elisabeth McAndrews' fortune was considerably less, but she had some "rainy day" money in savings accounts. They owned a cabin near a lake in New Hampshire which they would occupy during the month of July and rent out during August, usually showing a slight profit for the season. Their four children were brought up in an atmosphere of thrift, and in the first year of Bruce McAndrews' presidency of Spring Valley their first-born, Betsy, was a half-scholarship freshman at Wellesley. The three boys were in the Spring Valley public schools and, except for the youngest, Stephen, all doing well scholastically. Stephen was not stupid; it was only that he caught colds easily and missed a lot of classes. Douglas and Robert, the in-between boys, were healthy and industrious and partners in various gainful occupations. The family group photograph that ran in the October 1932 issue of the Spring Valley Alumni Bulletin received a great deal of favorable comment, some of which took the form of congratulations to the trustees for their wise choice. The well-loved Prexy Witherspoon already belonged to the past.

A few changes were desirable to indicate that a new man had taken over, but Bruce McAndrews moved slowly. To an assembly of the teaching staff he announced that at least for the time being he contemplated no changes in personnel. He did not specify how long the time being would last, but he indicated that there would be an evaluation of all teachers and all courses in the following June. "That should keep us on our toes," said one teacher.

"It should also give him one hell of a lot of work next June," said another. "And just when he's going on vacation."

"I've got tenure, ha ha ha," said the first man.

"I've got a book coming out, ha ha ha," said the second. "However, I'll trade you. My book for your tenure."

The changes that everyone expected were immediately apparent, but not revolutionary. "Economy is the watchword," said a little card that was hung in every class and dormitory room. "Please turn out the lights when not in use." A pat of butter in the students' cafeteria now cost a cent. With the cooperation of the chemistry department the water in the swimming-pool was made to last twice as long. A twenty-five-cent charge was made for catalogues to prospective students. The students' annual breakage fee of $7.50 was declared non-returnable. Administrative and faculty personnel were required to sign slips for all non-local telephone calls. Smoking restrictions were placed on the library, laboratories and various hallways, with suspension the punishment for infractions, thereby effecting a saving in insurance rates. "No matter what I do, there'll be some grumbling," said Bruce McAndrews to Elisabeth. "But at the end of the year they'll know one thing—at least the trustees will. I'll have reduced expenditures and added a little income, enough to pay my salary *and* old Witherspoon's pension."

"I hope Witherspoon knows that."

"He does know it. I saw to that. I don't want any criticism from that corner."

Bruce Clanronald McAndrews also saw to it that Witherspoon and many others heard about a personal gesture involving financial sacrifice. As the new president he attended regional alumni dinners—Pittsburgh, Fort Penn, Philadelphia, Cleveland, Wheeling, Erie, York-Lancaster, Hagerstown, New York, Chicago—and it was customary for the alumni and alumnae to give him a small honorarium above his expenses. The amount was always either $50 or $100. "Thank you very much," he would say, looking at the cheque and folding it neatly. "This will help a really worthy cause, and without this cheque my contribution would be very small."

"But that's yours, Prexy," the chairman would say.

"I know it is, but you won't mind if I give it to the faculty loan fund. You've no idea the good work it does. Hardship cases. Dignified assistance, and all done very quietly. Just since I've been at Spring Valley this fund has made emergency loans amounting to almost two thousand dollars. Keeps up faculty morale."

After his first year, in which his honoraria added some

eight hundred dollars to the faculty loan fund, Bruce Clanronald McAndrews deposited the money to his own account.
Expenses were mounting, what with a daughter at college
and orthodontist's bills for the boys, and he felt that he
had made the important alumni faculty-fund-conscious, in
the advertising jargon of the day. He had also silenced faculty criticism of his economies.

He was impervious to undergraduate criticism. "They
are congenital complainers," he would say to Elisabeth.
"Every year in September we get two hundred freshmen
that think they know more about running a college than I
do. And every June we get rid of a hundred and fifty seniors,
so glad to be graduating that I'm forgiven for what I did. I
am not going to be bothered by the carping criticism of
freshmen, sophomores and juniors. In the second half of
senior year they start getting sentimental and I've already
noticed that my harshest critics among them become the
mushiest a few weeks before commencement."

McAndrews made a point of attending football practice at least once a week during the season, and of having
his picture taken with the coach, the captain, and the graduate manager of athletics. For such pictures he wore a scarf
in the colors of Balliol College, Oxford, flung haphazardly
about his neck; standing hatless in his tweed jacket and
flannel slacks he looked more the coach than the coach did.
Sometimes he would get off a few forty-yard punts for the
photographer, and one such picture was used to illustrate a
little piece about him in *Time* magazine. This informality
apparently contradicted the growing legend of his aloofness,
but the legend persisted. No one lower in the academic
ranks than associate professor was encouraged to ask for
personal interviews. In respect to undergraduates' requests
to see him he would say "That's what we have deans for,"
and when instructors and assistant professors, men of John
Appleton's rank, wanted to see him he would suggest that
the man "take it up with the head of your department."
Inasmuch as the head of the department was sometimes the
last man an instructor wanted to see in regard to his prob-

lem, a certain amount of extra power thereby accrued to the professors, and they were not entirely ungrateful.

The head of the history department was Professor Benjamin Franklin Schuessler, A.B. (Spring Valley), A.M. (Penn State), Ph.D. (University of Pennsylvania), member of the English Speaking Union, The Pilgrims, and numerous learned societies. His course, The History of England, covered the political and social history of England and covered it well. He made human beings of the extremely human figures who had made English history and he did not hesitate to poach on the territory of the teachers of English literature. To his sophomores at the beginning of his lectures he would say: "I am always pleased to see so many ladies and gentlemen thirsting for all they can learn of Geoffrey, the Count of Anjou. No? Could I be wrong? I see no sign of recognition. Well, perhaps you know him better as the father of Henry Two. Henry Two you will recognize as founder of the House of Plantagenet. Ah, that brightens up the little faces. Plantagenet. Approximately one-third of you have heard of the Plantagenets. You will be hearing a *great* deal more, oh-ho my yes. Oh, you will be hearing *so-o-o* much of the Plantagenets. But later. Today we get acquainted, I with you, you with me. It will take me longer to get acquainted with you, because you outnumber me, but let me make it easier for you to get acquainted with me. Everybody knows that this is a pipe course. Schuessler flunks nobody, as long as you stay awake. Or so the story goes. We shall see, and I wouldn't count on it, if I were you. But there are perhaps two, and there may be as many as six of you who would like to come out of this with honors. To those of you I say, watch your dates. I am a son of a gun for dates. It's the quickest way I know to separate the serious students of history from those who are here, as they used to say, to cure a meerschaum. So be careful of your dates, memorize your successions, and one of you will graduate fifty dollars richer—the Robert Elliott history prize."

Benny Schuessler had been a friend of Charles and

Ethel Appleton, a frequent visitor to their house, a walking companion of Charles Appleton's, and godfather to John Appleton. He had spent most of his life on or within a mile or two of the Spring Valley campus and, like Rupert Hillenketter, he was an institution. A bachelor, he had lived for a while in one of the men's dormitories and for two years at the Faculty Club, but his dormitory room was too small and he did not like the feeling that at the Faculty Club he was subject to a subtle surveillance by Rupert Hillenketter. He took a room off-campus in the home of a retired railway engineman and ate his meals at the college cafeteria. He had three expensive habits that he did not regard as extravagances: he allowed himself a visit to England on every sabbatical; he bought books; and he was often tapped for small loans by undergraduates. Most of the loans were repaid, but not promptly, and seldom when he was in need of money. He had a savings account which he would not touch; he was afraid of poverty in old age, and he hoped to be able to save $10,000 so that when he retired he could live nicely for ten years on $1,000 a year and his $720-a-year pension and after that it would not matter; none of his immediate ancestors had lived beyond age seventy-five.

He had never been voted most popular professor by an outgoing class, but alumni who had been out a few years would say, on returning to college, "Let's go call on Benny Schuessler," and it was in many cases the only faculty call they would make.

Elizabeth Appleton could not understand Professor Schuessler, particularly in his behavior with John Appleton. "He giggles over nothing," she said.

"He was practically a member of my family. He knew me when I was in diapers. I wouldn't be surprised if he'd changed me when I was in diapers. He used to come for Sunday night supper and I can remember he always helped my mother with the dishes."

Homosexuality was a new mystery to Elizabeth Appleton and she looked for signs of it in the Schuessler relationship, but there were no overt indications and John

Appleton had freely told her of overtures that once had been made to him by a member of the football squad, by a washroom attendant in the Fort Penn railway station, by a well-dressed stranger on a Pittsburgh train and by a young Englishman who was a graduate student at Harvard. She knew that he had taken drinks from the well-dressed stranger and had gone to a hotel with him where he had allowed himself to be seduced but had been sent away angrily when he refused to satisfy the man in return. She was oddly unshocked by the revelation, merely curious as to the mechanics of the seduction. "It isn't the same as with a woman," John had said.

"Why not?"

"Because it isn't a woman."

"You mean a woman's body."

"Exactly. With a woman—there's some place to go, if you know what I mean."

"I know what you mean."

Nevertheless she remained obscurely jealous of Professor Schuessler and of John's fondness for him, and Schuessler gradually spaced his visits to their house until he stopped coming at all. Benny Schuessler was head of John's department and saw him daily, frequently at lunch, more frequently in the older man's office. There was never even the remotest mention by Schuessler of the fact that months and years were passing since he had been inside the house at Harvard Road and Bucknell Street. At faculty social gatherings he greeted Elizabeth as though nothing had happened, and indeed nothing had, except that Benjamin Franklin Schuessler had been casually and grievously hurt.

So long ago, so early in her life at Spring Valley, Elizabeth Appleton had given offense to two persons, and in neither case had it been deliberate offense. But the snubbing of Elisabeth McAndrews was more effective because it had been unintentional; and the absence of malice in her rejection of Benjamin Franklin Schuessler was even more chilling to the warm ebullience of the man. He asked only to be liked, and he did all he could to attain that small distinction. He could hate a villainous king long dead; for the recent living his range of feeling went from affection only as far as amused contempt. But it was unfortunate that one of his least favorite persons of the sixteenth century was also named Elizabeth.

VIII

❀

To be home with his wife and children at Christmas was all
the reward John Appleton wanted for the tedium and generally wasted years of his Navy career. He got home in November 1945, too late to resume teaching, since the course
schedules and teaching assignments were already in force,
but when he paid what he thought would be a courtesy call
on Bruce Clanronald McAndrews he was immediately offered the post of acting dean of men. "You can think it over,"
said McAndrews. "But you'll be doing us a tremendous
favor if you accept. In fact, John, you *could* start this afternoon. We really need you." In his delight at getting home,
at being in the old familiar surroundings and among friends,
he forgot about his half-formed intention to tell McAndrews
he would not be available until the autumn of '46. John
Appleton accepted the job of acting dean, and Elizabeth
was pleased. She thought he was doing it for her.

The official announcement was published under a four-column headline in the *Echo*, and John Appleton realized, from the emphasis that was put on his athletic and naval careers, that McAndrews was building him up as a strong man. He soon learned why.

Fraternity initiations by custom had taken place in February, after the results of mid-year examinations were made known, but the custom had been altered during the war and the initiations were being held after Thanksgiving. Phi Phi Alpha, a local fraternity that had never been successful in its petitions for national affiliation, was at the peak of its membership numerically and after twenty years of humility, near-extinction, and as butt of campus jokes, the Fifis were second only to Beta Theta Pi in number of major letter-men, almost even with Phi Gamma Delta in numerical strength, and had taken from Psi U the distinction of doing the most drinking. Most of the new members lived in dormitories and Quonset huts, and the fraternity house, a converted private residence, was so small that no single room was large enough for a seated meeting of the members. The result was that few meetings were held, and the organization was conducted by a committee of the fraternity officers and seniors. The fraternity house was simply a place where the members could loaf, play pool, drink, and have sexual intercourse with any willing girl.

On "goat night," the night of initiation, the full membership turned out to see the fun, and the goat-room in the cellar was crowded with young men who had been hazed in previous years. They were now armed with paddles in which were burnt the letters ΦΦΑ and most of the full-fledged members had supplied themselves with wartime gin or rum. The president of the fraternity read from the formal initiation ritual, but he was interrupted and shouted down by the members crying, "Let's get at these freshmen, let's give it to these goats." The president accordingly dispensed with individual ceremony, the twenty neophytes took the oath together, and the hazing began. This part, however, was not done in a group; each neophyte was

(218)

hazed separately; paddled, smeared with paint, pushed around from one group to another. The horse-play went on until it came the turn of one neophyte, a man in his late twenties. His name was Bob Ransdale, and he had been a marine. He was led blindfolded to the center of the room. The president spoke: "Most unworthy scum of the earth, you are about to be inducted into the sacred mysteries of the noble order of Phi Phi Alpha. Ransdale, assume the attitude."

Instead of bending over, Ransdale took off his blindfold. "That's a lot of shit," he said. "There's no son of a bitch in this room's going to whack my ass."

The room grew quieter. "What did he say?" someone asked.

"I'll tell you what I said. Don't any son of a bitch think I'm going to stand here and take it. Because I'm not. This whole thing is a lot of balls anyway. For kids, and I'm no kid. I joined this God damn thing because it's a place to get drunk and get laid. The rest is bullshit."

The president spoke: "The sergeant-at-arms and his assistants will proceed with the initiation."

Somewhat hesitantly three young men stalked Ransdale. They moved toward him slowly, and suddenly he half-wheeled and with the heel of his hand struck the nearest man on the chin. The man fell on the floor and did not get up. Ransdale ignored him and grabbed the second man by the hand and jerked his arm downward. The man screamed with pain. The third man, the sergeant-at-arms, punched Ransdale's jaw and immediately four others from the crowd began punching and kicking Ransdale. He tried to fight back but he could not move his arms, and in a few minutes he was limp and bleeding from the nose and from a cut over his right eyebrow. "Kill the bastard! Kick the shit out of the son of a bitch!" They yelled, they shouted. Some who could not get near enough to punch him spat on him. He was conscious, but he had stopped resisting. The vice-president said to the president: "What'll we do with him?"

The president said: "I can't hear you."

The vice-president shouted: "I said, what the hell shall we do with Ransdale?"

"Do you know where he lives? I said, do you know where he lives?"

"Yes. I know where he lives."

"Then get him out of here."

"You mean take him to his room? Not me."

"Then the two of us. You and I together. This isn't so good," said the president. He tried to quiet the crowd, but the yelling continued. He and the vice-president, wearing the silken stoles of their ritualistic offices, pushed through to Ransdale and each took him by an arm. The man whose arm had been jerked was sitting on the floor, moaning in pain. The man who had been knocked out came to, was given a slug of whiskey, and immediately threw up.

On the steps Ransdale stumbled and fell. "I think we'd better dump him at the hospital," said the vice-president.

"Dump him? You mean just leave him there?"

"Well, what would *you* do?"

"I guess you're right."

In the morning John Appleton went to see Ransdale in the hospital. "Well, Ransdale, how does it feel to be a member of Phi Phi Alpha?"

"I don't know what you're talking about."

"Come off it. None of that gangster code with me. That's the kind of kid stuff that you objected to. I hear you put Standish in the hospital. Dislocated shoulder."

"Glad to hear it."

"Yes, I'm sure. But Rumbaugh's partially paralyzed."

"What happened to *him?*"

"You tell me. You cracked a vertebra or something in the back of his neck."

"I did? What am I supposed to do? Send him flowers?"

"No, I don't expect you to do that. I came here because I have to. It's my job. Up to a certain point we have to protect our students."

"What point is that, Appleton?"

"This point. Do you want us to get a lawyer for you, or do you want to hire your own? The police are in this now, and we'll do whatever we can to help you, but I don't have to tell you, you're through. We don't want you around."

"Me, for Christ's sake? What about *them?*"

"You know what fraternity initiations are. You went in there with a chip on your shoulder and you got just what you deserved. But because you had a chip on your shoulder, a young guy may be paralyzed for life. Do you know what you are, Ransdale? You're a professional sorehead. And you're a professional marine. You were probably just as much of a pain in the ass to the good guys in your outfit."

"When I get out of here I'll give you a chance to say that again."

"No you won't. I had a prick like you in my gun crew. He was going to give it to me as soon as we got out of the Navy. But he didn't. He had the chance and he didn't even try. And you won't either. You're a lot older than most of the guys you were with last night, the oldest man in that fraternity house. And you behaved like a complete shit."

"Why don't you go fuck yourself?"

"Do you want us to get you a lawyer? Your father gets here late this afternoon."

"I don't want anything from anybody in this jerk joint."

"Sure you do. You're the kind of sorehead that will try to sue the fraternity. Well, much as I hate to tear myself away—"

"Appleton?"

"What?"

"Did you ever know a girl named Emily, her husband was a war correspondent?"

"Sure I did."

"She told me to look you up."

"Well, why didn't you? Maybe you could have black-mailed me before, but now you've got yourself in a nice jam, and nobody's going to believe a word you say."

"Not even your wife?"

"Write her an anonymous letter. Isn't that what you're thinking of doing? If it's anonymous, she won't pay any attention to it, and if you sign your name, why should anybody pay any attention to it?"

"I'll get Emily to write her."

"Do you think little Emily is going to write a letter to anybody? We could always send the letter back to her husband, and then where would she be? Ransdale, you're not only a prick, you're a stupid prick."

"She tells me you were no good in the hay."

"Does she tell you that you are? Ransdale, you get stupider by the minute. Here you are, threatening to blackmail me, and don't you know that every time you apply for a job or any position of trust, they're going to want to know what happened at Spring Valley. And you know who answers all such letters? Me. You shouldn't tip your mitt like that. You know, we have fitness reports here, too. Your record, not only your marks, but everything else about your character, and all I'd have to do would be to put down a few words to the effect that you were *suspected* of trying to blackmail a member of the faculty. Just suspected. Thanks for the tip, wise guy. I've got you by the balls and you pull one fast one and I'll start twisting."

"Ah, shit, I just wanted to see what you'd say."

"Well, you heard what I said. By the balls, Ransdale."

John Appleton that afternoon informally reported to Bruce Clanronald McAndrews on developments in the Phi Phi Alpha incident.

"It was bound to happen," said McAndrews. "It was coming. It's in the air."

"You mean you'd had some previous information? I wish you'd told me."

"I didn't quite say I'd had some previous information. I wasn't holding out on you," said McAndrews. "It just stands to reason that there's bound to be friction between the veterans and those that aren't. It isn't only the difference in age."

"I see. What do you think ought to be done about Phi Phi Alpha?"

"What would you suggest?"

"I suggest you call a special meeting of the Interfraternity Council, with the exception of the Fifis, and tell them that it's up to the fraternities to crack down hard, right away."

"A good idea, but it would be better coming from you. You're a Spring Valley Beta and I believe you were on the council as an undergraduate."

"I don't carry the prestige you do. And as a matter of fact, your being a Dartmouth man—I'm sorry, I don't know what fraternity you were."

"I was a Tri-Kap. Kappa Kappa Kappa, a Dartmouth local, second oldest fraternity at Dartmouth."

"Then doesn't that make you the ideal man to speak to them? I'm not being immodest when I say that ever since Deke dissolved, Beta has been the strongest fraternity at Spring Valley, and I don't want Beta, or myself, for that matter, to seem to be bullying the Fifis. When I was here the Fifis were a joke."

"That's entirely changed. They're the second biggest, as you know, and as soon as building materials are available they're planning to put up the biggest house on the campus. They have the money."

"Well, if they're getting rich I guess that entitles them to special consideration."

"I didn't say that, John, or imply it. I haven't liked the way things have been going at Phi Phi Alpha, and if I'd had my way they'd have been disciplined two years ago. However, what went on there also went on elsewhere, even at Beta, if you don't mind my saying so."

"What, for instance?"

"Well—do you know what a gang-fuck is?"

"Sure. Did they have one at Beta?"

"So I heard. Unofficially there was a report that a young woman took on half a dozen students, one right after the

(223)

other. I had your predecessor investigate it, but we got no-where. We couldn't take any official action because there were no complaints, either from the girl or her parents or the parents of any of our students."

"The same thing happened when I was an under-graduate. I won't say what fraternity. I've also heard about it happening at State. Didn't it ever happen at Dart-mouth?"

"Not while I was there. A few years ago, before the war, there was some scandal during Winter Carnival. The point is, we can't crack down on Phi Phi Alpha without stirring up a lot of trouble. And maybe the kind of trouble we stir up will be worse than a fight at a fraternity initiation. The Associated Press and the Pittsburgh papers have been after me all day."

"Then I think you ought to lose no time in calling to-gether the Interfraternity Council. You make a statement in which you say that the council has made the following deci-sion. That gets you off the hook."

"Well, you may have something there. But it will be better for the college if you handle it. If you speak for the college, it will get into the papers as 'Acting Dean John Appleton says,' and not 'President McAndrews says.' In other words, treat it as something on the dean's level. Once I get in it, the college itself is involved, but if you take care of it, it'll just be a disciplinary matter on a lower level. Sort of a family squabble."

"And not worth the attention of the president?"

"Exactly."

"Well, I guess that's part of my job, to take the heat off the president."

"I don't know that I like the way you put it, John, but that's my thought. I've had to do the same thing when I was at other colleges. You know, I could have ordered you to take this responsibility as part of your duties, but I don't like to order anybody to do anything unless it becomes ab-solutely necessary. We've had this discussion, so—*will* you call the Interfraternity meeting, and *will* you issue the statement to the press?"

"It's an order, even if it is in the form of a request?"

"Depends on your reply to the request."

"All right. May I use your phone?" John Appleton spoke to McAndrews' secretary: "Get me a list, I'm sure you have it there, of the presidents of all fraternities, and then look at their schedules and find out what classes they're in at this period, or the next period for those that aren't in class now." He hung up.

"Very efficient," said McAndrews. "You know, John, this is very valuable experience for you, although it may not seem so at the moment. Some day you'll be sitting on this side of this desk."

"I appreciate the compliment, but a lot of things can happen before I'd even be considered."

"Nevertheless, when you are considered—and I have a feeling you will be—I'll remember how well you handled this."

"Thank you, sir."

The meeting of the fraternity presidents was held during lunch hour in the visiting teams' dressing-room in the gymnasium, a room picked for its remoteness and because no one would be using it at that time of day.

John Appleton sat at the head of a long rubbing-table, the council members sat on benches. "Many's the time I've stretched out on a table like this—maybe this very same one," he began. "In any case, we have a great big charley-horse to iron out, so let's get to it."

Within the hour the council, who were as fair-minded and personable a group of young men as could be drawn from the student body, had come to a decision; and since most of the fraternity presidents were also on Student Council, their decision also had the effect of coming from that higher authority. Ransdale, who was not mentioned by name, was to be allowed to resign from Spring Valley College, and no other public statement was to be made by the Student Council or the Interfraternity Council, or by any individual member of either. The men present at the meeting then sent for Wilmer Dinsley, president of Phi Phi Alpha, and told him of the decision.

"I guess it's fair enough," he said. "I don't want to say anything against Ransdale, because I don't know whether he's a member of my fraternity or not. He was formally initiated, but we had a meeting this morning and expelled him. I guess nobody was ever a member of any fraternity for so short a time. However, it turns out that the whole fraternity has to vote on an expulsion. According to our constitution, which I read up on this morning, it takes a two-thirds vote of all the active members. I'll call a special meeting tomorrow, and I guess Ransdale will be expelled.

"However, gentlemen—Dean Appleton and gentlemen—you know the old thing in the Bible about casting the first stone. What happened to us last night could have happened to any lodge on the campus. And we all know that certain other things have happened that are a hell of a sight worse. If Dean Appleton doesn't know about them, I'm not going to tell him, but anybody that's been here for the last three years knows what I'm talking about. There isn't a lodge on this campus that doesn't have something to hide. If you had picked out Phi Phi Alpha, or mentioned us by name, I was ready to fight back, and we *would* have mentioned names. Names and dates. I'm glad I don't have to do that. I think too much of this college and my friends here, but I have a feeling that Dean Appleton, a Beta, had a lot to do with your decision, and if he did, I want to thank him."

"Dean Appleton had everything to do with it," said the president of Phi Gamma Delta.

"Right, right," said several others.

"I'm glad to hear it," said Dinsley. "Then in his presence I want to say this: we all, every damn one of us here, the presidents of all the fraternities, are good and worried about conditions. The damn war's over but we haven't got

(226)

rid of all the Ransdales. There'll be more of them, and the place where they're liable to raise the most hell is in their fraternity houses. There's the G.I. Bill that I understand will run till 1950, and after every war there's a collapse of moral values. All of us are the children of the Jazz Age made famous by F. Scott Fitzgerald and the Lost Generation made famous by Ernest Hemingway. We don't want to be that."

"Sociology major," the president of Beta Theta Pi whispered to Dean John Appleton.

"He's all right," said Dean John Appleton.

"But at least the screwballs in the Lost Generation and the Jazz Age didn't have the atomic bomb to play around with. But we have. We may not have it now, but we're the ones that are going to have the responsibility for it and probably other things a lot worse. Therefore, if we don't learn to take responsibility now, on little things, we're not going to be qualified to take greater responsibilities later on."

There was applause.

"The officers of Phi Phi Alpha didn't expel Ransdale because we were afraid of punishment. If you could have been at our meeting this morning you'd realize that. We were worried because we let a guy like Ransdale in in the first place. And by the way, some of you fellows ought to have red faces, too. Ransdale had bids from four other fraternities that I know of, and he could have been a—well, never mind. He went Phi Phi Alpha because he wouldn't have to pay national dues, and that's the only reason. He told me last week, one fraternity is much the same as another, and I guess I should have asked him then to hand over his pledge button, but I didn't, so *we* got him, instead of one of you four fellows at this meeting. Any one of you four could have been in the same spot I was in today."

"Dinsley, you're right, and we took that into consideration when we were discussing what ought to be done," said John Appleton. "Now, gentlemen, I repeat what I said before Dinsley got here. Everything that was said at this meeting is secret. Please don't divulge any of it, even to your fraternity brothers."

The details of the meeting were kept secret, but in twenty-four hours the campus and interested townsfolk had been told that John Appleton's handling of the Phi Phi Alpha affair was "masterly." John Appleton had become a hero overnight, particularly to the undergraduates who had not had time to form an impression of the new acting dean. His fairness appealed to the students, to whom fairness was a religion and in many cases the only religion.

"It could all change," he said to Elizabeth. "The first time I make an unpopular decision."

"You know better than that. Not while any of these students are in college," she said. "You've made your reputation, and they won't forget it. I'm interested in what Mc-Andrews said about your being on his side of the desk some day."

"I'd be interested to know what he thinks now," said John.

"Yes. Now he probably wishes he'd handled the thing instead of you."

"Well, I got him off the hook, and that's what he wanted. He almost lost his temper when I said that, and I shouldn't have said it. But I was sore myself when I saw how he was passing the buck to me. I had more to lose than he did."

McAndrews contrived to appear to have master-minded the solution of the Phi Phi Alpha affair, and at dinner said to Brice Ditson: "Several people have complimented me on the way I handled it." (This was completely untrue.) "But most of the credit should go to John Appleton. The only credit I do claim was in giving John a more or less free hand, and assuring him that I would back him to the hilt. That young man has a great future. I consider it a great stroke of luck the day I asked him to come back as acting dean. He almost didn't, you know. He wanted to wait a year, but I practically put it to him as a personal favor."

"Well, I'm pleased because Elizabeth will be pleased," said Evangeline Ditson.

The friendship between Evangeline Ditson and Elizabeth Appleton had not been disturbed by Elizabeth's renunciation of Porter Ditson. "A clean break, there was no other way," Elizabeth had told her. "Unless I intended to leave John and marry Porter. But John had a miserable time in the Navy, through no fault of his own, and to come home to nothing or worse than nothing—I couldn't do that to him. And Porter is strong, much stronger than John. I know he loves me, Evangeline, and I love him, but—oh, you see."

"You've really put your finger on it," said Evangeline. "Porter is much stronger than John. I don't say he hasn't been miserable, too, but he's better able to cope with the situation than John would have been."

The Phi Phi Alpha incident was absorbed into the history of Spring Valley College. Milton Rumbaugh wore a leather neck-brace for three months; and a year after the episode there appeared in the *Echo* a small item which had appeared earlier in the city newspapers: a man identified from fingerprints as Robert F. Ransdale, thirty years old, former marine, was found dead of shotgun wounds near Las Vegas, Nevada, where he had been living for several months with his common-law wife, Renee Reville, a chorus girl employed in a Las Vegas night club. Holder of the Silver Star and the Purple Heart, Ransdale, according to the Associated Press dispatch, had been released on bail earlier in the week on complaint of several tourists who had refused his offer to "protect" them. Under the Associated Press item the *Echo* printed a shirttail which said: "Ransdale was briefly a student here, entering with the Class of '49. He resigned from college following an altercation at Phi Phi Alpha on initiation night in Nov. 1945. His parents, Mr. and Mrs. C. Ransdale, lived in Coatesville, Pa. He was a graduate of Coatesville High."

IX

Elizabeth Webster Appleton was the mother of two children: a son, Peter, born in 1934; a daughter, Betty, born in 1935, but throughout the earliest years of their lives the children were hardly more than a statistical note on the Spring Valley campus. If Elizabeth Appleton was successful in her effort to keep herself in the background of her husband's public career, she was even more efficient in bringing up her children unaffected by public attention. To an undeterminable degree she was influenced by the tragedy of the Lindbergh child and the omnipresent fear of kidnaping that harassed especially those parents who had, or were related to people who had, money. This same fear had also had a subtle part in curtailing conspicuous spending by parents of small children; such spending had already been reduced by a widely held belief among the rich that extravagance—other than governmental—would hasten revolution, and the fear of revolution was very real in Western Pennsylvania. These factors—her desire to further her husband's career, the threat of kidnaping, and the angry sounds that came from Pittsburgh—were the immediate cause of her parental policy, but even without them Elizabeth Appleton would have been guided by her own upbringing. Until she was twenty-one and married John, Elizabeth Webster had departed only once from her parents' strict and strictly conventional pattern of suitable behavior: she had entered tennis tournaments that were not restricted to members of the host clubs and their invited guests. Although she never got past the second round in the major tournaments, nevertheless her name, Elizabeth Webster, Meadow Club (or Southampton), got into print in the newspaper articles by Hawthorne and Danzig —"Miss Palfrey had little difficulty in disposing of Elizabeth Webster, 6-1, 6-1"—and even that small publicity was distasteful to her mother and father. Elizabeth Webster Appleton had not rebelled against restrictions, and she saw no reason not to maintain them in her own capacity as parent.

When they were old enough the children were sent to the kindergarten and through the grades at the College Model School. The Model School children had a quasi-private school status—they were the sons and daughters of faculty and of nearby Hill parents—but in the case of faculty children, without a tuition fee. The Appleton children started piano lessons when Peter was eight and Betty seven. Along with other faculty children they were taught to swim in the college pool, and they went to the dancing class at the country club on winter Saturdays from two to four. They learned to play tennis before they were ten, and knew the college cheers and songs by the time they were six.

From the beginning Betty was better at studies and games than her one-year-older brother. She was kept a grade behind him, but only at the insistence of her mother. "I may not know anything about child psychology, but I do know that much," said Elizabeth. "She's bright, and he isn't, and if we let her skip a grade and be in the same class that he is, she'll call him a dumbbell."

"Maybe he is a dumbbell," said John Appleton.

"What if he is? He's a boy, and I don't think boys ought to be made to feel inferior to girls, especially brother and sister. You don't want your son to grow up to be a fairy, do you?"

"Is that what would happen to him?"

"Something like it, if you take the manhood out of him while he's still a child."

"So far I haven't seen much sign of manhood."

"Well, maybe that's my fault because he was my first child. Of course you're partly to blame, too. Betty isn't the ball of fire you make her out to be. I should think you'd have learned a few things from your own experience."

"My own experience?"

"Your father. You're doing the same thing to Peter."

"Oh, hell, all fathers do it. It's part of growing up."

"Does it have to be, because it always had been?"

"Ah, there, Elizabeth. You're getting modern."

"I am not."

"Yes you are."

"I *am not*."

"It sounds that way to me."

"I don't care how it sounds to you . . . *What* sounds to you? What are we arguing about?"

"I said that all fathers do the same things to—"

"Yes, and I said it doesn't have to be that way just because it always has been. I don't call that modern. That's any mother at any time in the history of the world. She wants things better for her children."

"Listen to you! You want these children brought up exactly the way you were."

"Not a hundred percent the way I was. I reserve the right to make changes when I feel they're necessary. Circumstances alter cases. Shakespeare."

"I don't think it was Shakespeare. Let's look it up." He

went to the bookcase and got out Bartlett. " 'Circumstances alter cases.' Let me see. Thomas Chandler Haliburton, otherwise Sam Slick, 1796-1865. It's from something called *The Old Judge*. I must get that out of the library."

"I never heard of Sam Slick or that other person. I've heard of Richard Halliburton. He went to Princeton and wrote books. My mother loved them. My father hated them. Then he was killed or something."

"He was lost at sea when some Yale men scuttled his boat. I think your father was one of them."

"You never want to help me when it's something that pertains to the children."

"I'd be glad to help you, any time. But I never get anywhere."

"Well then don't criticize me because I don't want Betty to make Peter look like a dumbbell. And he isn't a dumbbell. It's just that she's quicker. And a girl. Fathers and daughters, the old story."

"Yep. Jarvis Webster and daughter Elizabeth, all over again."

She laughed. "You bastard, honestly. You are a bastard."

During her affair with Porter Ditson she had tried not to be unusually maternalistic in her dealings with the children. She sensed that they would sense an alteration in her attitude, most likely in the direction of kindness, that they would find just as disturbing as if it were in the direction of cruelty. To behave toward them with precisely the same degree of fairness, sternness, and warmth, when at the same time she was living in a state of exciting anticipation from meeting to meeting and of euphoria after each meeting— this was her design. That she succeeded was an accident. The affair had not gone on very long before the war and military service intervened. It was a natural thing, then, for the mother to behave toward her children in a way or ways that were different from the way and ways that they were accustomed to in normal times. Any departure from normal ways would be—and was—attributed by the children to the great fact that their father was far away in the Navy. She read them his letters to her; family friends would inquire for him in the children's presence; and among the children's own friends the normal condition was to have a father away in the war and, frequently, a mother at home who was trying without complete success to make the best of the situation. Impatience, followed by affectionate demonstrations, followed by vagueness, became the normal conduct of mothers, and the Appleton children saw it happening in the homes of their friends and in her own home. Elizabeth's abrupt termination of her affair with Porter Ditson coincided with her announcement to the children that their father would soon be home, and to them this was a full and satisfactory explanation of her sometimes erratic behavior. All would be well when their father got home, and since the children had not seen their father in three years, and did not remember much of their life before he had gone away, all was well. And it was new. John Appleton was not a total stranger to his children when he returned to Spring Valley; but to Peter, who was eleven, and to Betty, who was ten, he was a familiar novelty, impressive in his blues, husky and strong in his new grey flannel suit, and they took some pride in the enthusiastic welcome that their father was given by his older friends. Within a week of his return, his presence in the house made their home life complete. And there was no doubt that he was glad to be with them again.

"Do you know what Alice said?" said Betty to her mother one day after he had been home several months.

"No. What?"

"She said Daddy is better-looking than Gregory Peck."

"Well, he is. But he doesn't look like Gregory Peck."

"Alice thinks he does, only better-looking."

"Well, your father is a very good-looking man."

"Don't you ever get jealous of the Amazons?"

"Look here, young lady, you're not to call them Amazons. Coeds, if you want to be slangy, but not Amazons. And you may be one yourself some day, don't forget."

"I'm not going to Spring Valley. I'm going to Smith."

"Why Smith?"

"Because Alice's mother went to Smith and she says Smith has the best reputation."

"For what?"

"What?"

"What has Smith the best reputation for?"

"I don't know. But Mrs. Robinson says it has, and that's where I'm going."

"You may change your mind."

"No I won't."

"Well, when the time comes, maybe you will go to Smith."

"Mum, why didn't you go to college?"

"I married your father instead."

"But you could have done both if you'd gone to Spring Valley."

"At that time I didn't know anything about Spring Valley. Anyway, I didn't take a college preparatory course. I don't think I could have got in Smith, for instance."

"Were you a society girl?"

"Heavens, Betty. I don't even know what you mean by that."

"You were. I know."

"How do you know?"

"Because you came out. Other girls don't come out, but society girls do."

"In that case, yes, I was a society girl."

"I don't want to be a society girl."

"That's up to you. There is no society in Spring Valley."

"Yes there is. Mrs. Ditson. And you. Only you're the real thing and Mrs. Ditson isn't."

"Really, Betty. Who's been filling you full of these ideas? Alice's mother? Whoever it is, she doesn't know what she's talking about. You mustn't listen to such nonsense."

"Mrs. Robinson ought to know. She lived in New York. She said you were the real thing and Mrs. Ditson only *thinks* she is."

"Mrs. Ditson is a very good friend of mine, and I wish Mrs. Robinson wouldn't say things like that."

"Well, I like Mrs. Robinson. She's more fun than Mrs. Ditson, I'll tell you. And you shouldn't say anything against her. She thinks you're beautiful and she says Daddy's going to be president of Spring Valley. She says you and Daddy are the ideal couple."

"Very flattering, I'm sure, but I wish she wouldn't say everything that comes into her head."

"Do you know what she said about Professor Hillenketter?"

"No, and I don't want to know."

"She says he's an old shit."

"*Betty!* I've never heard you use that word before."

"She said it, though. 'Hillenketter is an old shit.'"

"That's enough of that. You're saying it because you like to say it, and I want you to march right upstairs and wash your mouth out with soap."

"I will not. Mrs. Robinson said it."

"Well, somebody ought to wash her mouth out, too. You go right upstairs and then stay in your room for the rest of the afternoon. This instant."

"I don't know *how* to wash my mouth out with soap."

"Then go and rinse your mouth with Lavoris. Oh, never mind. Just go to your room and stay there till I tell you to come out."

The child started to cry. "It's not fair, and I hate you."

"Go on."

Elizabeth heard the child's deliberate kicking of each riser as she mounted the stairs, and then saying, quite distinctly, when she reached the second-story landing: "Hillenketter is an old shit." Elizabeth pretended not to hear, and the child, after a moment's wait, went to her room and slammed the door.

John Appleton laughed when Elizabeth came to their daughter's description of Rupert Hillenketter, but his laughter was brief. "Sylvia Robinson is getting famous for those remarks," he said.

"She ought not to make them in front of children," said Elizabeth.

"She ought not to make them at all. She's not helping Morrie, I can tell you. Or the Jews. We have one, two, three, four Jews on the faculty. Two in Morrie's department, physics. Shapiro in the English department. Sarah Fabrikant in music. Every time Sylvia gets off one of her wisecracks—did you ever watch Sarah when Sylvia's being a wit? She looks at her with a fixed smile on her face and you can almost hear her saying, 'Why don't you shut up, you damn fool?' The others, too. They listen, and then when Sylvia's finished they all turn away. And Morrie's no genius, you know. He's a good, workhorse sort of physics teacher, who if he were a genius wouldn't be at Spring Valley. In other words, he could be replaced, and probably will be. She hates it here and she wants him to get a job in industry at two or three times the money. He's told me that. But he likes it here. It's healthy for the children, and he likes teaching."

"Sylvia was on the stage."

"Yes, but in one show. Some little revue. I must say she has quite a shape."

"That's no secret."

"No, she fills a sweater. Not that you don't."

"I don't flaunt them the way she does, and I'm a lot taller."

"Well, be that as it may, I don't think the Robinsons are going to be with us very long. Sylvia will see to that."

"Oh, you think she's doing it deliberately, to get Morrie fired?"

"I have no way of knowing that, but that's how it's going to work out. Morrie won't have any trouble getting a job, but I hate like hell to see a guy giving up what he wants to do, in favor of what a little bitch of a wife wants to do. Frankly, what surprises me is that she hasn't been caught in the hay with somebody."

"Oh? Does she?"

"I don't know that, either, but have you ever heard any of your women friends express a longing to go to bed with Morrie?"

"No, but that doesn't mean anything. The women I see

don't express that about anybody. Do the men about Sylvia?"

"In guarded terms. Such as, 'How would you like to wake up with that in bed with you?' "

"Who said that?"

"Oh, several guys expressed the thought. But the one that put it in those words you'd never believe."

"Who?"

"None other than Bruce Clanronald McAndrews, B.A., M.A., Ph.D."

"No!"

"It slipped out. We were walking behind her across the Quad. I guess there's some hope when a man fifty-eight can react so spontaneously. Of course he's a rather young fifty-eight, and I guess with Elisabeth drying out in a sanitarium—I wonder what McAndrews does do?"

"Nothing, I would have said. But that's what surprises me about him and Sylvia. His even thinking that. And *saying* it . . ."

"Saying it, that's what amazed me. You don't say a thing like that to a man that you don't like, and McAndrews doesn't like me. He wished he hadn't said it, but he did. Well, I'm good for twenty more years, at that rate."

"Wouldn't it be interesting if they did have an affair, Bruce and Sylvia?"

"It'll never happen. Where would they go? It's as simple as that in Spring Valley. Where would the president of the college go to meet the wife of an associate professor?"

"His house, while Elisabeth was away," said Elizabeth.

"And everybody see her coming out?"

"Oh, she could go there at night."

"What would she tell Morrie? 'I'm going over to try a little screwing with Prexy?' Morrie's home at night."

"Well, it's not our problem."

"No, it certainly isn't, and it isn't theirs, either. It isn't going to happen."

"I hope not. I really can't tell you how I dislike that woman. I'm sorry if Morrie's going to be fired, but I won't miss her."

"Don't say anything about that, by the way. I'm not even sure of it myself. Pretty *damn* sure, but not positively."

"How do you know?"

"I knew you'd ask that. When he made the remark about Sylvia, Bruce said: 'But if *you* have any such plans you'd better hurry. I don't think she's going to be with us long.'"

"It sounds to me as though he confided in you a great deal."

"Well, as acting dean I see more of him than anybody else does, and that's a pretty lonely job he has. He has to have someone he can confide in, and he knows I keep my mouth shut. Except to you. God, when I think of what I tell you."

"I love it."

"It's a good thing you can keep a secret. And it's a good thing I have you to tell them to. There's a nice one cooking now. Does the name Marissa Bratting mean anything to you?"

"Of course. Queen of the Junior Prom, wasn't she?"

"Oh, and Student Council. It turns out that Miss Bratting is a howling Lesbian. The austere, cold beauty, the personification of our young womanhood. As far as we know she restrained herself till this year, and then when she was voted Prom Queen, which apparently was her ambition all through college, she let go with a bang. First her sorority asked her to move out. They found out about it but were keeping it a secret. Then she went after a freshman, seventeen years old. Bratting was safe while the sorority was protecting her, but not in the women's dorm. No secrecy there. The dean of women sent for her and she was brazen as brass. 'I know why you sent for me,' she said. Well, you know Mrs. Drew, the motherly type. She always wants to be helpful, but Marissa wasn't having any. 'Ship me home if you want to, but if you don't let me graduate, you're going to have to ship four other girls, too. *And* one member of the faculty.'"

"What are they going to do?"

"She was sent home this afternoon. Mrs. Drew spoke to her mother on the phone, and the mother knew about it.

She said she'd been hoping that sending Marissa to a coeducational school would be the solution."

"She was a real beauty, too," said Elizabeth. "What about the others that she implicated? The faculty member?"

"Mrs. Drew has refused to give McAndrews any names. She says the girl is obviously unbalanced and quite capable of making irresponsible accusations. But everybody knew who the freshman was, and she's been given the bounce. Fortunately, the freshman has such bad marks that she can be officially dropped for that . . . Well, we get about one a year. Or two. McAndrews told me that when it's two, and they aren't corrupting any others, the policy is to pretend it isn't there. But if a girl is a wolf, so to speak, Mrs. Drew has her in for a lecture and a warning, and if she doesn't behave, out she goes. We do the same with the fairies."

"They all ought to be expelled."

"Oh, sure." He held up his hand and pointed his index finger in the general direction of the campus. "But do you realize that up there, tonight, in dormitories and fraternity and sorority houses there are about seven hundred very young, reasonably healthy men and women. Full of sex, and probably at the height of their sexual urge. Living in close quarters. Half the male students and at least a third of the female students have had normal sexual experience. Been laid, at some time or other since they came to Spring Valley, if not before. And these young men and women aren't subject to any vows or sublimating through religion. Most of them are going through a period of having no religion at all. Now if you could see everything that goes on up there tonight, if you could be in every room between now and four o'clock tomorrow morning, and you expelled every man and every woman that was having some homosexual experience, well, maybe tonight you'd have to expel six. But maybe tomorrow night you'd have to expel fifty. And if you expelled everybody that had ever had *any* homosexual experience at Spring Valley, I hate to think what that would do to the size of our graduating classes."

"Oh, you're exaggerating. I'm thirty-five years old and no

woman has ever made a pass at me. Not one. I've been sent notes, but that's all. And I know I'm not bad-looking and have a nice figure. So I think you exaggerate."

"Possibly I do, but you never went to boarding-school. Hence the lack of opportunity. And I'm basing my theory on some pretty reliable stuff. The confidential records that I've seen since I've been acting dean, plus my own observations when I was in college and at boys' camps."

"Well, I just don't know."

"Well, I just don't know either. Let's go to bed like two heterosexual, very lucky people. You know, Elizabeth, even after fifteen years and two children, I'm still a little in awe of you. I often wonder what you really think."

"At the moment I think I'm very glad you suggested bed. You're not in awe of me there. Do you want a glass of milk?"

"Yes. Let's have a glass of milk."

"He's too old to spank, and too young to punch," said John Appleton.

"He's too big to punch, you mean," said Elizabeth Appleton. "He's awfully strong. *You* don't *know*."

"The way I feel now, I'd be willing to put it to a test."

"It would be awful if you hit him and he hit you back and hurt you."

"That kind of talk practically challenges me to take a poke at him. However, I know I *can* lick him, so I'm not going to," said John Appleton. "Tell him to come downstairs."

"Why can't you tell him?"

"Listen, are you and I going to have a brawl over this kid before I even talk to him?"

"Well, you said you'd deal with it."

"I did and I will, but your attitude toward me is decidedly unfriendly, and the only way I can explain that is that you're on the little bastard's side."

She got up and went to the foot of the stairs. "Peter, your father wants to talk to you," she said, and went out to the kitchen.

The boy came down and stood in John's study. He was fourteen, but already he was the tall son of a tall father and mother and had not yet shed his childhood fat.

"All right, you can sit down," said the father.

"Oh, it's going to be a long one." Peter slouched in a leather chair.

"It might and it might not. If you don't show some respect I might just pick you up and throw you out of here."

The boy glared at him but said nothing.

"Take your leg off the arm of that chair," said John Appleton. "All right, let's have your story."

The boy shrugged. "I don't know what you want to know. You heard the whole thing."

"Not from you. Let's have it from you, from the beginning."

"I don't know where to begin."

"Well, since you're so helpless, I'll start you off. Begin at eight o'clock last night."

"Eight o'clock last night? Eight o'clock I guess we were all at the movies at eight o'clock."

"All right, wise guy. You've begun. Proceed."

"Do you want me to tell you about the show? Who was in it?"

"You're asking for it, buddy. If you want to see how hard I can hit you, you're going to find out."

The boy knew that his insolence had reached a limit. "Well, we got out of the movies and went over to The Spoon for a malt. We played some records and then I guess about ha' past nine we started to walk home. We were passing the Elks club and we stopped to look at this car, a new Buick convertible Roadmaster, green, twin spots, white walls—"

"And the owner's initials painted on the door."

"Well, nobody noticed that at first. But somebody noticed that the keys were in it. So we took it and went for a ride."

"Wait a minute. Didn't you have any discussion about

taking off in a car that didn't belong to any of you or any of your families?"

"No. We just said something about getting checked out in the new Roadmaster, and I got in and started it and we went out Hill Street and this old guy in the Chevy smacked into us at the corner of Twelfth. It was his fault. He never even slowed down for the stop sign but kept coming out of Twelfth and into Hill without stopping."

"Then you all got out and ran."

"I drove the car over to the curb and parked it and yes, then we ran."

"And it was just your great misfortune that the old guy happened to recognize you and young Foster."

"Well, yes."

"And then you came home, didn't say a word about it to your mother, but retired to your room as though nothing had happened. That took real guts. Real courage."

"Well, if you'd been here maybe I might have told you, but I didn't want to worry Mother."

"Maybe you would have told me, then again maybe not. When I got home at eleven o'clock you didn't exactly rush down to tell me."

"I didn't have a chance to. The police got here the very same time you did. I'm not saying I would have told you, but you can't be sure I wasn't going to, because I wasn't even sure myself. I was thinking about it."

"That was the first thinking you'd done all night. Well, you're very lucky the car belonged to Mr. Ditson, because he isn't going to prosecute. But you'd have a nice list of charges to face if he did. Enough to put you in a reformatory. Driving without a license, stealing a car, speeding, reckless driving, leaving the scene of an accident."

"I know all that. Incidentally, not speeding. They don't give speeding tickets in town. Only reckless driving."

"You're absolutely right. We'll take speeding off the list and instead of that we'll put in assault and battery by automobile, a much more serious charge. You know so much about cars, what's your estimate on the repairs to Mr. Ditson's car and the Chevrolet?"

"Well, the right front fender on the Buick, and the body of the Chevy. A hundred dollars."

"Two hundred and fifty dollars for the Buick, I don't know how much for the Chevrolet. The chief of police told me your fines would have amounted to at least five hundred dollars. I'll have to pay the lawyer something, and we're only very lucky that there isn't a big hospital and doctor bill to pay. As it is, it's going to cost me four or five hundred dollars by the time we're through, and Dr. Foster the same amount for his son, although you were the one that was doing the driving. Two dollars a week allowance you get, twelve eights are ninety-six dollars a year. Roughly your entire allowance for the next four years. That's the financial end of it. But judging by your attitude, the worst damage wasn't financial. It's your complete lack of any regret or feeling of guilt."

"I apologized to Mr. Ditson this afternoon."

"That apparently was too much for you."

"Well, can't he get insurance?"

"Yes. Yes, he can get insurance. He can get insurance in a minute. All he has to do is file a claim *and*, Mr. Wise Guy, make out a police report for the insurance company and then the police have to act by arresting you and holding you on those charges. Mr. Tomaselli, the owner of the Chevrolet, is a respectable businessman—"

"Owns a shoe-repair shop."

"Has an excellent reputation, has never been in an accident, and his word is going to be believed rather than that of two young punks who steal a car and smash into him. The only reason you're not in the cooler tonight is that Mr. Ditson happens to be a friend of your mother's and mine, and he persuaded Mr. Tomaselli not to appear against you. If you were an undergraduate you'd be automatically suspended, have to stand charges before Student Council, and probably be expelled. That's in addition to the legal business. How do you think I feel about this thing, the Dean of the College? I'm the one that represents the college in disciplinary matters, and my own son, before he's old enough to go away to prep school, has his freedom only through the kindness of two men, Mr. Ditson and Mr. Tomaselli. And God damn it, you little snotnose, saying 'owns a shoe-repair shop,' as though you were superior to Mr. Tomaselli. What I'd like to do would be to make you work it out in his repair shop, but you'd be no damn use there."

"I'll work for Tomaselli, I don't care. Only stop preaching to me, I know I did wrong."

"Oh, you know you did wrong, do you? Well, when I see Mr. Tomaselli tomorrow I'll ask him if he can use your services as an errand boy, delivery boy. If he paid you ten dollars a week for July and August, that would be eighty dollars. I'll see if he and I can't arrange something along those lines. As to what you owe Mr. Ditson, he has no job to give you and I don't know how we'll work that out. But we'll work it out, don't make any mistake about that."

"Is that all? Can I go now?"

"Yes, you may go. But it's not *all*. It's going to be a long time before you forget last night's caper."

The boy went to his room and Elizabeth came to the study. "I heard most of it," she said. "I wish you wouldn't make him work for Mr. Tomaselli."

"Give me credit for some sense. I'm not going to. But I'm going to tell him that Tomaselli has no job for him. Really rub his nose in it."

"All right, if you think it'll do any good."

"It won't improve his manners, but it'll make him think twice about swiping cars. You haven't spoken to Porter Ditson, have you?"

"No, not yet."

"I was thinking that the least we can do is offer to lend him one of our cars while his is in the shop. I've already thanked him, but that would give you a good excuse to call him up."

"If you think I ought to."

"It would be nice. He'd appreciate it from you."

In the morning she telephoned Porter Ditson. "I'm terribly sorry about your car, Porter. John thinks we ought to lend you one of ours and I agree with him. Shall I drive it down to the hotel and you can bring me back here?"

"I would love to see you. I can get another car from the dealer, but I would love to see you."

"Ten o'clock?"

"All right, fine."

He was waiting on the curb, got in, and said: "Not straight home, Elizabeth?"

"All right," she said. "Where, then?"

"Oh, anywhere. Out toward the club."

They drove out of the business district before speaking.

"And a little child shall bring them together again," he said.

"I was wondering what you were going to say."

"Is it the same, Elizabeth?"

She nodded. "I didn't think it would be, but I'm shaking inside. Up and down my arms. Across my chest."

"That chest, that I don't call a chest."

"I want you now as much as I ever did, and it's three years. John's an awful damn fool to make me do this. I thought everything was peaceful and serene. For you *and* for me. But it isn't, is it?"

"Has there been anyone else?"

She shook her head. "No. But I'd go away with you now. You haven't still got the apartment in Fort Penn, have you?"

"Lord, no."

"Where do you take your girls?"

"What girls?"

"You must have some."

"I have a place, but you'd be taking an awful chance. Especially in broad daylight."

"Where is it?"

"It used to be a whorehouse. Under the new management it isn't a whorehouse, but they'll provide the room if you provide the girl."

"How far is it?"

"About fifteen miles."

"Chick Medina's?"

He nodded. "Used to be. Another fellow has it now. It's spruced up inside and out, and they call it the Sans Souci. But no, Elizabeth. Not in daylight. You have too much to lose. This time of day there'd probably be a brewery truck, a groceryman."

"You do love me, don't you?"

"Yes. You know it."

She suddenly turned off the highway into a side road. "I wonder where this leads to."

"Farms."

"Do you know a good place to stop?"

"Yes."

"Tell me when."

"Do you want to get out, or stay in the car?"

"Get out, don't you think?"

Presently they stopped the car and went behind a stone fence. "We won't have time for everything," she said. "Do you remember everything?" She removed her girdle and sat on the ground.

"Yes," he said.

"Al fresco," she said, and smiled. "Our first."

"Our first."

She lay back.

"What about your dress?" he said.

"The ground is dry. Only dust," she said. He smiled and she asked him why.

"Only the bare essentials," he said.

"Yes. Oh, I see what you mean. A kind of a pun. Darling, I think I'm getting a little nervous. Quickly. Oh, yes. Oh, my dear darling."

He sat on the ground while she stood up and put on her girdle. "I forgot what good legs you have."

"That's not a very nice thing to say."

"I know, especially when I think of their erogenous potential."

"What on earth does that mean?"

"Your good gams make me horny."

"Not now."

"Yes, even now. I couldn't do anything about it again so soon, but I'll bet I'll never forget you standing here and pulling on your *ceinture de chasteté*, in front of me and various birds and cows."

She lifted up her dress. "Have a good look to make sure."

"Thanks," he said.

"This is the wildest thing I've ever done in my life. Once I almost—"

"You almost what?"

"Oh, on my wedding trip, John wanted me to make love on the beach in France, but I was too timid. But this—this was my idea. I must be—I don't know what I am. I would have gone with you to the Sans Souci."

"I know."

"Do you wish now that we had?"

"No. This is like nothing else ever, and I'd have felt very guilty about taking you to the Sans Souci." He lit a cigarette and walked with her to the car. "Are you going to meet me again?"

"I don't know. You know that I'll want to," she said.

"I know that, yes, but I don't think you will. You're what, now? Thirty-eight?"

"Yes."

"And I've been your only lover in seventeen years."

"Seventeen years, and my only *love*."

"You probably won't meet me again, like this. This was lovely, Elizabeth, and I guess inevitable. But when you get home, it will be finis, without the telegram."

"I don't know."

"Yes you do."

"I guess I do."

(248)

"It isn't every day your kid is going to smash up my car. This is part of that."

She nodded. "Mm-hmm. It is. I actually don't feel unfaithful to John."

He looked at her sharply.

"I shouldn't have said that," she said, half asking.

"No, you shouldn't have."

"What made me say it? And why is it wrong to have said it? I know it was wrong, but I don't know why."

"Because it means that you're going to stay married to him. That this was nothing compared to your marriage."

"And yet I love you. You know that's true."

"Yes, I believe that."

"Well then tell me, what is it? Elucidate."

"It's simple, Elizabeth. You're a wife. And you like being a wife. You like being John Appleton's wife!"

"Somebody's wife, yes. Not necessarily his. I'd rather have been yours. But it's true, I like being a wife. I like being in a marriage. But you had to think that out for me. I never would have discovered it for myself."

"You didn't have to discover it."

"Porter."

"What?"

"I'll go back on the ground for you, I'll wait for you, I'll make love to you. Now, this minute. I'll stay out here all day with you. I'll take my clothes off."

"Yes, if I said yes, you would. But love isn't the thing with you any more, Elizabeth. As a matter of fact—as a matter of fact, it never really was. You were pretty young at the time, but when you married John Appleton, you were going by an instinct. You knew, really knew, that marrying him was a surer way of getting what you wanted than if you'd married one of the boys you grew up with. Or someone like me. You could have me as a lover but John Appleton was better husband material."

"But he was my lover before we were married. I had an affair with him."

"Why argue with yourself?"

"I wouldn't have had an affair with him if I hadn't been sure I was going to marry him?"

"Exactly."

"You're right. But you're wrong if you think I won't meet you like this whenever you want me to."

"How can I be honest about that? As long as I have any sex life, I'll want you. But a long time ago I told you that self-preservation is practically my whole philosophy."

"I remember. I've never forgotten."

"Your face, your body, yes. But you could make me die, Elizabeth. Not kill me, but make me die. I could very easily die of wasted love. Because my love for you isn't only sex, and yours for me very nearly is. I'll live off today for quite a while, but in a few weeks I'll go back to sex with nothing else, which is the way I've been living for three years, and did before I was your lover. You see, with me it would be sex and marriage, but with you they've become two separate activities. Fun, pleasure, with me, but marriage with John. I don't want to see you any more."

"Why can't there be both?"

"Is that a rhetorical question? There can't be both because you don't really want both. Sexy as you are, passionate and exciting and abandoned like today, the sex you get with John is really as much as you need."

She was silent. They were driving now, almost back in Spring Valley.

"Porter, my dear, you're married, too, you know. You're married to yourself."

"I guess you're right. That's a very profound comparison of the two of us. And it makes me feel better, less sad. It makes what we've had very sweet. And you're sweet, Elizabeth."

"No one in the world, in my whole life, has ever called me sweet."

"Nobody else ever knew that about you."

"I'll love you as long as I live."

"And I'll love you as long as I live," he said.

She reached over and took his hand and held it to her

breasts, each breast separately. "Yes, I always will," she said.

The incident with Porter Ditson became in time the point at which Elizabeth Appleton would date the end of her youth. The very circumstances of the incident gave it a youthful character. It was a young thing to do, to feel such desire and to act upon it so recklessly, to behave in actuality more recklessly than she had ever done during the years when her only concession to age was to consider herself a *young woman*. None of this had entered into her thinking at the time of the incident, but in her recapitulation she saw that the final act of her youth was more youthful than everything that had preceded it. The long affair with Porter Ditson had been *in* her youth, but not a youthful thing. Only once before in her entire lifetime had she nearly approximated the same degree of sexual impetuosity and that had been on the occasion of her first full experience with John Appleton. But she had known then that she was going to marry John Appleton, and it had been an unresisting seduction, a passionate formality, no less a nuptial item than was the selection of her bridesmaids or the choice of favorite tunes that Emil Coleman was to play at her reception. She knew it was not the case, but it was almost as though she had carefully saved the most youthful gesture of her life for the end of the time of impetuosity, romance, and recklessness. She could say: "Once in my life I stayed with a man just when I wanted to." The only youthful thing about the long affair with Porter Ditson had been the impulsive, rather cowardly termination of it. But the incident on the country road had made up for her earlier failure to see him one last time, to make love with him once more, before her own new start, and not her new start with someone else—John Appleton—could properly begin. The simple truth was that three years earlier she had been three years too young to make the parting absolute and the new beginning unencumbered.

Porter Ditson, she would always remember, was no longer young. When he had spoken of dying of wasted love he had been unconsciously convincing, not so much romantically as realistically. The steady drinking and the regular physical exercise apparently matched each other, and he seemed to be in good health. But his body was forty-three years old and the face that had looked up at her from the ground behind the stone fence was a face that had been wearied by more than the recent passion. His eyes, humorous and tender, were not yet old, and maybe they never would be. But the skin near his eyes had the first scratches of middle age and there was a lot of grey in the smoothly brushed hair. As truly for him as for her the incident was the termination of youth, and she would often wonder whether he so regarded it.

Now began for Elizabeth the system of conduct that in a year or so produced her permanent public character. It was a system that was not inconsistent with the public character she had previously maintained; Spring Valley, Town and Gown, had always regarded her, with reasonable accuracy, as a young woman from one world who had married into another, and was conforming to the rules and customs of the second. But beginning with the incident on the country road and her realization of its meaning for her as an end to youth, Elizabeth Appleton became more explicitly a recognizable American type; the wife who frankly and equally participates in her husband's career while making it plain that she wants no other career of her own. John Appleton became a cause, if not quite a crusade. She went with him wherever and whenever it was permissible. As soon as the children had gone to boarding-school she accompanied him on trips to other colleges, driving the car and putting in many boring hours alone in hotel rooms, but dining with him and his professional acquaintances and their wives. She was an efficient and decorative traveling companion and an unobtrusive guest who, as she well knew, happened to be the handsomest woman at most of the dinner parties they attended. At home in Spring Valley she gave small dinner parties that she always described in advance as "not a party—eight, with John and me" but that gave

Mildred Klein, who was a good cook, the opportunity to exercise her talent.

"See how you like this wine," Elizabeth would say to a male guest.

"Oh, you're asking the wrong fellow," the man would say. "I don't know the first thing about wines." But he would taste the wine, say it seemed excellent to *him*, nice body, dry but not too darn dry—and for $3.50 she had made a friend who would always respect Elizabeth Appleton's judgment.

The misfortune that had come to Elisabeth McAndrews had left the college without an official hostess, and visiting dignitaries were usually entertained at the Appletons' house. Elizabeth would keep track of the expenses and an itemized bill would be presented to Bruce Clanronald McAndrews, but the bills the college paid did not reimburse Elizabeth Appleton for the better whiskey, better brandy, better cigars, flowers, candy, that she offered to the sophisticated tastes of the traveling poets, United Nations delegates, hillbilly folksingers, United States senators, radio news commentators, flamenco dancers, science editors, and English authors who brought outside culture to the Spring Valley College "World Today" programs. The English authors and the radio commentators were the standard product of their environments, sure of their charm and eager to get on a you-and-I basis with their attractive hostess; the others who passed through Spring Valley on their way to cultural outposts in Pittsburgh or Fort Penn were sometimes arrogant, sometimes pitiful, sometimes negligible, but what they did for Elizabeth Appleton was considerable. In her girlhood she had been impressed by only two varieties of celebrity: the men and women of the stage and motion pictures—Marilyn Miller, Jack Buchanan, Fred and Adele Astaire, Hope Williams, Thomas Meighan, Charles Farrell, Janet Gaynor, Constance Bennett, Irene Rich—and by male tennis players—William T. Tilden 2d, R. Norris Williams 2d, Vincent Richards, Ellsworth Vines, John Hope Doeg, Henri Cochet, Francis X. Shields. She was impressed by Suzanne

Lenglen and by Robert T. Jones, Jr., but not by painters, polo players, politicians, opera singers, playwrights, poets, psychiatrists, soldiers, or priests of God. She was too young to have been invited to the parties for the Prince of Wales during his 1924 visit to Long Island, and her crush on him—she was fourteen at the time—did not survive the disapproving remarks she heard her mother make about the prince's extraordinarily democratic behavior on the North Shore. Elizabeth Webster Appleton thus went to Spring Valley with few personal gods, and in Spring Valley she acquired no new ones. She had no one to look up to but the historians who were admired by her husband, and since they were only names to her—disembodied names that were signed to volumes she forced herself to read—she had no desire to meet men and women because they had made reputations for themselves.

This rare quality made her a better hostess. As a good hostess she was polite to all her guests; as a woman who was not impressed by the reputations of some of her guests she put at ease the major and minor celebrities who came to her house by behaving toward them with a naturalness that was relaxing to all but the advanced egocentrics.

"I'm going to buy you a guest-book," said Evangeline Ditson.

"No, please don't, Evangeline. It'd make *them* self-conscious, and me too. And anyway, they're not really my guests. They'd never come to my house if Elisabeth McAndrews could entertain them."

Nevertheless she was soon the established *de facto* hostess of Spring Valley College, and as such she placed her husband in a subtly advantageous position for any higher ambitions he might have. He was not president of the college, but as dean, teacher, and now host he was the most active individual in the administration. Bruce Clanronald McAndrews had several years to go before automatic retirement age, and since he cared not the slightest who succeeded him, he hid his boredom with the job and its routine. He did what was expected of any man who held the job:

he made the ceremonial speeches at the opening of college in September and at the time of commencement; he appeared at the district alumni dinners from Chicago to New York; he took as many official trips as he could manage in order to get away from the campus; and he was glad to be relieved of the chore that he had bestowed upon John and Elizabeth Appleton. He was healthy and vigorous for his age, and his surreptitious study of Pennsylvania law had convinced him that as soon as he was retired he could quietly have Elisabeth committed to an institution and as quietly divorce her. He had discussed all this with the lady in Fort Penn whom he intended to marry at the proper time.

Barbara Speacht was a well-to-do woman in her fifties, widow and principal heiress of Christian Speacht, whose money had been made in street paving and highway construction. Neither Barbara nor Christian Speacht had made the top level of Fort Penn society, but his money had become respectable as it increased and Barbara had further respectablized it with her church work and philanthropies. The understanding between Barbara Speacht and Bruce McAndrews was satisfactorily *quid pro quo:* she would be able to leave Fort Penn as the wife of a college president emeritus, enjoying a standing that had been denied her by the women who had snubbed her. The advantages to Bruce Clanronald McAndrews were obvious. He would be able to afford the committing of Elisabeth and the divorce, the upkeep of the house the college provided for retired presidents, and—with the willing help of Barbara Speacht—they could indulge their fondness for travel. Meanwhile they spoke admiringly of their companionship, their mutual interdependence and growing affection. His visits to her were of necessity a well-kept secret. She owned the apartment building in which she lived, and when there was a vacancy on her floor the apartment was rented to McAndrews. They went to bed together originally as a defiant demonstration of their residual powers and desires; the intimate relationship continued because the limited past experience of both parties made any new experience a novelty and a pleasure. She exhibited a nervous sensuality that passed for youthful excitement; as to Bruce McAndrews, his sexual urge was no more than that; an urge that impelled him to perform a biological function which was accompanied by pleasure and was then put at rest until the reappearance of the urge. He was not a romantic man. He was not a sentimental man.

But he was a selfish man, and his selfishness amounted to an emotion. He was determined to finish out his tenure with an irreproachable record, and as he entered the final years of his presidency he was pleased with his achievement thus far. No one blamed him for the misfortune that had happened to his wife; if anything he was an object of sympathy. No one blamed him, he believed, for being less warm than Witherspoon, his predecessor, since the college had grown in size and what with the problems of expansion and the depression and the war, he could not be expected to devote much time to personal individual relations with students. And if there were some alumni who complained of the changes in the character of the college, they could not blame Bruce Clanronald McAndrews for the existence of coeducation or the relaxing of admissions standards which had taken place during Witherspoon's tenure. McAndrews had a ready answer for any alumnus who wanted the college to revert to its earlier character: "Give us the money, and we'll give you another Princeton—*or* a Kenyon, *or* a Haverford." He never made such a statement, but it was implicit in his defenses against criticism, and cautious alumni shied away from the statement before it could be made. All in all, he had given Spring Valley its money's worth, and when his time was up he would relinquish his post to a successor who would take over a going concern.

Although he did not care who his successor would be, he cared who it would not be. He did not want John Appleton to follow him as president of Spring Valley. Bruce McAndrews was not one to waste much time in wondering why he disliked a man, but he anticipated the day when he would be asked for an opinion of John Appleton as presidential material, and this would require a better answer than merely that he considered Appleton a show-off. He had disliked Appleton almost on sight; Appleton had the appearance of a man who was coming to coach the football team, not to attempt to teach history. He was, moreover, very, very sure of himself on the Spring Valley campus, as an alumnus, the son of a highly respected professor and of a popular alumna. As a teacher he had inspired respect for his subject and gained popularity for himself without making any cheap appeal for it. Bruce Clanronald McAndrews realized that nearly everything John Appleton did and was could have been cited in his favor; McAndrews therefore saw that he would have to provide himself with more acceptable reasons for his opposition to the Appleton candidacy. That there would be an Appleton candidacy was a foregone conclusion. "I won't have the final say in the matter," he confided to Barbara Speacht. "But just as a courtesy they're going to ask me if I have any ideas."

"What have you got against Mr. Appleton?" she said.

"Nothing. That's the trouble."

"There must be something, Bruce. It's up to you to find it."

"I know."

"Why don't you ask yourself why you don't want him to be president."

"That's what I've been doing."

"Not exactly. You've been asking yourself why you dislike him. Maybe it's the same thing, but maybe it isn't."

"You've hit on something. Why *don't* I want him to be president? Why don't I?"

"Ask your New England conscience. Is it because you think he'd make a better president than you've been?"

Her question angered him, but she was already too important to his future to risk a quarrel. "Maybe so," he said. Then he admitted to himself that there was truth in her question. "Maybe so."

"Then let me make a suggestion. I know something about politics. Christian made his money as much through politics as through building roads, and he always talked things over with me. If you honestly think he would make a good president, irregardless of you liking him or not, then the thing for you to do is support him. Especially if they're all thinking about him anyway. You see what I mean, Bruce?"

"Yes." He also saw that this woman who giggled and panted in bed was a crafty strategist as well as a sharp person in matters of business.

"Let them think you're all for him. Let *him* think so, too. And you start thinking so. That's what you want to do. You start thinking he's the right man for the job and one of these days you'll discover an objection. That's the way they'll look at it, Bruce. It's human nature to. And that way, if you discover an objection, it'll be a stronger objection than just not seeing eye-to-eye. I wish I could meet *her*, but there's no way to arrange that, and I guess I've known plenty like her, from your description."

"She's his most valuable asset."

"Oh, you never said that before."

"Well, I'm just beginning to realize it. There's nobody else on the campus that could take charge of things the way she has."

"And there's never been any talk about her? You know?"

"Never, not even during the war."

"And she's beautiful?"

"Well, yes. Not what they call a glamor girl, but good-looking. Pretty. Not the dressed-up kind."

"Your Junior League type."

"Yes, that's about the size of it. I was never much of an authority on the opposite sex."

"You wouldn't be as fine a person as you are today if you had been."

"Thank you, Barbara."

"Well, I mean it. Christian may have had his faults, but chasing women wasn't one of them. Has there ever been any of that kind of talk about Appleton?"

"No."

"Make a difference in a coeducational school."

"I know. No, I guess he's like me in that respect."

"What wonders me a little bit," she said. "Why does a New York society girl want her husband to be president of Spring Valley?"

"It's a pretty good job, Barbara."

"Don't take that personally. I'm just wondering what does she get out of it?"

"Well, it's as high as he'll ever get."

"Yes, but is she going to be satisfied with it? Look at it from her point of view. Where did you say they're sending their children?"

"The boy goes to St. Paul's and the girl to Farmington."

Barbara Speacht nodded. "You see why I asked you? Mrs. Appleton hasn't given up her old background, not if she's sending her children to those kind of schools. I know the kind of parents that get their children into St. Paul's and Farmington, right here in Fort Penn. Let me tell you, if this Mrs. Appleton'd been sold on Spring Valley, those children wouldn't be going to ritzy schools. Mark my words, that's where your trouble is in that family."

"Trouble? What trouble?"

"Every married couple have their disagreements on some subjects."

"But I never heard that John Appleton objected to where his kids are going to school."

"Maybe you didn't. Maybe he doesn't object, but I look at it this way. She wants to get her children away from Spring Valley and he doesn't realize what that means. It means that she doesn't think Spring Valley is good enough for them."

"Maybe so. I never looked at it that way. She has a lot of money and I just thought she wanted to give them a good education."

"She does. Better than they'll get at Spring Valley High. And you wait and see where the boy goes to college."

"By that time I won't care where he goes. How do you know so much about people you never even saw?"

"Oh, it only takes a little imagination. Christian used to ask me the same question. He used to say I could be the first woman governor of Pennsylvania if I had the inclination, but you'd never catch me running for office. Political, that is. Oh, I got elected to like charity things and church guilds. That's because I was good-natured and had the time and money. It was easy. If my parents had had the money to send me to Miss Holbrook's I could have been president of the Junior League. I have the knack for those kind of things, but I don't think it's ladylike for a woman to run for office."

"How do you feel about a woman that's trying to get her husband elected to college president?"

"In her position I'd do the same. That's why I understand this woman, Mrs. Appleton. If she can't be it herself, she's going to see to it that he is. Would you care for a bottle of beer, Bruce?"

"I was just thinking I'd like a glass of beer."

"I was always glad I had the money to do things for people. They said Christian got rich on graft, but those that said it were in it with him up to the hilt, most of them. And those that weren't wished they were, with very few exceptions. Another thing, nobody ever sent back a cheque of mine for their favorite charities, graft or no graft. I have no respect for a hypocrite. Would you care for a sandwich? I got some imported liverwurst that just came in today. It's almost as good as they used to send before the war."

"That would be just right."

"Is she one of those skinny ones, Mrs. Appleton?"

"No, I wouldn't say so."

"Well proportioned. Those skinny ones, I never trust them."

"No, she's well proportioned."

"I like a womanly woman."

"So do I."

"Oh, I wasn't fishing for any compliments. But I don't know what a man sees in some of those flat-chested creatures. You sit still and I'll be right back." She patted the top of his head. "But that's not saying I don't like a slender *man*."

As a Lutheran churchwoman Barbara Speacht had no legitimate reason to visit Presbyterian Spring Valley College; her husband had been a Penn State alumnus, she herself had gone nowhere to college. But she became mildly obsessed with the idea of meeting Elizabeth Appleton. She did not reject the possibility that Bruce McAndrews' animosity toward John Appleton emanated from jealousy and something like love of Elizabeth Appleton. He seemed unable to say anything finally disparaging about her, and the spontaneity of his calling her Appleton's most valuable asset was not lost on Barbara Speacht. She was not in love with Bruce McAndrews, did not expect him to be in love with her, could imagine nothing more than affection and companionship for a man and woman their age; nevertheless she had curiosity about Elizabeth Appleton, and if Bruce McAndrews was secretly or unconsciously in love with John Appleton's wife, prudence indicated an investigation of the woman before Barbara Speacht finally committed herself to marriage with McAndrews. He had not noticed, or he pretended not to notice, that she had never actually promised she would marry him. That was one of the things he apparently took for granted as an inevitable development of their intimate companionship, just as he took for granted that she was a rich woman without her ever having disclosed the size of her fortune. On that score he was in for a pleasant surprise: she had a large, comfortable apartment with a full-time, live-out maid; she owned a Cadillac for which she had a chauffeur; she dressed expensively; but except for the car and chauffeur she lived unostentatiously for a woman who was worth well over two million dollars, of which more than half was in tax-free securities. It was all hers.

One day, early in 1950, Barbara Speacht instructed Walter, her chauffeur, to order a Spring Valley telephone book, which was delivered to her by mail. She first looked up the John Appletons' address and then she began to read the alphabetical listings of the Spring Valley subscribers. She got only as far as the D's. Four listings for the name Ditson: Ditson, Brice, had a listing for business and another for residence; Ditson Hardware was the third listing; Ditson, Porter, gave as his address the Spg Vly Hotel. The name Ditson was not an unfamiliar one: Mrs. Brice Ditson's name appeared with Barbara Speacht's on the roll of the Women's Republican State Committee, and in all probability she had met Mrs. Ditson. But the four listings of the Ditson name, which stood out typographically in the Spring Valley telephone book, evoked something besides recollection of Mrs. Brice Ditson. She thought about it, and she recalled that Mrs. Brice Ditson was the daughter of a man named Frothingham or some such name, a very important man in Stratford County, but she was still not satisfied that she had found the reason that the Ditson name rang a bell, and so she paid a visit to the Fort Penn Women's Civic Club library and studied *Who's Who in America* and the Pittsburgh Social Register. In the latter she found what she was looking for: it was Porter Ditson, who lived at the Spg Vly Hotel, whose name had struck a gong. In 1942 and through 1945 he had been a tenant of hers in a small apartment house she owned. She immediately telephoned her real estate manager and asked him to send her all records on Porter Ditson, which included the confidential comments of the building superintendent: "Quiet. No noisy parties. Only 1 woman visiter. Come 2 or 3 times a month. White woman about 35 yrs of age. If they was all like Maj. Ditson I woud not complain. Do not think visiter was prostute. He called her Elizabeth but did not hear last name. Maj. Ditson nice gentleman. Very clean."

There were thousands, possibly millions, of Elizabeths. There were probably hundreds of Elizabeths in Nesquehela County. But Barbara Speacht was too shrewd a woman to reject the laws of chance. An Elizabeth who came to see a quiet, nice, clean gentleman named Porter Ditson two or three times a month, and who was not a prostute, was probably a married woman and probably a married woman from Porter Ditson's not too distant home town. Her name might have been Elizabeth, and it might have been Elisabeth. Her name might be Elizabeth Appleton, and it might be Elisabeth McAndrews. Barbara Speacht was sure she was on the right track—the right track of two tracks. She had never seen Porter Ditson, but from what she already knew of him she was doubtful that he would be having an affair with Elisabeth McAndrews, although such a situation would provide a pat explanation for Bruce McAndrews' ill-disguised intention to abandon his wife. No, the woman was Elizabeth Appleton; of that she was convinced, and she was equally certain that Bruce McAndrews had no suspicion of it. Barbara Speacht was delighted with her discovery, her detective work, and with herself. She had been snubbed too often by women like Elizabeth Appleton. They took her money, they allowed her to work for their charities; but when she went into their homes the hall carpets were covered with canvas runners as protection from the feet of hoi polloi and incidentally to tell the strangers where they might walk. The Ming and Meissen pieces were put away, out of reach of the clumsy peasants, and a maid was stationed on the second story where she could keep an eye on the curious who might open closets and drawers. Barbara Speacht hated what those women did to her, and she hated herself no less because she always went back for more. Soon after she had convinced herself that Elizabeth Appleton was the visiter to Maj. Ditson's apartment Barbara Speacht realized that she had developed a hatred of a woman she had never seen.

"How can I arrange to meet Mrs. Appleton?" she asked Bruce McAndrews.

"Why do you want to?"

"Just idle curiosity," she said.

"Do you just want to see her, or do you want to talk to her?"

"I won't say I know you, if that's what's worrying you," said Barbara Speacht.

"It doesn't worry me, except for your sake. I'm still a married man's all I was thinking," he said. "Why, I guess it could be arranged. And maybe it should be. Yes. Maybe you ought to start taking an interest in Spring Valley, then it won't come all of a sudden when we announce *our* plans. I'll give you the names of a couple of Fort Penn women, some that went to Spring Valley and some that are wives of alumni. You can begin to show an interest that way, publicly, and then it'll be easy as pie for you to visit the college."

In due course Barbara Speacht became a Friend of Spring Valley College, an organization of alumni and non-alumni, who were delighted that the well-to-do Lutheran widow could be so easily persuaded to help a Presbyterian institution. They well knew that Mrs. Speacht's initial contribution of fifty dollars was only a token of her interest. Barbara Speacht was a generous woman, and whoever it was that had originally spoken to her about Spring Valley College deserved a lot of credit . . . There was a special day in the spring for Friends of Spring Valley College and Mrs. Speacht seemed well pleased with her visit. She sat and talked with Elizabeth Appleton for more than half an hour, and at the faculty-Friends luncheon she engaged in animated conversation with Brice Ditson. At the suggestion of one of the members of the Friends board Bruce Clanronald McAndrews personally welcomed the newcomer to the organization and it turned out that Mrs. Speacht and President McAndrews had met previously. "People ought to do more for education," Mrs. Speacht said to one person and another. At her tea in honor of the visiting ladies Evangeline Ditson was flattered that this potential benefactor to the college, whom she vaguely remembered from some other gathering, had heard of the generosity of the late J. W. Framingham. "The next time you come to Spring Valley you must stay with us," said Evangeline Ditson. To which Barbara Speacht replied: "And I hope you'll call me up the next time you're in Fort Penn, although I don't see how you can bear to leave this lovely place. The *air* is so salubrious."

A few days later Bruce McAndrews said: "Well, Barbara, *you* were a great success. How did you like *them?*"

"Where was Mr. Appleton while I was there?"

"Tied up. This is one of the busiest times of the year for a dean. You got along fine with her, though."

"Did I? Is that your opinion or hers?"

"Mine, but based on what she told me."

"Yes, I can hear her. She probably called me an amusing little creature or words to that effect."

"No, she didn't say that. She said she'd had an interesting chat with you and that you seemed genuinely interested."

"Tell me about Porter Ditson."

"You mean Brice Ditson. Brice is a trustee, although he went to Princeton."

"Porter Ditson, not Brice."

"He wasn't there. He has no connection with the college. Why do you want to know about him? He's a loafer, a gentleman loafer, not at all like his brother. How did his name come up?"

"It didn't. I'm bringing it up now."

"Why?"

"I'm not quite ready to tell you, but when I do it'll be very interesting."

"In what way?"

"Oh, no. You don't get any more out of me till I'm good and ready, Bruce McAndrews."

"When will that be, pray tell?"

"When I'm good and ready, and have more facts to base something on."

"There isn't anything very interesting about Porter Ditson. He's a man about forty-five, never done a tap of work. He plays golf and in the winter he goes skiing and skates at the country club. The rest of the time he's at the Elks club bar. He hasn't got a brain in his head and if he didn't have a little money he'd be a bum."

"Never married?"

"Never. I've heard that he's a regular visitor at a roadhouse about fifteen miles from town. They have women there, I understand. I don't see how a man could lead such a useless life in the Twentieth Century."

"Do women like him?"

"There you have me. I don't see him enough to be able to tell that. But I never heard anything to that effect, and

(265)

he's still a bachelor. Why are you so secretive and yet want to know all about him? He doesn't fit into this picture."

"What picture?"

"The college. The people you're interested in, like Elizabeth Appleton. Or does he? No, there's nothing there. Never so much as a whisper."

"There's never been so much as a whisper about you and I, either."

"Is that what you're implying? That Elizabeth Appleton had a love affair with Porter Ditson? You're barking up the wrong tree, Barbara."

"I didn't imply anything, Bruce."

"I can tell you right now, the only talk there's ever been about Elizabeth Appleton was in connection with Rupert Hillenketter, a retired professor, and that wasn't much. Nobody ever took it seriously. She admires Hillenketter, God knows why, and he fancies himself as an old-fashioned eccentric type, but there was never anything there. I'll tell you a little secret about Hillenketter that I'm not supposed to know officially. He likes to get the women students to keep sex diaries. That's been going on for years. He tells them he's at work on some monumental treatise and he needs their help. When I first came to Spring Valley I heard about that, and I don't pay much attention to it any more. I do remember hearing that the girls in the sorority houses used to get together and invent things to put in their diaries but he caught on to that and flunked them, so they stopped. Nowadays they don't have to invent anything. He's no fool, Hillenketter. I don't like him anywhere near me, but he's no fool."

"Does he do anything with the girls?"

"I suspect that he does. But not before he's sure that the girl isn't going to make a fuss. Our dean of women, Mrs. Drew, can't stand Hillenketter. I respect her and she's had her suspicions about Hillenketter for years, but she's told me in strict confidence that the girls she suspected of relations with Hillenketter are naughty little girls anyway. Oh, there are always stories, always rumors, but nothing to take any action on."

"Where there's smoke there's fire."

"Usually is. But he's been at Spring Valley a long time and there's never been any concrete evidence against him, or even a situation that required evidence. Once a few years ago we shipped a girl home for being a Lesbian and at that time Mrs. Drew got an anonymous letter that said that the girl had described her experiences to Hillenketter. In fact the letter implied that Hillenketter more or less encouraged the girl. But Mrs. Drew and I never told anybody about the letter. As much as she dislikes Hillenketter, Mrs. Drew and I agreed to burn the letter in my office, and that's what we did."

"Quite rightly," she said.

"You have to have more than that to go on. And darn it all, you can't teach psychology without getting into sex. When I was a dean I'd say about a third of the problems that came to my attention had something to do with sex. You can't pretend it doesn't exist. Or you do pretend, we do, officially, till something gets out of hand. Then we're supposed to be experts, temporarily, and after the thing blows over, back to the old pretense. I'm only glad that Mrs. Drew and John Appleton have to deal with those problems and not I. One advantage of being president instead of dean."

"I wish I'd had a chance to meet Mr. Appleton."

"The next time you come up I'll see that you do," said Bruce McAndrews.

"When will that be?" said Barbara Speacht.

"Well, commencement's only a few weeks off. Let me think a minute," said Bruce McAndrews. "The Friends of Spring Valley visit the college only once a year, en masse. But I might be able to arrange it so that you and a few other potential benefactors . . ." He smiled.

"Can you fix it so that I stay at Mrs. Ditson's?"

"That's who I had in mind."

Evangeline Ditson, with her lifelong suspicion of

motives, quickly guessed that Bruce McAndrews had more
than a college benefaction in mind for Barbara Speacht, but
she had no objection to being used as a cover-up. She sent off
an invitation to Mrs. Speacht, who replied that she would be
charmed to spend the night as Mrs. Ditson's guest. The obvious choice of partner for Mrs. Speacht at Evangeline's dinner party was Porter Ditson; the less obvious choice was
Bruce McAndrews. Evangeline had them both, along with
the Cleveland millionaire who had been given an honorary
degree; the millionaire's wife; Harry and Frances Jeffries;
Mrs. Drew, the dean of women; Jake Rodeheaver, the
wealthy young faculty member; and John and Elizabeth
Appleton. Invited to come in after dinner were Rupert Hillenketter, Roy and Mary Leslie, the Charles Mosslers, Dr.
and Mrs. Frank Hopkins, Benny Schuessler, State Senator
Oscar W. Doppelganger and Mrs. Doppelganger; and the
two Meems sisters, middle-aged spinsters who were not
asked out very much but did a great deal of church work and
always went home at a reasonable hour, usually offering to
give a lift to from two to four others in their chauffeur-driven
Packard.

The college year had officially ended with the Class
Day exercises in the afternoon, and the sunset had brought
some relief from the 90° heat. Evangeline's dinner, begun in
half light, had ended in darkness broken by the hurricane
lamps on table and sideboard, and the good food and wine
had restored vitality to the company. The hurricane lamps
were carried out to tables in Evangeline's back yard, the
scene of the second half of her party.

"You'd never know you had this much room out here,"
said Barbara Speacht to her hostess.

"Yes, we go through to the next street," said Evangeline.
"There's no alley in this block, but we're the only ones that
go through all the way. That's our garage, that used to be
the old carriage-house. When I was a girl all this was wide
open, no fences, and all this space used to be one big back
yard, a sort of playground for all the children in the block.
But now we're almost the last private house in the block. The

only one with trees left, and I'm afraid they're dying off. But we love our house and I guess we'll stay here as long as we can."

"This was *your* house?"

"Yes, I was born in this house. My husband and his brother were mostly brought up several blocks from here. They were orphans, raised by an uncle and aunt."

"So I guess Mr. Ditson thinks of this as his first real home."

"My husband does, yes. My brother-in-law, Porter Ditson, that sat next to you at dinner, I suppose he's never really had a home of his own. Of course not. He lives at the hotel, something I could never do, but I suppose it's different for a man."

"I guess if they get used to it. A bachelor, isn't he?"

"Yes. Never married."

"A charming gentleman, too. But I guess some men are just not cut out for marriage."

"Don't meet the right woman, I guess."

"Or sometimes do, but she isn't free."

"Well, yes, there's that, too."

"I think that often explains it, why some men stay bachelors. By the time they're ready to settle down, they don't see anybody they want to settle down with except somebody that already has a husband."

"In some cases, but Porter seems to like being single. Of course he never tells anybody what he thinks or does."

"Maybe that's just as well, if you know what I mean."

"Well, he'd be the soul of discretion, Porter. He *is* a *gentleman*."

"Oh, that's written all over him. Gentleman. That would give a woman confidence if she ever decided to—well, *you* know."

"Oh, now here's someone I'd like you to meet. Just joining the party. He's a retired psychology professor, and very interesting."

Rupert Hillenketter was a new experience for Barbara Speacht, whose acquaintance with college professors was limited to four or five men on the faculty of Fort Penn University, friends of her late husband's. "I'm glad to see you back so soon," said Hillenketter.

"I didn't meet you when I was here before. I'm sure I didn't, or I'd have remembered," said Barbara Speacht, pleased but confused.

"*I* remembered. No, we didn't meet, but you must realize that I'm one of the old monuments around here. One of the landmarks, perhaps I should say. You must also realize that after so many years, I always notice a new face even among the Friends of Spring Valley. *If* the face is pleasing to the eye."

"Thank you. Thank you very much. I'm overwhelmed."

"And am I to take it that your being here so soon after your previous visit is an indication of, ah, serious intent?"

"Serious intent? How do you mean?"

"That you're more conscientious than some of the Friends of Spring Valley. I've often thought that many of them were fair-weather friends in the most literal sense. In other words, dear lady, this is a pleasant place to visit on a lovely spring day. But you've come to our commencement, and on a day that most people would prefer to strip down to the buff and sit, Buddha-like, in a cold tub. I confess that I have been doing exactly that. I came home from Class Day and took off every stitch, filled my tub with the lukest of lukewarm water, and cooled it and myself off. Have you been to Japan?"

"No, I haven't."

"I thought perhaps you might be able to tell me about the bathing customs there, which I'm told are extremely civilized. How much more civilized it would be if instead of having us all sit out here on this sultry night, our hostess had provided a tank or pool, in which we could all converse in comfort. I confess that I should cut short my conversation with Miss Cora Meems and her sister Miss Irma Meems, for aesthetic reasons. Indeed, I very much fear that I should confine myself to the amenities with our hostess. But I should go on chatting with you, with Elizabeth Appleton, little Mary Leslie, Mrs. Hopkins, and even Mrs. Jeffries."

"Goodness, I don't know why you should include me."

"Would I embarrass you if I were to tell you why?"

"You might."

"Then let me try to put it in a way that will not embarrass you."

"I haven't got their figures and I know it."

"Ah, but you have your own."

"Maybe we'd better change the subject, Professor."

"Very well. Now who among the men present would you exclude?"

"I thought we were getting off the subject."

"Off the subject of your figure, since you don't seem to welcome personal compliments. But can't we be critical of the men? Let me commence. I'm afraid my good friend and former pupil, Harry Jeffries, has been careless of his diet. So Harry would add nothing to our *soirée de bain*. Nor would our host, who can only be described as scrawny. What would you say to John Appleton?"

"He has a nice build."

"I agree. Porter Ditson?"

"Yes, I guess so."

"Who else?"

"Mr. Leslie. Not very tall, though."

"I agree."

"That's about all, I guess."

"Not Dr. McAndrews, our president?"

"Well, him, yes."

"Oh, decidedly. But I wonder why you didn't mention him."

"I guess I just didn't think of him that way."

"That may be more revealing than you know. However, the rather odd fact is that the man that most women find attractive, among those specimens of manhood present tonight, *is* the very one I had to exclude on aesthetic grounds."

"Dr. Jeffries?"

"None other."

"I guess some women would like him."

"Quite a few do. But of course our discussion wasn't so much their animal appeal, was it? We were discussing them from the point of view of standing in a tank with them and carrying on a conversation, a very different thing from making love. The man you might like to talk to might easily be the last one you would like to make love with."

"Not me. I have nothing *against* Dr. Jeffries, but he isn't my type at all. You expressed it when you said animal appeal. Not that he's an animal, but he looks all physical, if you know what I mean."

"Oh, I understand perfectly. In fact, I'm convinced that of all the men here, your personal preference would be Bruce McAndrews."

"I'm not saying one way or another."

"You require what might be termed the spiritual element in your love-making?"

"I'm a widow, Professor. I was only married the one time in my life."

"But as a scientist I have to keep an open mind, you know."

"Oh, sure. I guess everybody ought to, to a certain extent. Keep an open mind, that is."

"I think I'll promote you. From Friend of Spring Valley College to Friend of Education Everywhere."

"Thank you, but I don't know as I deserve that."

"Yes you do. The open mind is the first requirement to being a real friend of education. The open purse is close behind, but first comes the open mind—and I regret to say they don't always go together. The gentleman in the white dinner jacket with the artificial carnation in his lapel. He was given an honorary degree today."

"Yes. Mr. Marple."

"Gifford E. Marple, of Cleveland, Ohio. His purse is open, but not his mind. Although I fancy that to me it's an open book, a very thin volume printed in large type. He craves respectability, the tokens of respectability such as honorary degrees, in order to convince himself that he's innocent of his secret vices."

"Oh, dear."

"Yes. Without claiming to have any documented evidence, purely on certain observations, I would put him down as a pederast."

"I'm afraid I don't know what that is."

"No? Well, it's a sexual practice that was said to be common among the high Nazis. Roehm, for instance. Do you remember that period?"

"No, I don't, but I never followed European politics very closely."

"Well, pederasty might be defined as the substitution of a young man for a woman in the sexual act. That's not a scientific definition, but as a woman of the world you've heard of the practice."

"That's where you're wrong, Professor. I'm not a woman of the world. I don't know much about such things."

"Then I've been misled by your evening gown and your jewelry, your grooming."

"No, I'm very unsophisticated in such things."

"Misled, but not entirely surprised. Women often do hide their intense preoccupation with sexual matters by getting themselves up in the most sophisticated dress."

"I don't see how that would hide it. I should think that would call attention to it."

"It calls *my* attention to it, dear lady. But flamboyant femininity is so obvious that in our society we often make the mistake of thinking that an extremely well-dressed woman must be extremely well adjusted. Actually, it's the best disguise of all for a woman who has very serious problems. Most men seeing you for the first time, beautifully gowned, well turned out, would think that you were completely adjusted. But I'm afraid I couldn't agree with most men. I seldom do. I'm not a psychiatrist, but I dabble in the field, and I know you'd make a most interesting patient."

"Me a patient?"

"Everyone is potentially a patient, but some are more interesting than others. You'd be one of the interesting ones."

"Not me."

"Ah, now, I'm the better judge of that, dear lady. I could ask you three questions that would—"

"Well, don't."

He nodded. "The resistance is very strong. And you *don't* want to know about yourself?"

"No. Anyway, I think I know all there is to know."

"You weren't afraid of your father?"

"Oh, come on, Professor, that's just a wild guess."

"But you were, and much more afraid of him than you've ever admitted to yourself. So much so that it took a lot of patience on the part of your husband—"

"Now, Professor. Don't start *that*."

"Too late. I *have* started it. Your present relations with a gentleman who shall be nameless are much more agreeable than those you had with your husband. But haven't you asked yourself why? I'll *tell* you why. Your husband inherited, you might say, some of your fear of your father, and you never quite got over that, with your husband. But the unnamed gentleman, at this moment lighting a cigar for Gifford E. Marple, got the benefit of your husband's patience."

She was silent, then: "How did you know so much about me? I don't mean the psychoanalysis bushwa, but how did you know—oh, I guess I told you I was a widow."

"Yes, you did, and when you were here before I wondered what brought you here. Your husband wasn't an alumnus and neither were you, an alumna. You have a perfectly good second-rate university in Fort Penn, if education was your new hobby. Then why Spring Valley? Why not Dickinson? Franklin and Marshall? Colleges closer to home. *Cherchez l'homme*, dear lady. And by process of elimination, I found him. I think you will be very happy, when certain obstacles are cleared away. But you could be even happier if you knew a little more about yourself. Write to me if you ever feel like it."

"I have nothing to write about."

"Then I may expect a letter next week? Two weeks? You've forbidden me to ask you three questions, but will you answer one, just one?"

"That depends. I might."

"In this group, who of the men most reminds you of your father—wait, before you answer. Let me write down his initials." Rupert Hillenketter reached behind her and with his forefinger rubbed two letters on the glass top of an iron table. "All right. Who?"

"Dr. Jeffries," she said.

"Look on the table."

Barbara Speacht turned and saw the initials H. J.

"Harry Jeffries," said Hillenketter. "I could clear that up for you in a very short time."

"What could you clear up, Rupert? I have no doubt that he could, too, Mrs. Speacht. May I join you?" Elizabeth Appleton in a cotton print evening dress pulled up an iron chair.

"Oh, now, Elizabeth, you know better than to ask that," said Hillenketter.

"I wasn't really prying. Rupert is positively uncanny sometimes, his ability to see beneath the surface of things."

"I wish I could do that," said Barbara Speacht.

"Oh, I don't know," said Elizabeth Appleton. "What if we all knew everything about everybody? Wouldn't life be dull?"

"Not to me," said Rupert Hillenketter. "Even if I were omniscient, that is, if I knew everything about everybody at a given moment, the human mind is so responsive to so many, many, many influences that I still couldn't predict what would happen in the *next* given moment. That would keep life from being dull. We can predict, but we can't foretell. That's the difference between science and mumbo-jumbo."

"Now I *never* thought of *that*," said Elizabeth Appleton. "Did you, Mrs. Speacht? I understand it, but I never would have made the distinction. Predict, but not foretell. Rupert, you're very good tonight. Our visitor has stimulated you."

"Thank you," said Barbara Speacht.

"You always stimulate me, Elizabeth," said Rupert Hillenketter.

"No, no, Rupert. Not always. And not nearly as much as I did when I first came here. Now you know all about me, and I'm not a very interesting subject at best."

"I know a great *deal* about you, Elizabeth, but I haven't the opportunity to observe you that I once had. Elizabeth and I and young Mrs. Leslie and Porter Ditson used to meet for bridge regularly."

"And then the war came and put a stop to our bridge, but why didn't we ever resume after the war?" said Elizabeth Appleton.

"I suppose nobody wanted to."

"Mary, with two very small children. But I could have played, and I'm sure Porter could have."

Hillenketter shook his head. "It wasn't in the cards, if you'll forgive an atrocious play on words."

"Doesn't your husband play?" said Barbara Speacht.

"No, he never played after contract came in."

"None of us played very well. Mary Leslie was the best," said Hillenketter.

"Do you think so? At playing a hand, but Porter was better at bidding, I thought. He had that intuitive thing," said Elizabeth Appleton.

"When he was your partner. But when he was my partner, no. I wonder if that would still be the case."

"Well, let's have a try at it? No, I guess not till fall. The Leslies are going up to Lake Ontario somewhere, and you're going abroad, I hear, Rupert?"

"For a few weeks in August, after the big tourist rush."

"John and I will be here most of the summer," said Elizabeth Appleton. "Where do you go, Mrs. Speacht?"

"Oh, different places. I thought I'd try New Hampshire this year. I like to change around. Last year I went to California."

"I've only been there once, late in the war, when my husband was in the Navy. What I saw of the fabulous city of

San Francisco, I might as well have been on Fourth Street, Spring Valley. Well, not really, but almost."

Hillenketter laughed lightly. "Nevertheless it sounds as though you'd found what you went for."

"Oh, Rupert. *Yes.* That was the view from our hotel room. Rupert should have been a detective. What do they call that? Deductive reasoning. Five years ago, heavens." She turned again to Barbara Speacht. "Where in New Hampshire, Mrs. Speacht?"

"I haven't quite made up my mind. There are several good hotels, I'm told. I've never been there."

"Neither have I. My father went to school there, and my husband's family originated there, but I've yet to see it. I have a *boy* at *school* in New Hampshire, but of course I've been forbidden to visit him."

"Forbidden?" said Barbara Speacht.

"Oh my yes. When he first entered he didn't even want his father to go with him, but we drew the line there. His father went up with him, but neither of us has been there since. They're so independent, the modern children. Or think they are. Have you got children, Mrs. Speacht?"

"No, no children."

"I sometimes feel that I haven't either—well, not really, but they do push us out of their lives as soon as they can, or at least it seems that way. Rupert, I'm sure you have theories about that."

"Of course, by the hundreds. About children and about their parents, although I don't make as much of a distinction between children and adults as you do, Elizabeth."

"We're all children, is that what you mean?"

"Or all adults. Our childhood fears carry over through our adult lives, sometimes to our last gasp. Even the most superficial psychologist, one of my freshmen, soon learns that you must consider the whole man, the whole woman, and not start with the girl's first menstruation, the boy's first erection. You go back as far as you can, as far as the individual under consideration will let you. I've been very much interested lately in relating childhood sex play to the sex play that occurs late in life. I've been trying to determine whether there's a pattern. I've been getting some but not nearly enough help from one or two of the teachers in the Model School. Has to be surreptitious, so I won't mention the teachers by name. But if I could make some progress there, I'd have records that would be very helpful twenty years from now, when the children are grown, and forty years from now, when the children are no longer young."

"The Model School—" Elizabeth began, in explanation to Barbara Speacht.

"I know what a model school is. I went to Normal for a year," said Barbara Speacht. "But I'm glad to hear they don't allow you to keep sex records of young children. They learn about those things soon enough, without being asked questions about it when they're six years old."

"When would you call 'soon enough'? At what age?" said Rupert Hillenketter.

"To be asked such questions? Twenty-one. And I don't think anyone ought to have to answer at any age if they didn't feel like it."

"I agree with you, Mrs. Speacht," said Elizabeth Appleton.

"Then I'm afraid I must withdraw my compliment to your open mind, Mrs. Speacht," said Hillenketter. "Your mind is just as closed as Elizabeth's."

"Well, I'm glad I have company," said Barbara Speacht. "Nothing personal about it, but you modern professors don't seem to realize that women like to have privacy, secrets. And always did."

"Oh, I call that fig-leaf psychology. But we all know what's behind the fig leaf," said Hillenketter.

"Oh, no you don't. But you want to know, and men always did want to know and always will," said Barbara Speacht.

"It works both ways, dear lady. Women also have their own curiosity."

"That's what *you* think. But we don't. With women it isn't every man. It's one man. Isn't that so, Mrs. Appleton?"

"Yes."

"With men it's any and every woman," said Barbara Speacht. "A woman can be content with one."

"I'm afraid there's a great deal of evidence to the contrary," said Rupert Hillenketter.

"You mean women that are unfaithful? They wouldn't be unfaithful if the man was the right one. But men are, even men that love their wives. The darn trouble with you psychologists is that you don't understand women. You're all men, or most of you are, and you think you're being scientific and all that, but you look at everything from the male point of view. You twist your facts to suit yourselves. You'd like to think that women are as promiscuous as you are, but they're not. You've had time to think about all the women that were true to their husbands during the war, and compare that with the husbands in the army that slept with other women. That ought to prove something to you, but you don't want to think about that because it goes against your own pet theories. I'm not blaming the men that were unfaithful. They couldn't help it, because they were men, and men are naturally promiscuous."

"You've made several statements that I can't accept, but woman convinced against her will, and so on," said Hillenketter.

"And now let's talk about—the baseball game. Spring Valley beat Mount St. Joe's three to one, the first commencement game we've won against the Irish in five years. Did you know that, Rupert? Why are the Irish such good baseball players?"

"Because they have so many Italians on their teams, as you'd know if you'd study the lineups. And it was a boy named Leinbach who scored the winning run for Spring Valley."

"Don't be cross, Rupert," said Elizabeth Appleton. "You can't always have your way."

"No? I could still have my way, as you call it, if I wanted to attack such specious arguments, but what's the use on a hot night?" He rose and without another word to the women left them, said goodnight to the Ditsons, and was gone.

"He's sixty-five," said Elizabeth Appleton. "And he isn't used to having people stand up to him, especially women. But you have my admiration."

"I got so mad at him. Look at my hand shaking," said Barbara Speacht.

"Oh, you mustn't let him upset you. I was terrified of him when I first came to Spring Valley, but he's really an old dear."

"Does he always get on the subject of sex?"

"Quite a lot. But I'd rather talk about it the way he does than the whispering, gossipy way a group of women can."

"He still doesn't have to say some of those words. That's just to see what effect it has."

"Well, I wouldn't like him to say erection in front of my fifteen-year-old daughter, and he doesn't, but I'm not convinced that he says things to shock people. True, he is too—probing—on short acquaintance. But he does that for a reason. He does it because you don't expect it, and you're so taken by surprise that you find yourself saying things you wouldn't ordinarily say."

"Maybe you're used to him. I'm just—" Barbara Speacht did not finish her sentence.

"Ladies, may I?" Bruce Clanronald McAndrews took the chair vacated by Rupert Hillenketter.

"Sit down, Bruce. Mrs. Speacht has had her baptism of fire."

"Rupert Hillenketter? You forced him to retreat."

"I'm going to leave you two. Our house guest, Gifford Marple, is all alone," said Elizabeth Appleton, and left them.

"Are you having a good time?"

"Oh, Bruce, that awful man."

"Hillenketter?"

"Yes. Why couldn't you have come sooner? I tried to get your eye."

"He *did* upset you. The son of a bitch."

"Not only the things he said. But all of a sudden I realized, I have no one to go to. I wished I had a woman friend, but I haven't. I never made any real friends. I'm all alone, I never realized it before, till this terrible man—somebody to go to, to protect me. You don't *know*, Bruce."

"What did he say?"

"One thing after another. Accusing me of complexes. But it wasn't just the things he said, but making me feel this way. *Afraid.* I've never needed anyone before. Bruce, *will* you—let's decide on a date to get married. I don't care when, just so I get over this feeling of not having anybody to protect me."

"Of course. The divorce may take some time, but I can get it started as soon as they name my successor. That will be during the Christmas holidays sometime. Six months from now."

"If it's a question of money?"

"It won't be. Well, it will and it won't. I'll have to make provision for Elisabeth's support as long as she stays in a rest home. And I can't get a divorce in Pennsylvania, not on any of the grounds they allow. But we don't have to go into that now. We can be married before a year is up."

"That's all I want to know. It would be worth a million dollars to me."

"A *million?*"

She nodded. "Yes, I have that much. Twice that much. I'll see that Elisabeth is well taken care of. Anything to avoid a repetition of tonight. Bruce, I'll make you happy, I know I will."

"You do, Barbara."

"And we can travel and do all the things you wanted to do. Would you like me to give some money to the college now?"

"I'd rather you waited. Wait till after we're married. Even then I'd rather you left them something in your will than give it outright."

"I'm beginning to feel better."

"That's good. I warned you against Hillenketter, but I

guess it didn't take," said Bruce McAndrews. "Have you had much of a chance to study the others? Porter Ditson? John Appleton?"

"Well, they used to play bridge together, Mrs. Appleton and Ditson. *Without Appleton.* If they had an affair, I guess that's when it was. I don't think it's going on now. They have that look about them that means it's all over."

"I don't understand 'that look.' "

"I don't expect that you would. But they have it. She's back with her husband, and he's—he's just getting old."

"Old? He's only in his middle forties."

"I don't care, Bruce. He's an old bachelor, hanging on. Polite as could be at dinner, but as they say, just going through the motions. I saw him look at her once or twice, and she's a very attractive woman. I give her that. I don't want her for a friend, and she doesn't want me, but she is attractive, and yet there was something awfully dead about the way Ditson looked at her. The *other* men react to her. Respond, the way men do to an attractive woman. But not Ditson. And he means nothing to her. She's put him out of her life."

"Did they say anything? Were you together with them? What do you base all this on?"

She would not tell him that in her long friendless state she had watched people and thought about them, a substitute for companionship. "Oh, I guess I'm just like any other woman," she said. "I like to know what makes them tick."

"Well, you're darn good at it."

"It's what they call deductive reasoning, I suppose."

He smiled. "Well, it isn't quite, but I wouldn't like to start explaining why it isn't. When we're married I'll have time to do a lot of the reading I've neglected, and you can read with me."

"Are you going to educate me, Bruce? I'd like that."

"I won't educate you. You don't need it. But I can tell you what to read, we can read them together. Plato. Aristotle. And Descartes. Spinoza. Locke. Hume. Kant. I still have all my books from college. It'll be fun, although embarrassing to see how much I've forgotten."

"Let's start with psychology. I'd love to be able to come out with something that would make Hillenketter's eyes pop out of his head."

"He'd know where you got it. He's a faker, but he has read everything."

"He thinks I don't know anything, and I don't. But just once I'd like to bowl him over."

"It would kill him."

"I wouldn't have any objection to that, believe you me."

"All right. We'll plot his destruction. A nice old retired college president and his wife, planning murder by intellect."

"First we're going to make sure that Appleton doesn't get your job."

"That isn't going to be so difficult."

X

The defeat of John Appleton for the presidency of Spring Valley College was not accomplished by Bruce Clanronald McAndrews, by Evangeline Ditson, or by anyone else who consciously wanted him defeated. Nor was it caused by gossip, envy, Elizabeth Appleton's eager campaign, or any of the factors thus far noted that singly or collectively might be considered as having militated against him. John Appleton was defeated by a perverse exercise of power by a small group of men who resented and resisted Appleton because he was too frequently called the logical and obvious choice for the job; and for those men, the trustees of Spring Valley, to yield to such pressure would have been to surrender their most dramatic privilege. The trustees normally voted on the presidency only once in about twenty years, and many men had served on the board without ever having had a say in the election of a president. Year after year, four times a year,

(284)

the trustees would meet to transact their business, to speak their thoughts on high policy, financial affairs, new construction, honorary degrees, and such other business as might properly be brought up for consideration. The men would come to Everett Hall—some from considerable distances—for a brief morning session in the trustees' room; they would adjourn for lunch at a special table in a corner of Commons; and resume their meeting until late afternoon, when there would be a cocktail party for the trustees and a few administrators and professors and their wives. In the evening there would be a dinner party at the home of one of the local trustees. Few of the men from distant cities would stay the night in Spring Valley; they would motor back to their home towns, or be driven to Altoona to make train connections for the east or west.

The men were men of consequence, of varying degrees of achievement, chosen by the kind of men they admired for a chore that was dignified and dull. The honor of being chosen and the dignity of the job were barely enough to make up for the hostile criticism that was often visited upon the trustees, and a defensive attitude characterized the board's relations with faculty, student body, alumni, and the public. The routine work went unnoticed, but every non-routine decision came in for almost routine censure. Nevertheless no trustee had ever resigned except on orders from a physician; membership on the board gave opportunities for the exercise of power that were unique and highly respectable, however limited, and the habit of power was on all these men; the businessmen, the clerics, the men of medicine and the law. They were the elite of Spring Valley College, and this was to be one of their big years.

They all knew John Appleton, and they liked to think they knew all about him. He was a "campus kid" as a career colonel's son was an "army brat." Even his prolonged absences from the campus—at Harvard and in the Navy— were never regarded as more than temporary. John Appleton would always be back; John Appleton would always be there. The Appleton-Spring Valley tradition that John

*hoped to establish was already in being, in the minds of,
among others, the trustees. Also, it was hard to fault John
Appleton; his record was a satisfactory combination of var-
sity letters and Phi Beta Kappa key; popularity and the
firm hand (as in the Phi Phi Alpha matter); family man,
socially accepted wife, clean-cut appearance, young middle
age, Harvard lineage, no eccentricities. His one fall from
grace—the so-called Framingham lecture—was tolerated
by some and condoned by others: tolerated by those who
were aware that the Framinghams of the world are fair
game for college professors of the liberal persuasion; and
condoned by those trustees who were getting a little tired
of the Framingham domination of Spring Valley. And the
tolerant and the condoning did not have to be reminded
that the Framingham spokesman, Brice Ditson, was a Princeton man, a Framingham in-law, married to a Framingham
who had shown no disposition to continue the Framingham
benefactions. The Framingham lecture had done John Appleton no harm.*

*But the trustees were not to be dictated to by the logi-
cality of John Appleton's qualifications. More exactly, they
were not going to relinquish their power to select as well as
to elect a president. To an immeasurable degree they were
subtly influenced by the current Congressional cliché, "rubber stamp." They were not going to be a rubber stamp
board of trustees, and every time John Appleton's name
came up, they thought of someone else.*

XI

Mary Leslie drove away and Jean Webster Joralemon Roberts walked slowly up the herringbone-brick path and entered her sister's house.

"You, Jean?" came the voice of Elizabeth Appleton.

"It's me." Jean took off her coat and hung it in a closet and joined her sister in John Appleton's study.

"Did you have a good look at the town?" said Elizabeth. "John's gone for a walk."

"Yes, we went up and drove through the college and down to the business section, then out to the country club. Met an odd job called Porter Ditson. He knows my Bill."

"Why do you call him an odd job? And I want to talk to you about your Bill. But first tell me why you think Porter Ditson is an odd job?"

"Well, he's so pre-war, pre-depression. He's more like Father than anyone I've met in years."

"Like Father? I don't see that at all."

"Oh, he couldn't be more unlike Father in most ways, but there was always one thing about Father that impressed me more than anything else. His courtesy. Not just politeness or manners, but courtesy. Don't ask me to define courtesy, because I couldn't."

"But you've used the word. *Try* to define it, or explain it. Explain why Father had it and Porter has."

"Well, as long as you don't hold me to a definition. Father had beautiful manners. Everybody agreed on that, even Mother, but so have a lot of men. Beautiful manners. But you can pick them up or you can be taught them. But you can't be taught courtesy. That has to come from inside the person that has it. It's that knack I suppose you'd call it of making the other person feel that you're interested. Sixty-five thousand men can have beautiful manners and I can tell you of a lot of times when they used their manners to be rude and boorish and snub people. But no matter who he was talking to, Father always made that person feel that Jarvis Webster was speaking to him or her, and not just hearing himself talk. I used to see Father do that with caddies and big shots, and dull old ladies in Southampton. Everybody. Didn't you ever notice that about him? You must have."

"It's quite true."

"Ditson has the same thing. This Ditson, not the one I met yesterday. Today, for instance, he pretended to bawl out Mary Leslie. 'You knew I was heading for your table,' he said. 'Why didn't you have an extra cup for me?' Then when he was talking to me he told some story about Bill Collins. Two little stories, as a matter of fact. Nothing earth-shaking, but they were for me, because I was new here and he wanted to make me feel at home. And he wants to have a party for me."

"But why do you call him an odd job? That isn't exactly a compliment."

"I didn't mean it in an uncomplimentary sense, though. His clothes. Beret and coonskin coat. Knickerbockers. One of those tennis sweaters with a red-and-blue V-neck. I've seen older men dressed like that at Mill Neck, Tuxedo, and I've seen pictures of them at Davos, St. Moritz. But I didn't expect it at Spring Valley."

"We're used to it here. Always the same costume since I've known him. Been skating, I'm sure."

"Yes, he'd been skating," said Jean. "And you could see he was dying for a drink. Not tea. I imagine that in his quiet, gentlemanly way he's quite a lush. You don't get those veins in your face from unfortified tea."

"I've never heard it was a problem of his," said Elizabeth.

"Has he ever been married?"

"No."

"And he doesn't work, I gather from Mary."

"He has a small income and he lives free at the hotel, which is owned by his brother, the man you met yesterday."

"And who left just about no impression at all except that he's married to that very forbidding hockey player."

"She isn't a hockey player, Jean. She's a very good friend of mine. What else did Porter have to say?"

The question took Jean by surprise. "Oh—why, nothing else. He only stayed a minute."

"He said something about me, didn't he? What was it?"

"No, I've told you all he said. All I remember."

"Jean, ever since you've been one year old I always knew when you were prevaricating, but if you don't want to tell me what he said then let's change the subject. I want to ask you about your Bill, as you call him."

"Was he ever a beau of yours?"

"Porter Ditson? Of course not. What ever gave you that fantastic notion? Porter is everybody's beau, in a sense. I used to play bridge with him before the war, and he's invited everywhere. Did Mary Leslie put that idea in your head?"

"Not a bit."

"Then why would you say a thing like that?"

"I guess it was my clumsy way of getting around to

(289)

asking you if you ever did have a beau since you've been married."

"No, I haven't, and at forty I'm not very likely to change my ways."

"Forty's nothing these days, and you certainly don't look forty."

"I don't have to *look* forty when I have a son at St. Paul's and a daughter at Farmington."

"What I meant was that nobody asks that any more. A lot of men would much rather have an affair with a woman of forty. I've heard *that* discussed in great detail, by Mr. Neal Roberts, and his El Morocco friends. Their theory is that a woman of forty isn't encumbered by any silly morals."

"And they're probably not, the women they like. But I couldn't live that kind of life."

"Neither can I! That's why I'm here, Elizabeth. I want to study you and John and maybe get the courage to marry Bill. Right now, it *is* a question of courage. I couldn't face another disaster. I couldn't for myself, and I couldn't marry Bill unless I were sure it will last. He's forty-five, and he shouldn't marry again unless it's going to be permanent."

"Neither should you. Neither should anyone."

"Oh, but people do marry with some doubts about that. He wants to marry me on any terms, and when I give him this warning talk he says if he's willing to take that chance, why should I worry?"

"Then marry him. It's after all the chance everybody takes, whatever age they are. You're not deceiving him, and he's old enough to know what he wants."

"No, he's young enough to know what he wants, but he's too old to have two more marriages. In other words, if I'm a failure, say in five years, he'll be fifty, and two marriages in that period of your life—I want to be sure."

"You can't ever be sure. The only way you can be sure is if you make up your mind that you're going to stay married no matter what happens. Cruelty. Infidelity. Drinking. Temperamental differences. And even then you can only speak for yourself. You can't decide for him. *He* may want to break it off, and if he did, you'd naturally let him . . . I'm afraid I'm no help at all. I hear John. We'll talk about this some more later. *In your study, dear.*"

John said, "Hello, Webster Sisters, you look very charming, both of you."

"Thank you," said Jean.

"Thank you," said Elizabeth.

He went to a bookshelf on which were a bottle of bourbon, of gin, and of vermouth; several glasses, and an ice bowl. He poured bourbon over ice in three glasses, and handed two to the women.

"I didn't ask for this. Are you getting a cold?" said Elizabeth.

"I wish to propose a toast," said John Appleton. "To Ralph Ridgeway Ballard."

"Who's he?" said Elizabeth.

"The next president of Spring Valley College."

"*Oh, no!*" said Elizabeth.

"Now drink up," said John Appleton.

"I don't want to—and are you sure? You're positive?" said Elizabeth Appleton.

"Yes. Drink, Elizabeth. Even if you have a mental reservation."

"I'll drink to the man who should have been president, my husband, John Appleton."

"And I drink to my wife."

"And I to both of you," said Jean.

They half finished their drinks, and Elizabeth spoke: "I suppose there isn't a chance you could be wrong about this?"

"Not a chance. Naturally you're dying to know how I found out. Well, I was walking out Hill Street on my way home and Brice Ditson passed me with a carload of men. I didn't see who they all were but I recognized two. Trustees. Waved to them. They waved to me. Then about five minutes later Brice pulled up at the curb, alone. He asked me to get in, wanted to talk to me. It seems they *were* some of the trustees, and he was depositing them at his house. Which he did, then turned around and came back and picked me up. Apparently in the car when they saw me they decided that they owed it to me to tell me about their decision. It won't be announced officially until Christmas vacation, but they called Ballard long distance from Brice's camp, so Ballard already knows. And that is how the news got from Aix to Ghent." He bent down and kissed Elizabeth. "I didn't want it as much as you wanted it for me."

"A few years ago you didn't, but you did the last couple of months," she said. "It's rotten mean of them. Ungrateful, and stupid."

"I wanted the honor, Elizabeth, but I didn't really want the job."

"What exactly did Brice say?" said Elizabeth.

"Don't you two want to be alone? I'm in the way," said Jean.

"Hell, I'm glad you're here. You're family," said John. "He was very nice. He didn't say so, but I somehow inferred that telling me was his idea. He said, 'John, I think we owe it to you, since your name has been mentioned so often, to tell you that a final decision has been made, and the next president of Spring Valley is Ralph Ballard, Ralph Ridgeway Ballard, of Haverford.' Then he told me they'd been considering Ballard and two others, that I was one of the other two, but that there was a strong feeling that they wanted to go outside the Spring Valley family—that's what he called it, the Spring Valley family—for the presidency. He said the other man was not a Spring Valley man either, and that I was the only local boy that was ever considered."

"The only one they could possibly consider, he might have said."

"Well, he implied that. He said they, the trustees, felt that Spring Valley simply must do all it can to further relations with other small colleges, and that that was going to be the policy from now on. I didn't say so, but I thought to myself does that mean they're going to start raiding other faculties, and if so what's that going to do to further relations? He gave me permission to tell you, Elizabeth, but asked me to keep it secret from everybody else. So, Jean, don't you go calling up *The American Scholar* with your scoop."

"I'm just glad you're not disappointed, John," said Jean.

"Oh, I am, but *there's* the one who's most disappointed," he said.

"Disappointed and angry. Who is this Ballard anyway, aside from being a Haverford Quaker?"

"Oh, he's qualified. He's assistant dean and a full professor. Harvard Ph.D., which didn't hurt him any here. Married and has four daughters, one at Swarthmore and one at Bryn Mawr. His wife is a Bryn Mawrier. He was an administrative officer in the army medical corps during the war. And he played lacrosse and tennis as an undergraduate. Member of Gulph Mills and the Rittenhouse Club. I got all this from Brice, who rattled it off so glibly that I a little bit suspect Ballard is Brice's man. Well, I guess I never was, after I sounded off on old Jap Framingham, so the hell with it and let's enjoy our new freedom."

"You *are* disappointed," said Elizabeth.

He smiled painfully. "Only because I'd begun to take it for granted, and I knew how much you wanted it for me."

"Finish out the year here and we'll go away next June," said Elizabeth.

He shook his head. "No. This is where I finish out the rest of my life. This is where I belong, Elizabeth. I'm just this good and not a bit better. For some unknown reason, this is more my college now than it ever was before."

"How can you say that?" said Elizabeth.

"Because that's the way I see it. I'm a little like Samuel J. Tilden and a little like Jim Thorp. I'd probably win the popularity contest but that isn't what they pay off on."

"I think I know what he means, Elizabeth," said Jean.

"Yes, I'll bet you do," said John, turning to her. "And Elizabeth will know too, as soon as she gets over her disappointment. You have no bitterness—and I guess we have, Elizabeth and I. But you see why it's where I think I belong, don't you?"

"If you do, then please explain it to me," said Elizabeth to her sister. "If I got a kick in the teeth I'd feel I wasn't wanted."

"Not necessarily, Elizabeth," said Jean. "You used to go in those tournaments at East Hampton, year after year, and always get put out the second round, but you kept on going back."

"There's no similarity here. I never thought I was going to win," said Elizabeth. "But I was given the chance to do the best I could."

"There wasn't any similarity until you said that," said John. "But now there is. I was given the chance to do the best I could, and it wasn't good enough. Somewhere along the line I could have made myself so indispensable that they'd have had to give it to me, in spite of their wanting someone from another college. I could have been so good that I'd have won out over a policy. Well—I wasn't. I wasn't quite good enough for that. Also, I didn't try hard enough, and if people know you're not trying, why should they hand it to you on a silver platter? I *never* was *that* good. I have a place here. In fact, I have a place in my life that happens to be here, put it that way. If I'd been elected president, I'd have been a good one. But I honestly believe, and in all modesty, that I'm to this place what Christian Gauss was to Princeton, and still is even though he's retired. I'll never be chairman of the board of U. S. Steel, but I'm a damn good blacksmith."

"I wish you'd resign."

"No, Elizabeth, I won't resign. Unless—if a month from now you decide you don't want to live here any more, then I'll resign."

"They went outside the family, as they call it, to get Bruce McAndrews, and I don't see that he's improved matters any. I wonder how he stood?"

"Oh, I'm sure he wasn't for me, but I don't think that mattered. Bruce has had the title, but for a long time that's all he's had. Nobody pays any attention to him. I was about to call him a figurehead, but he isn't even that. I'd sure as hell hate to end up my presidency with as little to show for it as Bruce has. He has a house rent-free and a pension, but if he's smart he'll take the next bus out of town as soon as Ballard is installed."

"So would we."

"No. And by the time Ballard takes over you'll have changed your mind."

"You're more hopeful of that than I am," said Elizabeth. "I must get supper."

"I'll help," said Jean, then she saw John quickly shake his head, unseen by Elizabeth. "Or maybe I'll just sit here and keep John company."

"You and John have another drink. Supper'll be ready in ten minutes," said Elizabeth, and went to the kitchen.

"She wants to be alone," said John. "This is a very big disappointment to her, and at the moment not even I can take the sting out of it. She has to blame herself first and then her good sense will take over. But she's going to have to work that out alone, not by my reassuring her."

"Why would she blame herself?"

"Because this has been the big thing in her life the past couple of years, and I wasn't always very helpful. She'll be all right eventually, but it'll take a little time."

In a short while Elizabeth called them to the kitchen, where a cold supper was laid. "You two go ahead without me," said Elizabeth. "I'm going upstairs and lie down for a while. I'm all right, but I just have to think this whole damn thing out."

John put his arm about her waist and hugged her. "You go on upstairs and come down when you feel like it."

John Appleton and Jean had their supper and Jean washed and put away the dishes. "She's had almost an hour," said Jean. "I think that's enough."

"Yes. Go on up and talk to her. Maybe she's fallen asleep."

Jean went to Elizabeth's bedroom, which was in darkness. "Is that you, Jean? Come in." Elizabeth was lying on top of the bed, in her slip. She turned on one of the reading lamps as Jean entered. "Was there enough to eat?"

"More than enough. I put the roast back in the icebox. Still quite a lot left," said Jean.

"You never used to be able to do anything in the kitchen, but now you're very efficient," said Elizabeth.

"We weren't brought up properly. Every girl ought to know how to cook and sew."

"We were brought up properly if we'd married properly, but we were expected to move into a houseful of servants, and we didn't. Not that I regret it. I'm so used to doing things for myself that I could never go back to that old life. I wouldn't know what to do with myself. With the children away at school I'd have been lost but for the fact that I've been semi-official hostess for the college. The president's wife is a hopeless alcoholic and I've had to do the entertaining of the visiting firemen. Well, that's over, too."

"You'll find something to do," said Jean. "It's very important to."

Elizabeth smiled. "I detect a note of warning, yes?"

"I guess you do. You're a very attractive woman."

"That danger has passed, Jean. I *had* a lover."

Jean said nothing.

"Are you shocked?" said Elizabeth.

Jean nodded. "Yes, I'm shocked. I'm not surprised. There was something I didn't know, and I'm shocked that that's what it turned out to be."

"I had a lover for almost five years. It's been over that long, but now I'm paying for it. I can't help but feel that I'm partly responsible for John's not getting that job."

"Who knew about it?"

"One person. Evangeline Ditson. In those things I suppose you always have to take someone into your confidence, and in my case it was Evangeline. The man was her brother-in-law, the odd job you saw today."

"Yes, I thought that must be who it was."

"Why?"

"Oh—it would have to be someone like that. Your way of going back to Southampton, somebody the opposite of John."

"Yes. And we were in love."

"John of course never knew anything about it," said Jean.

"He suspected something at first, when there was nothing, but if he suspected anything later he never said anything."

"And I suppose he was an ideal lover, this man."

"Just that. And wanted me to marry him."

"Well, why didn't you?"

"Because I don't believe in divorce when the only reason for it is wanting to sleep with someone else. I'm not criticizing you."

"You're not in any position to now, Elizabeth."

"I don't agree with you. I'm in a position to criticize you, but I'm not in a position to take a sanctimonious attitude. I can criticize you, or myself. And I do criticize myself. I criticize myself now, as I often have before, for not feeling more guilty about my affair with Porter Ditson. But I don't feel guilt, at least not toward John. I have felt some guilt toward Porter. He was the loser in our affair, because it made him want to change his whole way of life. I wouldn't marry him, I ended the affair, and he's never been able to return to his old philosophy. He had a philosophy. It was self-preservation. He had it all worked out that he wanted to live to be seventy-five, and if it hadn't been for me, wanting him and wanting to be with him, he'd have held on to his philosophy. Now I don't think he cares any more. He doesn't care about anything, not even me. Porter Ditson was the loser. John didn't lose anything."

"You just said—"

"I hadn't finished. John never knew I was sleeping with Porter, and it never became public knowledge, so he didn't lose his he-man self-respect. The only thing he may have lost was the presidency of Spring Valley, if Evangeline influenced Brice Ditson's vote because I committed adultery.

(297)

But I'll never know that. You see, Evangeline hates John because he once attacked her father in a lecture, and even if she influenced Brice's vote, it may have been for that reason. All these years she's kept the secret of my affair with Porter, so I'll never know any more than I do now. Who ever said life was simple?"

"I never heard that anyone said it."

"No, but you thought it was. That's why you came here. To look at a happy marriage in a simple, college community."

"True."

"Well, you see now that it isn't any simpler here than anywhere else, and that a happy marriage, the kind that you're looking for, is an absurd, foolish dream. So stop looking for it."

"I wonder how much of this you'd be telling me if you hadn't lost out on the presidency."

"None of it. I'd have let you go on thinking that John and I were one of your *Ladies Home Journal* couples. They're usually named Stephen and Cynthia, and Cynthia is very wise and understanding about Stephen's old sweetheart, the one that turns up at the country club dance. And of course Cynthia cleverly outwits the siren and all is well. Nobody does anything nasty, like actually getting into bed. That's what you came here thinking we were, Stephen and Cynthia."

"Yes, I had an absurd, foolish dream."

"Well, if nothing else comes of your visit, I've at least punctured that dream. You can't marry a man of forty-five, and you married twice already, and honestly expect to live like a magazine couple. Good Lord, Jean, you're already having an affair with Bill Collins. What does an affair consist of? What are the physical realities of an affair? I'll shock you. I'll really shock you. The first time I ever slept with Porter Ditson was right in this bed."

"What are you trying to do?"

"You'll see in a minute. For two nights Porter came here and why do I say slept with me? He didn't sleep with me.

We had sexual intercourse and loved it and for five years loved it, and each other. Not a mean little kiss on a country club porch. And then we stopped. We gave up something that we wanted and needed."

"Why?"

"Because I chose to stay married to John. I don't know how many times he's wanted to go off with someone else, or *if* he has. But he always came back to our marriage, if not to me. Romantic love and sexual curiosity haven't been a part of our marriage for years and years. But I'm his wife, and that's how he thinks of me, habitually. I've hated him sometimes, and I'm sure he's hated me. He has no real guts, and he isn't all that intellectual, either. But we're a marriage. You surely don't think a mother gets any pleasure out of changing diapers? And washing them? And you surely don't think she loves and adores every single thing her children do. I know things about my own two that I haven't even told John, they're so disgusting. But I'm still their mother. It should be easy, you know, to have your pleasure with a man and let it go at that. Sixteen years ago I had pleasure with John, and produced Betty. Seventeen years ago, I had pleasure with him and produced Peter. I should be able to say that all that happened sixteen and seventeen years ago, and they shouldn't matter to me now. But we're caught, trapped, by something that happens to our glands, I suppose. A man and wife get to look alike, and that's been explained by the theory that they eat the same things at the same time and for a long period of years. I don't know. But I have found out that I could give up a happy, exciting relationship with the only man I ever loved, and go back to the only one I ever married. You think I never cry when I see Porter Ditson? That odd job? Oh, how cruel that was, Jean, without your knowing it was. Sometimes I'll be in my car, downtown, and I'll see him without him seeing me. He's saying hello to people, stopping to chat with them. Then he'll move on and stop to pass the time of day with someone else. They like to see him and talk to him, his little pleasantries, his courtesy, as you so beautifully described it. And I wonder if he loves me, but I really know he does, and that I love him. Then the traffic light changes, and I drive past him without waving, pretending I haven't seen him, and I wonder if he has seen me. I'm sure he has. And we'll meet at parties. 'Hello, Elizabeth, you're looking well.' The same thing he says to Evangeline or Mary Leslie. 'Hello, Porter, have you been away?' He never dances with me any more, and if I sit next to him at dinner he talks about nothing and never raises his eyes. What deadness there is to what we once had."

"It sounds to me as though you'd been paying for your affair much longer than you realize," said Jean. "Maybe that's why you have no feeling of guilt."

"Very possibly," said Elizabeth Appleton. "Instead of guilt and fear, I'm carrying a benign deadness. That's what he left me with. And pity. But I did say I felt guilt toward him, didn't I? I guess that's what I meant . . . Did John send you up?"

"Yes. He thought you might be blaming yourself for his not getting the presidency."

"Did he say why I'd blame myself?"

"No, but he thinks your good sense will convince you you had nothing to do with it."

"My good sense. John always counts on my good sense. Well, maybe it was thanks to my good sense that we still have a marriage. John *is* a bit of a Stephen."

"Stephen? Oh, *Stephen,*" said Jean. "And maybe I'm a bit of a Cynthia."

"Not in a thousand years. No Cynthia would ever marry a Tommy Joralemon."

"I guess I don't know what I am," said Jean.

"The future Mrs. William Collins. But just remember that when a husband wakes up in the morning, one of the first things he wants to do is spit. Hock-hock-hock. Spit."

"I thought that was just Neal Roberts."

"Oh, no. Stephen has to do that, too. Hock-hock-hock. 'Did you get it, dear?' " She got off the bed. "I think I'll wash my face. What time is it?"

"Five after seven."

"I'll wash my face and be right down. John will be listening to the Jack Benny show," said Elizabeth. "So there'll be no conversation before half past seven."

The carefully guarded secret of a new president for Spring Valley remained intact until the following Wednesday morning, when the *Echo* ran a streamer: NEW PREXY FOR S. V. C.?, and a story that read:

> According to unconfirmed but reliable reports, the Spring Valley board of trustees have chosen the successor to President Bruce Clanronald McAndrews. The new president will be Ralph Ridgeway Ballard, Assistant Dean of Haverford College. . . . No official announcement will be made until Jan. 1, 1951. Reached by telephone yesterday, Dean Ballard refused to confirm or deny the report. Further information, he told the *Echo,* will have to come from the S. V. C. trustees. . . . The decision of the trustees runs counter to campus sentiment, which was strongly in favor of the selection of Dean John Appleton. Interviewed yesterday in his office, Dean Appleton told the *Echo* that he had no official knowledge of Ballard's appointment. He declined further comment. In ignoring the wishes of the overwhelming majority of undergraduate, faculty and alumni sentiment, the trustees once again have shown a tendency to rule in absentia. It is high time, according to some observers, that changes were made on the board of trustees as well as in President's House.
>
> A protest meeting of undergraduates has been called for 8 P.M. this (Wed.) evening on the steps of Everett Hall. Leading undergraduates will speak. BE THERE!

John Appleton was still at the breakfast table when Bruce Clanronald McAndrews called him on the telephone. "You've seen the *Echo,* I imagine," said McAndrews.

"Just finished it," said John Appleton. "Elizabeth is reading it now."

"I was wondering if it wouldn't be a good idea for you to go to the meeting."

"What for?" said John Appleton.

"Well, it might get out of hand."

"Yes, it might. Some of the students are still celebrating last Saturday's game."

"Well, don't you think you ought to calm them down?"

"How?"

"Speak to them."

"What magic words shall I use?"

"Well, John, I leave that up to you."

"You leave more than that up to me, Bruce. Naturally I'll do nothing to encourage a demonstration, but I'll be damned if I'll take the rap for the trustees. Don't forget, officially I'm in the dark. I have no official knowledge of the trustees' decision."

"Maybe the story in the *Echo* is wrong," said Mc-Andrews.

"What?"

"I said maybe the story in the *Echo* is wrong."

"I heard you the first time, but I wanted you to repeat it. Why you lying son of a bitch, you'd let me go to that meeting and try to lie *your* way out of it. You'd let me get up there and make a complete horse's ass of myself. These kids have an honest sentiment, and they have a right to express it. But you want me to cheapen the whole thing with a cheap lousy lie. I've known for years that you were a damned fool, and a yellow-belly, but for you to suggest that I go and lie to these kids . . . What I'm almost tempted to do, and what I *could* do in their present frame of mind, I could send a very angry mob over to your house and see if you could lie out of that. You're chicken, fellow. You'd better be called away for a couple of days." He hung up without waiting for McAndrews' next words, if any.

"Good for you. What brought that on?" said Elizabeth.

"He tried to pretend that *maybe* the story in the *Echo* wasn't true."

"Oh, how disgusting. More coffee?"

"Sure! Give me some more coffee, and maybe I'll have one of our V. I. P. cigars. I feel good."

All day undergraduates would say to him: "Hi, Dean. You coming to the meeting?"

And he would raise his eyebrows and say: "What meeting?" No member of the faculty or administrative staff put into words the thoughts of commiseration or need for caution, friendly advice, and forlorn optimism that were in the individual minds. The words were not necessary, and in most cases an expression of the thoughts would have been indelicate. John Appleton got home shortly after six o'clock, and his wife and sister-in-law were waiting for him. "Caviar?" he said.

"Jean's idea. She went downtown and bought it herself. Wait till you see."

Jean Roberts brought in three small dishes, forks and spoons, and a Revere bowl filled with sour cream. On each dish were two small pancakes.

"Blinis?" said John Appleton. "This is the way to go."

"She wanted to have a party, and this is it," said Elizabeth.

"We ought to be drinking vodka," said John Appleton.

Elizabeth Appleton looked at her sister and smiled.

"I wasn't sure you liked it," said Jean, and took a new bottle of vodka from behind the whiskey and vermouth.

"Da, da, da," said John Appleton. "Arise ye prisoners of starva-tion. This is too good for the intellectual bourgeoisie. The *hell* it is. Nothing is too good for the intellectual bourgeoisie. Nothing is usually what we get, too. But all we want is a few simple pleasures, like blinis and caviar and vodka when we come home from the tractor works. This has been quite a day."

"I want to know everything that happened," said Elizabeth. "Beginning with Bruce McAndrews. Did you see him, did you talk to him again?"

"That was Triumph Number One. He left town right after my sound-off. He was supposed to preside at a meeting at ten o'clock, but when we got to his office we were told he'd been suddenly called out of town. No explanation except

(303)

that he'd be gone several days. That's happened before, when his poor pathetic wife has been worse than usual. But nobody really believed she was the excuse today. Not that anybody so much as mentioned the *Echo* story to me, but a lot of teachers went out of their way to say hello to me, men and women that ordinarily don't make a point of it. And the students! At least a hundred times I was asked if I'd be at the meeting tonight. All I said was, 'What meeting?' and that always brought a laugh."

"Is there going to be trouble?"

"What kind of trouble could there be? If Bruce hadn't blown town they might have gone to his house and raised a little hell, but my guess is that they'll have their meeting and there'll be some speeches, and when the crowd gets tired of the speeches, the meeting will break up. It's a pretty cold night to be standing around. It was just above twenty by the back-porch thermometer. It'll be down around zero by morning."

"Who were some of the people that went out of their way to say hello to you?" said Elizabeth Appleton.

He named a few teachers and described them for Jean, and he accompanied Jean and Elizabeth to the kitchen for the preparation of the evening meal. They had steak by candlelight in the diningroom, and dishwashing was postponed while they had coffee and brandy in the study. "I hope Ralph Ballard is enjoying himself tonight as much as I am. Although I guess he had his celebration Sunday night. By the way, Elizabeth, when you write to the kids, of course you won't—"

"Say anything about disappointment. No. I'll just mention in passing."

"Peter won't give a damn, but Betty would have liked me to be president."

"Peter would have, too," said Elizabeth.

"Did I leave the radio on in the kitchen?" said John Appleton.

"We didn't have it on," said Jean.

"Well then I'm hearing things. I'm not used to vodka."

"I hear *something*. A band?" said Jean.

"It *is* a band. And singing," said Elizabeth.

John Appleton concentrated on listening, and the others were silent. "Elizabeth," he said. "You know what that is."

"I think I do. It's the college band."

"And you know what they're singing, don't you?" John Appleton addressed his sister-in-law. "It's the Spring Valley Fight Song.

> Get outa the way!
> Get outa the way!
> We're coming down the hill.
> Get outa the way, whoever you are,
> Whoever, whoever the hell you are.
> Get outa the way, whoever you are,
> We're coming down the hill!"

"And it's getting closer," said Elizabeth. "I think they're coming down Bucknell Street. Let's go look."

"No, not yet," said John Appleton. "They may be coming here. I'm sure they are. But if they're not, I don't want them to see me. That might start something."

The band and the singing students now stood in front of the Appleton house. The band and the singing stopped, then changed to a chant: "We want Appie! We want Appie! We want Appie! We want Appie!"

"Who?" said Jean Roberts.

"Appie. Me," said John Appleton. "I have to show my face. You two go on upstairs. You'll be able to see everything from our bedroom window. I'll give them a minute more to blow off steam."

"Good man," said Elizabeth Appleton, and kissed her husband's cheek. Elizabeth and Jean went upstairs. They stood by the window in the darkened room, and they knew the instant John Appleton opened the front door as the chant changed to an undisciplined roar. It lasted a full minute, and then two young men and a girl with megaphones called to the crowd: "A long cheer and an echo for Appie. A long cheer and an echo, for Appie. Right-hand side, the cheer; left-hand side, the echo. Are you ready?"

"That's a very special cheer, almost never given for an individual," said Elizabeth.

"It's quite a production," said Jean. "What are they saying? Spring-Spring, Valley-Valley. Sort of counterpoint."

"I'm going to raise the window just a little. I want to hear John."

"Oh hell, raise it all the way. I want to hear him, too," said Jean.

The echo-cheer ended and there were individual calls for Appie, who now raised a hand, and the bass drummer thumped for silence.

"Ladies and gentlemen—" said John Appleton.

"That leaves out the trustees, Appie!" a voice called out, and there were rude noises and boos.

"Ladies and gentlemen—I am delighted to join you—in this belated celebration—of the smashing victory—over Mount St. Joe's."

There was laughter and cries of "Come on, Appie, you know why we're here."

"Good for John," said Elizabeth. "I was wondering what he would say first."

John Appleton continued: "Like most of you—I read about the victory—in this morning's *Echo*."

"What victory? Come on, Appie," cried the hecklers.

"Let him talk," cried others in the crowd. "Stop interrupting."

"I read about the victory—" John went on. "And as always, I wished that I had been in the game. I've spent most of my life here on The Hill. Next to my family, nothing in the world means as much to me. In fact, as some of you may know, Spring Valley at one time *was* my family. My father was on the faculty here, my mother was one of the early Amazons. And so, being so closely connected to this college, and having such affection for it, when I read the article in this morning's *Echo*—I wished that I had been in that game."

There was a small murmur among the crowd that quickly became crescendo as the implication took hold. John held up his hand again.

"But as a former right end, I can tell you that it isn't always the man that carries the ball who is responsible for the touchdown. As an end, I have taken out a defensive halfback while one of my teammates galloped on to glory. Also as an end, I have caught a pass and scored a touchdown that I never would have scored if someone else hadn't taken out the safety man. So I know something about teamwork and indispensability, and the distribution of the laurels.

"What's more, ladies and gentlemen, I long ago learned that you don't win games by interfering with the coaching staff. The coaching staff has its responsibilities, and they often get the blame when things go wrong. Particularly when, let us say, a star halfback is kept out of a game. They have their reasons for not wanting to let him play. And you can be sure that they're good reasons. And whatever the reasons, that we may not understand at the time, you can be sure that they're in the best interests of Spring Valley.

"Now if I may, I would like to abandon my somewhat ambiguous remarks about football, and make a personal announcement. I said earlier that I've spent most of my life here on The Hill. I would like to add that after your visit to me here tonight, nothing in God's world will ever get me to leave. I thank you for coming here and making it *impossible* for me to leave."

"And he means it," whispered Elizabeth.

There were cheers, in a deeper key, and a roll on the snare drums.

"The alma mater," said Elizabeth, and as the music began she sang:

"In the hills of Pennsylvania
Stands the college that we love

And it stands for all we hold so dear.
Looking down our alma mater, from the peaceful sky
    above,
Bids her sons and daughters, 'Be of good cheer.'
Spring Valley, Spring Valley,
We echo your song.
Spring Valley, Spring Valley
So true.
And until the day we die
We will wave your banner high
And cheer for the Gold and the Blue."

Jean leaned forward and saw John wave his hand as he called out, "Goodnight, goodnight."

"Goodnight Ap-peeeee. Goodnight," they called. Bits of flame appeared in the crowd as the boys and girls lit cigarettes and turned away. The band formed ranks and began playing the Fight Song, and in five minutes the Appleton lawn was deserted.

"I guess we can go down now," said Elizabeth.

"I'll stay up here," said Jean.

"Oh, no. I took Stephen and Cynthia away from you, but I have to give you something to take their place."

"What?"

"I haven't the faintest idea. But whatever you see will be the real thing," said Elizabeth Appleton.

John Appleton was in his study. "I decided to open a can of beer. Beer's better to cry in," he said. "Did you catch the whole performance?"

"Don't pretend it was a performance," said Elizabeth.

"No, I guess it really wasn't," said John Appleton. "It was right off the cob, but I'm always corny when I'm really being myself. I'm a very corny guy."

"You were very good, John, and don't spoil it for me," said Jean.

The telephone rang and Elizabeth answered. "Hello," she said. "Oh, hello, Porter. Yes, she's right here. For you, Jean."

Jean Roberts took the telephone. "Hello, how are you?

Yes, I remember you did. Well, the only thing is, it's very nice of you, but I'm going away tomorrow. I've had a change in my plans. No, I don't know when I'll be back in Spring Valley. You were very nice to want to, but I have to go to Philadelphia. I will. Yes, I'll be seeing him. I'll tell him. I certainly will. What? Goodbye, and here's Elizabeth."

"Yes, Porter?" said Elizabeth. "No, I'm afraid we're all just about ready to retire for the night. A very busy day, for all of us. Would you like to speak to John? All right, I'll tell him. Goodnight." She hung up. "He wanted to bring a bottle of Scotch and see how long you'd stay awake. He was thinking of that night when you made the Framingham lecture."

"God, that was ten years ago," said John. "Think he'll call again in ten years?"

"No, but he might," said Elizabeth.

"You see what our life is here, Jean," said John Appleton. "For instance, we can expect a call from Porter Ditson every ten years. And in 1960, the town will still be run by a rich woman."

"Evangeline Ditson?" said Elizabeth.

"No. An anarchist. Mildred Klein. She'll have all the cash."

"Now how did you know that?" said Elizabeth. "You've never had any dealings with Mrs. Klein."

"No, but I wanted to show you it doesn't pay to have any secrets from your husband," said John Appleton. "Jean, you remember that."

"I'll try to."

He stood up. "Thanks very much for the caviar, *and* the vodka. You're not really leaving tomorrow, are you?"

"Yes, I am."

"Isn't this rather sudden?"

"Yes, but well thought out."

"Well, I wish you great happiness. That's what it is, isn't it? Mr. Collins?"

"Yes."

"I hope he's good enough for you, and if you think he is, that's all that matters." He bent down and kissed her forehead. "The Webster girls make good wives. Maybe I'll see you at breakfast."

"Yes. For sure," said Jean. "Goodnight, John. You were very good tonight with that crowd."

"Yes you were," said Elizabeth.

"Thanks. Goodnight, Mom, in case you two want to sit up and talk."

"Mom?" said Elizabeth. "That's a new one."

"Yes. Yes it is. I'm a real cornball tonight." He hung his jacket on a crooked finger and slung it over his shoulder. "A real cornball."

"He looks tired," said Jean, when he had gone.

Elizabeth Appleton was looking straight ahead. "Oh, I'm sorry. What did you say, Jean?"